EVIL FROM BENEATH THE SEA

A lurid, red glow materialized out of the blackness above the submerged Cradle. It quickly strengthened, first into light and then into fire, an evil, lifeless fire that seemed to defy nature, aye, and possibility itself.

Tarlach of the Falconers watched in disbelief as Una of Seakeep, the determined noblewoman who had hired his company to defend her lands, walked forward to the burning *gate* which sundered the evening sky.

Within its glare was the suggestion of something, a great, misshapen head that appeared to be all jaws. The evil thing was not yet free. Tarlach could see it struggling. Even if it took his own life, he must keep it from harming the Daleswoman . . .

Una and Tarlach's story is but half of the
heroic epic told by the Chronicler of
Lormt in the stirring saga of the Turning,
STORMS OF VICTORY

Tor books by Andre Norton

Caroline with (Enid Cushing)
The Crystal Gryphon
Dare to Go A-Hunting
The Elvenbane (with Mercedes Lackey)
Flight in Yiktor
Forerunner
Forerunner: The Second Venture
Gryphon's Eyrie (with A. C. Crispin)
Grandmasters' Choice (editor)
Here Abide Monsters
House of Shadows (with Phyllis Miller)
Imperial Lady (with Susan Shwartz)
The Jekyll Legacy (with Robert Bloch)
Moon Called
Moon Mirror
The Prince Commands
Ralestone Luck
Sneeze on Sunday (with Grace Allen Hogarth)
Stand and Deliver
Storms of Victory
Wheel of Stars
Wizards' Worlds
Wraiths of Time

THE WITCH WORLD (editor)
Tales of the Witch World 1
Tales of the Witch World 2
Four from the Witch World
Tales of the Witch World 3

MAGIC IN ITHKAR (editor, with Robert Adams)
Magic in Ithkar 1
Magic in Ithkar 2
Magic in Ithkar 3
Magic in Ithkar 4

Storms of Victory

WITCH WORLD: THE TURNING
Andre Norton with P.M. Griffin

TOR
fantasy

A TOM DOHERTY ASSOCIATES BOOK
NEW YORK

This is a work of fiction. All the characters and events portrayed in this book are fictitious, and any resemblance to real people or events is purely coincidental.

STORMS OF VICTORY

Copyright © 1991 by Andre Norton, Ltd.
Maps copyright © 1990 by John M. Ford

A Tor Book
Published by Tom Doherty Associates, Inc.
49 West 24th Street
New York, N.Y. 10010

Tor® is a registered trademark of Tom Doherty Associates, Inc.

Cover art by Dennis A. Nolan

ISBN: 0-812-51109-3
Library of Congress Catalog Card Number: 90-49030

First edition: March 1991
First mass market printing: March 1992

Printed in the United States of America

0 9 8 7 6 5 4 3 2 1

Seakeep is dedicated to Maria Franzetti, a friend.
—P. M. G.

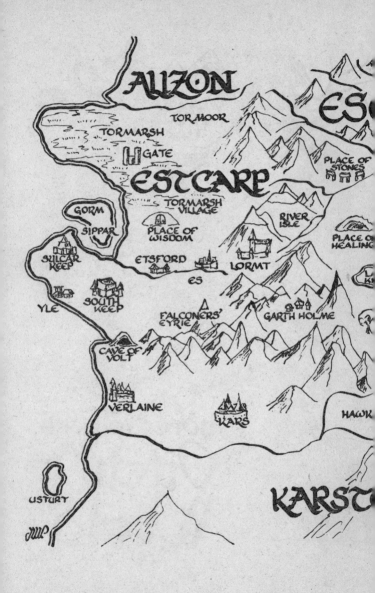

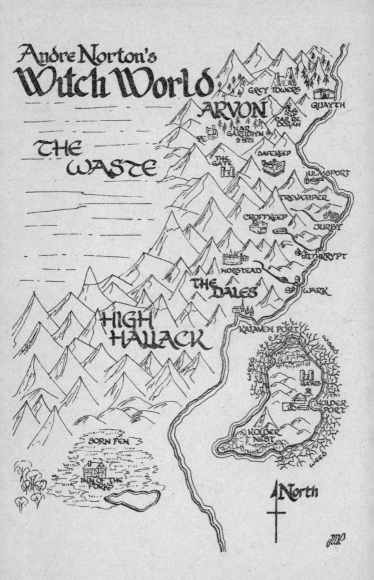

The Chronicler

THERE was a time when the hilt of a sword or the butt
of a dart gun rested more easily in my grip than this pen.
Now I record the deeds of others, and strange tales have
I gathered. That I find myself a chronicler of others' deeds
is one of those tricks which fate can play upon a man.

In the backwater of quiet which is Lormt a man must
make his own work. I have been fortunate in that I am
drawn more and more to the seeking of knowledge, even
though it chances that I am but a beginner and must do
so vicariously through the recounting of the deeds of
others. Though sometimes, more and more, it comes to
me that I have not yet done with an active role in that
eternal war of the Light against the Dark.

My name is Duratan and I am of the House of Harrid
(which means nothing now). Though I take commissions
these days to search family rolls for many divided clans,
I have never found any bloodkin to my house. It is sometimes a lone thing not to call any kin.

I came into Estcarp as a babe, having been born just at
that black time when Duke Yvian horned all the Old Race
and there was a mighty bloodletting. My nurse brought
me hither before she died of a fever and I was fostered.

From then my destiny followed the pattern known to
all my exiled people. I was trained to arms from the time

1

I could hold a weapon made to my measure—for there was no other life then when the Kolder devils loosed all our enemies upon us.

In due time I became one of the Borderers, adding to my knowledge of weapons that of the countryside and survival in the wilderness. Only in one respect did I differ from my fellows—I seemed able to bond with animals. Once I even faced a snow cat, and we looked eye to eye, before the impressive hunter of the heights went his way. In my mind it was as if I had dwelt for a short moment within his furred skin, kin to him as I was to no other.

For a time thereafter I was wary and disturbed, fearing that I might even be were, one of those who divide spirits—man and animal, able to be each in turn. Yet I showed no tendency to grow fur or feather, fangs or talons. So at length I accepted this as a minor talent—to be cherished.

In border service I met also the younger Tregarths, and from that grew in me a desire to something more than a triumph at arms and always more bloodletting. Of those two storied warriors it was Kemoc, the younger, to whom I was most drawn. His father being Simon Tregarth, the outworlder, his mother the Witch Jaelithe, who had not lost her power even when she wedded, bedded, and bore. There was also another unheard-of thing—that their children, all three, were delivered at a single birthing. There was Kemoc, and Kyllan, and their sister, Kaththea, who was taken for Witch training against her will.

Her brothers rode to prevent that but were too late. Kemoc returned from that aborted mission very quiet, but henceforth there was a deadliness in his eyes when he spoke of his sister. He asked questions of those who rode with us, and any we met. However, I think he gained little of what he wanted, for we who had fled Karsten had retained even less of the old lore than was known in Estcarp.

Then, in one of those swift forays which were our life, Kemoc suffered a wound too serious for our healer to deal with and was taken from the heights we guarded.

Shortly thereafter there came a period of quiet, almost a truce, during which our captain wished to send orders for supplies and I volunteered for that. With Kemoc gone I was restless and even more alone.

I carried the captain's orders but it meant a gathering of material which would take some time and I had nothing to do save find Kemoc. In me there has never been the gift of easy friend making and with him only I had felt akin. I knew that since his sister's taking he had been searching for something, and in that I also felt I might have a part. When I asked concerning him I was told that his wound (which had left him partly maimed) had healed well enough for him to go to Lormt.

Lormt was then to us mainly legend. It was said to be a repository of knowledge—useless knowledge the Witches avered—but it was older even than Es City, whose history covers such a toll of years that it would take the larger part of a lifetime to count. The Witches avoided it, in fact seemed to hold it in aversion. There were scholars said to have taken refuge within its walls, but if they learned aught from their delving they did not share it abroad.

I followed Kemoc to Lormt. It is true that one may be laid under a geas, set to a task from which there is no turning back. I had angered no one (that I knew of) with the power to set that upon me. But I was firmly drawn to Lormt.

Thus I came to a vaster and more unusual group of buildings than I had ever seen. There were four towers and those were connected by walls. Yet no sentries walked those walls and there was no guard at the single gate. Rather that was ajar, and must have been so for some time, as there was a ridge of soil holding it thus. Inside were buildings but not like those of a keep, and around, against the walls, smaller erections most little more than huts—some of which were a-ruin.

A woman was drawing water at a well as I dismounted and, when I asked her where I might find the lord, she blinked and then grinned at me, saying here were no lords, only old men who ruined their eyes looking at books which sometimes fell to pieces while they did so. So I went searching for Kemoc.

Later I discovered that the affairs of housing were managed by Ouen (leader by default of the scholars, he being a younger and more active man) and by Mistress Bethalie, whose opinion of the domestic arts of most men was very low indeed. There was also Wessel, a jewel of a steward. It was because of these three that Lormt flourished as well as it did.

Nor were there only males among the scholars. For I heard of a Lady Nareth, who kept much to her own company, and one Pyra, a noted healer, whose country and clan were unknown but who Kemoc revered for her knowledge and help with his own injury.

Five days I stayed with him, listening with growing excitement to his discoveries. Those about him were for the most part so elderly that they might have been our grandsires. Each had a quest of his own and no time for us.

The night before I left Kemoc faced me across one of the timeworn tables, having pushed aside a pile of books bound in worm-eaten wood. He had a small pouch in his hand and from this he scattered between us some beads of crystal which lay winking fire in the lamplight.

Without any thought my hand went out and I pushed one here, and one there until a pattern I did not understand lay before my eyes. Kemoc nodded.

"So it is right, Duratan, knowledge lies here for you, also. And believe it or not, you have talent."

I looked at him openmouthed. "I am no maid—" I protested.

He smiled at me. "Just so, you are no maid, Duratan. So let me say this to you. There may be secrets within secrets and the Witches are mortals for all their powers. There is infinitely more in this world than they know. I have discovered much here and soon I shall be able to follow my own road. Take these." He swept up the crystals, returning them to the pouch. "You shall find use for them."

When I left at dawn the next morning he was at the gate to see me forth.

"If peace ever comes to this land of ours, shield mate, ride you here again, for I think that there is to be found a greater treasure than any wrecker lord of the eastern coast can dream of. Luck be with you and fortune your shield."

But his wish did not hold. Within a month of my return to the mountains a rock moved under my mount's feet when I was on scout, to plunge both me and the poor beast into a narrow valley. The chance I would be found was slim and pain sent me drifting into a darkness I welcomed.

Yet I had not come to the Last Gate. I was discovered by a deaf-and-dumb beast of a man who carried me forth, though his rough handling was a torment. I awoke in the house of a wisewoman he served. With all her skill she fought to save my crushed leg. Heal it did, but I knew that I would never stride easily again and the Borderers would ride without me.

With a knotted stump of cane in hand I made myself walk daily. I had fallen onto a stool after such a push when she came to me, in her hand Kemoc's bag. She held that out and for some caprice I fumbled within and drew out a few of the crystals, throwing them on the floor. By some chance they were all of the same color—blue—and, as they fell, they shaped, as cleanly as if I had pushed them, into the shape of a dart head pointing to the door. I felt as if someone had given me a sharp order. It was time to be about business as yet unknown to me.

"You have," the woman said to me, "the talent. This is uncanny—ward yourself well, Borderer, for you will find few to welcome you." She tossed the pouch to me as if she wished it quickly away from her.

I decided it was time I searched for Kemoc in Lormt once more but first I helped that awkward servant enwall his mistress's herb garden. When I finally rode forth there was in me even a small hope that I might find knowledge to buy me freedom from my lurching steps.

Only Kemoc was gone when once more I entered that uncloseable gate. Ouen told me that Kemoc had been greatly excited when he had ridden forth a tenth day earlier, nor had he mentioned where he was going.

Because I did not know his goal and because I believed that my handicap would make me a hindrance to him, I settled in the room which had been his, paying into the common fund of the scholars the last of my small store of coins. For a short time a shameful weakness of spirit took me and I railed at fate.

But I roused myself to fight such despair and now and then I tossed the crystals. Thus I began to learn that I could influence the patterns which came, even move separate ones by staring at them.

That drove me to the reading halls, though I had no idea what I sought. I drew upon scraps I had found in Kemoc's room on which he had scrawled some results of his own delving. But I felt I faced a maze in which I could be easily caught, for I had no one purpose.

I strove to speak to one of the scholars who seemed more approachable than the others, Morfew, who welcomed me as a pupil.

When it seemed that I must have action, for it was not easy to settle into a niche of books and scrolls, I went into the fields of the farms which fed the establishment and worked, exercising my leg and forcing myself to walk without a staff. Though I had not sought her out, Pyra came to me and offered surcease from pain, greatly in agreement with what I strove to do for myself. She was a woman of great inner strength and it was only by chance that I discovered what else she was. For one day, when a stumble in a field brought back a measure of my pain, she found me sitting in the hall, crystals in hand.

I threw them in idleness and those of blazing yellow separated from the others and formed a pattern to seem a pair of eyes. Such eyes I had seen in a bird's head and these appeared to live for a moment and gaze at Pyra. I heard a quickly drawn breath and at that moment, as if I had heard it shouted aloud I was sure. I glanced from those eyes on the table to the eyes in the woman's head, and I said to myself, "Falconer!" Though few, if any, men not of their own breed had ever seen one of their women.

She put out her hand and caught mine, turning it palm up, and she studied that calloused flesh as one might study the roll on the table. There was a frown on her face; as she abruptly dropped her hold on me she said only:

"Tied, Duratan—how and why I do not know." Swiftly then she left me.

But tied to the bird warriors I was though I did not guess it then or for years to come. Time passed and I did not count the days.

However, my power grew. That which had stirred in me when I had fronted the snow cat strengthened by use even as did my limb. I began to put more thought to such things, casting my crystals, seeking out birds and small field creatures. Then I gained a liege one of my own.

There had been a storm and after its fury had passed I rode out to the edge of the wild lands. These were hedged by forest which made a living wall around Lormt save for where the road (somewhat overgrown) passed and where the river Es curled. There came to me a whimpering, and it was the space of several breaths before I realized that I had caught that, not by ear, but by thought. I took it as a guide and it led me to where, trapped much as I had been in the mountains, lay a thin, shaggy-coated hound. It was a beast of fine breeding though it was all bones and its long hair showed neglect. Nor did it wear a collar. As I knelt it drew lip to show teeth and I noted a mark across its muzzle as if a whip lash had left a scar. I looked into eyes which were fearful and I loosed thought to calm and comfort. It sniffed my fingers and then licked them.

Luckily it had shared my fate no further, for it was only a prisoner and wounded by the matter of a scratch or two. I worked apart the branch of bramble which was its

7

last binding and it arose to four feet and shook itself, took one step and then two away from me. Then it looked over its shoulder and came back, while from it to me flowed gratitude.

Thus I found Rawit and she was no common hound, but one that had been hardly used and had come to know my sort only as an enemy who punished. Though from the moment she came to me there was no barrier between us. Her thoughts flowed, even if sometimes they were hard to understand, but there was exchange between us and I found this a wonder which seemingly was as great a one to her.

We had visitors—mainly a trader or two who brought that which could not be raised in our well-tended fields, salt, scrap iron which Janton, the smith, used with great expertise. Also there were Borderers passing and from them we learned of the war. I asked of Kemoc and only once did I have news. That came from a horse dealer who had sold him a Torgian. But more than that I did not know.

There was a time when restlessness gnawed at me. I took to riding the woods' boundaries, Rawit running by my side. Though we were well away from the mountains and no raiders came, still I felt a need for such patrols.

Morfew told me once that the ancients who had built here had set over the whole site a guard of Power and those sheltering within the walls need have no fear. Still I borrowed a spade and smoothed out that ridge of earth which kept the great gate from being closed.

As my unease increased I fell into the habit of each morning throwing the crystals as I arose. Oddly, Rawit always came from her bed at the foot of mine to watch. And each day I threw only those which were the red of blood and the smoke grey of dying fires. Yet when I tried to share my foreboding with Morfew, he shook his head and told me the ancients guarded well their own.

My wariness was given credit when a troop of Borderers came. These were no scouts nor being sent to turn some raid. Rather they carried with them all that they

owned packed on ponies. From both men and animals—
even more from the animals—I sensed some strange peril.

Their captain gathered those scholars who would heed
him, and the farm people, to share the warning which
had sent them on the move. Pagar of Karsten had set on
march the largest army that men in this part of the world
had ever seen. Already their van had penetrated well into
the mountains across so wide a front that there was no
way Estcarp could hold against them.

"But it is no longer our war," the captain said. "For
the Council has sent forth the Great Call and we are for
Es City. If you would have safety prepare to ride with us.
But do not think we can linger long for you."

Ouen glanced from one to another of his fellow scholars and then spoke up.

"Lormt is guarded well, Captain." He gestured to walls
and towers. "I do not think we can do better than to
trust the guardianship which was set here when the last
wall stone was fitted into place. We have no life beyond
these walls. Also there is among us a wisewoman, Mistress Bethalie. She is strong in power though no Witch."

The captain grimaced and turned to Janton. "Your
people then—" he began.

Janton looked around but one head shook and then
another. He shrugged.

"Our thanks to you, Captain. But we've lived here
father-son, son-father, for so long we would be like wheat
pulled up untimely from the fields—to wither into nothingness."

"The folly is yours then!" The captain was sharp. His
gaze lighted on me and he frowned again. For, that morning having thrown the fire and ash twice and felt a great
weight of oppression, I had put on my scale shirt, and
fastened my arms belt over it.

"You—" I caught his thought and felt anger, then also
knew that he had the right to resent a fighting man to be
at this time apart from any troop.

I answered that thought easily as I limped forward.

"Captain, how came that Great Call?"

"The seeresses," he answered, "and the falcons of the Falconers. The Council move but they have not told us how or what. We have heard that Sulcar ships are in the bay and perhaps they wait for those who must flee."

Then he added, "Do you ride with us?"

I shook my head. "Captain, I found refuge here when there was no other to bid me welcome. I take my chance with Lormt."

They rode on towards the river and I heard them speak of rafts. I laid hand on the gate I had freed and wondered how well it would serve us as a barrier if Karsten fury spilled into this pocket nigh forgotten by the world.

The next day was awesome. I awakened before light and heard the whines in Rawit's throat, her shadow fear heightening mine. There was that about us which fairly shouted of Power, Power aroused, Power brooding, Power about to leap.

Even the most dreaming and woolywitted of the scholars felt it and so did those on the farms, for they came, family by family, to gather within Lormt's walls.

Ouen and I welcomed all within. Even old Pruett, the herbmaster, did what he could to bring forth those gifts of nature which would do the most good in times of trouble. While Mistress Bethalie and Pyra stood together, a strange look lay upon them both, as if they strove to see what lay before us.

So did it come, first like a vast drawing, and I saw men and women sway as they stood, just as I felt within me the same pull. The ponies screamed as I have never heard their like do before and Rawit howled, to be answered by all the farm dogs. Then—

I lived through it as we all did. But never have I found words to describe what came. It was as if the very earth strove to rid itself of us and all we had planted on her back. No sun broke through the fallen darkness. Those clouds were blacker than any night, except that through them cut great jagged blades of lightning.

Someone caught my arm and by a lightning flash I saw it was Morfew.

"They do it again—they move the mountains!" He clung to me so closely that I caught his words.

Much has been told of the Witches and their power, but in those hours what they did was greater than any feat of their planning before. Literally did they move the southern mountains, and Pagar and his invaders were gone, even as much else went also. Forests fell and were swallowed up, birds and animals died, rivers were shaken from their beds to find other courses. It was the ending of the world through which we lived.

There came a bolt of lightning which cracked the sky above our heads and struck full upon one of the towers. From the foot of that followed so great an explosion of light as was blinding. We huddled on the ground and strove to see, fearing our sight had been rift from us. Yet when dim shadows appeared again it was to reveal a continued glow of blue light which centered now on two towers. Then those stones, which had been so firmly set, began to fall and we who could gain our feet pulled others away from the crumbling towers and walls.

It seemed that that time of destruction went on forever. But there came a moment as if some great beast which had used its claws to ravage our world was at length tired of the destruction it had wrought, and the day cleared to a grey through which we looked once more on Lormt.

Perhaps, though the two towers were partly rubble and the wall which linked them only an unsteady mound, fortune had favored us. For no one had been killed and injuries were slight. Even the animals we had brought into the courtyard were safe.

There was something else—just as we had felt drawn by what we could not understand, so now were we all worn of strength. Those who dazedly found themselves alive moved only slowly. It was close to nightfall before we made our first discovery.

In their fall the towers, the walls, opened hidden places and rooms, crannies which had been sealed perhaps even at the first building were now visible. Our scholars went a little wild at what was displayed there. Forgetful of bruises, cuts, even hurts, which might have kept such old ones abed, they strove to climb tottering piles of rubble, to bring forth coffers, chests, sealed jars which stood as high as one's waist.

The rest of the ten days which followed was a strange time. From one of the remaining towers we could see that the Es had vanished from the course we knew. Trees in the forest leaned haphazardly one against the other. However, the houses which had been in the open were not greatly harmed.

That tower which had taken the first blow of all was split to its roots and I strove to keep the scholars away from it, for stones still rattled down into the depths. There was a dim glow there which flickered and grew less by the hour. Morfew joined me, wriggling out on his belly even as I to look down into the hollow.

"So the legend was right," he commented. "Smell that?"

There was dust in the air and a much stronger mustiness such as forever clung to the libraries. Still there was also another odor, sharp and acrid, which made us cough.

"Quan iron," Morfew said. "It is one of the old secrets. Yet I found one account last season which said that great balls of it were set at the foot of each tower and that is what was to keep Lormt from harm."

In a way it had, for we had been saved. However, we were careful of the unsteady piles of stone. After they had inspected their own homes many of the farm men came back and aided us, for the scholars had little strength and had to be discouraged from much they would do. In spite of my weakened leg I discovered that I could carry and push such as I would have thought I could not manage, as if some superior energy had come to me. So we were busied over many days, freeing the wealth of the hidden rooms and piling so much in the general hall that one could only follow narrow paths between.

On the third day I was heading for labor when Rawit whined and then her unhuman thought touched mine.

"Hurt—help—" She pointed her nose toward the ragged top of the second tower. There something moved. It flapped wildly back and forth and I saw it was a bird, caught by one foot so it could not right itself. Also one wing drooped while the other beat frantically.

To climb to that was dangerous, still I made the ascent testing each hand and foothold. The bird ceased its struggles and hung limp. Yet it was not dead, for I could just touch the edge of its thought and that was one of terror and helplessness. Thus I brought down at last a falcon, and no ordinary bird. This was a female of that same species whose males were the other selves of the Falconers, those dour fighters who had held the mountains for so long. Managing to loose the foot was easy once I had reached the trapped bird, but caring for the damaged wing was a task beyond me and only Pyra's skill brought it back to partial use again.

Galerider (I learned her name early) was never to soar freely again but she became as much of a companion as Rawit. Though she mantled warningly at any other, she allowed me to handle her. She had been torn from her nesting place by a sucking wind and had no idea how far or from what direction she had been borne.

At length we settled into a new life. There were refugees who found their way to Lormt, but none stayed past the time when they had regained their energy. Many of the scholars had disappeared into their cubbies with the newfound knowledge, so intent that they had to be brought forth for meals or rest, so enchanted by their finds that they might have been ensorcelled as we are told men can be.

There came news. In that mighty task of turning, many of the Witches—nearly all of the Council—had been killed or so emptied of power that they were only husks in which a life flame burned feebly. One such as brought to us by a young woman who begged our aid. But there was nothing yet uncovered which could answer her need.

The Witches remaining no longer in command, we were told by the leader of a scout troop sent south to assess damages, Koris of Gorm was now declared leader. It was the scout captain also who brought news of Kemoc—saying that he with his brother had managed to free his sister and they had all disappeared.

If they fled toward the mountains—had they been caught up in the torture of the land? I often wondered that when I had time to think of anything except what was happening in Lormt. By chance I had become a keeper of bits of information about the present not the past, and wayfarers who came down the old road would ask concerning this kin, that holding, and the like. So I began to assemble records and my knowledge of clans and houses became known so that some came from a distance to see me and ask of their kin.

Then one came in a dream.

Parting a haze with a sweep of his arm as one might pass through a curtain Kemoc stood before me. There was surprise on his face but that faded and a smile took its place.

"Duratan!" His voice—did it touch my thought only, or did it ring in my ears? I could have sworn to neither. However, there was much he told me to add to my store of knowledge and be of greater aid to those who sought me out.

For he and his brother and sister had dared the east and found what they sought—the land from which our blood had first come. There was struggle there, for their own coming had unsteadied a balance of power. They now fought great evil and those who serve the Dark. Thus they wanted aid from any willing to give it—let such only travel east and they would find guidance.

When he had done he drew one hand down the haze against which he stood and said, "Look you here, shield mate, and you will know my words are true and you are not dreaming." He was gone and there was darkness, but that was the edge of waking and I opened my eyes.

Rawit was on her feet—her hind feet, her front paws

against the wall—and she gave a sharp bark. But I had already seen it—a streak of blue running down the stone as if a finger had drawn it there.

Nor was that the last time that Kemoc sought me so, and what he had to tell me I kept record of. Twice I was able to tell seekers those they sought had gone over mountain to the east. It appeared that some ancient bond which had kept those of our race from thinking of that direction had been swept away. We heard tell of whole households—all kin together—gathering their possessions and setting out in that direction. Of each I made record.

So there was still war, though now largely of another kind. For the Dark which had slept or been sealed in Escore, as Kemoc said, stirred and awoke, not only within that land but elsewhere. Thus one of the tales I have to set down here was given me by Kemoc himself when he returned from a-voyaging into the unknown, though it was not his tale alone, and he but added somewhat to it before he gave it into my hands. Through it I learned of the sea—of which I knew little—and of dangers which might abide there.

Port of Dead Ships

by
Andre Norton

It was in the month of Peryton and there was already the sharp bite of coming winter in the air. We had finished the last of the harvesting and I could turn once more to what had become my main interest in life, the work on my Chronicles of Lormt, when there came a party to us, even though Lormt lies even more afar from the road east than it did before the Turning.

The leader was Kemoc Tregarth, my former comrade-in-arms among the Borderers. He brought to me a valiant story, of a hunting of the Dark to the far south, which is as unknown to us as once was Escore of the east. Thus I speedily thereafter added this to my ever growing collection of tales concerning the lives of many after the great wars of the Turning. A little more we push back ignorance and bring forth the light of knowledge.

1

*T*he lead-dark sky was as gloomy as the age-encrusted thickness of walls in the west watchtower. There had been a heavy drizzle of rain all night and dawn had brought very little light. Nor did the two lamps in the room within do much to penetrate the general murk. The young man who had been sitting on the wide seat the wall provided under the window did not turn his head when he spoke but continued to stare at the bleak sky.

"Four within the four-month—" He could have been musing aloud. Then he added a question: "And before, what are your records?"

The tall man seated at the foot of the table shifted in his carven chair. "None such since the Kolder times. Oh, yes, we lost ships but never were they all in one part of the sea, nor did we have the floating proofs of evil then. There were six so lost and five of them discovered in the Year of the Winged Bull—my father's time. Osberic was intending to send out a search force—but then the Kolder took Gorm and we had other things to think on. Though I have sent to Lormt—to have the records searched. Your Chronicler, Lord Kemoc, has promised us a hearing and as soon as he can assemble what information is there—"

"Lormt may have little knowledge concerning events of the sea. Though I agree if there is aught to be learned Duratan will dig it out. Do you have other legends of such happenings before the Kolder?"

The tall fair-haired man shrugged, spreading his hands apart in a gesture of not knowing. "Our records were in the Keep. When Osberic destroyed that, and an army of the Kolder slave-dead, what we should know now went also."

"It is always the same general part of the sea which seems to be thus cursed, your people say?" The woman

17

wearing a long plain robe of a grey-blue leaned a little forward so the lamplight awoke sparks from a brooch at the neck of the robe and the girdle which held it close to her slender waist.

"Always to the south," the fair man assented. "We have established trade with the Vars and it is a good one. Look at this." He put out a hand to the stemmed goblet before him on the table, turning it a little. As had the gems the woman wore answered the light so did this produce a flicker of rainbow as it moved. The bowl top was a perfect oval but the support was formed of a branch of flowers, frosted stem and petal touched with a small beading of gold.

"Var work," he continued. "A toll of twelve of these brought back unchipped, sold at auction, and a ship need make but two runs a year. You have seen the fountain in the garden of the Unicorn. Bretwald brought that back— and on his next voyage he was ravaged by a Kolder raider. All his charts and knowledge—" The man shrugged again. "Gone. It was not until after the Kolder nest was broken once and for all that any of us ventured southward again. Varn may not be the only port which it will pay a trader to visit. Now we have this: ships afloat, uninjured in any way we can see, yet deserted and with no sign left of what has happened to the crew. I say, and there are those who agree with me, that this is of Power—and evil Power at that. Or Kolder—"

The group gathered around the table all moved a fraction at that last word. Kemoc had turned his head at last to watch them. He who spoke was Sigmun of the Sulcars, a captain noted among his fellows for "lucky" voyages and who had served valiantly two springs back against the nest of pirates and wreckers who had set up a foul headquarters on islands off the southern border of Karsten. The woman at his right hand was the Lady Jaelithe, and that was a name to awaken many memories. A Witch who laid aside her dominion over Power to wed an outworlder, the same man who now leaned back in his own chair, his half-hooded eyes on Sigmun: Lord Simon Tregarth. Though he wore no mail this day, yet there was that about him as always seeming that he might be summoned at trumpet call to reach for arms.

He who sat at the head of the table had had an extra cushion added to the seat to bring him to a level not too far below his guests. Koris of Gorm was now in all but name ruler of Estcarp. Beside him was the Lady Loyse, who had in her time wrought well in battle also.

The last at that board, beside the empty chair where Kemoc had been seated earlier— He watched her carefully now, perhaps trying to judge whether it was near the time when she must leave, reach the pool in the center walled garden five stories below and renew herself with the water there as her Krogan blood demanded. She caught her lord's anxious glance and the slightest shadow of a smile reassured him.

"The Council will do nothing." Koris was blunt. "They seek only to regain what they have lost—more of their kind, more of the Power which was torn from them at their turning of the mountains."

Sigmun laughed harshly. "Oh, aye, I was told that speedily when I asked for audience. But I say to you— there is evil loose to the south. And evil unchecked grows always stronger. If the Kolder—perhaps a pocket of them who were afield when the nest was destroyed—are on the rise again . . ." The hand which had touched the goblet so delicately now curled into a fist.

Koris reached forward to smooth out again the thin sheet of parchment which covered a third of the table top. He ran a fingertip along the border of Karsten (an age-old enemy now fallen into chaos) tracing bays and indentations, the mouths of the river which drained, through tributaries, clear back to the base of the eastern mountains.

"So far we know." Sigmun watched that moving finger. "And for a space beyond." He drew his belt knife and leaned well forward to push its point even farther south. "This be wild coast and treacherous—also it seems uninhabited. There are no fishing boats to be seen, nothing shoreward to hint at any holding. Above Varn, here"—he stabbed the line marking the shore where it became a scatter of dots and no firm line—"there are tricky shallows and reefs which might have been set up purposefully to catch the unwary. Reaching there we head out to the open sea. No one has mapped the coast. By all indications, Varn is very old. Its people are not of Karsten, nor of any race we Sulcar have seen elsewhere. They do not like the sea—rather fear it—though why we do not know."

Kemoc stood up. "They fear the sea. And it is on the road to Varn or near there that ships disappear. It would seem they have good reason to fear it. Have they no tales then—the kind which are told in taverns when a drinker forgets caution in speech?"

Sigmun grinned crookedly. "Oh, we thought of that also, Lord Kemoc. We think we Sulcars have hard heads and steady stomachs, but we have yet to see one of Vars blood in the least tipsy. Also they are a clannish people and they do not mix much with strangers. They are civil enough in their greetings and their trading, but they do not add aught to the bare words demanded by that."

"Kolder . . ." Lord Simon said that word as if it had seeped out of his thoughts. "There were rumors not long since that such as they linger still in Alizon, their old overseas ally. Yet this which you report does not fit their pattern of attack."

Lady Jaelithe shook her head. "Did you not say, Captain Sigmun, that ships were so lost before the Kolders moved upon us? No, I think here indeed lies a different puzzle."

"The question remains." It was Koris who spoke now. "What aid can we give you, Captain? Our forces are mainly for use ashore. Also, we still needs must watch Alizon with patrols. We have none except the Falconers who are trained to fight on both land and sea. And of them we cannot raise more than a company, for they have their own problems. They wish to establish a new Eyrie—in fact there is talk of one overseas. That is their affair and I do not think that they will be quick to answer any summons to fight an enemy unknown and unseen, save to those who have disappeared. I cannot strip my borders on such a slender evidence. The ships you command are wholly yours; Estcarp has but fishing boats and a small merchantman or two. So what do we have to offer?''

"True, all true," the caption answered promptly. "What I seek is knowledge." Now he looked directly at Lady Jaelithe. "I believe, and so do all those who have discussed this matter in our Sea Council, that some of this, perhaps all, is a matter of Power. If those of Estcarp will not aid us in this, then we must seek elsewhere. I have heard of what you have battled in Escore—can it not be true that in the far south, where we have not been, that land curls about to face the sea, giving easy coast-room to some of the Dark? What say you, my lady?'' He tapped the parchment map again with knife point. The section which lay so there was blank except for a wriggle of line which might be part of an island, and more of the dots signifying the unknown.

She whom he had addressed leaned her head back against the high back of her chair, her eyes closed. All knew that though the Witches would not restore her jewel to her, the Lady Jaelithe had not lost what she could command before her wedding.

When her eyes opened again she looked beyond the table, and they sought the dark corner where I sat on a stool, watching this council as one might watch a harvest playlet. That I had any right there at all was a question which might well be asked.

"Destree m'Regnant—'' She hailed me by a name, and maybe the old story was the truth—that when one's name was used in a matter of Power, one is captive to another's will. For I found myself walking to the table, all eyes upon me.

Sigmun's were hot, his lips tight, as if he kept words locked within him by great effort. In this company he was the one most likely to be my unfriend. The Sulcar

21

have their own ways of Power but those deal only with the sea and perhaps a little with the weather. Also their few wisewomen are very proud of their calling and do not welcome outsiders any more than do the Witches. Of the others there I had no way of judging. Save I knew that in their own manner each of them had broken some pattern of their people and so were not mind-bound against the strange and new.

"M'lady." I gave her the traditional salute which went with her onetime rank, my head bowed above hands held palm to palm breast high.

To my surprise she returned that salute as if I were her equal. I found that a little daunting for I wanted none ever to believe that I was more than I truthfully claimed to be.

Orsya, of the water-dwelling Krogan, pushed her chair back a little, allowing me to approach the table closer. Once more Koris's hands went out smoothing flat the chart which lay there.

"What do you 'see'?" Lady Jaelithe asked sharply.

My hands were cold as the tremor which ran along my back. What if I failed now? True enough she had tested me alone and then it had been easy, not that I could or would ever claim that I had full command over this small power of mine. Now I drew a deep breath and leaned forward to place both hands palm down on the unfinished portion of the chart. I strove then to think of the sea, to paint in my mind the ever tumultuous waters, the birds which dipped and soared above, that other life which came and went below its surface.

Suddenly I could feel the touch of wave spume on my cheek, taste from the air the smart of salt, hear the never ending murmur of the waves. It was as if I trod well above the water, not soaring as a bird but rather as one who could walk some invisible layer of air.

I was searching out what lay to break that surface below. There were islands—as many of them as if some giant had seized up a handful of pebbles of all sizes and flung them out without care as to where they might fall.

Some were merely rocks hardly showing above the wash of the water. Others were larger. Yet there was nothing growing on them—nothing but rocks on which lay sea things now dead and stinking, as if these islands had been spewed forth by the sea itself.

Not too far away there was a sullen fire in the sky. I willed myself again and toward that I went. There was molten rock spilling down the sides of a cone, lapping out into the water which boiled with its heat.

Besides all this I "saw" something else—an unnatural threat which was being torn and rent by some process of its own formation. That which I touched ever so slightly was formless but it was apart from what I watched. There was the feeling of birth here, of a purpose. And that purpose held no natural cause in what it wrought. It was something so alien to me that I could not even set name to it. Yet I also knew that it was a threat to all which I looked upon—even the restless and heated sea itself.

I was back again in the tower chamber and I looked only to Lady Jaelithe.

"You saw?"

She inclined her head.

"You felt?"

"I felt," she answered.

I lifted my hands from the parchment. Suddenly I was weak, tired, I may have even wavered as I stood, for Orsya's hold tightened on my arm as she guided me into Lord Kemoc's empty chair.

It was the Lady Jaelithe who had pulled the Var goblet to her and poured into it a measure of wine from the flagon near to hand. She pushed that towards me. I was fearful of lifting that treasure, it might so easily shatter in my unsteady hands. Then someone else took it up and held it to my lips so that I could drink. The wine allayed my sudden thirst, warmed me, for I was chilled as I always was when I used my gift.

"There are newborn islands." It was Lady Jaelithe who answered their unvoiced questions. "Also there is a volcano sprung from the sea depths—"

23

"That we have seen at times," Sigmun put in as she paused.

"Also—there is something else—there is unknown purpose!"

For a moment there was silence and then it was Sigmun who spoke and I was not too exhausted to see that his hot and angry eyes measured me. I had been brought here despite his protests and to him this use of my talent must cut like the lash of a length of broken rigging.

"Lady, does one trust a faulty star course?"

"Destree"—she stretched her hand across the table and I reached out mine to hers, to have her warm fingers close and hold firmly—"has seen and I followed that seeing. Do you then agree with those late companions of mine that my gift is now worthless?"

He flushed, but I knew there was no softening towards me, nor would there ever be. I was weary of the dread and suspicion which might always follow me.

Sigmun's lips parted as if he would voice further condemnation but it would seem that he thought better of that. It was Lord Simon who brushed this aside as one who would keep directly to the point of the matter.

"What purpose? Who can control enough Power to bring to life a volcano?"

"Who controls enough for the churning of mountains?" Koris asked grimly. "And that we have seen in our own time and place."

"Witches—farther south?" Captain Sigmun seemed to bite upon that as one would bite upon the tartness of an unripe fruit.

Kemoc had come to stand behind his lady's chair, his hands resting on her shoulders. "We have met in Escore," he said, "one adept to whom our Witches would be as untaught apprentices. And he was not the only one of his kind in the days when those fought together for dominion. We do not know who or what lies to the south. But I say this, we shall have to discover and that speedily. If men disappear and ships act strangely, there is purpose enough to learn. However, the Lord Koris was right when he said that we have no forces to send unknowing of how they must be used. As it is on the land, so it must be by sea—there must be scouts sent out.''

Captain Sigmun nodded vigorously. ''That is so, and with them someone who has the gift. Volcanos and new islands, those we can understand, but if they are born by the will of someone or something—then I say we must have aid of Power to make sure.''

I think we all looked to the Lady Jaelithe now, for certainly she was first among us when it came to considering the uses of Power.

''That is a matter to be thought on,'' she returned.

''And by the fifth hour—'' Lord Koris had begun when Lord Kemoc moved, sweeping his lady up in his arms. She had gone even paler and her breath was light and fluttering. Without a word he hurried towards the entrance to the tower room and we knew that her Krogan heritage demanded the water that was theirs since their race had first come into being at the interference by some adept with nature's laws. Perhaps the very appearance of a Krogan among us was an argument that Power could call fire and molten rock out of the sea.

Captain Sigmun stood and said that he had to meet with three of the Sulcar commanders. It seemed that the company took that as a signal to break up. But Lady Jaelithe remained where she was, though Lord Simon and Koris had gone out, my hand still clasped in hers.

''What story is yours?'' she asked in a low voice which was perhaps for my ears alone.

I looked away from her eyes and studied the goblet from Varn for a long moment before I answered.

''You named me fully, my lady. Have you not also heard where my shame lies? I am only half of the House of Regnant—who my father was not even my mother could say before she died at my birthing. The ship on which her clan sailed was tolled ashore by wreckers—''

I had half forgotten the Lady Loyse, but now she moved and asked sharply:

''Off Verlane?''

"Not so." I shook my head. "It was across seas. There was a nest of pirates who boarded or wrecked many vessels. Those of the men who got ashore had the sword put to them, the women—" I was silent for a moment and they understood me well, I could feel it. "The Sulcars sent three ships against that hold and they had with them a true seer and a force of Falconers. They found my mother in a place of—of—the Dark—the real Dark. She had been given to— My lady, she could not even tell what had befallen her in that place except that she had been the plaything of something that wrecker lord would placate and be friends with, so she, and others before her, had been the price.

"She was—mindless. It would have been well for her if they had had pity and cut her down instead of bringing her back. But Wodan s'Fayre was her betrothed and he had led the breaking of that nest. He would bring her back and see if she could be healed.

"There was a healer in Quayth then, one of the Old Blood of Arvon. And my mother was taken to her. But she would not aid—she said that my mother had been overshadowed by evil and that she who had been Wodan's betrothed was gone, what was left was only a living husk. But he did not believe and arranged that she be taken to an island that he had knowledge of and there be tended by his sister and her maid-sister. They did so until I was born. Then she, who had at least worn my mother's body like a cloak, died and I lived. Only since then, Lady, there is no trust among the Sulcars for me. My gift came early, when I was just able to talk. I farsaw and I foresaw—until I realized that it was not a gift but a doom— for my foreseeing placed ill on people who asked it of me and never good.

"Last year Sigmun's blood brother became foolish from much drink at a tavern in Es City and he saw that I was also there, for I had come to ask of the Witches whether it be true that I was of some Dark blood. This is truth: if I forsee for myself, and sometimes that seems forced upon me and I cannot deny it, I profit but others pay hard for my gain. This Ewend caught me in my chamber, having seen where I went, and he said that there was one way to lay a Witch and this he would do and I might thank him for it. But when he laid hands on me—I foresaw and that I cried aloud. And he was afeared for I spoke of a thing he believed very secret. So he loosed me, for I added to that seeing my only weapon, the threat that I would forsee a death of dread for him and that would come to pass.

"After he had let me go, while he was still muzzy-headed from what he had drunk so deeply, he was found by Sigmun, who had been hunting him. And he told Sigmun what death I had threatened. And, Lady, believe me in truth, I had not cursed him, nor built any spell against him, but within a month that very death came to him.

"Sigmun believes that I can kill with my tongue and my thought. Those of his clan fear and hate me. Yet he brought me here for I think he believes that if there is work of the Dark within this trouble then I, who am of the Dark, can perhaps be used as a weapon or an unwilling hostage. His people fear spells, except those of their healing women, and some to do with wind and wave. They believe that a man can be ill wished and that is why I still live, I think, for they believe I could leave some curse behind me which would pay in horror what they had done in blood."

"And you," asked the Lady Jaelithe, "what do you believe? That you were fathered by something of the Dark and so a danger to all those of the Light?"

I rubbed my hand across my forehead as if I would erase so the pain which gnawed at me, always did so after I had used my talent.

"Lady Jaelithe, I know not what to believe. This much I know—in the Dales of High Hallack there be many places of the Old Ones—some for good and some for evil. It is said that the evil cannot be welcomed by the good. When I was a maid just taking on womanhood I went to one of the places of Gunnora, she who all say is a friend to womanhood and truly for all good. I entered in, nor did any force of assault on my body or my mind drive me forth. I asked there that I be let to know what I am—that if I be evil let me be brave enough to turn steel against myself—that if I be good I be sent some sign that that was true.

"This came to me, falling from above, whence I could not see, coming straightly into the hands I held out." I groped beneath the shirt latching at my throat and brought out that which never since had left me, a stone smooth and cool to the touch, with worn lines upon it which I had never been able to see clearly. For, when I stared at them or strove to copy them onto parchment, they seemed to slide and move. The pebble was the color of ripened grain and bore a drilled hole near the top so that it was easy to string it upon a wearing cord.

The Lady Jaelithe looked upon it and then, as if she was drawn into that gesture from a force she could not resist, she held out a finger, not quite touching its surface.

There was a sharp exclamation from the Lady Loyse, for there was a spark of light which shot between flesh and stone. The Lady Jaelithe was still, very still for a long time—or what seemed so to me. Then she said:

"Be at rest in your heart, for none who are tainted within can wear that. And I think that this is a promise that there will come a time, Destree, when you shall surely know . . . much."

2

What more assurance she might have given me I was not to know for there was a shout below and a messenger came running up to our council room so fast that he near stumbled flatfaced before us. What he had to give was a summons and we three followed him down into the courtyard. There stood a horse lathered from hard riding. He who had pushed the beast so was speaking to Lord Simon while Captain Sigmun came at a swift stride back to join us.

". . . strange ship—unlike any we have ever seen! Harwic of the *Wave Skimmer* has brought it in. There were none aboard. . . ."

"By the barge we go quicker—there are enough to man the oars!" Sigmun caught at the messenger's shoulder. "When did they come to port?"

"At dawn, Captain," the messenger, who was plainly Sulcar, answered promptly. "I have changed mounts twice—"

"To the barge is right." Lord Koris gave the order. "The crew is already gathered there. I planned to have gone upstream to the second watchtower."

Thus we speedily found ourselves afloat, for no one gainsaid any who had been in that upper chamber against going. Even Lord Simon, Kemoc and the captain took oars as we pulled out from the wharf. Lord Koris was at the tiller and set our course. For the moment it was a tricky one, for Es River is a highway in itself and many use it, both for traveling, and for the carriage of goods. Between the city and the coast it is always crowded and we swept past many a deep-loaded barge, they pulling aside in haste to give us clear voyaging as the messenger sounded a warn horn from the bow. Our own small vessel was crowded, since we had shipped a double quota of oarsmen, they trading places at intervals.

Even so it was past twilight, well into the deeper shadow of night, when the coast wind came to promise that we were near our journey's end. There was the gleam of torchlight gilding the water ahead as we closed in upon the landing for the official barge.

During that time there had been little said among us. We might all have possessed the farsee talent and been hard at labor marking out what lay ahead. Yet if that were so, none spoke of what they viewed.

From the water's edge we went straight to the small keep which was the place of the port governor. Him we found in the lower hall seated before a table which was piled high with rolls of parchment, cups used, some still half full, and plates which bore crumbs and smears of hasty meals. When he saw Lord Simon and Koris, who were to the fore of our party, he hastily got to his feet, his sword clanging against a metal flagon which he inadvertently swept from the board.

His hand lifted in a quick salute and he called over his shoulder for servants to clear the table, though he kept his hand in guardianship over the rolls. They brought up chairs from the darker corners of the room for the Tregarths and Koris. But the rest of us, save Sigmun, who remained standing, were satisfied with two benches. One I shared with the Lady Loyse and the other seated Kemoc and his lady, who, though he still kept a supporting arm about her, looked well and alert again.

"The ship?" demanded Lord Simon without delay.

"It is anchored off Gorm, my lord."

"Soooo." It was a long-drawn word, almost a hiss.

Gorm was a place of the dead, the small party of guard who drew that duty (it was always left to chance drawing by the leaders of squads) never stayed there more than a tenth day. And they kept away from the heart of the doomed and long-dead Sippar (a city which once had outrivaled Es City itself in wealth and inhabitants), taking position only in the tower by the seawall.

A place accursed was Gorm, where the dead-yet-walking hordes of the Kolder were finally released from the hideous spell laid upon them and the power of their captors broken in the east. No ship willing went to anchor in what had been the prime harbor in the old days. That Harwic had so left his find there suggested that there was good reason not to bring it closer to a cleaner portion of the land.

"A large ship, my lords. But it has no sails, nor any sign of there ever having been a mast raised above deck—"

"Kolder?" Lord Simon interrupted.

"If Kolder, then unlike their other ships such as we

have representatives of," replied the port officer. He
thumped the rolls he had been consulting and Koris drew
the nearest from under his fingers, pulling it out to its
full extent.

Though to my view it was upside down I could see the
drawing very boldly painted there and recognized it from
cruder pictures I had seen copied among the charts of
Sulcar seamen. This ovoid form which seemed to be entirely without any superstructure, more like a queerly
shaped bladder blown and sealed, had traveled under water, as ready as any native killer of the sea to lurk below
the surface in its hunt for victims.

The same servants who had cleared the table so deftly
at command returned with trays bearing plates and gob-
lets and these were shared out among us. I had not realized that hunger had made a hollow within me until I
looked at the bread and cheese, the pannikin of well-
baked fish pudding on the plate I balanced on my knees.
We ate and drank in haste as ones who are at siege and
must speedily return to their posts. Yet it was tasty and
I licked the spoon from which I had eaten the pudding.
The crumbs left on my plate were very few indeed.

I nursed my goblet after taking only a sip. This was the
wine of sea port, potent stuff, and perhaps befuddling to
one not used to it. Nor did the Lady Loyse drink deeply,
though like me she cleaned her plate.

"This Captain Harwic, what story does he have for
us?" asked Koris.

"He has been sent for, my lords. You may listen and
judge for yourselves what unknown thing has been
brought to mystify us." The port officer had never ceased
to frown since we had entered and I believed that he
indeed considered that Es Bay might well be threatened
by what was now at anchor in it.

"This he brought to me—" The officer now pushed
something across the table into the fuller light of the lanterns which now shown clearly, for it would seem that
this defense tower was not equipped with those ever-
burning moonlike lights which studded walls of most of

the old part of Es City. "This," he repeated, and pulled back his hand more quickly as if he found even the touch of the thing in some way dangerous.

It looked to be a box, but inset in the lid was a round disc of glass—fully transparent—and below that was a dial which bore strange markings. There was a needle suspended so it trembled over that dial, and it swung easily as Lord Simon took up the find. I saw his face become set and he beat a tattoo on the side of the box as if striving to move that arrow. Though it quivered, it did not shift.

His lips formed words which he did not share with us and he arose so suddenly from his seat that his goblet overturned and the dark river of wine would have smeared over the edge of the parchments had not the officer snatched them away.

"This was found on board the ship?" There was an incredulous note in Lord Simon's voice.

"So Captain Harwic said."

We were all staring for it was plain that the box had delivered some shock and it must have been a mighty one to so affect this man noted for his many forays against the Kolder and the ancient evils of Escore. For shaken he plainly was.

He put the box down with care, almost as if he had held something which might spout fire, as had the mountain from the sea in my farseeing. If he were going to explain what he found so overpowering he did not have time before another Sulcar wearing both a mail shirt and the winged helm of a ship's captain came in, pausing by the door until the port officer waved him forward.

"This is Captain Harwic," the port officer named him.

He was older than Sigmun. I had heard of him, that he was one of those born with a very restless spirit, to whom the finding of new sea paths was more needful than the trading with any people he might encounter on unknown shores. Yet that he could do also, as stories of his unusual cargoes were well known, encouraging others to try for such. He was what was known to his fellows as a "lucky captain" and those who berthed on his ship were envied.

Now he sketched a salute as his eyes swept from one to another of our company. I believe that they mirrored that chill which I expected from his people when they touched me.

"You have brought in a ship." Lord Simon stood with his fingertips just touching the box which had amazed him so, as if to make sure that it really lay there before him. "One," he continued, "which is a craft strange to you."

"Very strange, my lord. And I have been north to the Islands of Ever Ice and south past any chart we know."

Lord Koris looked up to him. "Kolder?"

For an instant or two Captain Harwic hesitated. Then he spoke with careful slowness as if he were not certain himself. "It is unlike the Kolder ships which were seen at the taking of Gorm. This one was not meant to ride beneath the waves, but with them. Yet how it could sail at all I do not see—there are no masts . . . and never were, by the look of the deck. And there are no oars, also it was not designed for rowers. The Kolder ships moved by their magic, perhaps this does likewise. Yet it was a derelict, floating unmanned and answering to no tiller when we found her."

"And there was no one on board?" Lord Simon asked.

"No one, my lord. Still two lifeboats swung on the deck. Yet it would seem when we searched her that those who had been there had been called away by a sudden order. There was dried and rotted food set out on a table, and the bunks had been slept in. Also in the place where the captain must have been there were charts out which we had never seen the like of, two cups had stood there but had rolled and spilled across the charts. And that"—he pointed to the box before Lord Simon—"was on the floor skidding back and forth with the roll of the vessel."

"What was the cargo?" The Lady Jaelithe spoke for the first time.

"Bales of something which had once been a plant of

sorts, my lady. That was swelled by the water which must have come through the hatch in some storm. It was. rotted and without value. Nor did it look as if it had been grain.''

"And where did you find her?" Lord Simon cut in.

"South, my lord. We were well south of the Point of the Hound. There hit a storm out of the northwest and that carried us well past waters which we knew. When we were left afloat after the fury of that subsided, we took a star sighting and tried for a shore. But there were reefs and islands and those we dared not venture among with the *Wave Skimmer*. We put out the longboat and Simot, my first officer, took four men, two of them Falconers, and they oared towards the islands which were large enough for a landing. The falcons were loosed, but the birds reported nothing but the bare rock. Not even lichen seemed to grow there.

"That night there came a distant roaring and there was fire in the sky. The like of that my father had once seen and the story he told very often. It must have been fiery rock from beneath the sea, shooting up. So we took sail away from there, for who knew where that troubled rock might rise next?

"It was midday as we sailed westward that we saw the ship. We lifted signals but there was no answer. Then he who commands the Falconers sent his bird to spy closer for it looked very strange. When the bird reported none on board we closed and took her in tow. Though that was difficult. We have found derelicts before but they have been Sulcar, and once or twice a round-bellied merchant coaster from Karsten too far out from their usual coastwise sailing. Never have I heard that any have brought into port what we have.''

"It seems, Lord Simon, that you have seen that before." The port officer pointed to the box.

"Not an exact match to this, but like it, yes. It is a compass.''

"And that, my lord?''

"A direction finder of sorts. This needle"—he tapped

the bubble glass under which that lay—"is supposed to point always to the north—thus one can keep a path. At sea such were always . . ." He hesitated for a moment, looking to the Lady Jaelithe before he continued. "This all of Estcarp and Escore knows—I am not of this world by birth but have won through one of the gates. This is something which my own time and place knows. And if so—" Again he fell silent; it was Kemoc who finished for him.

"Thus this derelict can be from another time-place? Can there be gates on the sea also? If so—what can win through them? The Kolder was an evil which near finished Estcarp in their time. Must we fear that some new disaster may come from the sea?"

"We can only learn though what has been found," Lady Jaelithe said. "And what the Power can tell us. Perhaps there are answers for us aboard that ship."

"We shall see." Lord Simon's expression was grim and now he gave a push to that which he called a compass, sending it out from under his hand. "The sooner, the better!"

Though the night was dark enough, our way was lit down to the quay by lanterns so that most of the shadows retreated to the farthest reaches. Captain Harwic had a ship's boat waiting and we all crowded into that. He gave the order quickly and we were shoved away from the quay, heading out into the dark of the bay. I had thought that we must return in his own vessel and that would be worked out towards brooding and damned Gorm. But instead his men plied oars and we pulled apart from the last of the anchored ships, heading on toward the full darkness since it was a moonless night.

I thought of Gorm and what it meant to those who were chosen by lots to garrison the watchtower there. The streets where the dead had walked under the control of the Kolder lie forever deserted, still the horror of what happened in Sippar, the great port, must remain always in memory. It had been more than a generation ago that Lord Simon and his following had fought the great battle there—and I knew that the Council had sent Witches with Power for cleansing. Yet it was still a place deserted and accursed.

Lord Koris should rule there by right of birth. He had been a self-exiled one when Sippar fell. Did he have any inner ties now to a place so blackened by the terror and despair of utter evil?

I saw by the dim light of the boat lantern at our prow a white hand move and touch upon a shoulder. Lord Koris—the Lady Loyse—both had been deprived of their birthright, yet it would seem to all whoever saw them together they had made their own kingdom of inner faith and strength.

On the still-distant island I saw the spinning beam of the great light, its sweep from side to side across the sea entrance to the bay. We had that for a guide and our men were quick and strong. It was not long before I picked up the wink of much smaller lights, those which must mark one of the great quays to provide landing beacons for anyone coming to Gorm.

It was towards those that we were making our way now. Beside me Captain Sigmun stirred. That we shared seating had come by chance and I knew that he was finding that an unhappy fortune. Only now I was better aware of something else.

That stone which I believed was a gift to me in Gunnora's shrine was warming against my skin. Such had chanced once or twice before. Power—remnants of Power—must still lie ahead. I raised my hand to press over the stone where it lay beneath my shirt. I wore Sulcar dress which afforded freedom from the long skirts and robes-of-state one sees in Estcarp. And because, except for my eyes, I looked Sulcar, my otherness was seldom apparent to those who had not heard the whisperings which followed in my wake when I went among the people who would not own me.

The short, loose breeches were an aid when we came at last to the quay in the dead city. I swung ashore with ease which matched that of Orsya, whose tight-fitting, glittering, short tunic was like scales, and truly I believed was fashioned from the skin of some large aquatic creature. She stood beside me looking towards the dark lump-mass of the city. Then she wheeled and faced the sea.

"This is a place of the Dark," she said. "I—" Her hands went to cover her ears, pressing tightly on either side of her head. Kemoc swung up beside her.

"It is well—!" I caught his thought and swiftly raised barrier, for never did I read unless that was asked of me.

Lord Simon might have some of the Power, bred in him in that other world from which he came. And Lady Jaelithe was surely Witch. Two of their three children were gifted in spite of sex and nontraining. All knew that Kaththea was a Witch in all but formal acceptance, and, as for Kemoc—he had dared to summon that which had not been called upon since the beginning of time of Estcarp itself and had not only survived but been answered for the aid of others. Warlock he was named, though he did not use regularly the gifts. While his brother, Kyllan, who had been named "warrior" at their triple birth, had mind send and some forewarning to draw upon, but his skills lay mainly in the meeting of battle.

The quay on which we stood was cracked and in one place part fallen from its support to be awash by waves. Not too far ahead there were two lanterns set and between them a ladder hung against the side of a ship. Lord Simon's stride lengthened and his pace was close to a run. While the Lady Jaelithe, wearing the riding dress which gave her more freedom, was quick to catch up with him.

He stood, his hands on his hips, his head turning slowly from right to left as he studied what was visible of the derelict in this light. The craft was large—near the length of a smaller Sulcar vessel—and I wondered at the skill and labor which had been expended to bring it to anchor here. There were two decks—the smaller upper one having a forward section placed higher still. Toward the stern behind this there were two lifeboats still snug set as Harwic had reported.

Lord Simon paced down the quay beside the ship. There were portholes but they were dark, dead eyes and no one could see through to what lay behind. As if the rest of us were invisible he caught at the ladder to climb to the deck. There was a lantern aloft there which gave some light.

Still without speaking he caught that up and a moment later disappeared into the cabin. The rest of us followed more slowly. Indeed this ship had never been meant to sail after the fashion of those of Sulcars. No mast had been ripped out by a storm; there was no place to set such.

Beside the door where Lord Simon had vanished more ladderlike steps led up to the smaller top deck. Sigmun and Harwic went in that direction. The rest of us followed Lord Simon. Here was a long cabin first which had portholes like windows on the sides. Ahead was a table set for four, wooden partitions marking out each place so that the plates and cups there would not slide to the floor during any attack of storm.

These showed remnants of a meal which certainly had not been finished, judging by the amount of food dried and rotted on the plates. We went on to visit other cabins. The walls were of well-rubbed wood, a rich red-brown. In two of the smaller spaces undoubtedly meant for private sleeping quarters, there were brightly colored garments on the bunks, which more resembled beds, and such things about which suggested women had been quartered here. Yet there was not any untoward chaos which would mark looting by pirates. In fact, Lady Loyse picked up a necklet of shining stones as rich as any worn for court in Alizon, where they flaunt their wealth. It was simply that the owner had gone as if for a moment of time only.

Back in the largest cabin at last, Lord Simon caught up with an exclamation something lying on the padded seat along the wall. It was certainly not a reading roll nor one of the rare books made by fastening separate strips of writing material into a common back made of carven wood or engraved metal. This was back-fastened right enough, but the strips were larger and seeming of a lighter material than any parchment.

Yet looking over Lord Simon's shoulder as he flipped this apart, glancing at each square as he turned, I thought that the markings there—though totally foreign to any script I had seen, must be runes of a kind. There was a picture of a woman dressed in strange garment which hardly covered even a quarter of her body. The clothing—if it could be called so—was a vivid red. Her hair was long, tossing free about her shoulders with no constraining ribbon or net. And she was lying belly down, her legs stretched out, her body resting on sand except for her head and shoulders, as her arms held her so. While behind her was a stretch of blue which might be meant to suggest water and out on that was just such a ship as the one we had boarded, water curling back on either side from the bow as if a knife blade were cutting through the waves!

Lord Simon snapped the reading record shut and studied the cover. Here was another picture, also of a woman, smiling—her hair, cut very short, was as black as that of the Old Race, but she certainly was not of Estcarp, and the robe she wore left her shoulders bare though she had jewels at her ears and her throat.

With his finger Lord Simon was tracing a line of what surely must be runes above the picture and suddenly he dropped the book to stare at his own hands.

"Simon—!" Lady Jaelithe set her hand upon his nearer wrist and was looking into his face with concern.

He started, as might a man awakened out of an absorbing dream, or one who was farseeing. Perhaps the latter was the truth for he said, as if speaking some unbelievable thought aloud:

"Fifty years! But it cannot be fifty years!" Still he looked down at the hand where his lady's fingers had slipped to grip his. The skin was brownly weathered but taut. Into my mind came then—perhaps his thought reached us all—that he expected to see grooved in his own flesh the signs of great age.

It is well known that the Old Race do not show marks of age (and they live longer than many other peoples of our world) which are common to those other races until just before they die. Yet the Lord Simon was off-time as all knew and it seemed he expected to be otherwise.

"This ship, Simon, is it true that it—"

"Of my own time and place?" he asked harshly. "Yes— of my own place—not my time. It seems that the latter moves faster elsewhere. A gate—in the sea?"

"Perhaps," she answered him. "But one which would take a ship without the crew? That I think is another matter."

3

I had slept during the latter part of the night after we returned to the port tower. Our quarters were not equal to those of the citadel at Es, but they were better than many I had known in my wandering life. If I dreamed, no warning from that carried over into the daylight. A patch of sun stamped on the stone floor a little away from the small bed told me that the hour was indeed late.

There was a washing place off the sparsely furnished room and I made use of what that offered, standing when I was through to look into a mirror of polished metal on the wall. In my mind there had flashed memory of that picture on the cover of the book Lord Simon had brought back with him into our quarters.

My fair hair, bleached even lighter by the summer sun, had been chopped off at shoulder level—for I found the long braids a woman must care for a hindrance. My skin was also colored by summer heat a brown which met the white of my body usually covered to form a definite line. I had the high cheekbones of the Sulcar also, but my chin was not so square and my mouth was certainly too large to give me any claim to even good looks, let alone equal comparison to most of the women I had seen.

It was my eyes which proclaimed the most sharply my alien status among the people whose blood I half shared. Where theirs were blue or in some cases green, mine were overlarge and of the color of well-forged steel. Being browed and lashed with black instead of that color which crowned my skull, those eyes appeared doubly prominent in my face, and, I thought, showed as chill as those floating hillocks of ice which could be often sighted in the far northern sea.

I held up my hair with my hands, straining it back so I could see what I might look like if I were shown as that pictured woman. The effect was in no way flattering and I went in to clothe myself thinking again that indeed I was not particularly favored by fate, physically as well as with those gifts which had done me more harm than good.

My hands sought Gunnora's talisman, which I settled carefully into place between my small breasts, I not being endowed in that direction either. It had been warm last night, but now it was cool and I latched my shirt high. There was a tap at the door of my chamber and I hurriedly went to answer the summons. The Lady Loyse stood there. She was small, making me feel suddenly too large and clumsy.

"Destree, we meet again. Jaelithe has something she wishes to ask of you. Also they have brought in the morning food." She smiled.

It was something I had thought about much since I had been so drawn into this circle of old friends and kin. It had been the Lady Jaelithe who had had me summoned to the first meeting back in Es City. These famed ones who had wrought in their own ways—Jaelithe, Loyse, and Orsya—to bring peace into places of the utter Dark had accepted me without question, spoke to me as if I were almost bloodkin, or at least a battle comrade from another time. It had been that feeling of trust which had led me to tell the Lady Jaelithe of my beginnings, and the

41

Lady Loyse had heard those same words. Yet she had not turned from me, jerking away her robe where it touched my sea boots as if evil could be scraped by such an encounter.

This acceptance was so new, and because of the past, I could not wholly accept it. What did I possess that these could use that they spoke me so fair and came to call me in person to a meal when a servant could well have been sent? I kept my thoughts veiled, yet they added to that cloak of depression which I had worn so long it had become a very familiar garment.

"It is a good day," Loyse said. She paused by one larger inner window which gave upon the center court of the keep. There was a plot of flowers that seemed out of place guarded by such massive stone walls. But we could look down to three benches set near together, well away from those walls as if any who so gathered had some uneasiness about being overheard—as if the walls might sprout ears. Save for Sigmun I saw that those who had come from Es on that call the night before were helping themselves to food from a table set on wheels.

We joined them speedily and they all gave me matter-of-fact greeting as if indeed I were a longtime comrade in some action of importance. Lord Simon sat drinking from a cup but his eyes were elsewhere, upon what rested on his knees: the book from the strange ship. But he looked up as Orsya put out her hand to summon me to a seat beside her. Kemoc sat cross-legged at her feet, watching his father with compelling intensity, as if he would force some information out of him by eye power alone.

It was the Lady Jaelithe who put down her own cup to look directly at me. I was instantly alerted. Now it was to come—what they wanted from me.

"You have farsight—and foresight—"

"Foresight," I returned quickly and perhaps more sharply than I should have done, "I will not use—"

I saw both Lord Simon and Kemoc shaken out of their own preoccupation to look at me. But the Lady Jaelithe

42

was continuing. "Have you also the talent of finding the origin of something from afar? That talent is often tied with the seeing."

I was silent with surprise. In my years of roving—though those had not been too many—I had never tried to set my gift working in that direction. Now that she spoke of it I had memory of small flashes of knowledge about people and things which had seemed to just coast into my mind when I took belongings into my hands. Yet I had always believed that that was merely my sensitivity to being more or less outcast and caused by my imagination, not any talent.

"Take this." Lady Jaelithe drew the alien book from her lord and actually thrust it at me with such a sharpness in her voice that it might have been an order she did not intend to have refused.

The book was very smooth to the touch and I found myself running my fingertips, as it rested on my own knees, back and forth across those lines of runes. They were neither incised nor standing above the surface as a touch on parchment might have found writing as I knew to be. In some way they were a part of the surface on which they appeared.

There was a stirring, not quite like the call to the seeings I knew so well, but of another kind. I closed my eyes and strove to open a mind door I had not been entirely aware I possessed.

There was a storm, such as even the most canny Sulcar sailing master would find difficult to fight for the life of his vessel. Also there was fear—so overpowering and wild a fear as ran close to the borderline of sanity. I crouched in the large cabin of that strange ship. Foul sickness arose in my throat. I could see another shadow—for the lights in the cabin had failed—and knew it.

"Miggy." I mouthed a name but I could not hear my own voice, so savage was the storm. It had seemed to spring out of nowhere.

"Jim!" Again a name, and, with that, came an even greater gust of fear if such was possible. Jim was gone—

he had been licked into the sea as if a wave was a giant tongue lifting him up to gulp down.

Before the storm—I strove to reach that—what had happened before the storm? Somehow I managed to force memory to reply. There was sun, hot on a reach of sand. And a short quay to which there were several of the alien ships tied up. Miggy and Jim—they had been whispering together. There was some act which had a danger of its own. Yet danger made it interesting. It had to do with a boat—a boat and, out at sea, a bigger ship from which something would be transferred. That was the secret, one which was the source of danger. Still that danger was a lure. Now I saw the interior of the cabin—there were four people there. They were not uniform in appearance as were the Old Race and the Sulcars, carrying their kinship on their faces for all to see. She whom I knew for Miggy (and what manner of name was that?) had red hair. While Jim's was brown, with silver patches about his ears, and cut short, as was Miggy's also. But the other woman sat combing hers, which was streaked weirdly with several strands of silver through black. And the second man, seated by her, was burnt very brown, while his close-cropped hair was in the beginnings of curls against the scalp.

They were arguing but I could not hear what they said, only feel tension in the air—it was about the danger. Then—

Once more I was back in the storm, the ship in wild swing. There burst outside the ports, from the rims of which water trickled now and then to wash the decking, a lash of light which blinded. There was nothingness, then—

I opened my eyes to find that all the party was looking to me. Slowly and trying as hard as I could about details, I recited what I had learned. If I *had* learned it and it was not born of some imaginative feat of my own. At that moment I could not be sure of anything, for I was spent. If I moved my head it seemed the whole courtyard took on the dizzying sway of the ship storm-tossed.

"The gate." Loyse spoke first when I had finished. "How did they get through the gate? How can there be a gate in the open sea?"

I shook my head very gingerly, afraid to bring on an attack of vertigo. "The storm—and before that the beach— There was no more."

Lady Jaelithe reached over and took the book from my now-slack hold.

"They sensed danger, these whom you saw. What danger was it? Perhaps the gate—"

"No." That much I could answer. "It was something to do with another ship at sea. A much larger one, I think."

"Sand and sea and many ships tied at a wharf," Lord Simon said slowly, then he caught at the book and went flipping through its queer pages in a hurry. He had found another picture and held it for me to see. "There were trees like this to be seen?"

The one he pointed out had a long bare trunk, its branches all at the top, wide leaves made of many tapering strips set together.

"I saw no tree."

For a moment he looked as one who had thought he had found a thing of value only to discover it was worthless.

"You knew of such a place in your own world?" Lady Jaelithe asked.

"Yes. Also there was a place in the sea which had strange legends of disappearing ships—legends which had been known for centuries. A sea . . ." he said musingly.

Kemoc added a question. "But if a ship comes through, where is the crew? We know well the gates—have we not had personal knowledge of them? But always it was that people came—alone."

"It remains," for the first time Lord Koris spoke, "that of this we must know more. Do we want another invasion from such as Kolder? Let us make sure as soon as we can of what chances in the south that such ships as that can appear there. The Sulcar will support such a venture,

45

since they believe that they will be the first threatened as
they have already been. What of their ships found derelict without crews? Can it be that perhaps the gate opens
also the other way, dropping Sulcars into your world,
Simon?"

"Who knows what has happened. But as you have
said—we must learn what we can. And to learn that we
need ships willing to sail south, though what perils await
there who can say?"

I think that all there would have volunteered for such
a voyage but there were still duty to hold a man. Lord
Koris had taken the rule of Estcarp, and for him that remained the fact he could not deny. In the end there were
five of us—Lord Simon, the Lady Jaelithe, Kemoc and
Orsya, and I—because in me something said, This you
must do. Though I believe that the Sulcars, had it not
been for those I was to company with, would have refused me on board. Legend grows greater than action in
the telling and I was considered to be one of the enemy,
or at least tied to the Dark, by most of the captains.

There were two ships chosen, Sigmun's and Harwic's.
Beside the regular kin crew they each carried a detach-
ment of Falconers, those dour fighters. But some precautions they did take. Though the Sulcar always sail in
family groups, living more on board their ships than on
land, this time they set ashore their children and such of
their women as were pregnant, Lord Koris seeing all were
well settled in comfort at the port.

There was one time of difficulty when one who was a
seeress aboard Lord Harwic's vessel showed temper and
teeth to me, saying that I was so ill-omened as to bring
the fate feared the most on any person—so what would
I do with a ship?

Then the Lady Jaelithe took command, and so much in
awe was she held by all, even more by those who possessed some bit of talent, that the woman gave way
quickly when it was made clear to her that that vessel
was to bear Lady Jaelithe and Lord Simon. While I was

to sail with Sigmun and Kemoc and Orsya on the *Far Rover*.

With a cargo of wood and very well provisioned, we set sail at last after two ten days of hard labor, heading out into an ocean under the first colors of dawn. Over us the seabirds wheeled and called mournfully and under a fair wind our sails bellied, so that we were fast past the dismal shadow of Gorm with only the wide sea before us.

We had made other expeditions to Gorm to explore the derelict and Lord Simon had consulted the charts and other records found on board. He had names for a crew of six, but there had been others on board—the women I had "seen" and whose clothing and belongings were still in one of the cabins, a double one. Of those he could learn nothing save that they had been aboard. While there were no notations in what he called the ship's "log" which explained either the purpose of the voyage or the reason for carrying the rotted vegetation which had been stored in the small hold. As for the reclaiming of the ship for any service he explained to Captain Harwic that the running of it did indeed depend on neither sails nor oars but on a complicated machine, such as the Kolders knew, which needed to be fueled with a liquid unknown in our world. Thus the vessel remained at Gorm's dock for the present under the guard of the small garrison there.

Though I am of half-Sulcar blood I had never been taken in to any ship's clan yet I had worked passage on many vessels, doing the lowliest of labor, never trusted to any position of skill or direct need in maintaining the voyage itself. This time I was left with nothing to do for my passage. Or I would have been had Orsya and Kemoc not sought me out in the first day. The Krogan girl was deeply amazed by the very fact that so much water lay always about her now. Her people in Escore depended upon streams and ponds, lakes and rivers, limited in their exploration on land because of their need for that same water to renew their bodies from time to time. Before our sailing Kemoc had made plain to Captain Sigmun that the ship must tow a boat from which at intervals Orsya could descend into the sea and swim for the space needed to restore her energy.

Since I was anything but welcome on board myself I yielded at once to their invitation to join them in the boat. Kemoc was a strong swimmer, though his one hand and arm bore still the signs of the harsh wound which had made of him a left-handed and perhaps less efficient fighter. But he could be a child paddling in a puddle when his best efforts were compared to Orsya. Since her gills went into service in water she could dive and stay unseen for lengths of time which no one save a member of her own race could equal. Though Kemoc made her swear that she would not venture far from the boat. There were grim tales enough of what might lurk in the depths— strange water beasts and reptiles of which we knew very little were rumored to have their hunting grounds there.

To my surprise Kemoc had questions for me. I did not think that the Lady Jaelithe or the Lady Loyse had repeated the story I had told them, the first time I had ever revealed the whole of it to others, but that the Sulcars considered me an outcast was plain, and also my reason for being in Es City, a wish to consult with some Witch, was generally known. He had seen me use a fraction of my talent and now it appeared that he wished to know the extent of my birth gift. There was no reason to hide aught from him; we were by fate members of a company sent for a task and it was only just that each of us knew what might be expected from the others with whom he or she marched—or rather sailed.

I said that I had farsight, and foresight (which I also made plain I considered a flawed talent upon which I had no intention of depending) and, as he had seen, I had the reading sight after a limited fashion. But that I had any other of the talents I doubted very much.

"Sometimes one cannot be sure," he said musingly as if he had thoughts he did not share. "The Council thinks little of Lormt but there is much that can be learned by delving into the past. When the mountains turned, Lormt suffered the fall of two towers. But that same shifting of very ancient stones uncovered hidden rooms and spaces which held records no one had looked upon for uncounted years. A comrade from the Borderers of my early fighting days now deals with some of these finds. When we return, seek out what Lormt may hold for you, Seeress."

"You give me a title which no Sulcar will grant, my lord. What I can see they distrust, even as they keep me apart—"

"Would you be one with them?" It was Orsya who asked that as she combed her silver hair, freeing it in part from the water which had sleeked it over her shoulders.

"I—" But I got no further for as I tried to weigh my desires, order my thoughts, I made a discovery which should not have surprised me. Did I want to be one with the women of the ship's cabins, labor at sails and all which kept the cabin home afloat, be at the orders of those who were masters and mistresses of waves and servants of winds?

I looked up to the ship behind which our boat swung into the waves the *Far Rover* sent back to trouble us. Never would I be accepted aboard with anything but grudging consent. If I was of the true blood I would long since have been wed and one with kin whose single purpose was to advance the ship in seeking and discovering new markets, or plying stolidly back and forth between cities well known. There would have been nothing more for me than that advancement which was shared by all. I could not be a seeress; they, too, were bound by even tighter ties into the pattern of voyages. I was too long a wanderer on my own to accept any such commitment to the will of others. It had been a long time since I had felt any envy. Perhaps it was true my nature was twisted from birth and I was a ship without a home port or a rightful captain, always a-search.

Now I looked directly to the Krogan girl. "I think I would not be one with them unless I had been course set by them from birth. Though that I have never thought or said before.''

"Each one of us has many roads ahead; we make choices sometimes without asking our hearts if this is rightful for us," Kemoc said slowly. "Nor can many of us live to walk a path another has chosen for us, no matter how schooled we may be to accept another's will." He turned his head a fraction and smiled at Orsya, taking one of her slender hands to hold it to his cheek. "Twisted indeed was our own path once but we came at least to where it ran straight and true. Though even now there lie shadows across our way—or so we must believe, being who and what we are. Still we would not have it otherwise. So," now he spoke a little sharply, his eyes for me again, "you have three gifts that you are aware of. And how do you polish them? By careful use as is well?"

I shook my head determinedly. "I do not seek to know the future—"

"But," it was Orsya who interrupted me, "you can see only one future—there be many for the same viewer. If one awakes one morning and does so, then the day will end with that future carried out. But if one arises making another choice the day will run otherwise. Then which, foreseeing, can you choose?"

"That is an argument I have used with myself," I told her. "Only the few times I have foreseen for others—and that almost always against my will—the evil waiting was what they met. They say my foretellings are curses compelling someone to meet the fate I outlook. And—for myself . . ." I shook my head. "Such foreseeing as that is always murkey, seeming like a picture which has been slashed into tatters, this part or that part visible as in a dream, but no orderly progress I can view for my own enlightenment. No, I can foresee—blackly—for others, and that I will no longer do. For myself there is nothing to make choices for."

"That is the way of all who foresee—to lack the Power to set their own life forward," Kemoc answered. "But that you always foresee evil for others and that comes to them thereafter, that I cannot understand."

"Say then that I curse them, my lord. Not that I do so deliberately, with malice. That is my Dark heritage perhaps."

My hand was at my breasts feeling for Gunnora's amulet and again I clung to the one small hope that had brought me. A seeress who cursed—that was *not* my destiny. That path I could choose not to follow.

"My father," Kemoc continued, "has the foreseeing, but it comes to him as a warning and only shortly before the peril it heralds. He also can bond with us when there is need, feeding what talent we may use with his strength. With my mother he can be one-minded even at a distance. But that he learned later; it was not a birth gift."

"And you"—Orsya dropped her comb into her lap and drew her hand caressingly down across his scarred flesh— "you meddled in what you did not even know, choosing a path of great peril—yet it was also one of safety."

He was frowning, looking to the sea rather than at her. "I did not know how much a fool I was to use what I did not understand. And what I have learned thereafter has made me only more aware of that."

"My lord—" I began, and then he smiled at me and returned:

"Lord? No, I was a simple fighting man of the Borderers and I am still a fighting man when there is need. I have no lordship nor do I want one. I am Kemoc first and so I remain."

"Kemoc," I corrected myself. "What chances in Escore?"

"Now that"—again he smiled a little—"is a very large question and I can only answer a small part of it. It is thus with us—"

4

$\mathcal{H}$e talked then of battles, of evil driven back, only to have its forces surge onward again, of how it was to live eternally on guard when one rode forth from those islands of safety which had always been under the protection of the Light.

"Still," Orsya said (she had tossed her hair until the sun, which was growing warmer, had dried it), "there are now times of peace and those are growing more and more, longer and longer."

"Is it, could it be true," I wondered aloud, "that Escore curves westward in the south, to touch upon the sea?"

Kemoc shrugged. "Who knows? We have ridden and fought our way far westward. My sister lives now upon another sea of which we of Estcarp had no knowledge in the old days. Judging by the extent of what we know nothing, it could well be that southward the land comes to an end and that sea is part of this one bordering the east as well as the west."

"Be still!" Orsya was leaning over the side of our small boat. There was a look of such concentration on her face now that a seeress might wear when in a self-summoned trance.

I stared into those waves but nothing could I see. The ocean was not like the clear water I had trudged beside inland, through which one could sight sand and bubbles, the coming and going of the creatures which made that course their natural home.

Kemoc did not glance at the water, rather his face was fixed in the set look of he who mind searches. All those who have any of the talents can develop mind touch to some degree. They cannot always communicate or receive direct messages from another but they can know where life runs, hides, or lies in wait.

Tentatively, with all the caution my own use of gifts taught me, I sent out a quest-touch tendril. Because Orsya still looked into the sea I strove to send in that direction.

For a second I flinched. What I had caught the fringe of was hunger, a mighty hunger, rawer and greater than any rage, and perhaps the more dangerous for that reason. There was no real thought, or if there was, the hunger overbore that.

Kemoc turned and caught at the rope which tethered us to the *Far Rover* and my own grasp was with his only a second later. We pulled with all our strength and our small craft answered, heading for the side of the Sulcar vessel. Orsya still kept her post as if she listened (could one name it so) to the thing which lurked out of sight.

I could keep in touch with it only slightly for the vibrations were too close to the edge of my ability to read to afford me more than that. However, I knew that the thing had certainly now turned its attention to us, that it had altered its swimming pattern and was following our skiff. I thought of a fish intent upon the swallowing of some bait and that lent more strength to my pull on our lead rope.

Now Orsya settled lower in her place, her chin propped upon her folded arms, which rested on the gunwale of the boat, her head forward, staring as if to force the swimmer below into view for all of us. That consuming hunger was now as sharp in my own mind as a shout might be in my ears.

We slid into the shadow beside the *Far Rover* facing the ladder dangling from her deck. Kemoc gestured to me to climb, but I indicated Orsya. He shook his head and I gathered that the Krogan girl might in some manner of talent be better armored than either of us. I sprang to catch the dangling cordage and was up and over unto the deck. Kemoc followed and then turned to reach a hand to Orsya.

"It comes!" she cried out as she dropped to the deck.

Three of the Sulcar crew crowded in as there was a flurry in the water below. I caught sight of a black shadow just beneath the surface and then there gaped out of the water a mighty head larger than the boat in which we had been. Great jaws ringed with pointed fangs, two rows of them, closed upon the wood of the boat and that sank out of sight in a rush as the thing which had so surfaced returned to its own place. Lengths of splintered wood whirled upward. It must have crushed the stout timbers of the boat, which had survived storms, as one could take an egg between one's teeth and splinter the shell into bits.

"What was that!" Captain Sigmun leapt down from the quarterdeck to join us. A moment later the *Far Rover* lurched in the water. The menace below had signaled its disappointment by a headlong ramming of the vessel.

Sigmun shouted orders and our ship veered a fraction from its course. However, there was no way in what we might defend ourselves from the unseen monster. I wondered if the seams of our hull could take such a pounding were it to continue. Then I saw that the rope which had moored our boat to the *Far Rover* was stretched tight and that the ship was actually answering to that determined pull. Turning, I snatched one of the boarding axes which were never far from hand in the racks, kept ready in strange seas. With all my strength I brought the blade down on the rope. It parted; the one end lashed back to rip my sleeve and cut into the flesh beneath.

Once more, even as I folded my torn sleeve over the wound, the ship shuddered at a ramming attack from below. Then that did not come again. Orsya stood close to that rail, grooved where the rope had cut, her head slightly aslant as if she listened. Then she spoke:

"It has dropped below."

The captain stared at her. "What is it?" he demanded. "Never have I heard of any sea thing which was large enough to trouble the *Far Rover*. Will it attack again?"

"It hungers," Orsya answered. "I know nothing of its kind. Only I think that such hunger will drive it far. It senses us."

Sigmun glanced about the deck as if he sought something which might be used in attack. The *Far Rover* mounted two of the dart machines which had been fashioned in imitation of those the Borderers carried. But they could only be used against a visible foe and had not been intended to shoot into the sea but rather across it. There were other aids to battle which might be used—the balls of glass which contained a blueish power to bring fiery death to man and sometimes ship when loosed from nets slung around to give them speed. The *Far Rover* was as well equipped as any Sulcar fighter-merchant could be and all that in the way of defense and offense had been checked, resupplied and made ready before we sailed.

There were harpoons set like spears in another rack on deck but one of those would be no worse than a splinter of the boat for that lurking below. We had a fair wind and the ship loosed of the small drag the boat had kept upon her cut the waves cleanly beneath billowed sails.

How we might have fared with a final attack we were not to know. Orsya sped across the deck, seeking the cabin she shared with Kemoc, and when she returned she held a bundle between her hands. Kneeling on deck she unfastened the strings of a stuffed bag which flopped open on the planking to show within a number of packets. One of these she caught up just as the water beast once again struck at the ship, this time dangerously close to the rudder. Kemoc, as if he well understood what she would do, tore off his shirt as he knelt beside her, holding the cloth as taut as he could against the planks. Onto that surface she poured a small stream of sandlike granules. They were dark and might have been the remains of well-crushed pebbles. Reknotting her first packet she took out another. From this she shifted a powder of blueish green. Kemoc took his side knife from its belt scabbard and with the point of that she stirred the mixture thoroughly. Then there was a last addition, this time of pebbles about as large as my thumbnail, of which she selected three of red and then six of blue.

Kemoc rolled and knotted the shirt into a bundle. I saw her lips moving as if she recited some spell or called upon a Power to serve her, then she ran, mounting to the upper deck where the steersman stood with a shipwoman beside him on either side to lend strength if need be.

Orsya drew back her arm and with all the strength she could muster she sent the package hurtling out over the water. It whirled downward at a speed I would not have granted it since it had no great weight. Touching the waves it sank like a stone. Orsya stood by the rail staring into the depths as if she could see the success—or failure—of her defense. There was a stream of bubbles boiling up through the water where that unwieldy package had sunk.

I longed to search with mind touch yet I feared that that very act had been what had aroused the creature in the first place. Then, without my searching, it struck at me, just as it must have Captain Sigmun, who was standing at arm's distance away, for I saw him sway. Not hunger this time but anger, a rage so great and dark that it near cut at one as might a sword. After that—nothing.

Now I did dare to search—the hunger had vanished. If the monster still waited below, it was not because of a desire to shake us out into its waiting maw. Yet Orsya still stood intent upon the water, Kemoc beside her, his own gaze fixed upon the ripple of the waves.

Captain Sigmun shook off what had held him prisoner for those few moments out of time. He shouted orders and the ship came to life—all of those on deck seemingly having been held in the same spell. It was then that the Krogan girl came away from the rail, Kemoc's arm still about her, supporting her. I guessed from her drawn face that she experienced, at least in part, the same overwhelming fatigue which came at the end of any use of the gift.

"Is it dead?" Sigmun paused beside the two of them.

Orsya shook her head slowly. "I do not think so. It has taken the Xalta inside it. But that will only confuse it for a while. It lies very deep now on the bottom of the sea and it is as if it sleeps. But for how long—what can I tell you? This is a defense made for use against creatures of the Dark who infest lakes and rivers—what it will do for one from the sea none of my people can guess."

I saw a bird arise from the foredeck, a falcon wide winging, and I knew that one of the Falconer marines on board was doubtless sending so a message to our sister ship, which was so far abeam that we caught only a glimpse of topsails. A warning—we might only hope that the thing with which Orsya had dealt would still lie in the depths long enough for both of our small squadron to be well away before it roused.

I saw Orsya glance in my direction and then speak to Kemoc. He beckoned to me, and, with Orsya between us, we sought her cabin, I pausing only to take up the bundle she had brought from there earlier. Once within she insisted on treating that burn the snapping rope had delivered to me, smearing it with a reddish stuff which had the consistency of mud and smelt acridly enough to make one sneeze. This hardened as soon as it was applied and that small pain I had only been dimly aware of during our encounter with the monster was instantly eased.

Kemoc went to the porthole and stood looking out. He was plainly troubled, and, when Orsya had finished with her heal-craft, he spoke that trouble aloud.

"You dare not swim again—"

Then I knew what fear was rising in him and it was echoed in me. The Krogans must have water for their bodies. To remain dry for a length of time was as fatal as to remain without water to drink while one traveled in a desert region. If there were dangers hiding in the sea how could Orsya survive?

"Perhaps I cannot continue to swim," Orsya assented, "but I can stay beside the ship with a rope about me to haul me forth speedily should any danger come. Also—" She brought out of that bundle which had held the materials for driving off the monster a jar which she untopped. Almost instantly the cramped cabin was filled with a scent which set me to coughing and brought that same response from Kemoc. "This can be used." She made a face and sneezed violently herself. "It would seem," she commented, "that this sea air has made it all the stronger. Nothing in any water of Escore will approach the source of this. Perhaps it is true also of sea creatures." She speedily resealed the container but for moments afterwards we continued to cough.

"We have time enough"—she put the jar away—"to consider many plans, for the water need will not be on me yet a good while. Before I try to answer that there can be a searching." Hanging her bag on a hook driven into one of the beams overhead she settled herself cross-legged on the bunk. Kemoc leaned back against the wall of the cabin and I edged forward a stool and seated myself.

Orsya reached up and took Kemoc's maimed hand in hers. She closed her eyes and I felt the surge of Power that went out in search—of what? The monster, to make sure that that was not coming to once more attack the *Far Rover*?

Awkwardly I set myself to match her pattern. One had first to close off the touches of life energy which marked members of the crew and the ship clan. However, one who has used the gift speedily learns how to do that. An entirely open mind would be a torment to the one who owned it if one did not quickly learn to center such a search on something else. Still here we—or I at least— had no quarry. I closed my eyes also, to picture the endless surging of the sea, the waves which spun white lace as the bow of the ship cut through them. Even this far from land there were birds overhead—those kerlins who were said never to seek solid shore except for their nesting and who slept upon the rocking waves far out from any land.

There was life. I caught sparks of energy but none I tried to follow. For I was seeking something else—a hunter out of the depths. That fierce hunger which had struck as a blow the first time I encountered it was not there. Perhaps Orsya's counterattack had worked better than even she had hoped. However, it was easier to center on something which one could mind-picture and I had seen no more than a portion of the monster's jaws as those crunched upon our boat.

Without willing it my far gaze opened. Even as I had hung on thought above those grim rocks of islands when I had used it at the Lady Jaelithe's bidding so did I now once more forge ahead—or so I believed—and found—

The islands of rock again. They were scattered—rising from the sea in a half circle, one end of which reached to what was either a true shore of our own continent or else an island much larger, older, and—

Energy poured around me. That was not aimed at me but over the outflung islands. There was Power here—to entrap! Hastily I drew back, closed down my searching tendril of seeking thought. The islands and the land behind them were gone. I did not yet open my eyes and admit defeat. Rather I fastened upon one corner of the land I had seen so momentarily—not among the islands, rather that portion of the shore. Into that effort I poured more striving than I had ever done before as in me there was growing a need for haste.

Now I no longer saw the sea, rather I looked down upon a range of sharply pointed teeth which in the guise of land mimicked the jaws of the sea creature. These formed an outer wall but farther in there was a blot of shadow. It was growing more and more difficult to hold that picture in mind; I was tiring. I was—

I was seized by a Power source far beyond my own against which I could raise no defense. Back spun my farsight over the sprinkle of islands. There was no distant fire this time—had the volcano I had seen before been quenched by the sea?

The force which had entrapped me swung back and forth as if it also combed the islands for some object. I halted my struggle, for now I knew it for what it was— the joined wills of Orsya and Kemoc. There was a leap of heightened energy. Island and rock reef passed under my "sight"; we were returning to the shore of that other mass of land. I realized that these other two were riding on the edge of that force I had earlier encountered, only to fear and flee from.

There was a bay spreading below us—for now we three were one. Far more sharp and clearly came the sight. In that bay were gathered a vast fleet of ships! But there was no touch of life arising from those. We had only an instant of that view and then we snapped away. Even so we did not go so swiftly that I had not caught that warning. It was like a whiff of stench from some battlefield where all had perished and none remained alive to bury the dead. This was death itself, and not a clean one.

We were—caught!

I have seen nets spread for fish and the silver bodies leaping therein frantically and without hope. Somehow I knew that withdrawal could not come without a struggle. I resisted, and just as I had been drawn to them so now did they swing with me. Now I was a spear point and they the shaft behind. Though I had never been so entangled before I instinctively fought to change what lay beneath me. Bit by bit, aided by surges of energy from the others, I slowed our flight inland. This compulsion was something such as I had not met before. The stench of evil was in it, but I could not locate its source. That this was a device of the Dark I did not question, and to seek out its nature might well draw us farther into its hold. Instead I fought to mind-see the ship, the cabin—

With the farsight one is never aware of one's body—only of what one sees within. That in-seeing might be the only aid for us now. Ship—there was still the ship. Again the rocks and bay, now that swing of barren land; I strove to build instead the picture of the ship, of the cabin which reason told me still held that which was the flesh envelope from which I had ventured. For return I fought and with me those two others.

A ship, yes— However, it swung in and out, alternating with sight of that country unknown. Perhaps I could not bring the whole ship into being, but the cabin was smaller and we had roots there. For wherever one has slept and lived, even for a short time, that site takes on a measure of one's person. On such a link the farsight can fasten for a guide.

I built those walls, the narrow space between them. I saw Orsya, Kemoc, their linked hands— It was as if they had not quite realized what I could do but now understood. Once more they poured into me the force which they were capable of raising. I had a body—I opened my eyes.

Orsya leaned against Kemoc's shoulder, her eyes closed. There was limpness in her poise, which brought fear. Then Kemoc stirred; I heard his mind voice call:

"Orsya!"

He opened his eyes just as I stood away from the stool, before the Krogan girl. My hands were up on either side of her drooping head. With all the strength I had left I mind-sent the picture of where we truly were. Yet she did not stir. Was she still caught in that web of the Dark which had entangled us? Still in my back swing I had not felt any diminution of energy, and surely I would have known if we had left her alone!

Kemoc pushed my hands away. His own went into place the same way. I knew that the tie between them was such that he could reach farther to draw her back. Also, was he not reputed to be indeed a warlock, one who dipped into ancient wisdom generally forgotten?

His face was grim-set. Orsya fell back on the bunk as he withdrew support. Now he bent over her still using that hold between them. All of a sudden she sighed. That sound gave me such relief I, too, felt weak and sagged back against the cabin wall. Her eyes opened and she looked up into his face.

"It—it—waits—" Her voice was hardly more than the shadow of a whisper.

Kemoc spoke nearly as softly in reply: "It is not here." And, as softly as he spoke, there was still authority in his tone.

However, it was toward me she looked and not to his face so close now to hers.

"It hungers."

At that moment I knew the rightness of her choice of words. That strong pull was as much a part of hunger as the force radiated from the sea thing. But it was not a hunger of body—

For the first time something which was not a conscious willing on my part twitched my thought aside, that was a path I must not follow. In that moment I also realized that, for once, fortune which was good not ill had worked through me for others.

Orsya, her gaze still holding mine, nodded. "You do not know your strength, seer-sister."

"But do not try it too far!" Kemoc broke in upon the two of us. "No more of—"

"Such journeying?" I interrupted him. "Be sure that I will swear oath to if you wish it. Though I believe that we three this hour have seen that which we seek—"

"So be it," Orsya returned. "That is a place of death." She shivered, turning her face from both of us as she spoke.

There was a rap on the door at my back. I looked to Kemoc and he nodded assent so I turned and slid aside the door of the cabin.

Yakin, the mate, stood there.

"Captain Sigmun wishes speech with you." He did not look beyond me, but rather *to* me as if he brought an order. Because of the tone of voice he used when he said that I believed that it was. Though I was none of Sigmun's clan this was delivered as if I did owe allegiance to him.

I stepped without, moving slowly, for again the toll that farseeing had taken had drained me. Also there was apprehension of a kind, for I was very sure that Sigmun would not look kindly on any use of talent by me. Had he in any way been aware of the far journey from which I had just returned?

5

*S*igmun faced me in the narrow slip of cabin, the only private space afforded in a ship which was both a way of travel and also the permanent dwelling place of a clan. His eyes were the dark blue of the shadows one sees lie stretching out from snow dunes, and certainly there was no lighting of grimness which held his features in a harsh set. However, he waved me to a small stool which was the only other seat in that blade-wide space.

"There has been spelling!" he spoke abruptly. "We will have no more awaking of those from the depths."

"If spelling called such—and there was no calling—then it was also spelling which sent it away," I pointed out.

There was no lessening of his set jaw, of the bitter lines which bracketed his mouth. Now he brought his hand, fist tight, with force against his knee.

"I will not have the *Far Rover* endangered!"

"She was kept from danger, was she not? The water magic of the Krogans may be more powerful than we know."

He did not answer that, only continued to stare, as if by his will alone he could bring out of me some oath which would reassure him. Inwardly I was wary. Sigmun had been in favor of our present expedition. There had been certainly warning enough that this was no easy sail upon an unnaturally quiet ocean. This being so why had he now apparently changed?

"Does that thing follow?" he demanded.

That he would willingly ask the help of my farsight was so strange as to set me on guard. I answered him then with the truth:

"Captain, my talent you hold in abhorrence, why do you now wish to use it?"

63

"There is reason to consult any chart when one is sailing blind."

He meant it then. His fear for his ship had broken down, at least for now, that strong-held barrier which the Sulcars had always kept against me. Farsight could not bring any fate upon us as my foresight might; I could dare such a reading and not—

Sigmun had turned to pick up an object from the floor. This he held into the light which came through the single port breaking the cabin wall. What he so displayed was a piece of wood about the length of my arm, splintered at either end. That it was part of that skiff which had taken the assault of the dweller in the deeps was plain.

"You read from such as this." There was no warmth in his voice, only urgency. Nor could he deny him after my one such seeking. Only I was already weary from the farsight. To use what little strength I had gathered since that to a new test was perhaps futile.

Reluctantly I took the broken length of wood in both my hands, resting it across my knees. Closing my eyes, I willed to see, to read—

A murk closed about me. Through that was movement. I might have been entrapped in a thick fog in which there was other life astir. Yet so concealing was that fog that I could not be sure of the nature of the things which flitted, only momentarily, close enough to catch my attention.

Not fog—but water! I was thought-deep in the sea and those which flickered in and out of my land-trained sight must be fish—sea creatures. There was a sudden flurry as a near cloud of swimmers flashed past me. Fear lived in the fog, now.

I had not seen enough of the monster who had hunted us to be sure of its shape, to be able thus to center my sight upon the object I hunted.

This thing slid forward ponderously. I had seen many kinds of sea dwellers, some so very grotesque that they might have been fashioned by deliberate intention to frighten, but this held no echo of anything I had ever sighted before.

Though it was hard in this murk to judge sizes I had the impression that the thing was near as long as the *Far Rover*. The body was scaled but those overlapping armor shields were large enough to give the appearance of being shell hard and solid. I had once seen a creature, brought from the north, which possessed a similar body but that had been quite minute compared to this. Though there was something of a fish about it, yet there was also that which was totally strange—no finned tail, no fins for side and back. Rather thick, taloned extremities protruded to make swimming movements. The head was near the same size as the body and most of that head was mouth which was widely agape now as it plowed forward after the fleeing fish. Though it seemed to labor at its swimming it closed upon that flight and snapped up mouthful after mouthful of prey so small in comparison with its bulk that it must near spend most of its lifetime eating merely to keep life within that hideous body.

I dared to probe.

I could not have uttered a cry, for the throat which should shape that, the lips which would utter it, were not there. Instead I cut the cord of the "sight." When I opened my eyes I was no longer in the murk of the deeps but still seated on a stool in the captain's cabin while he held me with that fierce, compelling stare.

"You have seen it!" No question that, a statement of fact which I could not deny. "Does it follow?"

"There are no charts in the depths," I returned, struggling to retain at least my surface confidence. "It is feeding—following schools of fish."

He was silent for a moment and then he nodded as in answer to some thought of his own. "But there is more, that is the truth, is it not? You found something other than a sea thing feeding on its natural food."

So I must have betrayed myself. How much dare I say to this man who had accepted me with nothing but distrust? He could well believe that I was attempting some trickery. Only those who have the talent themselves realize that that which one learns through it cannot be assumed, it is always stark truth.

"The thing is—was—a guardian. It has—by some means—perhaps the coming of boiling water from a volcano—been driven from its place and it is lost. But it is not native here. And it was set to a duty—"

He did not smile at what he might deem foolishness, instead he was frowning. Then he turned again and I saw behind him a small chest. This he drew across the planking which was between us and snapped up the lock, throwing back the lid. From the interior he pulled out a roll of very ancient parchment, the edges of which were so tattered that they might be fringed. Closing the chest again he unrolled a small fraction of the scroll he held.

The marks upon it were very faded. I had to lean well forward to see what had been so revealed. Though some of the lines were missing, and the whole needed several guesses to give it full body, I might have been looking at a very crude representation of the thing I had seen feeding.

"This," Captain Sigmun said, with something close to solemnity in his tone, "is Scalgah."

I stiffened. That he meant what he said—that the much-faded picture was intended to represent a legendary monster so ancient that only a very few legends so much as mentioned it—I had to accept. I had heard enough from those who had visited Escore—that in that shadowed land many of the old legends did have actual life—so perhaps this was possible. Only Scalgah was not of Escore, nor even of the legends of the Old Ones.

From whence the Sulcars had originally come no one knew now, even our bards and seers could not tell. Only there was with us the belief that we, too, had won through a gate, in so far a past that the stones of Es had not been yet cut or laid when we came. Why we came, that we did not know either. Those of High Hallack say they were hunted by enemies through the gate which brought them to the Dales. The Kolders warred, one part against the other, and forced their own gate that they might plunder what was waiting on our side to furnish them with the means of setting up a world empire of their own.

However, the majority of those who are recorded to be dwellers from Outside arrive one or two, or perhaps a small clan, together. Even as had Lord Simon in his time.

Sulcar legend did not say that we were hunted. Maybe we came by chance or for the adventure of seeking the new. However, there was no return and that was made certain by the appearance of guardians. Those who listened to the oldest songs knew naming those:

"Theffan, Laqit, Scalgah—" I found myself reciting those names—all reverences had long since fled that rhyming now. It was a game song for children—used to "count out" this one and that from a dancing ring.

I saw Sigmun nod and then he rolled up that ancient record to replace it in the chest.

"So now we go to the gate?" I ventured, although I knew that he could only equal my own guessing.

"Perhaps. I would like to know if Theffan and Laqit also exist."

"Water and fire, earth and air," I repeated. "In the heart of death is the core of life. He who holds the—"

I had gotten just so far in that other ancient saying when his hand shot forward and closed upon my wrist in a crushing grip. "How know you that?" He spoke between set teeth as does a man before he bears steel.

"I—I do not know!" Yes, those words had risen easily in me. However, when they had first become a part of my memories I could not tell now. I had long been a wanderer. The Dales I knew, and the Waste, and even part of Arvon. I had guested in halls, and slept under stars when other wanderers came together around a camp fire to seek out for a space the companionship of kind, for that we would hunger no matter how lone our lives. I had listened to the tales of merchants and, yes, had even served for a single voyage now and then aboard a Sulcar vessel when the ship clan did not know my story. I had talked and I had listened, and, though my years were not yet many, I remembered more than perhaps even the hard-faced man I now faced, whose laced fingers brought twisting pain to my wrist.

I could not understand why a scrap of ritual had struck him so profoundly. His other hand arose a little and his forefinger moved in the air as if he wrote there some message which only the initiated could read. I then knew what I had done. In some way I had used words which were the pass sign for one of the Kin-by-Sword companies among our people. Though such a one as I was barred from any these.

"I do not know where I first heard that, Captain. I claim no fellowship which is false." My other hand sought that amulet hidden beneath my worn shirt. Who was I indeed who could claim common blood, kin bond with any? Yet Gunnora had not refused me this sign of hers.

Did he believe me? I was not sure. But he released his hold on me and snapped the lock on the chest before he pushed it back into the shadows from which he had drawn it.

"You would be wise," his voice was very sharp and cold, "not to repeat that again. If it was mouthed in your hearing at one time that was, in itself, a call for discipline. So you say Scalgah—but does he follow?"

"That I cannot say, Captain. The farsight does not measure—" Then I remembered the board I still held—it had not been altogether by the farsight that I had viewed those murky depths. I laid my hand palm down upon it but I did not seek.

"I can only watch through this," I told him.

"Let it be so," he said curtly and I read in that tone that I was dismissed, so arose from my stool, the broken board in my hold.

Nor did he call again upon any gift of mine. Also, after speaking with Orsya and Kemoc, I did not seek again on my own. They were deeply interested in my report that the creature of the depths resembled one of legend, however, and told me of those other survivals of what had once been termed myth yet lived on in Escore.

Orsya's need for water was answered ingeniously by two of the Sulcar women, who brought forth a length of stout canvas carried to repair storm-torn sails. This they sewed at either end with their stoutest of waxed thread. Then we caulked it on the inside with tar, working until we had a crude trough as long as Orsya's body. Water drawn from the sea filled it at intervals and the Krogan lay within that, renewing herself as she must for life itself.

The days were fair and the wind was steady from the north. It seemed to me, who had long ago come to question any singular run of good fortune, that we were a little too favored. It might well be that the Dark forces were playing with us, as, according to legends, they had in the past, waiting to deliver some blow when it would be the hardest for us to stand defense against it.

We did not seek with farsight again. But Kemoc spoke often of the lore he had learned at Lormt. Though then he had gone for one purpose only, to search those incredibly ancient records in order to discover a place where he, his sister, and his brother might take refuge from the anger of the Council, there were other records stored there. He shook his head now over the fact that none of our party had sent for information there concerning the far south. It might be a case such as Escore where a part of our world had been walled away for protection. We could well have been better prepared had we known what lay perhaps forgotten in this time.

Now he asked of me every scrap of knowledge I had before he went to Captain Sigmun. Upon demand he was shown the full of that roll of learning. However, the runes, worn away by the years, were in another tongue and Kemoc could learn little from it. He asked once if I might hold it and so go far-seeking in the past but received such a decided "No" that I think he was astonished. As for me, I kept out of the captain's path as best I might so we had no more talk together.

The fair weather and the increasing warmth of the days as we sped south brought many of the clan to the deck, where they busied themselves with the care and restoring of wardrobes, the repair of weapons, and those small tasks which lie always to hand. Orsya mingled with them and showed one who made belts trimmed with shells a new pattern to work by.

Alone of our trio I had the least to do. Until, driven by sheer boredom, I took knife and began to work on that piece of half-splintered board which Sigmun had left with me. I was no master carver but once I had wintered in a dale where there was a woman so gifted with her hands and she had wrought from large gnarled roots all manner of strange creatures. From her I had learned enough to shape, far more clumsily, some object hidden in the wood which my eyes told me could be raised for the sight of others. My belt knife was keen and, though I began at first clumsily, my fingers once loosened to such a task grew the more skillful. What I brought forth from the wood was a likeness to Scalgah as my farsight had marked him.

It was Orsya who first noted what I was doing, kneeling beside where I sat cross-legged peeling off slivers of the wood. As I paused to measure my work she put forth a hand and touched lightly the whittled wood. Her fingers were snatched quickly back and I heard a small sound so that I looked to her inquiringly.

"It is . . . death." She had hesitated before she said that last word.

"Yes."

"Yet you give it life. For what purpose?"

I did not understand at first and then I guessed that she meant the "life" I was bestowing by the carving which was coming at my insistence from the formless wood. Purpose? I had thought to employ my hands, not wishing to be idle when all those about me were busied. Still there were always warnings to be heeded in such matters.

Whatever is wrought by our hands carries in it something of our own energy and talent. A man could be tracked, even identified, by a sapling he had slashed to find his way through a wilderness. Someone, with the gift the Lady Jaelithe had led me to believe I had, could read the maker's body and spirit (a little) by taking into hands something wrought by the other.

"I do not know why," I answered slowly. "I thought to busy my hands, but there are indeed many things I might have chosen to see within the wood to lead me to free them so. Only it was only this which I was minded from the first to carve."

"A guardian." She had settled herself by me. "A guardian of a gate?"

"Who knows? The Sulcars have been long here. They have forgotten their coming and the reason for it. It has been only since the Tregarths found Escore once again, and the displeasure of the Council no longer matters, that people have questioned things as they be and speculate as to what might once have been. Also the mystery of lost crews and kin, as well as such surprises as the derelict Lord Simon recognized as being from his own world, if not his own time, makes one wonder what else there remains which might be a threat."

Orsya was combing her hair again, shaking it free of the water, for she had only recently climbed out of that liquid bed. Drops of moisture flew and a few pattered on the wood I held.

"There is never any peace now," she said. "Even in Escore, where for a time when we have beaten off the Dark and it seems had the best of a mighty victory—and such we have had many times over—we are not allowed long to go our own way and rest from battle. Always the Dark gathers new force, that which is of the Evil, and readies itself, so that once more rises a cry for swords and spells and keen eyes, ears, and mind to listen and arouse. Once my people were content with our streams and lakes where none troubled us—though we ourselves

71

make the substance of such tales to be far different. Only I have not before heard that any gate has a guardian—"

A long shaving curved away from the blade of my knife. "Scalgah was a tale—as Escore he has taken on life again. But he is far away from the place where he should lie in wait. There was a troubling of the sea which even he could not withstand, some disturbance which has driven him from his proper place—"

"You have read this from him?"

"In part, yes."

She tossed the curtain of her hair back on her shoulders. "Did he know—were we more to him than food?"

"I do not know. He requires much to fill his belly." I tapped on that part of the carving with the point of my knife. "Only I begin to think that he knew that we reached for him."

"Does he then follow?"

"Again I do not know. But this I am sure of, I shall not seek him out without great cause. Nor would Sigmun and his kin take kindly to such action. I am no seeress of their choice but someone they have reason, or so they believe, to look upon with suspicion." With my other hand I again sought that amulet of Gunnora's. Only by that could I keep my own dread fear at bay. We were sailing as fast as a good wind could carry us toward that place we had seen, of desolate sea-born islands, fire mountains, and the bay of dead ships. What also might await us an active imagination could well supply—but never on the side of the Light.

I looked down at that on which I had been working. Had I a talent for such or not, that which was emerging under my knife indeed possessed a kind of life. Almost at that moment I was moved to hurl it into the sea. Yet something within me kept it within my grasp as if the time for such was not yet come.

Not yet come! My thought caught that. Perhaps the same sudden idea was caught by Orsya for again her hand came out towards the carving yet she did not quite touch it.

"There are weapons which are not steel," she said slowly. "Yet I would not carry this one openly if I were you."

I stroked away another bit of shaving and glanced up—to the afterdeck, where Sigmun stood beside the steersman. He did not wear mail or helm here and the wind pulled at his loose-braided hair. His attention was aloft at the sails which filled with the ever present wind in a manner which could arouse uneasiness in any shipmaster—it was too constant, too well faring. It was as if there had been a summons which only the *Far Rover* herself could answer and she did. We had veered course slightly that morning—another twenty hours or so of such a tail wind and we would be nigh past Karsten—though we could see nothing of that ill-omened shore from where we coursed. There would come then the Point of the Hound and beyond that only Varn was truly known.

Our sailing plan had been to harbor there, at least long enough to hear any news which those of the edge of our world might have gathered about what chanced beyond. Though the people of the city were mainly silent with strangers, the presence of the Lady Jaelithe might loose minds if not tongues. The Vars had ships, small fishing boats of shallow draft. They did not go to sea beyond the sight of the coast.

6

*N*either of the Sulcar ships had sailed from Escarp cargoless. Having Vars' needs in mind what they carried was fine woods, selected either for color or scent. There were large slabs of spicy pine and longer lengths of redheart with its vivid coloring, the more slender logs of wence, which were gold-yellow and near as hard as steel, taking on a metallic lustre when polished. As well as small quantities of others with which I was not familiar save when they grew in the far hills.

The land around Varn was treeless, the largest growths on the plain which fanned out from the sea being large brush, thorned and forbidding, generally carefully avoided by man and animal alike.

Unlike other peoples, those of Varn did not explore inland nor spread far from the single city which was the heart of their own civilization. It seemed that their population never increased very much. There were indeed some families or small clans who left the safety of that stone-walled hold to cultivate fields well out on the plain, also tending flocks of sheeplike beasts that were much smaller and longer of limb than the species known in High Hallack, but produced a long-hair wool which could be converted on looms to a cloth which actually withstood moisture—and which the Sulcars coveted for boat cloaks, though very little of it was ever sold.

Though I knew the procedure well I had never seen used so carefully before the sensing of a harbor entrance. Sigmun had no seeress aboard, but one of his crew, a straight-backed girl, looking to be still in later adolescence, took her place at the bow of the *Far Rover* as we nosed in towards the shore. It was according to her hand signals that the man and woman at the wheel did their duty during a lengthy advance with most of the sails lowered, leaving just enough canvas above to give us slow movement.

Although there were no reefs breaking the surface of the sea here, this caution suggested that we were creeping through a maze of obstructions to enter the throat of the bay.

Cliffs loomed high on either side. Sigmun pointed out to Kemoc certain breaks near the tops of those natural walls which he believed held some manner of defense if the city should be threatened from the sea. Twice the path the water-see girl set for us brought us enough to one side to move directly under one of those.

At mast top we were plain marked with a Sulcar trade

flag. However, on board near the wheel and its guardians our small force of Falconers had taken a stand, ready to defend the helmspeople should trouble arise. One had released his bird to spiral upward, well above the crests of the cliffs, keeping position in the air to sight any activity which might suggest danger. It was an excellent commentary on how wary the Sulcars were of the taciturn people of Varn that they continued such action even though there had never been any hostility shown.

Behind us the *Wave Skimmer* had closed in. For the first time we were close enough to see those on the deck of our sister ship. Their water-seer was a man and they were just entering the crooked path down which we had steered when the *Far Rover* emerged into the open bay.

That was bowl shaped, surrounded by cliffs except for a space directly before us. There the walls of nature gave way to an open space in which was fitted, as a worker in gems might fit a jewel into a setting, the city itself—running from the base of the cliff on the north to that on the south.

The bay was not empty of shipping. Two wharves ran out and to those were anchored several small boats, one masted for the most part. Their sails made a brilliant splotch of color for those were dyed (though they were lashed down now and not showing their full brilliance) red, yellow, green, and even mixtures of those colors.

As the sails so were the buildings of Varn itself. Though the coloring there was more subtle. The whole city might have been a canvas by some giant artist because the dwellings on one level were of one shade, those of the next a second, blending so that from the bay the town actually appeared to be striped, beginning with shades of blue a little lighter than the sea surging about the wharves and then going through green, violet, wine red, rose, and so to gold and then a pale yellow.

I had heard that Varn was unlike any other city the Sulcars visited, but this wide display of color was breathtaking to one who was used to ancient stone, always greyed. I heard Orsya beside me at the fore rail give a little gasp as she looked upon the prodigality of color.

Not only were the walls of each and every building done so but there were flags of different sizes cracking in a breeze which swept seaward over the town to touch on us.

The *Far Rover* was brought to anchor some distance away from the wharves. Sigmun had disappeared into his cabin, only to come out again wearing a mail shirt, a winged helm in the crook of his arm. He had given us all the instructions he had learned from ship records. We did not go ashore without invitation and we might have a long wait for the delivering of that. Those of Varn moved only to their own customs and made no exception for any visitors.

The *Wave Skimmer* moved in to anchor a couple of ship lengths away. We watched them also lower the trade flag to raise it again with a streamer of white now above it. We could see people on the wharves but none of these appeared to halt what they were doing to even glance in our direction. Clearly one cultivated patience here. I had near decided that we were going to be ignored forever when a group came along the wharf nearest the *Far Rover* to embark in a boat which skilled oarsmen sent through the water at a good pace towards us.

Despite the color of their city those in the boat were dressed uniformly in a silver-grey and they all wore strange headgear in which a pointed cone was the center of a securely wrapped length of scarf thick enough in the overfolding to shield most of their faces.

At first I thought they had well-weathered skin much as a far-voyaging Sulcar would show. Then I saw that their color was so uniform they must naturally be dark of countenance. All but one of them sprouted a nubbin of beard on the projection of the chin and their eyes were unusually large and also dark—being artificially enlongated by black marks on the skin curving upward toward temples. Though I thought the Sulcars were tall, these Vars appeared to unlatch a spring within their thin bodies as they got to their feet, one by one, to catch at the rope ladder Sigmun had ordered over the side. When they reached the deck the shortest of the party of four who had come to receive us was almost half a head taller than the captain.

They looked to neither the right nor the left, concentrating on Sigmun and his first mate. Before him they spaced themselves in a line so straight they might have been measuring it by their toes planted along one of the cracks between the boards.

There were doubtless differences among them. However, at first meeting, they looked so much of a match, one to the next, that they might well have been deliberately patterned to do so—like the manikins which are sold at fairs in High Hallack at harvest time.

Captain Sigmun and his mate saluted them with hand held up, palm out in the universal sign for peace. However, they made no reply in kind. One of their company spoke then, using that broken trade speech which the Sulcars had devised early on their meeting with other peoples.

"Ship come—why?"

Sigmun pointed upward to where our flags played, snapping in a breeze growing ever more brisk.

"Trade." He was as terse as those from the city.

They had been inspecting our company unblinkingly. It seemed to me that their gaze was not so much for the Sulcars but rather centered on those of us who were not members of the crew. Kemoc had followed Sigmun's example and wore mail, cradling his helm against one hip. Orsya's scaled, tight-fitting garment was covered by an unbelted robe of so light a blue that it was near the same silver as her scaled garb, which showed as the wind flapped the robe's skirts, as if striving to drag the whole thing from her shoulders. I had made no alteration in my own garb and looked quite drab, which had long been my portion in any company. A very lean purse does not warrant anything more than durability. My hair was

sheared short at shoulder level and, though I had no mail,
there was a serviceable long knife in sheath at my belt.

"Who?" The leader of the Vars pointed directly to us.
There might have been curiosity in his ocular examination of us, but there was certainly no warmth or any alteration of expression on his features.

"Lord Kemoc, Lady Orsya, and . . . Destree," Sigmun
answered with the fewest possible words.

They were silent and motionless, except for the
spokesman, who stretched forth one hand. There was
what appeared to be a round stone resting in the hollow
of his palm. At first sight it was as silver-grey as the garments they wore. Then it began to change color, at the
same time giving off a glow which tinted the flesh on
which it rested. Blue, and the intensity of that hue grew
more dramatic in less than a breath of time.

The owner swung his arm in a short arc. Now the stone
pointed directly at Kemoc. The blue appeared to fade a
fraction, but it did not altogether withdraw. The second
swing was toward Orsya and the color rippled across the
surface of the indicator as a stream might ripple across
some pebble in its bed. At last it was before me. At first
the color faded even further than it had with Kemoc, but
an instant later it came flooding back until there was such
light that it might have given off a lamp's radiance.

At the same time the amulet beneath my shirt warmed,
the warmth rising to the heat of stone new-raked from
the fire, so I was forced to fumble and bring it away from
my skin into the open. Its honey shade might have been
a fire of golden flame to answer that of the blue.

The man from Varn was plainly astounded, as were
those with him. I saw the serenity of their faces crack
and astonishment break through their indifference. He uttered a stream of words as if he voiced an incantation or
a formal greeting. Then he clapped his other hand over
the stone, hiding it from view. Toward me he inclined
his head, a gesture copied by the three others with him.
Then to my surprise he pointed directly at me and made
a question of one word.

"Trade?"

Did he wish my amulet? Or did he wish me? I wanted to try mind touch, but was too cautious to attempt that with a race who might not be so gifted and so would believe it an invasion which would then endanger any rapport.

I left it to Captain Sigmun to answer since it was he in this instance who headed our small command. The brilliance of the amulet was withdrawing being no longer confronted by the stone. I had no intention of parting with it since it was to me an abiding weapon against the Dark in my own thoughts, a promise that however I might have been fathered I was not a daughter of evil.

"Ask it of her." The captain deftly passed decision to me. The leader of the Varn deputation appeared disconcerted, as if they had fully expected Sigmun to be in full control of all. However, obediently, the spokesman looked again directly to me expectantly.

In answer I deliberately slipped the amulet back beneath my shirt to rest warm between my breasts. Then I strove to carefully select words from the trade lingo as I had picked it up during my journeying.

"To me only—Power." That that word might mean as much here as it would in the north, I had no way of telling. One never does claim any hold on Power which cannot be proved should the need arise. Perhaps even here they might have heard of the Witches, even though the Council had no records of Varn. Would they deem me a Witch and so expect from me what one of those dedicated and withdrawn personages might do? That would be fatal for all of us. Yet I must make sure that the amulet remained mine and not a thing to be bartered for. Power comes by the choice of some one or thing greater than any born of flesh, bones and blood, and to the one any such is given has to bear the weight of it without question—or in some cases relief. I would not, could not, part with that. Luckily I felt no touch of any mental probe. However, at the same time, I sensed that they had accepted my refusal and would not quarrel with it. Instead, to my discomfort, they turned nearly as one and bowed, touching the bands across their foreheads, their lips, and finally their breasts in what was undoubtedly a form of very formal recognition or greeting.

Then the spokesman looked again to Sigmun.

"Trade," he said once more and this was uttered as half order, half promise. Turning again a little from the captain he once more gazed full-eyes at me and added:

"To Asbrakas, High One—" It was not quite an order but it was certainly a summons which he did not expect to have refused.

We had talked of Varn before we had sailed. Since the Sulcars had found it to be most southern of all the lands they knew in which there was a native civilized people, it had been decided that if we could we must learn what was known there which could pertain to the mystery we sought. Did the Vars know of the derelicts? Had they any tales of volcanos or any other strange things about the sea? That I should not refuse this invitation was plain.

"I come—" I agreed.

Orsya caught at my sleeve. "Not alone!"

I looked at her and at Kemoc, who was frowning as he watched the speaker. Had I any right to involve others if this was a trap of a kind, if that speaker had meant not my amulet but *me* when he had said "Trade"?

"She is right." That was Kemoc. "After all, they have tested us and I believe that we have passed some ordeal. They cannot object to three of us when they have a whole city to face us down."

So I pointed to Orsya and then to Kemoc and I said. "With these—we come."

For the first time I saw the Vars leader blink but he did not refuse. Kemoc spoke to Sigmun:

"Let my father know what we do."

The captain eyed each of us, and the gaze he turned on me was as chill as an ice-dotted northern sea. It was plain that he was yielding against his own will when he nodded and stood aside. The Vars also made way for us so that we descended first into their boat, they following after.

Oars flashed, sending the light craft shooting for the quay from which it had earlier come with nearly the speed of a dart. That rainbow of a city loomed higher and higher above us as we approached the shore so that now we were able to see that it had not really been erected on any level ground but arose by tier as if each line of colorful buildings was a step in a great stairway. We landed and walked along the wharf to the width of pavement which separated the first line of buildings from the curling waves.

There was not only the color to set those apart from other cities I knew. This close we could see that doorways and every window opening were surrounded with a wide band of intricate carving. The base was a pattern of vines but what sprang on stems from that innermost representation were circular designs—not like flowers but rather discs very closely engraved with lines which could be runes.

There were no streets as we knew them in Es City, rather steepish ramps which had a landing at each level of the buildings and then ran as a level way from each side of that central rise. Here were indeed people but we moved as if we were invisible, none turning their heads, or pausing to watch us pass. All we saw were men. It was as if this was some Falconer Eyrie in which no female dared ever set foot.

Windows facing the way of our climb were curtained. Yet I saw one of those curtains twitch as if there were the watchers who were indeed interested in strangers.

At weary length, for the necessity of climbing those steep ramps wore at our muscles so long had we been at sea, we came to the topmost level. Here were buildings three times or more the size of those below and their walls might have been of burnished gold, for the paint here gave back a glitter.

Two, which were the largest, fronted the space at the top of the ramp. We were pointed to that on the left-hand side, once more to face steps, a wide flight of them rising to a columned space. Those columns also were entwined with the same intricate carving we had seen below, these, if it were possible, even more tightly designed. Between such was an open doorway for which there appeared to be no gate nor guard.

The spokesman of the party which had brought us hither stood aside indicating that from here on we were to go unescorted. So we climbed, not hurrying our pace, in fact taking time to look about us from side to side.

I had none of that warning which comes to those in the battered northern lands where, through centuries, the Light and the Dark have battled. There was none of the sickish effluvia which assaulted nose and nerves when the Dark was near.

Longing very much to release a probe of mind send I came to stand before that opening. Though the sun gave us a full light here there was no light ahead—perhaps some curtain denying that hung there. Yet I could see no hint of such. To be sure I drew the amulet once more into the open. As it had when confronted by the stone of the spokesman it began to glow.

Then—the suddenness of it nearly sent me stumbling back—there sounded a single great brazen note. I have heard the small gongs which the Sulcar seeresses use when they call upon a favoring wind after a ship has been too long becalmed. However this sound was the gathering of a multitude of such notes, combining them all into one mighty burst.

Kemoc was shoulder to shoulder with Orsya. His hand was on the hilt of his sword in reaction to that sound which must have shattered all calm in the city. I saw the Krogan girl's hands move in a suggestion of waves upon the surface of a stream. We did not even exchange glances but I was aware that they were one with me here and now. Three abreast we approached the cavern of the entrance.

There was indeed dark—not a tangible curtain such as one could grasp with the hands and hold aside—rather one like water into which one had dived—swallowing us up to keep on going blindly ahead.

We had taken perhaps four strides when we stepped out of the dark as easily as we had entered it.

There was light enough, though not as clear and bright as the sun outside. It hinted of the moon rather than the sun but still it awakened brilliant beams of rainbow light from all about us. For we stood in a single huge hall or room, and, surrounding us, was the work in glass which had made Varn famous ever since the first Sulcar trader had brought evidence of it back to the north.

The walls had niches and in each of these was some wonder, while the shaded colors of the city without were reflected like gem lustre from each piece. In addition to these embowered along the walls there were pillars scored with color, around which wound vines with leaves here and flowers seeming so delicate that they might be shattered by a very breath on them. I thought that all the best which could be produced by the workers of Varn was here visibly enshrined.

At the far end of the huge chamber was something unlike all else which kept it company. We found ourselves hurrying, for there was something about the glimpse we had of that which drew us. Then we came to a halt and I think that all of us gave an exclamation of wonder.

Here a throne of green-blue glass, transparent in spite of its rich color, stood high-backed. It was occupied by a figure which was enwrapped in bands such as formed the headgear of the Vars we had seen. These were of silver-grey and soft enough to show the contours of the figure they were intended to conceal. It was plainly that of a woman, but even the head and face were wound about and its blindness was somewhat daunting as we looked upon it.

Only the hands were free, and those were held level with the breast of the enwrapped one. On the side-by-side palms there rested a stone four, six times larger than that used to test us on shipboard. It was crystal clear at first, then small swirls of color moved in it as if it were a vessel holding water and that water answered to some disturbance.

7

During my wanderings I had seen other statues which might once have represented the Power for forgotten peoples. Still this one, so enveiled from sight, gave an impression, not of being fashioned by the hands of others, but rather of a living thing entrapped and hidden. Certainly that which sat there could not be alive so bound with only long, slender hands bare, slightly greenish perhaps because of the reflection of its throne, remaining as still as if they, too, were indeed carven.

Why we had been sent to observe this goddess or ancient ruler, or whatever the seated one represented, we had been given no hint. I glanced at my companions and saw Kemoc's lips moving, though I heard nothing, and I did not try to make mind contact. He might have been calling upon some Power which he had known in Escore. Orsya continued to move her hands in the pattern of the gliding current of a stream.

As for me—here my limited talents gave me no chance at learning what we might face. Farseeing and foreseeing—neither were of use. However, once again I brought forth Gunnora's amulet and fire blossomed in the heart of it. While that swirl of color within the great stone the enthroned figure held grew brighter, and wove a faster pattern within the boundaries which contained it.

I might well be holding one of the ancient light balls of Es City so did Gunnora's gift glow. Always that was matched by the glory of the huge gem the hidden one held.

Once more, out of the very air about us, sounded that great boom of some gigantic gong—a sound strong enough to make our ears ring. The surface of the strange gem was certainly expanding, or else we had been subtly ensorcelled to see it so. Out of its heart burst a fountain of rainbow light which trembled, rose and fell as might the water which fed the fountains we knew. Up and up, now a portion of it was directly opposite the band-hidden face of the sitter. It climbed again, and spread as it climbed, a constant flowing light which was nearly akin in girth to the columns of the hall behind us.

Then it leaped!

The beam faced Kemoc for a dazzling instant, swept on to confront the Krogan girl, and last of all fronted me. But there was no danger in it—rather a welcoming as if something long banished from all it knew stood now before the entrance to its own place and joyfully came home.

A tendril of that blue-green flame was outflung, the very tip of it touching for only a breath space of time my amulet. Within that I felt movement, not that Gunnora's gift wished to be free to leave me, but rather that a part of it hailed something akin. My pendant stone might be lips sucking at liquid which was not only new to it but which promised nourishment beyond any it ever hoped to have.

While I—sight entered my brain, not because I summoned it but because I was the vessel made to hold certain Power. Much of what I saw I could not understand for it came in the form of waves of color, whirling, self-knitting, self-loosening again. What I did know was that this was truly of the Light though of another kind, which on this earth had been in exile and which now had found heart-kin.

The fountain leaped again, up and up. Our heads went back on our shoulders drawn by the rise. Up and up—About us the glass enhancement of the hall beamed out in answer.

Then—

It was gone! As a flame might be blown out by a gust of wind, the fountain vanished. Only where before Gunnora's gift had gleamed gold when awakened, it now rippled with added hues—green, blue. While from it there poured into me sensations I could not set name to. For the first time wariness, the shadow of fear, pricked at me. I was too ignorant; this was too alien to find easy berth in me. Both physically and mentally I flinched. For a moment or two I wanted to turn and flee from this place, to shed my amulet and leave it with the silent one, refusing what it might have now to offer me.

For the third time the gong note sounded. This time it was followed by a reverberating echo which I dimly felt must ring through all Varn. That gem which the seated one held was colorless, not even the reflection of the throne could now tinge it slightly.

Around us there was a dimming, deadening of the glitter from the glass. But there was more, too. That figure on the throne—the bands which cloaked it were looser, or else that which those covered was losing substance. The body outlined only moments earlier had had the seeming of concealing firm flesh, youthful contours. Now there was a shriveling as if age had suddenly struck where it had been long refused touch.

The two hands suddenly fell to the lap though they did not loose hold upon the gem. Now the ball of the head nodded forward until that which must mark the chin rested on the breast.

Who was I watching that change? I was disoriented, confused. Taking two steps forward I was now within touching distance of that figure. Was it about to crumble into nothingness? If so what penalty would be wracked upon the three of us for the dissolution of what or who must be an awe-producing figure to Varn?

I grasped the amulet tightly and ducked my head to loose its cord. Then, guided by something outside any conscious act, I held out Gunnora's gift and allowed it to dangle down, to lie upon the surface of the deadened gem.

Instantly within me I knew that what I had done so unconsciously had been necessary, a gesture desired, a last test perhaps, set by that I might never be able to understand.

From where the amulet and gem touched there flashed a spark of vivid blue fire. Down into the gem it swirled, bringing with it life. Only the original color was now crossed and entwined with Gunnora's harvest gold. When I drew back, the gem lived once more, but was changed. However, the amulet showed no reduction of its own life. I half expected that we might again see a change in the hidden one, but that was not to be. It still sat, head forward, its bands loosened, its head turned downward as if blinded eyes could see, could search out what might be in the heart of that which it still held.

There came a light wind out of nowhere, wrapping us about, tugging at my short hair, raising Orsya's loosed locks. Softly it brushed against us. The breeze brought scents of growing things, all the richness of high summer. Such had I smelt within Gunnora's shrine; here it was even richer, caressed the closer. Then it was gone and its going seemed to have released us from that spell which had lain upon us since we had first been brought into Varn's shrine.

We turned to retrace our way between those columns. I looked over my shoulder. She who was seated on the throne still nursed her gem and that held the mingled color which had entered it on the touch of the amulet.

When we came out of that palace, or temple, or place of Power, whichever it was to Varn, we saw that our escort from the ship had been augmented. There was Lord Simon, helm on head, his fingers laced in his sword belt. Beside him the Lady Jaelithe, in mail and riding dress, her hair bundled into silver net after the fashion of the Witches. With them were more of the men of Varn—and I thought I could see a far greater number of people on the ways which separated the tiers of the city.

I had not returned the amulet into hiding but held it up against my breast as had the hidden one once held her gem. The colors which had come into it did not this time fade, but swirled to the outmost edge of the stone hungrily, as if that light wanted forth into full freedom. I heard from below a murmur of speech and the crowd of

Vars divided, leaving standing there in plain sight a robed and cowled one, face as hidden as had been that of her in the temple.

Arms raised and wide sleeves fell back, showing the same long and narrow hands which held the gem, and above them rounded arms, so I could not help but believe that this hidden one was also female.

"Thrice blessing." Into my mind came that greeting. "Power calls to power, Light to light, even as the Dark can call shadows. Peace is not yet won, but there is now a beginning—"

"Well to Varn." I made do with the best I could think of then. "Nothing have I done, only through me, through this." I held the amulet a little away from me, turned down my fingers so that all might see the light still within it.

"We are all but servants of the Greater Ones." The hands against the rich blue of the other's cloak were moving back and forth as if waving to me some tangible blessing. "That which is planted cannot grow, not even continue to live unless it receives nourishment and tending. We have been long without that which you have brought to us."

Now she put her hands together, bowing her cowled head, giving me such reverence as one of the Council would expect. Only that made me uncomfortable. Would she address me so if she knew what our coming had done to the hidden one within?

"To everything its season," she answered me as if my mind were fully open to her reading. "The guardian has kept watch for lifetimes, weariness is not alone for us."

We descended that last flight of stairs. Those of Varn, save for the cloaked one, drew back.

Lady Jaelithe's gaze was for the amulet. She traced a sign in the air. There were lines as blue as those of the throne within, and they held for all of us to see. She looked now to me.

"There is a burden." Her voice sounded troubled, as if she saw wrong instead of right in what had happened.

"From any act comes consequences," I said aloud. Yet I was aware that, in a fashion I could not find words for, the amulet was becoming, with every breath that I drew, a weight of which I was most aware.

The cloaked one put forth her hands as if she held them toward a fire for warmth. Though she did not presume to actually touch what I held. Once again she spoke to us.

"For every trade there must be something offered in return. What will you ask for out of Varn?" Now her hands gestured as if she would include the whole of the rainbow city in her offering.

While I was moved, without any prompting I was aware of, to answer her. "What we would have is news—from the south."

Her hands were stilled and I thought I could sense wariness, a hesitation. But I also knew approval from those of my own company.

Then the cowled one nodded. She made another gesture which was plainly an invitation to follow her and she went to the right and the building there which flanked the temple in which we had visited.

There was a ponderous door which might have been built up with layer upon layer of thick glass, the whole infused with a silvery light. That was drawn back at our coming, though there was no sign within of any who welcomed us. Once more we faced a columned hall but all the decoration was of the same clouded glass vined with a silver brilliance like the shine of the moon at full—giving good light to a circle of high-backed chairs established in what looked to be the exact center of that space.

The cowled one fitted herself and the width of her robe into one and signaled again for us to choose our own, to be seated. While from the back of the hall there came three of the city men much like the others, only with gemlike stones on the peaks of their headgear. This trio took their place in the circle facing the robed one. As usual they turned set, expressionless faces to us.

Once we were settled the cowled head turned a fraction to face the Lady Jaelithe and, even as her hands had moved earlier, so now did those long fingers rise to write upon the air. There were three signs so made and that in the middle I knew though I had no Witch training. It was the signal which appeared on the door of Gunnora's shrine. The Witches in their proud ranking of Power had never called upon the Ever Nourishing One. She was of another time, one which, even with the opening of Escore, the knowledge of Arvon, they refused to acknowledge. Too far had they journeyed apart during the unnumbered years.

Only the Lady Jaelithe, no longer bound by their prejudices, replied to that with a like pattern. Though I was the more amazed for I had always believed that Gunnora's rule was largely for the Dales and Arvon, with only traces remembered perhaps in Escore and among the humbler folk in Estcarp.

"We have hungered," the cowled one spoke to our mind. "There has been dire troubling and we have beseeched a sign. This is the second year time when the rains have not come and in the fields seeds dry or their sprouting withers. To the will of the Great Ones we have appealed. But always there has come only a greater burden. Were it not for the bounty of the sea Varn might be shattered and we all be as dust."

"From where has spread this troubling—from the east?"

Could it be true in the south Escore curved around the coastal lands a part of the proper coastline? Certainly there had been "troubling" in a plenty in that riven land.

"To the east there is nothing but the mountains. No, what threatens lies south. There have been many signs and portents of shadow. We have dreamed ill dreams. Those grow longer and touch more of us each nightfall until some who have been greatly afflicted are brought into the Place of Light that they may have renewing sleep outside the Shadow. The food from the sea, which holds us to life since our fields do not yield, is sometimes gone, and our boats return with empty nets, or within those strange monsters which can deal death with claw or tooth.

"Those who had sought farther for food have seen afar the light of fire rising from the sea. While all men know that neither water nor fire can hold together, that one must always conquer the other. There have been no traders in our bay. Six moons ago the fishing boat of Zizzar Can was passed by a great ship, wind in its spread sails to carry it on but no man tending those sails, nor standing vigilant at the steering—a lost ship with none aboard. He and his men would have boarded it to seek out the meaning of such a mystery, but they had no way of climbing aloft. Soon the winds had driven it on. But it came from the south."

"Was this the first ship you have seen so?" asked Lady Jaelithe.

There was a moment of silence and then the cowled one answered:

"In the Founding Years of Varn 6783 there was a similar time and then there came a wind from the south, searing with a heat which lay waste all the fields just before the harvest. Then four of the fishing craft were lost and the crew of the single one of that fleet which returned swore before the Waiter that all steersmen save their own, for they had followed some distance behind the other vessels, had set a southward course. Though they shouted and signaled no one on board those gave them heed. Nor did they return. Far off, against a dark sky as if some storm broke there but did not reach to Varn, there was a fiery light."

"And how long was that since?"

"This is the settlements year 6810. But this time there is that added to the ill which was not reported then—the dreams, and five or six days ago the Mirror of Keffin Du, set to guard the south wall, cracked and fell in shards when the guards, who answered the alarm, strove to dismount it for mending." Now the Cowl indicated with a nod one of the Varsmen and he went swiftly toward the back of the hall to disappear through another doorway.

"What do you seek south? Are fields over which you look also blasted? Are your ships taken?"

"Our fields are fertile still," Lady Jaelithe made answer, "but to the west there has been a mighty war of the Light against the Dark, and recently we have been told that here southward are strange acts which may mean more trouble—"

The man who had left the room returned. He was bearing before him a thick slab which he bent over to place on the floor so that all of us seated there could see that. The oblong was of glass, the underside of it murky, the upper part clear. While embedded between those two—

I have seen some of the horrors of the Shadow as run in Escore and Arvon—or representations of such. But this was enough to bring a gasp out of me. It was surely not a bird—though it lay in its transparent prison with wings outstretched. But those pinions were not feathered, rather they had the look of leather. The body was neither feathered nor furred, but thickly overgrown with stubby upstanding points like greatly thickened hairs. However, it was the head which was the worst. That had the likeness of a demonic-faced, miniature human. The mouth gaped a little—there seemed to be no visible lips— showing four large fangs, two up and two down, in the jaws. The nose was almost as prominent as a beak and slightly hooked.

Though it must certainly be dead the open eyes appeared to still hold life, as if it was staring at us all, marking each as future prey. On the head was an upstanding comb growth of the same bristles as clothed the body, but longer, like a ragged fringe.

There appeared to be no arms, unless those were marked by the bones which stretched the wings, but the legs and feet were again obscenely human in contour, though there was a tail wrapped loosely about the knees.

"This"—the cowled one nodded to the exhibit—"was one of a flock of such. They came, as if hurled by the savagery of a storm, from the south and they attacked the harbor birds, tearing them to pieces, so that blood and flesh fell from the skies.

"Having so wrought that there was nothing flying aloft save those of its own kind, they dropped landward—and they can walk. Into Varn they came and our kin died, for it seems that, savage as their bites are, they also carry poison at the roots of those fangs. People of the city died before we could net and kill. And these we have never seen before—have you?"

It was I who answered her and it was with a name I had always thought part of legend: "The Theffan."

I looked up from that small monster to find the others all staring at me.

"Where?" Lord Simon's single word was a command for enlightenment.

"Nowhere," I was forced to return, "save in legend— in stories which children use for a-frightening one another. There were guardians— One we have already met in the sea. The second was described as this thing before us, save that it was alone and only one. It is out of Sulcar tales, but very ancient—near forgotten. And there was also a third—"

My eyes had dropped once more to the small horror imprisoned for all time. To me it seemed more than ever that those red eyes held life. Now they centered directly on me, as if the thing wished so to set me in its mind that I would never be forgot when a time came for a reckoning.

8

We stayed a full ten days in the harbor of Varn. Three times we spoke with the cowled one whose face we never saw and with the trio who seemed to be the lawgivers of this city. Meanwhile Captain Sigmun and Captain Harwic had the cargoes of wood brought out and there was brisk bidding among the shore merchants for what was to them rare and precious wares. Only what we took in return were stores rather than the precious glasswork. There were dried, gnarled roots which certainly did not resemble food but which the Sulcars ground and made into a lumpy meal which in turn was again dried into journey cakes. But there was little else in the way of food, for the people of Varn were on short rations for another year.

There were coils of rope, supple and yet very strong, and the smiths of the city went quickly to work to cast bolts for dart guns, beat out long knives with cutting edges so keen that these might split a hair dropped from above. Also each ship had a second and a third row of containers added to the water storage and filled from the streams in the valley. For as fierce as the crop-parching winds from the south might be there was no lack of water which poured from springs in the mountain walls about.

All this preparation had little to do with us. Rather we gathered with both the officers of the city and with the fishermen who still went forth to draw nets and do their part for the very life of Varn. What we labored on were charts taken from our ships—those charts which were so empty to the south.

Captain Sigmun sat in on one such conference and he asked a question that seemed born of all the puzzlement of the Sulcars who were such super seamen:

"Lord, what of the ship at Gorm, how can such travel without either sails or oars?"

"Because it comes from a world like unto the Kolders' home in this much, them who are native there had machines of metal to serve their people—"

"And you, Lord Simon, coming from this world, would those machines obey you?"

"No, for it is necessary to feed the machine with a certain liquid which is like oil to a lamp. Without full tanks of that it cannot run. And such tanks within that vessel brought to Gorm were totally empty. It might well have been that, once brought through the gate, the ship ran on until it had used all that which made it mobile and then it drifted until Captain Harwic chanced upon it. We have not the means of bringing it to life again.''

''Then it was like those great ground crushers, the ones brought to break the walls of keeps which Alizon took to High Hallack. It was proven then that, while the Dalesmen could find nothing which would stop them, after a time they halted of themselves and did not move again. So that those of Alizon needs must fight hand-to-hand in regular battle.'' Captain Sigmun nodded. '' Things which are of the Kolder are evil. I trust that that ship at Gorm be taken to sea and sunk. Whether it lives or not it may have other hidden dangers.''

As if he had called some peril by his words there was a sudden movement in the room about us. Two windows crashed back against the wall, showering dangerous shards of glass around about. There came another blow which set the floor rocking under us. Kemoc threw out an arm and swept his lady away from the table, even as the rest of us withdrew in a hurry from our stools. The ceiling was shaking from side to side, even as did the floor under us. Above our heads solid surface cracked and debris rained down. I saw a pillar actually bend as if some unendurable weight had been pressed down upon it before it broke.

Two of the Vars had blood streaming from face cuts. The glass, which was so much a part of their life, now shattered to bring injury and death. Then the shuddering under us grew still and for a moment only there was utter silence. Breaking that came cries of pain, horror, rage. I edged to the now open window and looked out.

It might have been that Sigmun's words had roused up those long-dead devices of the Kolder. Houses had toppled; Varn could now be a city taken after a long siege. I looked to the bay and I knew I cried aloud.

A hand fell upon my shoulder, jerking me back and away so that Sigmun could stand in my place. He in turn cried out. A wave was coming across the bay, such a wave that I believe the most fierce of storms could not have raised. The Sulcar ships were in its path; they would indeed be lost.

Higher than the tip of the tallest mast was the sea. A hammer of water, it fell. We could see nothing but spray and ravening smaller waves. At the mouth of the bay a second wave was lifting—

Thus the terror of the sea fell also on the city, the water rising above the first two tiers of buildings to smash down. How many driven from shaking homes had been caught and swept away? When the wash of water retreated it must have pulled with it many of those who had been alive only seconds earlier.

I think we were all frozen by the very horror of what we witnessed. One of the Vars wailed, throwing his arms wide, rushing for the window next to the one where Sigmun stood. It was Kemoc who caught him and held fast against the blows rained upon him by a man who could well now be mad.

Sigmun held to the window frame, leaning forward, peering out towards that welter of water, now slipping back into the sea and taking with it much from the city.

Against what had once been the quay at which we landed there was dark wreckage, larger than any of the fishing boats that had been tied up there. And nosing against that, as if the two ships had sought each other when they had been overwhelmed by the water, was the second.

Neither had been drawn back by the rush of the returning water, nor were they sinking. The masts which had brought them, with wide canvas spread flying south were snapped, huge splinters arising from their decks to mark where those had stood. That any aboard them could still live was unbelievable.

Now from the city itself swelled wailing cries which carried all the sorrow of a stricken people. We went forth to see what could be done, Captain Sigmun to hurry down to his *Far Rover* if she were not now sinking where she clung against the wreckage of the quay.

That the worst of nature was not yet through with us

was made clear when there came two afterdisturbances of the land, bringing more buildings, already weakened, cascading down, until to walk any street was peril. Yet all those who were not caught by death in Varn were already striving to discover the full extent of the damage, to rescue and get into the safety of the plain to the east of the city all who could be carried, or could walk on their trembling feet.

We went to help as we could and became separated in the throng as we strove to bring entrapped living out of tangled masonry, call and hunt for any who might answer.

The sky, which had been open and blue before this evil struck, was darkening and there began to fall from it a shifting of grey-brown dust becoming so thick it threatened to smother us. We tied cloths wet in pools of the seawater over our mouths and noses. Those masks had to be constantly shaken free of the mud which resulted and wet again. And we carried more strips at our belts to be used by any of the survivors we found. Many such clawed at the ruins, trying to dig free some kin or friend.

Many of the dead and the badly injured were women trapped in the houses, for the Vars isolated their women folk in inner rooms and they had not been able to get out of their quarters in time.

I worked with a group of men, two of whom wore the tight silver suits, now encased in the falling ash, of authorities. They had ripped apart their head coverings, using the bandings to make the masks we wore.

The fall of ash grew deeper. Where the waves had licked it formed a firm cover in which we had to dig using shards for shovels. Only too often those we uncovered were already dead.

There was no end to what we did. As the darkness gathered someone brought a lantern burning oil and this was our only light. I grew weary so that my hands shook as I helped shove stones to one side, or used my own fingers to dig away the ashes so we might find someone entrapped. My nails were torn and the seawater in which

I wet my breathing mask from time to time settled into cuts in fiery torment.

We were on the first level just above the sea when I leaned against a half-tumbled wall to catch my breath, so faint that I could hardly keep my feet. For the first time I looked up and around, not keeping all attention only for what was immediately before me.

There were other lights visible, pools of fire here and there. We had by chance come near to where the quay had once stood. I looked out over water which I could not see, only hear in the slurp of waves against the wreckage. More lights showed not too far away—the ships!

That they could be still above water I could not really believe. Surely the wave had crushed them like eggs in a careless hand. Still those lanterns were clustered and swayed in the dark as if they were mounted on some standard which was unquiet.

"Destree!"

I blinked. The mind call had somehow broken through that shell of concentration on what we did, as if someone had grasped my arm and supported my aching body.

I was dazed enough to wonder if my talent had wakened only to deceive me when the call came once more:

"Destree!"

As one could recognize an audible voice so did I recognize the Lady Jaelithe. I pulled around a little to face squarely those lights bobbing above the water which was full of now waterlogged debris and I blinked as my eyes teared to wash away the still-falling dust.

I made my way in a swaying shuffle toward those bobbing lights. This was one of those nightmare dreams in which one is under some compulsion and yet one's body refuses to answer one's mind. Coming to the end of what was left of the quay, tumbled rocks and the wreckage of two fishing boats, I clung to a pile of stone and tried to see through the falling dust what lay beyond. A form rose out of the murk, climbing out of the filthy water at my very feet. A hand caught at mine where it dangled limply at my side and gave a gentle tug.

"Destree!" Not Lady Jaelithe this time but Orsya. And she was willing me to come with her.

I did not have energy enough to refuse so found myself floundering in water. Though I feared to be struck by some floating debris, a hand locked in the collar of my shirt brought me forward. With the ash so thick upon the surface it was like swimming through stew. Then a hand took one of mine and lifted it so that my fingers could find and curl around a rung of a rope ladder, as choking and coughing from my dip into the mud, I managed somehow to climb. Then other hands closed on me and I was drawn inward to sprawl upon an ash-dusted surface.

There was enough light here to see faces, that of the Lady Jaelithe and with her Kemoc, while a taller shape beyond must be the Lord Simon. I levered myself up and saw that beyond our small group Sulcar crew members were working to sweep up the all-present ash and send it overboard where a smashed bulwark made an opening to the water. I shook my head trying to loosen the mud plastered about my mouth mask while clawing to get that off that I might breathe again.

Before me appeared suddenly a bottle held in a steady hand and I managed to get that into my own shaking grasp and gulp down the sourish wine which the Sulcars used to renew strength, steeped as it was with healing herbs.

That was the last act I truly remember.

Lights tossed and were gone; I was laying flat.

There was an imperative call, a command I had to obey. Though every part of my body screamed for rest it was not yet to be found. Save, I realized through the fog that encircled me, I was not in body. Through no conscious order I was speeding nearer and nearer to a light brighter than any I had seen since we had entered the glass-lined temple. This was true fire rising pillarwise into the air.

It gave aid to the sighting of what lay about its base.

There was molten stuff, thick, pure flame-crested, as it flowed away from that stem, growing duller as it made a way slowly but inevitably into water. The steam from that meeting formed clouds as thick as those which might hold a storm.

There were other dark humps rising from the water. One long saw-toothed stretch still had water trickling from it, though this bore no fiery crown. I thought I saw some creature lying on it writhing in death. But of that I could not be sure.

It was not what I saw but what I felt which counted now. The use of Power, not that of nature's own cataclysm but summoned by some intelligence, sent waves out into the world even as the tidal wave had been loosed on Varn. Power was here to twist and tear. I have seen a lorka, one of the men-devouring creatures of the north, caught half in a web trap yet fighting so hard with tooth and claw that it could, and many times did, free itself, to rave on against those who were trying to defend themselves against its rage.

Here it was Power itself which seemed partially trapped. The energy which burst from it fanned outward, to transform what lay about—even as once the combined might of the Witches of Escarp had turned the southern mountains to save their country from invasion.

Yes, there was Power here, hampered enough so that it almost became an entity which had a purpose and identity of its own. I feared trying to tap it, or to follow it to its source. That it could snuff me out as one pinches the flame of a candle, of that I was sure.

Yet that which had sent me—or had pulled me hither—was not content to let me linger. My farsight swept on, past the volcano lifted out of the sea, away from that glowing pillar.

Beyond was darkness. It might be an empty night, save that which still struggled to free itself wholly was still there. Upon that my talent fastened. I, or rather my sight, moved steadily forward. There was enough reflection from the sea fire even here for me to see cliffs rising from the streaming water. They looked stark as if they had been new made.

I wafted above them only to see that this was all high land, well above any wash of the sea. Far ahead there was a point of light, red glowing as might a coal in a dying hearth fire. It was from that came the surging, fighting Power.

Still I dared not test it, even use a fraction of the far-sight to scan its source. The thing was too raging, too eager to seize. Yet there was something about it which grew into more and more of a puzzle. I had sensed Power many times before, even traces of it in individuals who did not know they possessed any such talent. Then there had been limits, curbs. No one I had ever known, nor heard of, would so expend what was a gift in such an awesome striving for mastership— For it had not been from a desire to rework the earth and water of its world that that energy had struck. No, the destruction was only the by-product of another need. It had been a flaw which produced the breaking of nature's bounds here, not the sustained effort of will.

Yes, there was a reason and that was only partly fulfilled. What happened to the sea along the path that force had taken was only a side product to its desire. Not dipping in it, but daring to keep in touch with that I could sense I spent farsight more recklessly. I knew now my purpose and need, that I find the source.

The rot of it came so suddenly I shot beyond and needs must return. There was very little light here; what lay below had a dead blackness which might form a hole reaching into completely nothingness. The farsight was not the same as body sight. I could sense-see that there was below me a structure of some sort, totally lacking in any opening, much apart of the rock on which it squatted like a dour devouring demon out of the spirit Dark.

Just that—nothing more. I hovered above it striving to pick up some emanation of identity, some hint of who or what was spilling forth that great blast of energy. There was nothing—save the energy itself. Yet I well knew that that was impossible; each hint of talent, and certainly this was far more than a hint, must have its root.

Still I was justly cautious and I would not venture into what might make me a part of the fierce battle. As my opposition arose I tried to build up the strength of that and return.

A goal—the *Far Rover*? But that might well have succumbed to the wave. A person? Lady Jaelithe! As I had trusted to Orsya in the water, so now I trusted to she who had been a Witch and had infinitely more talent than I. Instead of looking to that dark blot mounted on ragged cliffs I pulled into mind, with all my effort, a picture of her.

Into me folded, strong in its way as the wave which had struck into Varn, Power, as if I now stood under a fountain of it. Only I was not pulled back as I longed to be. Rather was I held steady. Then there came a second surge of the well-honed strength, a third, a fourth. I knew that all the company were united and that I was only the point of a dart aimed straight for that thrust outward which was striving to overturn our world.

As one we attacked. I felt as if I was a bird torn lose by a tempest from some firm perch, to whirl out helpless in a storm it could not ride. I attempted to stiffen, to hold. Somehow I did.

The cliff arose as I whirled, or was dashed earthward, and the sober bulk was there. Power—energy—but—life?

No matter how trained a Witch or a seer may be she cannot so lose herself in what she would do that the fact she exists somewhere else is denied. Here was nothing— or so I first thought. Then I caught it—flashes so quickly found and lost that they sped like the sparks from a fire. There was—or there had been—true life, yes. But the force possessed the life, not the life the force. And to any of that talent that is as great a horror as was the dead-alive army of the Kolders. It was a negation of all which the Light taught.

I had not felt the Dark as part of this before—it had seemed neutral, neither Light nor Dark—more like a storm bursting by the will of that which we cannot understand and which is outside our learning. But that it caught within it those it bent to its will so that they no longer were in command of their spirits—this could only be of the Dark. How cunning and unnatural must be the mind which conceived this that it could not be detected—only showed traces of what must have once been beings of freedom.

It was my horror at that which brought me back, spinning through the nowhere dark. I opened my eyes and saw Jaelithe's face. Her features measured my own horror as she gazed down at me. Then from behind, for I was lying my head pillowed on another's knees, came a hand holding within it something which I could not see clearly but which was wiped first across my eyes as I shut them again, then my forehead. There was the scent of the sea in that and also of the land, herbs well dried after they had ripened under the sun. I breathed deeply and felt only thankfulness that I had returned, that I had not been lost, bearing the others with me, as had been those piteous others set rigidly to the service of the Dark.

9

The *Far Rover* had survived the fury of the sea better than her sister ship, though that was still afloat, but barely so. Of our number we were now less than half of those who had sailed from Estcarp. All the crew members who had been on deck when the wave struck were missing, as were some who had been wharfside at the coming of the water. Captain Harwic was gone but Sigmun had survived. Going over the injuries of both ships when the deep black of night was turned into the grey of day (we never saw the sun and the ash still fell, though to a lesser amount) it was discovered that the *Wave Skimmer* would never be seaworthy again but timbers and parts of her could be used for the patching of *Far Rover* and her kin-crew voted by voice that should be done.

The fact that the masts were torn out of both ships was what concerned the united crew the most. Without those they could not hope for any real escape by sea. Certainly there was no timber in Varn land which could be used to restep those. Nor was there anything in the city ware-houses, those which remained intact after the quake, which could be substituted.

Three of the fishing craft rested now high and fast dry-ing on the second tier of the city. I saw Sigmun and the chief surviving officer of the *Wave Skimmer* walking around those as our own small party started back up the ramps to the upper town. What had been learned during my venture in farsight must, Lady Jaelithe decreed, be shared with the Speaker for the Seated One. A force which could not be understood, located in the south, able to stir the very earth, air and water of the world itself into such action, was now an enemy to be considered. Perhaps what we had been through this past day and night was only a forerunner of future attacks.

Some of the city dwellers had come back from the open land. They reported a drastic change in the main river which supplied their valley with water. Where before it had vanished into a cavern within the cliff wall some dis-tance from Varn it now ran straightly, for the cliff had split, rocks peeling away near to the original drain hole. A Falconer on duty with aiding townspeople away from the city had dispatched his bird to scan what might lie ahead there and reported that the water now entered di-rectly into the sea some leagues away from Varn Bay. But exploration in the direction had not yet been undertaken. As long as the water remained within their own sphere the people of Varn were satisfied. Also a party of them, driving their short-legged, long-haired animals up into the upper pasturage, had had a brush with the flying mon-strosities which they had barely been able to win. The creatures dived to savage both animals (who were better protected by the weight of hair from which they were soon due to be shorn) and their herdsmen.

Two of the herdsmen returned with severe bites, already carried by their companions in poison shock from the attack. What care was known to the city was given them but they raved and tried to rise and win back the way they had come, their fellows saying that they had had great trouble in the early period after they were wounded to keep them from trying to climb the southern cliffs.

Meanwhile we sat in conference with that robed one and two of the city elders. I was enjoined to tell in detail my assay by farsight. A question was speedily thrown at me:

"This thing which you sensed, is it strong enough to strike again?"

"I do not know. Nor was I able to learn the reason for its outbreak."

One of the city councilors turned his face fully, so that his cold eyes were hard upon mine.

"You from the sea"—a small gesture of one hand indicated the whole of our shrunken party—"seek this thing, is that not so?" Unlike his fellows met earlier he spoke trade language easily. "We have heard talk of guardians which are to be found in the lore of your ship people. It could well be that you have drawn the attention of this thing, which is so unknown to you, upon Varn and we now lie under its eyes ready for a second blow! The sooner you are forth from Varn the more we shall be pleased!" There was enmity in his voice which was as chill as the glance with which he held me.

Into the silence following that statement came another voice. For the first time she who wore the cowled robe spoke aloud. Why she chose the form of oral speech I did not know, unless it was because she wanted to cut any closer contact with us, in that she might agree with the councilor.

"You have sworn to the truth of this upon the very talent you possess," she began and I nodded. I had slept after my ferrying forth to use the farsight but still my strength had not fully returned. My mind I opened deliberately. If she wished she could so tap the mind send, know that there was no guile in that I had reported.

"One guardian met with you to the north, before you came into Varn waters," she continued deliberately. "Therefore if that were a scout, or messenger, your coming was already known. There might be excellent reason for preparing this which has been sent against us as well as you."

Lady Jaelithe gave answer as the other paused: "Yet these flying creatures were not sent upon you after our coming but well before, even perhaps before we raised anchor in Es Bay."

"I have heard," the cowled one made now direct answer to that, as if she was now summoning all she could use as evidence against us, "that one among you found floating derelict a ship which was not of any race we know and that he took that to Es. Perhaps he so robbed a power of its prey. Have you thought upon that?"

"There have been other ships, and those were Sulcar, which have in the near past been found floating so. It is the reason for that which brought us south. You think that they could also be prey reft from some enemy? Have you not also lost fishing boats?"

There was a long moment of silence. One of the councilors moved in his chair as if he found it difficult to sit there, perhaps because he was near Lord Simon, towards whom he darted glances now and then as if wondering why he had come armed to this meeting.

"We have lost boats—and fishermen," the cowled one conceded. That muffed head turned a little in my direction. I wondered how she could see when those folds fell so low as to mask her face. "You speak of others caught in the full power of this force. What did you mean? Could you have called out the names and been answered?"

I shook my head. "There were sparks of life within that, yes. But none dared I seize upon. It was like a great net," I used an example of her people, hoping both she and the councilors could understand the better, "full of struggling fish being drawn swiftly at the will of the net-ter."

Once more the cowl altered a fraction and now its dark opening faced the Lady Jaelithe. "This farseer has testi-fied that the all of you with the gift joined her in seeking. What thought you of this matter of 'sparks of life' sup-posedly netted by an enemy you cannot describe?"

"They were there." The Lady Jaelithe's hands moved, and there was meaning in their movements, though I could not read it.

Out of the long sleeves which hid her hands when she wished came those of the cowled one. She fitted fingertip to fingertip at breast level and then, in a sudden gesture which I was sure was one meant to repel, she swung the palms out as if they now formed a shield.

"You call upon that which I do not know, Witch. I am no spell-sister of yours! We be of different blood, far dif-ferent. I think you indeed meant no harm when you an-chored in our bay. But also it is very easy to believe that it was because you did so this mighty disaster came upon us. Yes, we have lost fishermen and seen the coming of other evils—such as the flying things—and so, it has been recorded, has happened before. But never have we paid such a price to any power as was rift from us this time. It would be well for you to go forth from Varn as speed-ily as you can, one way or another—"

Lord Simon broke in upon her now, with no sign of usual courtesy, speaking rather as to another warrior who had reported some peril to come:

"Our ships are not seaworthy. The *Wave Skimmer* will never sail again. Nor does this land here offer that which will repair the *Far Rover* enough to make it seaworthy. How then do we go? Men cannot walk on the waves and there is no path along the cliffs to be followed—"

Again the cowl swung and this time it was turned to the one of the councilors who had not yet spoken. He cleared his throat gratingly as if it were full of the dust which had fallen outside. His hands were resting on his knees and I saw both of them clench into fists as if he prepared to face some attack.

"There is another ship . . ." He hesitated and then swallowed raspingly again.

I think astonishment held us all for a moment before Kemoc leaned a little forward in his chair to demand:

"What ship—a fisher's craft? And where?"

"The spy bird that serves your fighting men has reported such. Near where the new river gate to the sea has opened."

"A wreck—" began Lord Simon.

"Not so, this one has not been battered. It floats well—"

"We were not told of this!" Lord Simon snapped. "Is it one of yours?"

"Not so!" And the councilor used something of the same heat in his reply. "There is still life on board, or so your bird spy has reported."

"Thus comes your means of travel." The cowled one spoke up quickly.

"Sulcar?" Lady Jaelithe did not ask that of the Varn people but of me and I knew I must seek again.

I closed my eyes and strove to put all from my mind but a picture of the *Far Rover* as an example of what I must seek. Then I sped forth the weary power of send as a trader might work a sea jewel out of its shell. I felt the familiar sick queasiness which came when I was foolish enough to use the power again far too soon. The hazy picture in my mind grew sharper, more fixed. I was indeed looking down upon a ship. The masts were two and to their yards still clung fluttering tatters of sail. But there were differences between this and any Sulcar ship I had ever seen. It was smaller, yet not a fishing boat. Now it rocked a little in the wash of the sea but there was a reef extending which kept most of the force of the waves from pummeling it. Except for the loss of sails it looked to be still seaworthy.

The falcon had reported life on board. I could see no one on the deck—in fact that was in a state of disorder.

Lines trailed from where lifeboats must have once been hung.

Delicately I probed, seeking that life—was there someone below injured by the sea, left behind when the crew had taken to those missing boats?

Life—yes! But at the same second I caught that small glow of energy I also knew that it was not human. Nor was it of the sea, or air. Rather an animal and one that had long associated with the human. It hungered and now it hunted, tracing out a trail of another creature smaller, wilder, a traditional prey—or foe. I strove to sense that other spark also and then jerked away my probe from a meeting with sheer savagery. There were more than one of these—there was a hunger in them also, avid, and they waited for that which hunted, thinking (though their way of thought was so alien that I could barely touch it) to make the hunter food for their own empty stomachs.

I made myself pull aside from a coming battle, striving to rise from the ship itself, mark points of reference around it so that we could come at it more easily.

"An island schooner—" Lord Simon's voice brought me out of the seeking and I knew that once again we had linked and they had shared my picturing of that ship.

"You know this then?" The councilor who wished us forth from Varn was quick to catch on that.

"I have seen its like—elsewhere."

"This then is a part of that which you have been seeking?" the cowled one asked swiftly. "You will be about your business with it." That latter was no question, rather a statement which was almost an order.

When we reported to Captain Sigmun the finding of the derelict he was instantly alert to what might be a promise for all of us. By main force of will he was able to get a fishing boat which had not been utterly smashed hauled away from the city tier where the waves had deposited in and into the water. It was still a damaged craft and there must be constant bailing to keep it afloat. Nor would it hold a large party. Thus we needs must split our forces.

Most of the Falconers who were left would march with Lord Simon, the Lady Jaelithe, and some dozen of the remaining Sulcar crew, from the inner valley down the newly opened river which now had a gate into the sea. From what we learned of the falcon's report the ship was in an almost landlocked, smaller bay now very near where river met the ocean.

Kemoc, Orsya, and I would go in the very crowded fishing boat fighting a way along the coast towards that same spot. We did not leave at once—the fishing craft must have all the repairs our Sulcar seamen could give her. While there was also a need for supplies.

Twenty of the Sulcars under the mate Simot of the *Wave Skimmer* must stay behind to nurse hurts, broken bones, head injuries, slashes left by flying glass. To my surprise those same city rulers who wanted us forth did not object to us leaving our injured behind. I believe that they thought getting rid of the five of us who had given evidence of Power was the imperative purpose now.

There had been during the night two more aftershocks, but neither did more harm than shake more broken masonry from precarious perches here and there. We had done our best to help the townspeople while Sigmun saw to the preparation of the boat, and I think that our services did not go unnoticed. Yet there was plainly a growing feeling among all those of Varn they would be glad to see the last of us.

That fall of ash which had been so choking had been laid by a steady rain which heightened at intervals into a drenching downpour. But that washed away the ash, except for muddy residue in corners, and, having known the stiffling attack of the dry particles, we were pleased enough even though we went soaked.

That night we slept in the hall of the council chamber and not alone for many of the Vars shared our quarters. Tradition and custom had been banished by the catastrophe and their women came with them out of concealment in the inner chambers, many of which no longer existed.

It was on the morning of the third day after the disaster that we left. Those to go overland included the majority of the Falconers, only two remaining with us, their falcons ready to act as scout. It seemed to me that far too many were crowded into the boat Sigmun had salvaged. He himself had taken over the command of our party as if it were his right, and none of us disputed that with him. We all, except Orsya, were ready to take our turn at the oars which propelled us out of the bay; two of the crew were stationed on either side of the bow to fend off masses of floating debris.

Within the bay it was relatively calm but once we were out in the open sea we found that the waves had to be constantly fought if we would keep on course. Luckily the owner of our boat had managed to save his single sail by furling it well before the quake wave struck and, with that raised to a brisk wind, the rowers were released for a space.

There was a stench of rottenness which the wind brought and we saw large sections of the ocean surface covered with floating isles of dead fish turned belly up. That some of the inhabitants of the depths had survived we had proof. For there were sudden whirls in those masses of the dead and gaps left where the already rotting fish had been dragged under.

I watched these closely. Very much in my mind was the memory of Scalgah. If that monster had indeed followed us south would this vast meal be to its taste, or would it turn its attention to the boat? When even the *Far Rover* had been shaken by the battering of that huge body we in this cockshell would stand very little chance. Still I hesitated to probe, lest by doing so I would attract the very danger I hope we might avoid.

The cliff line, as raw and sharp as ever, lay to the east as we sailed south. I believed that I could detect scars along the sides where more of that natural wall had been battered and lost to the sea. The clouds of sullen rain hid much except the general outline.

We bailed with a will, throwing overboard as swiftly

as we could both the fresh water from the sky and the salt from the sea coming through cracks even the Sulcars could not caulk. There was a chill wind, and that, blowing against our bodies through well-soaked clothing, brought us shivering, choking and trying to wipe rain and spray from our eyes.

With the arch of a dull grey sky over us we could not tell the time. We had speculated that the sea party might well reach the point of rendezvous before the company using the river as their guide could arrive. Twice we were delayed by having to make farther into the open sea to avoid fangs of reefs spilling out from the land. On one of these was evidence that some must be newborn for there lay sodden and dead under the spill of wave and rain the body of one of the valley herd animals.

The Falconers who had come with us watched the cliff crowns narrowly. It had been the bird of one that had found that the river had made itself a new bed. Now he brought his feathered comrade from beneath the edge of his cloak where he had carefully sheltered it and, having adjusted the device strapped to one of its slender legs, he tossed it aloft with a hunter's gesture. The bird circled the boat once and then soared up and on, toward the cliffs. Once more we had to edge into the sea to escape a water-washed ridge, and then took to oars to send our craft east again.

Here the water was murky. I saw a tangled mass, which could have been a large bush dug from a bank, wallow by. The water actually stained across the sea. While that outward-flowing current made it difficult to keep on course. Then I heard Sigmun shout and saw him pound the shoulder of the man beside him.

Out of the gloom rose the bare masts of a ship. The vessel swung a little back and forth as if it was anchored none too skillfully. There was no mistaking it—this was the ship of my farsighting.

Sigmun headed our craft straight for it. About us the rest of the Sulcar crew, except those busied with the progress of our own boat, were eagerly talking and pointing. Though now I could see a stretch of broken rail, and the main mast was certainly shorter than it should be, this vessel had not been too hardly used by the storm which had brought it here.

With the practice of their craft, at which, admittedly, none others in this world could do more than faintly equal, the crew brought us alongside the stranger and I saw one of the crew women leap up and make a line fast to the deck, holding us beside the greater vessel. That done she turned around to look over the prize.

A moment later she cried out, and kicked furiously as something near the size of her own foot dashed toward her.

10

*B*oth the two who had joined her, a man and a woman whose width of shoulders well matched his, had their long belt knives out even as their feet thudded solidly on decking. I saw more of the small creatures darting out from what were places of concealment, as if they were sentient enough to set ambushes for the first comer. They were certainly alive, and, like that monster of the sea, what they projected now was ravenous hunger.

The nearest Falconer dropped his cloak in the boat to free his arms and then leapt on the swing of our craft to climb into what was plainly a battle. It did not take the rest of us long to join him.

Those things which leaped to draw red, bleeding scores across the bare skin were furred, nothing from out of the sea. The long tails trailing on the deck were naked of any hair and the open mouths showed teeth ready for attack. There was a shrill squealing of a battle cry from them.

Knives and the Falconers' swords bit down into that frenzied pack, hacking—hurling mangled bodies back into the mass of attackers. Those injured or dead straightway became the center of balls of their loathsome kind feeding both on the dead and the dying.

We cleared the deck, sweeping the last of the wicked things into the sea, only at the cost of ragged bites and wounds which Orsya insisted must be treated at once with the supplies she had with her, for such creatures might well have carried poison in their fangs. Where the fallen had been the victims of their own fellows there were only now scattered bones.

I probed for life as I think that Kemoc was also doing. There was nothing more which had that avid hunger to mark it for us. However, there was still life on board. I swung around to set hand on the mast near me as I sent out a mind call, putting into it all the reassurance I could project.

There was a sound from overhead, almost a wail. From the rolled canvas of a sail a small body emerged. It was twice the size of the creatures we had slain, but I knew that that would not have saved it had that ravening force caught it. This was the hunter I had earlier detected.

It swung around and began to descend the mast, sinking what I thought were good and sharp claws in the wood as it edged its way down. We had made a circle about its refuge, eager to see the nature of this other seafarer.

Once I had seen a snow cat of the upper mountains, a thing of sinuous grace and wild beauty. This newcomer was perhaps a third of that as to size and I recognized it as one of those animals known in High Hallack and Arvon, an animal that, in the old days, had held a position of esteem with those of the talent.

In color this one was black as the eye paint worn by the town women of the Karsten ports. Though, when it jumped from its climb hold at last to land on the deck, one could see a triangular patch of pure white on its upper chest. For a long moment it eyed our company until it came to trade gazes with me. Then it uttered a small cry into which it was easy to read a demand for help. As the famished horde we had cleared from the deck it hungered.

I went down on one knee upon the bloodied decking and held out my hand. Slowly the cat edged forward far enough to sniff at my fingers. How it had come aboard this strange ship and what purpose it had here I could not guess.

Opening the larger pouch at my belt I pulled out a length of dried fish which served those of Varn as traveling rations. This I broke into small pieces, strewing them between me and the cat. It set to eating at once. Apparently it found no harm in us and was willing to let down its guard.

Captain Sigmun paid little attention to the cat; he was already at the way which led to the cabins and space below. While the Falconers, bared swords in hand, and two of the crew were quick to follow him. I broke up a second fish stick and was content to remain where I was.

The rain curtain had lifted. There was still a misty feel to the air but we could see the cliffs which here extended into the sea offering some protection to the derelict—and also mark that brown ribbon of current which betrayed the issuing of the inland river into the sea.

Orsya knelt beside me to watch the cat. "This is one such," she said slowly, "as the Old Ones knew—truly a cat. Only it is smaller. Lord Simon said that such were also known in his world."

It mouthed the last scrap of fish, even drawing tongue across the board where that had lain, and now it sat licking one paw and using that to wipe chin and lips, plainly washing after eating. This was the first time I had seen one of its kind before, and it fascinated me. Having completed its washing it yawned, to show an impressive set of teeth and four fangs two above and two below well set to tear. Its eyes were yellow, almost the shade of gold. With these unblinking it continued to stare at the two of us as if it now awaited any question we could care to ask.

I tried mind send. There was no pull of hunger to be read now; mainly the cat was curious. But the band level of its thoughts was far higher than that I was used to and it was hard for me to make contact. Tentatively I tried a question:

"Who are you?"

At first I was favored only with another long stare. Then there grew in my mind a hazy picture of the beast engaged in combat, tooth-and-claw battle, with another creature I did not know—not even distinguished clearly.

"Warrior?" I guessed

The battle scene did not fade.

"Fighter? Killer?"

"Black battler?" Orsya offered in turn. "Mighty killer?"

The cat's jaws opened to give forth a hissing sound. It was plain it did not consider us intelligent enough to reply properly—there was certainly about its whole body now an aura of contempt. The picture vanished and instead there built up a second scene in which our black find stood tall and several of its own kind crouched low about it, plainly in awe and respect.

"Lord?" I asked.

However, it was Orsya who found the proper word, mainly because, I later discovered, there were nonhuman allies in Escore and each of these species had a leader who attended councils from time to time. "Chief?"

The cat uttered another sound to answer that, a rumbling, throaty noise. It took a step or two forward until it could bump its head against the hand she also held out. Orsya dared to touch the fingers on her other to its head, rubbing the sleek fur behind and between its alert ears.

"Chief!" I echoed, this time aloud. Now it came to me for the same attention Orsya had given it.

We were still in the process of getting our communication clear and straight when those who had gone to explore the ship returned. The cabins showed signs of recent occupancy even as had those in the strange vessel brought into Gorm.

Kemoc had a roll of charts under one arm and Sigmun and his crew were already inspecting the stowage of the sails. Unlike that other ship, however, ropes over the side told of the embarking of the lifeboats, the ropes which lowered them trailing into the water.

Orsya slipped over the side and brought back the information that there was indeed an anchor holding it. Seemingly the ship must have dragged that until it caught between two rocks under the surface, the chain to which that was made fast now went taut or loose depending on the swing of the ship in answer to the waves.

Our searching brought to light other things. There was food aboard. Some of he containers had been gnawed open and their contents were long gone to feed that ravening horde which had welcomed us. However, in metal containers were hard biscuits and in glass jars we could see colored contents which might be fruit. There were also cans but the thin slips on their sides had been torn and the metal itself bore the sign of tooth marks. Prying knives opened a few of these and we discovered vegetables and more fruit, once a drink.

Though we were travel-wise enough not to exhaust this bounty in a single meal, we shared out enough to take the taste of Vars fish out of our mouths and mostly enjoyed the novelties.

There was still no sign of the party who had gone along the river path and we decided to wait them out on the ship rather than seek any possible camping place at the foot of the cliffs. Sigmun made sure that lanterns, a pair of them, were set so that any emerging in the river current might see them.

We made a more detailed examination of the derelict. There was clothing in some of the cabins—oddly fashioned shirts which seemed to be knit as the women of the farms knit winter coverlets. They had blankets but those had been stowed away in a sleek textured material which we learned resisted water and so meant a way of protection against damp. All which was found was carefully examined and put aside for future decisions.

The charts which had drawn Kemoc were again meaningless to the Sulcars who eagerly studied them. But Kemoc pointed out certain features which he declared, and Sigmun agreed, were like those found on board the ship at Gorm. The cat sat quietly watching our prowling about and annexation of the contents of the cabins. Orsya had settled cross-legged on the deck in the limited light of another lantern, smoothing between her hands a long strip of very soft material which carried a pattern of shells. These had not been stitched onto the cloth, nor painted on, but were a very part of it.

Kemoc was watching her, a smile about his lips, when Chief appeared out of the dark into which he had vanished earlier. He settled down beside me, that rumbling mumble to be both heard and felt as I stroked his back. On impulse I tried to contact him. Did he know where the crew had gone? What had sent them off in the small boat, leaving an undamaged and much safer mode of travel behind?

I thought that perhaps I could not reach him, and, then, though his rumble did not cease, I received again a hazy picture.

This was certainly part of the very deck on which we now sat. Tall figures moved at the edge of sight and then vanished. There was one who dropped down to sit even as Orsya now did well within Chief's range of sight so that she became clear to me. *She* certainly, for there was a wealth of loose hair, played with by the wind, and of a color which was indeed different from any I had seen, being far more red than Sulcar yellow. She had extraordinary eyes, huge and black, and one could not see into them. Then she raised a hand and brushed against those hidden eyes and the dark circles arose, she pushing up to her forehead what was like a mask under which her eyes were normal.

She picked up from the boards beside her the same strip of cloth with which Orsya had been playing and with that bundled up her hair.

I opened my eyes then and I reached out, catching the end of that scarf. Orsya must have guessed the importance of what I would do from my expression, for she let it free into my hold. Once again I could see that other woman. But there was something else—perhaps rising from the strip of cloth I held. I was suddenly aware of a compulsion. The woman I watched was on her feet. The laughing happiness which had been hers when first I had reached into the past was gone. I could see her mouth open as if she screamed, the lips shaping an ugly gap.

There were feet running past her. Now a darkness fell, though I also knew that that was no natural dimming due to the time of day but something else. She stumbled a step forward, her hands outstretched as if she had had both of them caught up in some unseen grip. She tossed her head, the scarf slipped from her hair, those strange other mask eyes fell away also. She twisted and fought. Her fear was like a lash reaching through the unknown between us to strike at me also.

Then there was a man beside her, his arm tightly holding her. I could see fear and concern in his eyes. Whatever possessed her had as yet made no assault on him. She got one hand free and struck at his face and head, her red pointed nails grooving deep scratches down his cheek. There came a second man and together they made her a prisoner. Only that which was her inner core—that—

I broke the mind tie instantly. That could have been a bridge between the possessed one and me. She had a fraction of gift, untrained, unguessed, and that had opened the way for that which had fallen upon her. They who held her were dragging her with them toward the passage which served the cabins.

As suddenly as the attack had been made on her, so did it also snap free. But I knew it had discovered what it had sought, an instrument through which it might act.

If this had indeed happened on board this alien ship, how much the quicker could it come and perhaps conquer those of us who were the greater gifted. It must be guarded against.

I looked with the outer sight to Orsya and Kemoc and I could see that at least some of what I had seen and felt had been projected to them. My fingers were busy with the seashell-patterned stuff, rolling it tightly. Many things can serve as keys to that which we would have remain imprisoned. If this was such, it must be put where it could do no harm.

"Give that here—" Kemoc reached for the scarf. He held the roll as gingerly as if it might be about to burst into flame, and then he wrapped it in the nearest possible covering, one of the charts he had brought to study. Could any of those, in turn, provide us with other entrances into the past and make understandable what had happened here?

However, I was not about to suggest that. Let such decisions await the coming of the Lady Jaelithe. I could produce the sight but I was well aware that all the guards I knew against what might be aroused by tampering with the unknown were as a straw compared to the training of a true Witch.

It was late afternoon when the falcon which served as our distance eyes brought news that the river-traveling party was within a short distance of the sea. At that time there was a brief conference as to the wisdom of remaining on board and bringing them hither or leaving a vessel on which certainly something uncanny had recently happened and prepare to establish a camp on shore.

The only difficulty with such a decision as that being that the incoming tide had already swept far enough along to lap against the cliff foot and there was no vestige of beach where we might shelter.

Then we could see figures on the move, not at the level of the sea but some way up the cliff itself, as if they followed a trail laid on a ledge we could not mark from the sea. Thus, using the boat which had brought us here, the Sulcars made two trips in and out and thus, returning both times crowded, the whole of our party was again assembled, this time on the unknown ship.

We filled it past the point of comfort, but at least our refuge was better than trying to see the night out either in the fishing boat or on the cliff side. There was some stability under us, provisions, and the light of several lanterns, until Sigmun ordered those to be doused in order to save the oil which fueled them.

Once more Lord Simon identified the charts. Though this ship was very different from that at Gorm, it was from his own world. Also, he explained, this craft, as well as sails, had the same kind of machine which would send it forward even if all wind failed. It was he who led a most systematic search of the cabins and that space where the wheel and the charts were.

Lady Jaelithe came to me where I sat in a small corner of the deck though not alone. The cat, Chief, had curled himself beside me, his head resting upon my knee.

"You searched—"

"Until I knew what I might stir with such a reckless questing," I returned.

She seated herself opposite me as if we two were about to engage in bespelling, with perhaps a scrying bowl between us. The rain clouds of earlier hours had split and withdrawn to the north. There was a rising moon and it looked very bright and almost harsh as to light. To everything there is a twin—one light, the other dark. The moon is for the weaving of women spells, which we are born knowing if we have the gift. But there are also two moons and one can be pitiless. I felt that that which rose this night was one which might be named such. Even the light can be cruel upon occasion.

The silver beam reached across the waves toward our new ship and that brightness resembled a claw waiting to hook about us. I was cold as if I sat full in the blast of a winter wind. And, at that moment, though my hand on one side touched soft, warm fur, and I looked to one far more versed in Power than I could hope to be, I was caught up in utter loneliness of spirit. It could be that one from the other time and place, whom I had watched struck by a fate I could not understand, trying in turn to meet familiar things here.

Even voices which reached easily about us because of the crowding sounded far-off and the words which they carried had no meaning. That sensation of being isolated increased. I began to breathe faster. This was being enclosed in thick glass into which even the needful air did not reach.

"Destree!"

My name sounded very faint—far away. Yet the knee of the Lady Jaelithe was close enough to brush against mine. I saw some movement in the half-light. I swayed a fraction as hands fastened to the fore of my shirt.

Light, not that pallid moonglow, was warm and yellow as the rising sun. Warmth spread from the now free amulet to break that shell which had been about me, ever thickening. I gasped, drew full lungfuls of air, and was alert to my own time and place once more.

The Lady Jaelithe's face was lighted by the flow piercing upward from her two hands held a little below my chin. I knew that what she so brought out of hiding was indeed Gunnora's amulet. Moonlight could call that power, even though it was of the sun also. But this time it spoke for another moon, a lightsome one, not a ghost light meant to only arouse the dead.

My own thoughts surprised me. This strange otherness was new; at least it had never visited me before. Had I indeed retained from my seeking something of that horror which had apparently sent into madness the woman of the ship?

I found myself spilling forth what had happened and I knew that Lady Jaelithe listened with all the strength of her art.

"Not again!"

I nodded, knowing well what she meant. Not again was I to spread wide my gift without knowing what guards must be held. But I had a question:

"What brought the madness?"

"My lord has said that those of his own world do not cherish the gifts. Those who are born with them are treated with disbelief. They have no discipline nor training to aid them in the proper use. We can believe that this woman whom you saw was one in which some of the Power slumbered. Perhaps she was entirely unaware that any fraction of gift was hers. Then there came a reaching—"

"From where? And how?"

"And why?" She added a question of her own to the two I had already asked. "We of this day do not understand the gates. We believe they were first wrought by those adepts who were seekers. Those of Escore who are closest to the old ways tell of wars and struggles and that there were summonings which brought into this world strange things. A number of the adepts opened such portals because they themselves would go a-exploring. Only their gates, once erected, remained sometimes traps.

"My lord says that in his world there are disappearances which cannot be explained. That there is a section of the sea about which are legends of whole ships which vanish. His people also fly through the air—using ships made to cruise so—and those also are gone, nor can any trace of them be found later.

"Thus there may well be a gate. For there is no other explanation which so fits the new facts we know. And if there is a gate in action which is great enough to draw in a ship, then the power which has fashioned it and which operated it is a mighty one. The Kolders found such a gate and they came through it, not singly as has happened with Simon and some others, but as an army riding moving fortresses able to bring down walls of a keep or even of a town.

"We have seen the sea raised to a force to assault Varn even as those Kolder machines attacked in the past."

"Do we then face Kolder once more?" Almost I could be at ease if she said yes to that, for the evil one knows is far better than a brooding shadow one cannot pierce.

"Simon thinks not. For in his time and world there was no Kolder. What we seek now is very different. But its strength is not to be questioned. I think that the woman you saw felt that strength and was greatly afraid, as well she might be. It was perhaps the first breath of that which lies beyond the gate through which this ship came."

"And she, those sailing with her?"

The Lady Jaelithe made a sign of protection with one hand.

"That we do not know—yet."

Chief roused and moved his head between us. His eyes seemed to glow in the night. I was tempted to try a second time to reach the past through him but I knew the full folly of that.

11

*I*n the end which was a beginning we did not sail south again with only one ship, or two—we were part of a motley fleet. The *Far Rover*, which had weathered the storm still afloat though lacking masts, could not take to the quest again, that was apparent. But those of Varn had been persuaded to trade for the more damaged *Wave Skimmer* five fishing boats. One of these Captain Sigmun, who now commanded by default the whole of the Sulcar contingent, sent north to ask for help in repairing the *Far Rover* and to convey also a plea for assistance for Varn.

I think that the townspeople might have even hunted us out of their ruined city had it not been for their seeress, she of the hidden face. She urged upon them in one meeting, which the five of us were ordered to attend, the consideration of the fact there could well be some agency, rather than the haphazard overspill of nature, behind all their city had suffered, and that if there was such a reason for the assault on Varn it should be learned and that speedily. It is always best to know as much of the enemy, before the onset of any engagement, which can be discovered.

The Lady Jaelithe herself went a-seeking by mind and contacted the Lady Loyse by dream control. Though Koris's lady had no talent of her own she had been comrade to Jaelithe so long that there was a mind tie between them and one which could be exploited if the need was dire enough.

Thus we could be sure that news of what had happened would reach Estcarp. Though, unless forces there could be talked into a perilous voyage, we could expect little in the way of immediate help. That we might abandon what we had planned never appeared to be in any mind.

Sulcars are born with a need to explore. The speculation that the danger which had taken so many of their number and one of their ships might be a planned visitation of the Dark had only strengthened their stubbornness. In the past they had wrought, even to their own sorrow (as when Osberic sacrificed Sulcarkeep to break the power of the not-dead sent by the Kolder), to fight against what were often apparently overwhelming odds. I knew that many of them believed that, in spite of Tregarth assurances, we once more faced some manifestation of the Kolder evil.

Sigmun put the situation into words when he bargained for the two largest of the fishing craft which could be repaired and made seaworthy once again:

"If this be of the Dark, and it has that stench about it, then will you think to rest here safe if you make no move to attract attention to you? Have you already been safe? You have spoken of your fishers who have disappeared—you have seen the fury of the sea and other portents. The Dark has such powers as can rack a world apart. For Power is neither good nor evil itself, it is only to be used, and it is how it is used that is what in the end matters. The Witches of Estcarp brought such a wrenching to the mountains of Karsten—though it broke them. Think you burning a mountain is any less a deed than what we have experienced here?"

One of the council muttered about Witches and Sigmun caught him up quickly.

"It is not Estcarp which brought fire out of the sea and all the rest to fall upon you here. But I say this—if a gate does exist, and it seems that is true, it can well bring further disaster upon Varn. Think you that it might not happen again and again? We know that there is trouble in the south—you yourself have said that. It is that trouble which we seek. I have heard you say that trouble followed us hither as if it was a scout of the Dark—is that not so?" He paused to look from one of those gathered there to the next and the next, as if he were prepared to challenge an adversary.

"Very well," he continued when there was muttering among them but no hearable answer. "Would you not rather we go forth into the very face of that which threatens so that it does not need to cast its lines hereabout to net us?"

So we gained four fishing craft (counting the one we had used to reach the derelict) to form a fleet. The derelict itself had been very carefully examined and some repairs made. It had, in addition to the sail, that manner of propulsion akin to that of the ship we had left at Gorm. But Lord Simon, having inspected that, explained again that apparently the ship had continued under that—and not the battened-down sails—until all the food for the mechanism had been exhausted and the fittings were now useless. However, there were other things on board which were an aid, such as those boxes which could set clear courses, the provisions we had already discovered, and the like.

There were records also and those Kemoc studied, the Lord Simon from time to time explaining this or that. The charts were a matter of envy to Sigmun, being much superior in every way to those known to him, but because they were of unknown territory those were no aid now.

I did not try to "read" again. The Lady Jaelithe herself kept very close watch on the seeress from the *Wave Skimmer*, a woman of middle years who studied me with hot, angry eyes whenever I crossed her path. I know she might arouse such anger against me as would have put me in danger, but she feared the Lady Jaelithe and would not try to cross one who had been a Witch and was still rumored to hold Power in both hands.

It was the Lady Jaelithe on our voyage back to Varn from the river bay who impressed upon me the dangers of interference with the unknown. Only that I knew and had already accepted. Captain Sigmun agreed that it was best not to bring the salvaged ship into port at the city, thinking that its presence there could well arouse more feeling against us. It was the Sulcars who worked on the vessels, preparing them as best they could for the open sea. Their badly injured stayed in Varn and Sigmun gave up the whole of the *Wave Skimmer*, with the consent of what was left of her kin-crew, to the people of the town so that their guild of boat builders went to work replacing the fishing ships.

Because she did have authority by the reason of her onetime office, the Lady Jaelithe seemed to have come into favor with the cowled spokeswoman of the council and, invited to share her quarters, took up residence in a suite of rooms within that impressive temple where we had faced the blind guardian of Varn. But the rest of us returned to the derelict and there did such labor as we could turn hand to. I was no stranger to Sulcar ship tasks and was more than willing to help. However, what Sigmun asked of the three of us—Kemoc, Orsya and me—was the clearing of the cabins below, to strip them of everything which might have been personal possessions of her vanished passengers and crew.

Chief accompanied me on my work in one cabin, curling up on a bunk which more closely resembled a comfortable bed. I had found two bags or cases which I thought were for the carrying of clothes and it was into these that I folded and pushed all wearing apparel, also anything else which might have been personal belongings.

The clothing, which resembled what I knew only superficially, was of unusual fabrics which I examined closely by eye but did not touch except with gloved fingers. I was not sure that I could indeed be pulled into "seeing" by touch alone, without clearing my mind, preparing myself to be receptive. However, I was taking no chances. When I had done the two bags were filled to overflowing. In fact it was necessary to obtain a length of rope to fasten one. For I had taken not only clothing and the like, but also bedcoverings which might have touched another's body.

I thought I was finished as I stood looking about the stripped cabin. The bunk was bare to its mattress, even the small curtains meant to hide the ports had been taken down. I was about to pick up one of the bags by the twisted rope handle I had devised, when Chief uttered a sound which was not quite a mew but clearly intended to attract my attention. He was standing up on the bunk, his hind legs on its surface and his forepaws against the wall behind. Twice when he saw me watching he butted his head against that wall.

I knelt on the bunk to examine the surface. It was paneled as was most of the cabin, but when I ran my fingers across the wood I felt what I was sure was difference in the depth of one of the joinings. If there was some compartment there it was clearly meant to be secret and the trick of opening certainly was not mine. However, with the point of my belt knife, I was able to force a small door which splintered under my gouging to show me a very shallow recess in which there were two boxes covered by material very soft to the fingers.

Still kneeling on the bunk I used the knife point most delicately, this time to raise the lids, taking care, as warned, not to handle the boxes more than I could help. What had been so carefully hidden by its owner must certainly be of value and thus even more closely tied personally to the one who had vanished.

There was a necklace in the form of fragile flowers of gold, each given leaves of small green gems which glittered, even though the light was not very bright. The heart of each flower was also a gemstone but of a deep golden shade. While between two of those flowers there had been set a pendant as a curling stem of gold, more of the green leaves, and a single much larger flower, the petals of which were not gold as the others in that chain but rather a stone which was both blue and green.

I have seen cherished jewels worn by Keep Ladies in High Hallack, some very ancient heirlooms treasured by Old Ones of high birth, even pieces found by those who dare to loot ruins of the Waste in Arvon. But the like of this never. The second of the hidden boxes revealed a bracelet, or so I thought it, as the chain was too short for a necklet, a ring, and a pair of matching pieces which, by the hooks on their backs, were meant, I believed, to swing from pierced earlobes.

This was indeed a treasure hord and I hunkered down to study it. I knew what would become of the things we gathered from the dismantled cabins. They were to be poked deep as they would go into a cliff crevice and left where no taint from former ownership could reach us. But to let this vanish so—there was protest ready on my tongue.

For as long as I could remember I had worn coarse clothing, mainly the castoffs of more prosperous and less unlucky Sulcars. The few new things I had ever managed to purchase had been the very cheapest I had been able to find, for most of my scant earnings had always to be saved for food to carry me through periods of lack of one kind of work until I could find more. There had been Sulcar kin who had allowed me passage for one reason or another, or because my story was not common to the port where I tried to sign on. I had also labored in the fields with the peasant farmers of High Hallack, and helped with harvests in Estcarp, where, since the wars, there was a dearth of steady hands and stout backs. I had also ridden guard for a convoy of merchants or two— men who had not been wealthy enough to hire blank shields or Falconers, but who had heard of the fighting ability of Sulcars and were willing to take a chance on one, even a woman—all knew that the Sulcar women stood ever ready to lend their strength on any ship or to the fore of a raiding party when their people had harried Karsten and Alizon in the old days.

Also I had seen rich loot rift from the coffers of pirates and wreckers, yet never had I seen anything to equal this. While to pitch it into a rock-walled pocket of the sea—

Though I had listened to all the warnings, and knew for a fact that there was good sense behind such, still, at this moment, I could not even close the boxes to conceal what I had found. Unconscious of having willed it my hand went out to pick up the ring. It lay in the hollow of my palm and when I raised it so that more of the light of the port touched it, there followed flashing rainbows of light. Truly if this was meant for bait it was such as would pull any eyes, hold the finder with desire.

I turned the ring about with fingertip. It slipped up and on my finger. The circlet might have been made to my measure so easily did it go into place. Against my tanned skin where small scars left by field labor still were to be seen, where the nail of the finger which it encircled was broken down and roughened, it was not where its beauty entitled it to be.

Nor did I seek mind touch. However, that came upon me. I saw another hand in place of my own, smooth of skin—the nail long and oval, unbroken, and even painted a deep rose. Happiness flooded in upon me as just beyond my sight stood the one who had given these treasures to me. And between that one and me there was a binding— They wed in Estcarp with words, and in High Hallack by cup and flame, among the Sulcar by naming of kin-clan. She who had worn this was wedded. Not to garner treasure or higher-born kin but because there was that of herself which reached and touched another. Together they had been so bound that in many ways they were one.

The jewels were treasure, yes, but what their owner had to hold to her was even a greater gift. I knew envy, not for metal and polished stones, but for the fact that there were some who were able to find this happiness which lay beyond the tangible.

There had been no cloud to shadow that happiness. I saw my own hand wearing that ring reach out into the air of the cabin and I waited to feel my flesh grasped by the firm fingers of another. Then—

Even as happiness had crowned me without my seeking, so did there follow the shadow. There are many beliefs within the world. Some swear by the Flame which dances on the altars in High Hallack, some by the teaching of even earlier gods and goddesses. We come into life and we leave it—some early and some later, some in illness, some by the cruelties of war—some even by assault of the Dark, and those be the truly unfortunate. Because we are what we are we have to make for ourselves hope— we must believe that there are things—or personages— greater, wiser, more honest and just, than we can be, and that, when we make an ending, it is in truth a beginning of an existence we cannot, because of the flaws which lie within us, really understand.

She who had worn this ring as a symbol of happiness, who in her joy and contentment had dared to believe for a while that there could not be any end to what she held—the fate which is with us all came to her and ties were broken, the light was overcome by dark. So did her pain and sorrow swell within me that I found I was weeping, and that I have not done since I was a small child forced to face what I was and what I must expect— loneliness, hatred, and perhaps even lying down with evil as its handmaid, though that I would fight.

I drew the ring from my finger and put it within its box. Yet I also knew that I could not give to the sea this I had found. The sealed niche which I had pried at to open was plain for the seeing. I knelt on the bunk and rammed it home again as best I might. It still showed the marks left by my knife and there might well be need for explanations. I looked down to the mattress on the bunk. Chief had moved forward and was crouched, with his forepaws on the larger of the two boxes. He might have brought some prey to prove his prowess and now dared me to take it from him.

It was easy to pull up the mattress and with my knife point rip stitches there until there was a space. The cat moved a little, allowed me to take the boxes and those I pushed as far into the opening as I could.

This was folly—already my obsession with the jewels was fading, with them out of sight. Still the stubbornness in me was not argued down by any foreseeing. These I would trust to fate. If any found them in their new hiding place and took them to destroy—I hoped only that I would not be near when that happened. For I knew my protest would be quick.

Looking around the stripped cabin I could see nothing else of its late occupant which I had left. So I took the bags I had filled and carried them up on deck where I found a small mound of similar well-filled containers. None of the Sulcar would touch them. It was left to Orsya, Kemoc, and me to drop them down into one of the ship's boats. The Lady Jaelithe, she who alone I feared might pluck out of my mind that which I wanted now to conceal, was not there. I gave a sigh of relief as we were rowed shoreward and pointed to the crevice which had been selected to hide it all, perhaps forever. Hide it we did, making several trips back and forth across the small strip of shingle the outgoing tide had uncovered, to see the possessions of the lost into that which must lose them even further.

I slept that night on deck. Chief was not with me, which was strange, as, after my return from Varn, it seemed he had taken liege oath, or perhaps kin-oath, with me and never strayed far from my side. Still, even with his warmth gone from beside my shoulder, where it had lain before, I went easily into slumber, nor did I dream as I half expected to do.

It was Sigmun himself who made the last inspection of the ship, Lord Simon and the Lady Jaelithe sharing his search, that no vestige of personal belongings of those who had once voyaged in her remained. I waited to be asked concerning the knife-gouged panel but there were no questions. Thus I was left a little uneasy. Not having the jewels before me to bedazzle, I began to think they might have been used in some fashion by that which wished us ill and perhaps I had opened more than a wooden panel. I strove to quiet my misgivings with the thought that if aught did occur in the way of sighting of the Dark it would be easy enough to pitch those boxes into the sea.

That I wanted the treasure for myself, as a fighter might conceal a better piece of loot from his comrades, that I was sure was not what ruled me. There was something else, a feeling that I could not cast aside such beauty on a mere guess that it could bring trouble. I looked once that day at myself in the burnished surface of a shield one of the Falconers had been polishing.

There was certainly nothing reflected there to awaken vanity in me. I was sure that if I decked myself with that which I had found I would speedily resemble a wild pony striving to wear the saddle of a prized Torgian stallion.

There did come to me now and then so strong a desire to look again on my find that I had to battle with it. I muttered, or thought out, scraps of the learning which I had picked up during my wanderings, and even took surreptitiously to sniffing some old and brittle leaves from Orsya's store of healing materials, those meant to clear the head and mind.

It was certain, I decided after the fourth attack of that need to seek what I had hidden, that it came the strongest at those intervals when Chief was by me. Though I dared not attempt to grasp any thought from him. However, I became very sure that the cat had some link with what I had found through his pointing the way.

The weather cleared and the days were fair. We had no more warnings out of the sea of trouble to come. It was on the twentieth day after we had set to work to prepare our oddly assorted fleet that we at last set sail for the south.

Once again, even as it had when we left the bay of Gorm, the wind was in our favor, filling the sails of both the salvaged vessel and the newly prepared fishing smacks. Falcons were sent above at intervals, only to relay the reports that there were no other vessels a-sea.

If Scalgah had followed us south perhaps the rage of the sea had been too much for him. I knew that Orsya kept watch on what lay under-wave but she reported nothing but the passage of regular inhabitants there—only saying that there were fewer of these than she would expect. Considering the masses of dead fish through which we had fought a way in the first days after the disaster, that was not to be considered strange.

We did not go too far off coast in our voyaging. The wall of cliffs continued to stretch a dark rope along the horizon to the east. To the west there was nothing but open sea. The one strange thing which the crew began to comment upon was the absence of seabirds. Perhaps they, too, had been drawn away by the abundance of dead fish. I was Sulcar enough to understand the uneasiness caused by their absence. The hardy fishers in the ocean have, from remote times, been a part of all voyaging, and certain types of them—a snow-white, wide-winged one, for instance—were considered to be lucky. We had legends of such birds guiding storm-warped vessels towards land. I knew many ships that carried paintings of that breed on the main sail.

It was on the fourth day out that the falcon sent on scout duty came with a report of land ahead. Whether that could be an island or if the shore took a wide outward pointing here we did not know.

Well before sundown we could see a dark line ahead of us, as well as still to the east. Sigmun ordered sail taken in to slow our advance. Two more falcons went aloft. This time they returned with the report that we were bearing down upon islands. As darkness closed in, a lookout on the main mast announced there was light ahead but veering more to the west.

It only required the stench which the shifting wind brought us to tell that we were not too far from a volcano. Though there was no spouting of wild fire into the night air, as most of us expected to see.

Sigmun had all sails in, those captaining each of the fishing boats following his example. The moon did not break through gathering clouds that night and our content of the past three days was gone.

Chief hissed when I would stroke him, and padded towards the bow of the boat as if he would stand lookout there. I followed him, coughing at times when the breath of the distant eruption reached us. There was uneasiness in the very air and I think that all of us were on guard, though exactly against what I believe no one could say.

12

Perhaps all of us spent that night uneasily. From where I made myself a place at the bow of the ship with Chief I saw people pass beneath the lantern glow on deck, and I had only drowsed a little when I was joined by another, and then a second—Kemoc and Orsya. The latter made plain her presence by the herb scent about her which even the acrid odor of the air could not banish. It was she who spoke first:

"What have you seen?"

I replied with the truth. "Nothing, for here I do not reach ahead." Nor had I even been aware of my talent since I had put the jewels into hiding, striving to make sure that I could not be trapped into using that which might bring upon us such notice as we wished most to avoid. That there lay more before us that night—hidden by dark—I had only to look to Chief to see, for he was crouched, staring outward as if, with the infinite patience of his kind, he did sentry duty by some den opening in which crouched prey he intended to seize upon.

Orsya dropped her cloak on deck. I had to guess more at what she did than what I saw, for the lantern light did not reach so far. She was upon the rail and then she slipped over, seeking that water she must have or she would die. Kemoc leaned well across the rail but he did not attempt to follow her down. She was entering an element she well knew, one where he could follow with the difficulty of those who breathed only air. Still I knew that if they were not joined in body they were in mind, and he stood sentry for her protection.

I had laid a hand on Chief's hindquarters and now I felt him quiver as if he prepared to spring. Though it was perilous I opened mind. I was on my feet, the rising wind whipping back my hair, hand on knife hilt. No stroke had come to me from a mind send, an attempted invasion upon that level of contact. Rather there was that which I sensed otherwise. Even as Chief might creep upon his chosen prey, so did there steal out of the dark south a feeling which was like unto a tendril, perhaps testing for some point of weakness. Yet it was not of a living thing!

That dark shadow which was Kemoc stood straight, his shoulder near touching mine. His hand had sought steel. We waited; after the scout might come the attack. However, there was none. That thing which had made my flesh tingle along the backbone had vanished.

I had heard tales of the undead—those which the Kolders had slain in spirit and yet still used in body. There were other stories, as grim, of certain sites to be found in places where the Old Race was once young and powerful. Yet what had stolen upon us that night was not even so allied with our own species or could share our thought or feelings. If it possessed life, and I was sure that it did—or at least purpose which moved it—then that life was such I did not know.

Kemoc had ridden against the Dark in Escore. His deeds there had already become the stuff of bard ballads. My own journeying had not been so far into the country half alive still with nigh-forgotten perils. So it was to him turned my question:

"What is that, warrior?"

"Something I cannot give name to," he answered as promptly. "Yet it is such that I would not have watching along any trail I take."

"Yet so does it watch, I think."

It was too shadowed where we stood for me to see his

war-broken hand move. On the air gleamed for a moment a sign, which first burned blue and then appeared to fold together into a blot, that showed first yellow and then red about its edge, before it snapped out of existence.

"So we know," he said quietly, but with the tone of one who had expected no less. It could be that in Escore he had made such tests before and been so answered. For his gesture was of that Light, and that which closed in upon it was clearly Dark.

At that moment I wondered for the first time at the folly which had brought us here. We had, all of us, from the first prepared for this journey as if we marched to an engagement from which none of us would stand back. Even the Sulcars, who fought clear of the use of talent, seemed to have agreed that there was naught else to be done but to hunt out what might be a long-held lair of evil. I had heard no voice raised in argument against what we did then, or a few days ago when we had put together this small and perilously weak squadron to go a-hunting the unknown. Had something reached all the way into the Council chamber in Estcarp marking us down and enslaving us without our knowledge?

I had faith in the Lady Jaelithe, perhaps the strongest of Power among us. They said of Kemoc that he had been long enough at Lormt to learn even older lore, though he was reputed to depend more upon his sword than such learning. While of the talents of Orsya I could not assess what she might know and be able to do for she was of another kin. Now I broke forth with a second question:

"Have we been as mountain sheep led to market?" For certainly to some powers rumored alert in the past we might well be as the stupid grazers of mountain meadows.

"If so," and he was not denying that thought of mine, "we have yet to see the shepherd. Though we may not be far now from where such may abide—"

There was a sound which brought my hand up, blade drawn and ready, only to know that Orsya was climbing back out of the sea, again able to abide in the air for a space. She clambered aboard and Kemoc picked up her cloak to toss it about her shoulders. While I saw the motions in the dark which I knew was her shaking her hair to rid it of the water.

"There is emptiness below," she said. "Life is not here, neither wearing fins nor shells, neither creeping on the floor nor swimming. It is a place in which fear has hunted and gone, leaving nothing behind."

So she set a seal on our unease. Nor did she and Kemoc go back below, but we three dropped to the deck together to remain—not on guard perhaps, but waiting—and for what we could not tell.

Morning broke again with a dull sky, no sun to break away that greyness. We came slowly up to the islands the falcon had reported. There was no green growth on them; they were barren rock with traces of the sea still set as if they had been raised from the depths, and not too long ago.

Again we missed birds; such isles as these in the north provided nesting places, oft time so thick with birds defending their own territory that there was fighting among them and the screams and squalls keeping up an ever rancorous clamor. Here the land might be long dead and with no life touching it. As Captain Harwic had done before us we chose two of the fishing smacks to do the exploring, selecting picked crews for them with Falconers for in-fighting if the need arose. In one I was at the bow. Sigmun might not trust me, but since I was favored by the Lady Jaelithe, he could not protest and all of us were well aware that this was not just a matter of sight and sound but also of the talent. The lady herself and Lord Simon were to the fore in the other boat, but Kemoc and Orsya remained with the ship as our common linkage.

Before we pushed off I was startled by a leap from the upper deck and Chief joined me, once more crowding past to take his place at the very point of the bow. There was a linesman who heaved over a weight and called out the clearage existing below, and the captain of the craft stood by the wheel as intent on those calls as we were in surveying the islands.

We had chosen the eastern way, while the other craft headed for the western sprawl of islands. Both craft moved by oars rather than trusting to breeze here. Adjusting our course by the soundings, we swung around the tapering end of the first island. I felt nothing of that which had striven to touch us in the night. The world was as empty to my mind seeking as it was to sight and ear.

But we were barely past the reef which pushed out from that island when we sighted the first proof that we were not the first to venture here. Piled up, its bow lifted high on reef rocks, was the remains of a ship. Its broken sides were patterned with barnacles and there was other encrustation which argued that it had been brought up from the sea after a long immersion. To my eye the design of it was strange. The small square ports, showing along its near side which was upturned to the sky, suggested that, large as it appeared, it had depended mainly on oars.

We did not approach it closer, but it held attention for most of us until we were well by. Certainly it was a warning that one went this course with caution. The leadsman's voice rang ever louder as we left that reef and its burden behind.

There were other islands ahead. Also that distant line indicating the coast of the mainland appeared to be moving east, as if throwing out an arm to encircle these blasted isles. The next two islands were smaller but— save they lacked a warning wreck—were no different in general appearance from the first.

It was as we drew closer to the next, and that was clearly the largest we had sighted—that Chief growled deep in his throat. While I stared at that mound of rock hunting sight of anything which might explain his unease.

My skin had begun to tingle oddly. There was a shimmer which came and went as I watched those rocks.

Twice I passed my hand across my eyes as if I would sweep aside some veil. Now I heard exclamations from the crew behind me. The three falcons which had accompanied their battle-comrades uttered ear-tormenting shrieks.

I waved eastward with my hand, hoping that the captain would obey that gesture and take us farther from what seemed now to be wild scatter of rocks. As I had marked at daybreak this was a morning without sun yet from between two of those ridge rocks on the island came a glint like that of light upon well-burnished metal.

One of the Falconers sent his bird aloft. It spiraled about, well above the dark blot of the island. The communicating device which the birds wore should pass a message of what might be there—for clearly it was not the black-grey rock which caused that patch of light.

As we veered out of line with that, I became aware that the prickling of my skin lessened. It was as if that spot had been hurling out in our direction some unseen assault which had manifested itself so.

"There is a thing of metal there." The Falconer whose bird was scouting moved up beside me. "It is not like anything Warwing has sighted before. He will not go closer for he fears it."

"Perhaps some defense," I returned. Knowing that anything which one of the war birds of the Falconers would avoid must indeed be a danger.

"Defense for what?" Since I was a woman it was odd that one of the Falconers would even notice me enough to ask that.

Defense for what was right. There was no sign, save for that long-ago wreck, to tell us that any had ever been before us on such a journey. I could no longer sight that glint among the rocks, but still I felt the prickle of skin, the sensation that there was a-lying in wait a threat to us. The reef into which the island turned stretched well out and we edged along, depending upon the leadsman.

More islands ahead—and something else! I heard an exclamation from the Falconer who still kept his position beside me, although his bird had come in to his wrist. At first sight that which broke the wash of the waves was only another of the rock mounds.

Only nature had not formed this one. It was four-square, fitting exactly the rock, on which it was so firmly foundationed, to the very water's edge. I knew well the age-old towers of Estcarp, and had seen many scattered remains which outdated even those across the sea in the land from which the Old Ones had long gone. None of those gave such a feeling of the far past, and of the alien as this.

To our sight, from the sea, there were no cracks in the four square walls, nothing to indicate that it had suffered from either blows of nature or of time. The huge stones which formed it were still cunningly set, and the lines of the two walls visible to us were broken only by what must have been left by the builders to serve as windows, dark oval hollows.

Those were all on the upper part of the building. At ground level there were no breaks in the surface at all. Entrance must have come from above. The stone from which it was wrought differed from that of the island foundation. It was smooth, unpitted, and in color a rusty red—almost, my thought supplied, the shade of dried blood. The roof which arose three stories above the sea was crenelated, the narrow embrasures perhaps intended for usage by archers.

Our craft did not change course to approach it closer. Nor did any of us suggest exploration. One of the falcons arose again to bear to our companion in exploration the news of what we had found. I studied it closely. There was that which suggested at any moment there might be a face showing in one of those blind eyes of windows, or that we would hear the whistle of an arrow, such as those of Karsten use for hunting, the snick of a dart, released to warn us off. I longed to probe but knew better. Such an invasion might well awaken something which time had lulled into a stupor.

We carried on, past the tower island. Ahead was a scattering of smaller lumps of barren rock. Farther yet lay an unbroken dark line across the horizon which could only mark, I was sure, the swing of the shore farther eastward into some cape or arm of another bay as that on which Varn had taken root.

We counted four of these lumps dotting the water, and two of them were surrounded by treacherous underwater reefs, so that we had to edge farther and farther west in order to avoid them. I think that none of us liked thought of that silent fortress behind us, nor the mysterious guardian which Chief had first sighted on the other island.

The silence of this part of the sea was oppressive. Yes, there was the wash of the waves, and the small sounds we ourselves made on board, but the wind had dropped and the single sail of our craft hung limp, also the absence of birds continued.

Just as my mind fastened upon that there was indeed a sound from overhead. Not the scream of a falcon but a hoarse, hacking call. There had come, seemingly out of nowhere, to hang above us one of those flying horrors which had harried Varn. One of the Falconers launched his bird and that spiralled up to hang above the dark noisome thing which made a landing on our mast, clinging to the very tip of that seemingly by some hook claws in its wings. It screeched and made grimaces at us, paying no attention to the falcon which indeed sheared off, not dropping upon it for a kill as one might expect it to do.

The Theffan instead gave all its attention to us. Chief growled deep in his furred throat and left my side, slinking along, belly fur brushing the deck, until he was immediately below the thing's mast perch. Then he gave the scream of rage his kind would utter when faced by a deadly enemy. One of the Sulcar took aim and fired a dart. The thing, with an incredibly swift twist of body, almost escaped injury. However, the dart cut through a bit of the leathery wing, pinning it fast to the mast while the thing shrieked and thrashed, striving to win free.

There was a froth dripping from its jaws. I thought of

venom and was about to urge the crew back, for several had joined Chief at the foot of the mast, when he who captained our expedition warned them off.

Dark blood spattered at each wing jerk, then the creature tore loose. It strove to mount, the falcon flying in wary rings just out of reach, but the tear in the wing seemed to prevent that. Fighting hard for altitude it coasted instead down toward the sea, but with a last effort it won to a hard landing on one of the rocky islets. It was screaming with rage and pain and its clamor filled the air. The falcon circled, and then swiftly it checked the second round of its flight and came arrow true back to its comrade.

Though the first of the winged things had appeared so suddenly, we had warning of the coming of its fellows. They skimmed in from the south as a flock, giving voice to cries as they swept down at the ship. Then we were fighting, striving to defend ourselves from these flying menaces. Swords scored as they swung upward, but I heard one man scream and saw him put hand to eyes, blood spurting between his fingers. Two dropped for Chief and, I think, would have taken him aloft. I cut the head of one from its hunched shoulders and the same blow continued on to slice at one of the other's wings. For some reason they did not come at me straightly as they flew at the others. I did not have time to think of anything but the fight at hand. The Falconers in their mail, and those helms with the metallic throat veils, were better prepared for them. Two stood one on either side of the wheelman, using sword and shield not only to protect themselves but in addition see that no harm reached him.

There was a scream piercing enough even to sound through the cries of our attackers. I saw the leadsman fall into the water. Twice I struck out at the enemy to reach the rail and then went over after him.

The water was murky and warmer than I expected to find it. But I got my one hand on the collar of the fellow's stiff shirt and brought his head up far enough for him to get a full breath.

We must keep afloat on our own, for there was perhaps no one on board who had seen our swift exit from the fight, or had time to drop us a rope. The smooth side of the ship offered no handhold—our nearest chance was one of those dots of rock which were part of the sprawl of small islands. Towing the crewman I headed for the nearest. Sulcars swim as well as any fish—or that is their boast. With most of their lives spent at sea, that was part of their heritage. But the one I now companied made only feeble efforts to aid himself. At least he had not clutched me in full panic.

I encountered rock sharp enough to tear through one leg of my breeches and felt the teeth of that outcrop even more as I dragged myself up to a position from which I could turn and pull the other behind me. He no longer made any effort to help himself and I found it an almost impossible task to get him out of the water, lying on his back. His eyes were open but fixed on the sky above as if he were aware of nothing. There was a long wound reaching from forehead to jaw along one cheek. That bled the more with every movement his supine body made as I tried to drag him higher. On his throat was a second gap in the flesh and that oozed freely. I put fingers to that and strove to halt the loss of blood while I looked up and around to sight the ship.

I had not thought that our struggle in the water had brought us so far but the craft where the battle still raged was a good way from our perch. Now I eyed the air for any of the horrors who might have left the greater engagement to make sure of the two of us. Luckily there were no stragglers, the pack of them appeared fully engaged at the ship.

My attention snapped back to my fellow in misfortune. Though his eyes still stared unblinkingly aloft, his face was convulsed by a grimace and I saw that the blood now rising in his head wound was darker, almost black, also it had thickened. That which I was trying to staunch on his throat was also dark. His hand arose from his side, fist clenched, to beat at the air, so I had to release my hold on the throat wound and struggle with him to keep his body from sliding off into the water again. His legs jerked and kicked. Yet he uttered no sound, nor did he look to me.

His mouth fell open and breath whistled out. Then his head arose a few inches from the rock only to thud back again, as, with that, his arm loosened and his feet did not move. He was dead—though neither wound should have been deep enough to let out his life. That the creatures we fought had the power of using venom as a weapon was so proven.

I stood up, steadying myself as best I could on the very uneven surface of that islet. The craft was even farther away and I could hear shouts and cries from it, making plain that the battle was still in progress.

My own position was totally exposed. Even if the flying horrors were beaten off, and I did not doubt that they would be, those retreating could well head for me and make sure that another of their enemies would be taken care of.

On the other hand to take to the sea again and swim for the ship would not be an answer, unless those on board were aware of my difficulties and could drop me a line. The perch which I now shared with the dead was a small one; it might even be more awash with the coming of the tide.

I looked towards the larger island to the north, one we had just passed when this attack had been sprung. It was guarded by reefs and no ship landing could be made there.

To the south then?

Reefs again, for now many of these showed above water. Those led almost like stepping stones to another and much larger island. I stooped and drew the body up as well as I could, leaving as much of it out of the water as possible. A Sulcar fighting crewman deserved a Sulcar funeral and perhaps we would later be able to give him such.

Then I stooped and washed my hands vigorously in the water. I must rid myself of the thick, poisoned blood. Having done this I looked ahead south. There was an expanse of water before the rise of the reef which I hoped would lead me to a firm place of refuge. I slipped into the sea and started to swim for that bit of water-washed rock.

13

$\mathscr{A}$lmost, except for the effort I must expend, this was like crossing a stream by stepping stones. Each time I pulled out of the water on a point of reef or an islet I looked for the ship. Always its course was farther away from the source of my own troubles. I saw no falcon rising from the air-ship battle. Had those valiant comrades been wiped out by the monsters as had happened with the birds at Varn?

This was a grey day wherein we had dueled with those aerial horrors and now rain came, fine as a mist but enough to slick down even those rocks above wave level, making it necessary to carefully watch one's footing. Mine was a painful progress now. As all on shipboard in such heat I had discarded sea boots for loose sandals. Those had been lost in my dive overboard. I could thank past poverty now for the fact that I had often, through lack of supplies, gone barefoot on land, so that the soles of my feet were calloused into nearly the same toughness as a boot. Though walking across the broken ridges of these islets had been and was growing more so a painful experience.

The water of the sea stung all small grazes into life. On my third emergence I shed my jerkin, worried a ripped seam to a great hole and so made clumsy coverings for my feet.

When I crawled out at last on the large island which had been my goal I stumbled and limped to the highest point within the immediate vicinity to look for the ship. Some current of which we had not been aware must have seized upon it while the battle was in progress, as it had been borne even farther to the east and even appeared adrift. Had the monster attack so thinned defenders that the ship could no longer make any headway, was as lost as the derelicts? Could all on board be . . . dead?

The swift death from poison which I had seen the leadsman suffer—was that the fate of all? Surely if any Falconer still lived his bird would be aloft, seeking—

Then, for the first time, my assurance was badly shaken. Had anyone seen my plunge overboard? Or if they had, would I now be deemed dead? That possibility had not crossed my mind—now it fastened tight in my thoughts. I wondered if I dared try send contact. Any of those on board whom I could picture in mind would serve as a target but, on the other hand none that I knew of were trained to receive. The Falconers had such a hatred for the Witches that they built, during the generations they had lived on the fringe of Estcarp, shields against any such touch. I might be able to contact one of the Sulcar—

Even as I considered that the worry which had been with me since I left the ship so unceremoniously developed at last. There were flyers in the air, only dots as yet, but they came from the direction of the far drifting craft and they were headed in a seaward sweep, as if they already knew that I waited for them, easy prey.

It was the nature of the island which saved me. The rocks which formed it were ridged. Gullies ran between some of the taller ones and there were other slabs which were tilted enough to form shelter against anything overhead. I speedily worked my way into one such niche and waited.

My exertions had begun to tell. In addition to my sore

feet, my back and legs ached. Also I realized it had been some time since I had eaten. In fact, so long ago had been my awaking from a doze on this morning and the taking of some very dry biscuit and a scrap of salted fish, I had gone without food for some time. Even more than the pinch of hunger, the need for water closed upon me. It was a sorry jest that I should be surrounded by liquid I could not drink. The realization of that made me twice as thirsty.

In a little the rain helped. I could reach out of the hollow in which I had taken cover, rub my hand across one of the standing rocks and bring it back wet to lick. Though that was indeed far from slaking the need in me.

However, hunger, certainly at the moment, was the least of my worries. My knife sheath was empty. I had no weapon, and from overhead came one of those ear-shattering screams of the flying horrors. One of them swooped down close enough for me to see, and counterwise it sighted me. Still to reach me it would have to drop so close to the ground—where there were upstanding threats of broken rock—that I think this problem did impress any mind the creature possessed, no matter how heated the thing was by rage.

I reached around and found several pieces of stone. Then my fingers caught under the edge of something larger, and I struggled to free a length of what could only be metal.

Its corroded skin flaked off in my grasp, but there was still a hard core. When I had it fully out of the ground I discovered I was holding a length which would compare favorably with a sword, although it lacked hilt or cutting edge.

To have even that made me bolder. I tried to count from the entrance of my fort the number of the attackers. To withstand such a pack as had descended upon us earlier was more, I knew, than was possible. They need only leave a token number of sentries on guard and wait for thirst and hunger to either weaken me or drive me out.

Yet I could only count five who skimmed back and

forth, and two of them had wounds. This was a beaten enemy, still that very fact might make them only the more set to take me.

One of them alighted on the crest of the rock perhaps a good stone's throw away from me. The fiery eyes were fixed and it threw back its grotesque head, giving voice to a throat-searing scream. I picked up one of the stones I had earlier loosened against just such a chance and threw.

The fragment of rock struck a little to the right of the thing, and shattered, one piece apparently ricocheting to hit the body of the flyer, who now leaped up and down as if rage filled it so fully it could not remain still. Another bound took it into the air and it arose quickly out of my field of vision. However, they were certainly very far from giving up the fight.

Two more swooped down to also alight, farther back than had stood the earlier one. These no longer screamed, but mouthed harsh chittering noises as if they were engaged in planning some coming difficulty for me.

I drew the rod I had found back and forth with one hand, scraping at it with the edge of another stone, wanting to clear it of all marks of corrosion so that I could see if there was any weak place along its length. It was not solid but rather bent under pressure, as limber as a whip.

The stones I had garnered earlier I made the best use of that I could—and was able to hit another of my attackers foursquare, sending it flapping and squalling to the ground, from which, though it made attempts, it did not rise again. However, I did not put an end to it. That was left for its own fellows. Two of them dived and, to my sickened disgust, caught the wounded creature by the wings and literally tore it apart. Why they turned on their own I could not guess, unless in frustration at not being able to take the fishing craft.

From the earlier mist the rain became a thudding downpour. Water spouted off the rocks, running seaward through the gullies. Under dark clouds we passed into a kind of twilight through which I was unable to see far beyond the crevice in which I sheltered.

There came no more screams from my attackers and I began to think that they had also been forced to seek some kind of shelter. At least the running stream of rain which fell to invade my hideout gave me drinking water. I sucked up palmsful, hoping that such a fill would also ease some part of my hunger.

The darkness was thicker. I had no idea of the hour. It could well be that night was really upon me. There was a rising wind which, at intervals, sent the rain slicing inward to my poor shelter. I was soaked to the last thread on my body and, though certainly my life had never been lightstone and I had known a number of miserable times, it now seemed to me that this was the worst I had yet met.

The falcons, if those intrepid birds still lived, would not be winging aloft in the midst of this. While had the ship kept to the last course I had seen before it, it must be going farther and farther from me. Once more I was greatly tempted to try the mind touch. If I could not raise anyone aboard the scouting craft, might I be able to contact either Kemoc or Orsya? Those with whom I had so lately sailed might well believe that I was dead—fallen into the sea and so totally lost.

I reached within the shirt the rain plastered so tightly to my body and brought forth Gunnora's gift. Though my flesh was cold, and I was beginning to be wracked by shivers, the carven stone within my palm was warm. I stared down at it. I did not know if it was meant to be used for scrying, and I still did not altogether trust my talent at piercing distance under a vague but perhaps deadly threat.

Still I tried to concentrate my full thought upon it, seeing first the stone, and then transposing Orsya's face upon that base. The amulet seemed to swell larger as I concentrated, but I was still aware that my hand held it. However, that connection with the real world faded. There was only the stone. Orsya—my thought went out—I tried to use it as a Falconer might use his bird, sending the mind search questing for our mother ship and she who was on it.

Only that search I could not complete. As fingers inserted in an ear can shut out sound or deaden it to the faintest of murmurs, so did my talent meet a barrier which turned it back upon me. The result of that return flow of energy was like a dagger thrust. Though I had heard that this might happen in times of stress, never had it been so with me before.

Swiftly I cut my thought search.

Still, on the surface of the amulet there was a swirl of movement. The outlines of what could be a head were forming. And I knew that it was not of my calling!

Two dark pits of eyes, a nose, a mouth which was set in a grin like that of a dead man struck down in battle. Only this was no warrior—at least any nation known to me. That rictus grin was softening, the lips no longer bared teeth to the full. While the blind pits which marked the eyes were filling, growing more and more like part of normal features. I was looking at a face which was no longer of the dead, but the living. There were eyelids closed across the onetime skull pits and slowly those were lifting. Then I was staring into eyes which seemed as large and knowing as my own.

This was a woman. That I guessed and knew it for the truth. I could see no hair above a high brow, nothing but the fact itself. Now the lips were moving again not to utter speech but in a smile which seemed to hold in it true welcome.

Gunnora? For a fleeting moment I held that thought. Then it was gone. No, not the All-merciful One—but a personage of Power, of command over my own kind even as the Harvest Lady ruled from her women-sought shrines.

There was satisfaction in the look I met. A fisherman might survey so a full net. I felt greater unease and I strove to cover the amulet with my other hand. Only to discover that I had no longer any command over my own flesh and bone.

Though it had grown very dark within the space where I crouched there was light about me—the warm gold of the sun. The warmth spread from the amulet to my whole body. I was aware of this but it did not matter. I was alert, waiting, as a messenger for some warlord might wait, impatiently, to be dispatched with orders to initiate some important maneuver.

Then—

The light in the eyes went out—candle flames puffed by a breath which was not mine. Once more the face changed to become skull-like—death out of life. Now I held only the stone. Yet from it radiated the warmth. In me there was something else becoming more sharp and distinct even as the face had grown.

In spite of the storm, the fact that the remaining flyers might come at me, I pulled out of my defensive pocket and stood under the thick curtain of cloud, rain plastering my hair and my torn clothing fast to my skin. I stooped and picked up the supple metal wand I had uncovered. At least in that much my own mind still obeyed me. For the rest—I was a game piece moved on a playing board.

I slipped and slid. The earth between the rocks appeared to have a greasy film but the covers I had tied about my feet answered for my progress. Though I expected to attract the flyers, to be a target for them, I heard no cries, saw nothing save the remnants of the body of that wounded one which its own companions had slain.

Now I reached the highest point of the island. So dark was the storm that I could make out very little. I had been brought here by a will I could not break.

The amulet still glowed. I glanced at it from time to time, watching for any change, but that did not come. Moved by that other will I turned around, cautious about my footing, to face south. The island on which I stood extended in that direction and it was that way I must go.

Thus I set out, climbing over ridges, striding through runnels between them where the streams of rain washed nearly calf high as I splashed along. Loneliness pressed on me more than it ever had in my life of roving. I think that I felt that because I was well aware that I went in submission to a command I did not understand. Though I went slowly with due care for every step lest I stumble and fall. A broken bone suffered here might well mean death.

On I went. Twice the way I followed narrowed to a rough ridge where the sea washed on both sides. It would seem that here the islands I could not see anymore in their entirety were like beads loosely set on a chain.

I do not know how long that journey lasted. In the darkness there was no way of measuring time. My body ached, and now I swayed dizzily from one handhold of upstanding rock to the next, striving to keep moving. For on me the pressure was growing heavier.

At last I fell and a wave broke over me, setting me coughing—as the water filled my nose—spitting the salty liquid out of my mouth. Under me as I lay there was no rock—luckily. Rather my hand swept across what felt like sand. I caught my breath and then crawled on my belly, so spent at last I could do no more, away from the lapping of the waves, well up into what appeared to be a rising mound of the sand, and there I lay. With great effort I pulled the hand which held the amulet to my now aching head, and darkness closed in so there was no longer any thought or feeling.

Did I sleep or swoon? At least I did not dream, or I did not carry into waking any such memory. I awoke to warmth on my nearly bare shoulders and I pulled my arms under me to help lever my body up.

The clouds and the rain were gone. A sun was in the sky and the heat on my body was such that I felt I lay half in a fire. I twisted around to survey my surroundings.

There was sea before me with reefs reaching out. Seeing those I marveled at the fact that I must have so blindly taken that road. It was not one I would have followed had I been given full sight. The island from which I had started was well out toward the horizon.

Remembering, I looked skyward. There was no winged thing to be sighted. However, here in the open I felt very exposed, so crawled as might an infant back to a wall of stone which arose up and up, a formidable barrier to any further retreat. To the west that wall continued. Farther along there were no reefs and the sea washed directly at the foot of the cliffs. I looked eastward and from what I could see I had reached that part of the mainland which curved out.

My stomach cramped and my hands shook, the right letting fall the amulet so it swung once more against my breast. By some chance, for I could not remember that I had intended it so, I still held the length of rod I had found on my first place of refuge.

To me at present the first need was food. Not far away were rock pools doubtless left by a receding tide. I crept to the nearest. There was a fish of some size who must have been dumped into that basin by the earlier inroad of the sea.

My past had taught me many things, one never to disdain anything which might be food because I shrank from eating it raw. It took me some time to catch the intrapped fish and kill it with a sharp pointed stone. I scraped the scaled skin free with the same weapon and ate, making the most of my prey to the last scrap of meat.

Where I was now the cliff was sheer and I had no intention of going west where it arose from the sea itself. But there was a fringe of dark grey, sanded beach to the east and the cliff showed broken in places. Still unsteady on my enwrapped feet, from which the improvised coverings were near worn away, I started on in that direction. This was a very empty world to which I had come. Save for some sea creatures to be found in a tide pool or two along the way, there was no life here.

Fortune favored me, or else that which pushed and kept me on my bruised feet watched over me for purposes of its own, for I came to a real break in the cliff. Down that poured a stream of water which fell in a miniature cascade into the sea at that point. I scooped the liquid up in both hands and drank my fill. It seemed to me that where the stream had cut a path would be the best place to attempt to go inland.

For a while it was a difficult climb and I would rest now and then, the water spreading about me, my body trembling from the demands I made upon it. The cliffs arose on either side to shut off any view of what I might be climbing into and my fear of being surprised by the winged things kept me going, hoping to find some kind of shelter once I reached the upper reaches of those walls.

At length they began to fall away, widen out, so there was room on either side of the water. Then I saw the first growing things which I had sighted since we had sailed from Varn. There was a greenish network across some of the rocks, wet with spray from the stream. It was not moss but rather resembled a netting, such as a spider would have fashioned. When I tried to pick up one end of a piece I discovered it was most securely rooted. These nets became larger and denser as I advanced. Then, ashore, in the grey soil showed stalks of a pale yellow-green—long narrow leaves outspread upon the ground with a center stem standing high. Those ended in a round knob and from them came a sickly odor. Stuck to those knobs here and there were insects, some still struggling for freedom.

At length the last of the cliff walls opened well out and I found myself at the edge of a wide stretch of rolling open land. As it was in the valley of Varn there were no trees. Clumps of brush gathered here and there, tangling branches from one to the next, forming a growth which nothing could penetrate. Some of these strange copses were of quite wide extent. The leaves were dark in color and, though there was no hint of breeze in the air, these were in constant, trembling movement.

I continued to follow the stream as about that the land was open and looked to offer the easiest going. Also there were signs of life within the water itself. I overturned rocks and found armored things which were near enough to what I had seen on sale in northern fish markets as to reassure me of their food value. Though I had nothing in which I could stew them as was customary for their proper serving. Once more I ate raw flesh, forcing it down. I had seen no signs of those herbs which grew along stream banks in the lands I knew.

Once as I wavered on I saw a serpent whose red-yellow scales made a bright patch to serve as a warning. I stood very still using the one end of the rod I carried to thump against the ground. The reptile, feeling the vibration, fled, as all his kind will unless one by chance corners them. But this was another sign that the land I had come to was not a healthy one for travelers.

The sun was well down the sky and I could not pick out any stretch of the land ahead I thought fit for a camp. Thus I squatted down beside the stream to rebind the coverings on my feet and try to make some plan for what was to come. With me still, perhaps even more pulling at me, was that feeling I must go on, that there was something waiting for me which must be faced.

By now I had surrendered to it so long I did not think I could ever break out of the spell it had put on me. We all know of geases and what those ensorcellments can do to the unfavored who have been so cursed. Was this in truth a geas? If so, who had placed it on me and for what reason? I could only belive that it was one which would not do me well and I longed at that moment for the company of the Lady Jaelithe, for perhaps she alone in all this world could read that which held me, and so aid me in what must be some coming battle.

14

$\mathscr{I}$ disliked being completely in the open, yet the nearest copse was so entangled, vinelike branches embracing one another, that I knew I could not find refuge there. Nor could I see anywhere within the range of sight a place as satisfactory as the rocks among which I sheltered before. At length I decided to go on. The sky above was clear and as far as I could calculate this would be a moon-crested night. Underfoot the ground was promisingly level and I had the stream for a guide.

My pace was slow. I wanted nothing so much as to squat down for rest on one of the patches of sandy soil which spotted the valley floor. Yet move I did, until I could no longer place one foot before another, so came to sit by the running water from which I scooped enough to satisfy thirst. I had heard many tales of the Waste of Arvon—had seen a portion of it when I had gone a-hunting Gunnora's shrine.

The foundation of that was iron-hard clay with drifting sand about weird, heat-tortured growths of strange vegetation or the skeletons of such which a touch would reduce to powder. This was a different kind of blasted country but I could not help comparing it to that other which now lay a sea away.

In spite of all my efforts, my head nodded and my eyes closed. At some point in that struggle sleep won and I must have fallen forward on a pocket of sand.

Through the dark in which sleep held me there came sound—a thin wailing which had all the great sorrows of a country spun into that single thread. I thought I had dreamed it, but when I blinked awake, bemused and disorientated, not sure of where I was, that wailing continued.

There was a night wind blowing from the south and its

strength must have carried that plaint. The moon was up but its light was not reassuring. As I looked, bleary-eyed, around it seemed to me that the copses I could clearly see cast very odd and disturbing shadows on the ground. Something a-wing blundered near me. I was instantly alert, picturing in that air one of the monsters. But if that were so the creature made no attack. Rather it dropped in a hunter's strike and a thin squeal cut the pattern of the wailing for an instant, before the flyer arose again, prey which was no more than blot as far as I could see clipped between its taloned feet.

I heard then a clicking which came from upstream. There were stones heaped there, so thickly drawn together (and absent elsewhere along the water's run) that one could believe that tumble was the last of some ruin so far gone that only traces remained. Out of what seemed to be the heart of that tumble was something emerging. I got groggily to my feet, but for the moment I moved no farther.

There was a patch of full moonlight uncut by any shadow between me and that place of stones. To my eyes the creature pulling itself out of the rubble was large, and growing larger as it continued to scramble free. Once it slid down the fringe of the stone it stood erect!

The thing was humanoid from the outline of its dark body and it walked on two hind feet, its upper limbs swinging free by its sides. Then it passed from out of the fringe of the stone into that patch of moonlight. There it stood, hunched over, its head thrust forward, seeming to rest on very little neck but rather on the shoulders. There was no bulk to it, rather it was painfully thin, both upper and lower limbs hardly more than skin-covered bones, though the body was bloated and as round as if it had swallowed whole a rock such as those it had sheltered among.

The thing was female. Once it might have worn clothing, for there were a few remaining tatters of foul stuff hanging from a belt which confined the top of that paunch. Long hair was matted on the head and fell in clotted strands about face and shoulders. In fact the face was so veiled by that that I could not make out the features.

Not until the thing threw back its head and opened jaws to give forth a howl such as might rise from some starving animal. As with the arms and legs the facial skin was drawn tight over bones, the lips so stretched as to show teeth even when the mouth was closed, as it was after that ululating cry had gone forth.

I tightened grip on my rod as the head moved forward a fraction. At that moment I found myself unable to either attack or retreat. Yet I knew that it had seen me. Arms moved, hands with long nails, some raggedly broken, came up, those fingers spread as if to tear at my throat.

It leaped forward and I slashed with the rod, which struck one of those hands so that the arm fell limply to the creature's side. It did not howl this time, rather it slavered words which I did not understand. Then it halted to begin a short sidewise movement.

I turned also, to keep facing it. It was plain that even if my blow had given it a wound, it had no intention of abandoning the hunt. For that was what it was doing—it played hunter and I was the prey. Since I had left Estcarp I had seen the creature of the sea, and the airborne hunters, both unnatural by the standards of the northern lands. But this was not wholly strange; it was the worse because it aped my own species, and yet it was such a foul thing as I could not imagine any woman of my kind becoming.

It snarled. I saw the shoulders hunch a little more and I was sure that it was preparing once more to attack. This time I went to meet it, swinging my rod with a whistling note in the air. I landed a second blow which fell on shoulder.

It cried out and strove to raise the injured arm, with the fingers of the other hand making clawing motions in the air as if it thought to reach me but was miscalculating the distance between us. Once more I raised the rod—

This time it cowered back, halfway into a blot of shadow. It was mewling like a voiceless beast, yet here and there came a sound which was not unlike a word. When I took a determined step forward it retreated, backing towards the rock pile from which it had come, stumbling over one of the stones and falling to its knees.

Shaking its head from side to side, it clawed at the stones seeking aid to get once more to its feet, yet that effort seemed too much for it. Then it squatted there unmoving. Its head went back so that the face was wholly exposed to the sky. I could see tear trails on its sunken cheeks. Bracing a shoulder against the rubble it held forth its unhurt hand, not in menace as before but rather as if begging mercy or help. For a long moment we faced each other so and then it slipped sidewise, going limp upon the outer fringe of stone.

Its breath was coming in flutters and it clutched at one of the flat breasts on its bony chest. Twice it raised its head a fraction, the sunken eyes fast on me, and both times its mouth moved to shape what I thought must be words.

The hair-matted head fell back as the breast heaved once, twice, and then the creature was very still. I waited but it did not move again. Then I ventured on towards it. I had been aware earlier of the stench, but now it seemed a hundredfold and I could not bring myself to touch the quiet body, even being near it I gagged and fought nausea.

I circled to approach the pile of rocks from which this foul caricature of a woman had come. There was a dark hole there like a well opening. When I reached it from the back, on the opposite side from that point where lay the dead, the smell was even worse. However, I sighted something which continued to draw me.

Between two or three of the stones on this side of the pile there was a faint glow of light which had not been cast by the moon. Its source must lie within that pile. That the dead had some form of light, a fire, was hard to believe. I only knew that that was a treasure worth the peril of invading any den it might have used.

So I climbed the pile of stones with all care and stood by that well entrance. The odor was near overpowering yet, looking down now, I could indeed see that glimmer. I lowered myself into the hole. The moaning on the night wind, which had awakened me, continued but it was interrupted now and then by stretches of silence. During one of those I entered the den, listening for any sound which might suggest that there was a second inhabitant.

The stones were so roughly set together (yet they did not shift under my weight) that it was like descending a ladder. I was out of the well passage and into a room. That it was a room I was sure by the regularity of the walls and the fact one could trace the joins between massive blocks. This was indeed a remnant of some ruin made for defense or living quarters. The light continued to hold my attention. On the floor stood a cylinder, part glass— at least it was frosted and yet the light came through— and part metal.

It had been set close to a heap of what looked like broken-off branches of the copse boughs and mashed wads of the net stuff I had seen on the stream rocks. In that noisome nest there lay a shrunken thing which I looked at only once and then turned from in a hurry. Whatever the huntress had once been she had not stayed alone in this den—those were the remains of a child!

I caught up the lamp in a hurry and went to reclimb into the night. In me there was turmoil. I could not believe that the mother had lived such a beast life—what had brought her to this hole with her child? Of what people was she?

Outside I put aside the lamp on the ground, finding by experimentation it could be turned on and off by pressing a button on one side of the base. Leaving it off and setting aside my rod, I pushed myself into a task I could not leave undone.

Though my whole body shrank from what I did, I made myself pull the corpse of the woman back to the edge of the well. Having no rope nor any to hold me I could only push it over, to fall to the floor of that age-old chamber. Then I hurried to move stones, to cover over that opening. I was weeping when I had done, for sorrow had grown within me as I worked. After I had set the last stone to close that tomb chamber I took forth Gunnora's amulet. There was no glow from it, but, as always, it was warm in my hand. I held it out and passed it back and forth across the heap of stones.

"Let that which is of earth return to earth." I drew from memory words I had heard in the past. There had never been a time when I had said such for any I had ties upon, for even when I had been a fosterling, I had not been heart welcome to those with whom I abode. Why should the dreary death of that creature which was no longer human put such a spell on me that I must do this thing?

"Let the inner spark which is life return to THAT WHICH SENT IT. May she who lies here be troubled no more and may SHE WHO GUARDS all womenkind welcome this one into the House of Peace through the last of all gates!"

In my hand the amulet blazed, the blue light of it seeming to seep through the cracks which my rough covering had left, as might spring rain falling to nourish waiting seed. Then that which had come from Gunnora vanished and by the pile of stone, with the morning star shining slowly, I was alone.

That pile of stone was not the only sign that once there had been more here than barren land. As the sky grew lighter, and I was able to see farther ahead, I noted other heaps of rubble fanning out from the river into the plain. Yet only the stones eroded by the ages remained and none of them held anymore any shape from which their original purpose might be read.

I had no desire to search farther for any remnant of life for I was sure that she whom I had found here had been alone, starving, and hopeless. Had she like me been brought here through some disaster at sea, marooned on this coast without any hope of rescue? Could she even have been from such a ship as the derelicts which had been found? There was no telling now.

Once more I hunted in the stream and made a meager morning meal of the armored things which lurked among water-worn rocks. With such to hand why had the dead one starved? Unless she had had no training at all in living off the land.

In me once more awoke the urging to be on my way. Still I did not yield to it at once. My meeting with the victim of this place might have loosened in a little the geas laid on me. I cupped the amulet and for the first time dared that which the Lady Jaelithe had warned against—I sent out a mind call, striving so to find the craft which had brought me here. Had that kept on the course which I had last seen it follow it must already have touched the shore—perhaps finding some temporary anchorage there—before I myself had made my perilous journey.

So recklessly I sought a mind, any hint of there being survivors of our expedition within range of my sending. And I picked up—

No! That was none of what I had always known as human kind. This was Power of a sort but none that I could put name to. And it came not from the seashore behind me but rather from some source to the south of where I stood in the rising of the sun.

I jerked back instantly and strove to raise my shield, expecting a probe in return. None came. It was almost as if the source was asleep or so engrossed in some purpose of its own that my touch had not betrayed me. I still could not think of it being emitted by something that had life as I knew it. However, for all my wandering, what did I know of this world? Not even the Sulcars had plied their trade this far south—or if some ship had recklessly penetrated hereabouts it had not returned to tell of it. Only Captain Harwic had seen the barren islands and he and the *Wave Skimmer* had not lingered long.

I thought of Laqit, that fabled last guardian in our lore.

All the tags and tatters of very old tales which I had heard during my wanderings had never hinted at the nature of Laqit. I was tempted to use the amulet, to try to raise again that face which I had seen. That, indeed, had human features. But there were entities of whom I had heard that had the power of full glamorie, who might take any form they wished and so present themselves to those they wanted to beguile, even as there were beasts do battle in either human or animal form. Though those did not become their animal parts except when danger threatened. And what danger could I be to anyone with my half gifts, one of which always carried calamity with it?

One thing did follow my reckless meddling, there descended swiftly upon me now the full force of that compulsion which had set me traveling. Whether I would or no I strode among and between those piles of rock heading not due south but angling to the west more than I had the day before.

This trail was taking me away from the stream upon which I had come to depend both for the food and water it could offer and for a guide which could not be lost. I fought to keep beside it, only to have increasing pressure applied on me to leave it behind.

There was no way I could carry water with me. As for food—the dead-alive land about me gave no promise of any successful hunting. I did have the unusual light I had found in the dead woman's den slung to my back by a cord I had made from the networks on the stones twisted together. That I did not need with the sun climbing higher in the sky at my back. It did not take long for the heat of that to become an evil instead of a welcome good. The rays striking my skin through the tatters of my skirt were burning worse than even those of the harvest fields. Yet except for those dire-appearing copses of interlaced, towering shrubs there was no place which promised any relief from the sun.

I had perforce left the stream well behind me and could pick out a dark line to the west which marked a continuation of the cliff wall when I caught a small touch of life force. One more step and it was as if a portion of the ground itself, directly before me, took wing and flew ahead but no higher than I could reach with my rod, uttering sharp cries. For a moment I nearly tripped over my own feet. The flying thing was clearly some species of bird, having nothing of the winged monsters about it. Nor did it keep to the air long; perhaps it was not accustomed to extended or soaring flights for it settled back to the ground and immediately thereafter it vanished. The plumage which was its cover was also its defense for that was the same greyish shade as the earth, even carrying spots and lines which mimicked that of the ground thereabouts. However, having once seen it, and had its life spark register on my mind, I was able to take this gift of fortune with a swift blow by the rod. Preparing it for the eating was a much harder task, and there was no way of cooking it. Again I ate raw the fruits of a hunt.

Having once picked up this touch of life force I was sure I could pinpoint it again. I went on pulled by that tie, yet relieved that I did not face such a fate of sheer starvation as had that pitiful thing back by the river.

Water I came across at the same time as I made my kill, in fact the bird fell to my blow because it must have been absorbed in appeasing its own thirst. It had pulled up the soil from around one of those repulsive insect-capturing plants to bare a large bulb that was studded with holes and oozing liquid. With infinite care I put finger to that moisture, smelled it. To my nose it had no scent, and then I licked on that dribble of sap. It had a sharp, sour taste but it allayed my heat-born thirst. I had the whole bulb out of the ground swiftly and punched a larger hole in it. The liquid actually spurted and I caught and swallowed as fast as I could the bounty it yielded.

So having my bodily wants answered, I went on—though my unwillingness to going so at another's will grew. I did not struggle. There might be a very good reason for me to conserve such Power as I had against some future confrontation. I knew only too well how helpless

I always was after I had drawn upon my talent to the utmost. Nowhere here were to be found the herbs and tending which a farseer must have after such an ordeal.

Though whatever moved me apparently had care enough to allow me to rest and take my own pace. It was late afternoon and the sun was a blow against my face and eyes when I stumbled forward a last few steps and came to my knees in the shade of a tall outthrust of what was mingled hardbacked clay and stones. I sat there, panting, for some time, looking but not seeing, content just to have this much alleviation from the burning heat I had been facing this day.

I do not know just when my unseeing stare tightened into a seeing one. There was a curved length of what could only be bone protruding from the side of that hillock. Beyond that marker there were other such, some half buried in the ground, some lying in the surface. While within reach there was a skull, its empty eye sockets turned toward the wasteland over which I had been traveling. These were not the remains of just one body. On my hands and knees I crawled partly around the hillock that I might see the other side.

There stood another such outcrop and beyond more reaching back to the cliff which did rise again before me. While bones were piled thickly about, some lying one over the other. There were whole skeletons which had been laid out correct to the last small bone and in other places bones were scattered as if flung about heedlessly.

Only what caught my eyes now were not these remains but what lay among them, about them, under them. There was the glint of metal, even the brilliant flash of gemstones, and shreds of cloth, rotted and rendered colorless by time.

I did not feel as I had when I had buried as well as I could that wasted body by the stream. So old and fleshless were these that I felt no kinship with them. Thus I dared now to do what many of my species would have done, I foraged among the long-dead.

It is a firmly held belief among the Sulcars—and per-

haps among the fighters of other races also—that to take
up dead-held weapons was to invite into one's own inner
life he or she who had last borne the sword, or knife, or
spear. I would be deemed unclean, doubly suspect to
Dark blood, had any of my late shipmates watched me
now.

When I staggered again into the shade of one of those
clay-and-stone mounds I had three knives, lacking any
touch of corroding rust, a sword with a gem-set hilt, and
an armlet with a sheath for a throwing knife, that light
and murderous weapon still within its hold.

As I had searched for what I needed I had decided that
this was no battlefield. Swords had not been drawn,
knives still lingered in rotted belts. Oddly enough the
metal was in no way corroded nor rusted, but clothing
and belts and boots remained only as fragile remnants.

I had not seen on the skeletons themselves any sign of
wounds. Each skull was entire without a break. There
were no dart bolts or arrows between ribs thus placed to
show that they had been shot into living bodies. Also I
believed that those dead here had not been killed all at
one time. It was as if various companies had been brought
to this slaughter place, sometimes years apart, and finished off, left to lay where they had fallen. Nor had any
visitor despoiled the bodies. Not only were unused weapons lying among the bones but I had seen jeweled brace-
lets, necklaces and the like, still upon the framework of
those who had once been their owners.

There was one way I might solve this mystery, perhaps
so learning how I myself might avoid a similar fate. Yet
I shrank from employing it. I sat there as the sun dropped
below the western cliffs and the broad banners it had left
flying began to fade, drawn one way and then another.
Would such an act as I contemplated draw me deeper
into the hold of that compulsion which had brought me
here? Was it worth such danger I could only guess at and
should be able to understand?

Gunnora's amulet was warm again in my hand. I put
my palm back down on my knee cupping the stone firmly

and then I reached for the first of the knives I had gleaned. It had a longer blade than most; the hilt was, I thought, fashioned of some kind of horn, and that had marks deeply incised within its substance.

Picking that up, I laid it across Gunnora's stone, then I shut my eyes and threw open my mind swiftly, that I might not turn from the task.

15

I did not slide into darkness—rather it was as if I were standing on a height looking down into a pool of grey mist. Here and there that was broken by an upstand of rock—so that all this might be again rock islets rising out of a dull, turgid sea.

There was stirring in and through the mist—I felt a blanket of fear, muffled fear, which kept one moving. Some part of it stood between those who so moved and a complete understanding of who they were and how they had come here.

There was a company entrapped, striving weakly to break forth. And I had been a part of them, only, by some freak of my own nature, I had been able to break bonds in this much, that I had climbed out of the cloying and imprisoning mist.

Who was I? Memory was dim, broken, had faded. A ship, the sea, and then a breaking open, a tearing apart of the normal world. Afterward the command laid upon all of us on board—that we steer for—

A harbor!

Yes, but though we made that landfall we were even more deeply caught in the net of some unknown fisher. We had come ashore, marching together, moved by the need for answering that call. Only in me had something twisted and strove for freedom. I had repeated words I had learned—held on to my sense of oneness—was not yet absorbed into the collected prey of whom I was meant to be a part. I had thrown myself aside just before those who were my fellows set climbing a long flight of stairs and I had fought my way—fought it indeed, for it was as if I moved through some thick morass into which I might be engulfed at any moment. Still I had turned from those steps up which the others climbed, their faces without expression, their eyes set in unblinking stares, all which had made them the comrades I had known either wrung from them or sent into an unwaking inner slumber.

So I fought and forced a way among dried carcasses of ships which had run ashore. Only still that compulsion gnawed at me. I put my hands over my ears, as I might shut out some order, which hearing, I would be forced to obey, as I zigzagged back and forth about the time-eaten relics of seagoing races seeking ever to get beyond the reach of that which commanded this port of the lost.

Then for a space I was free, still I felt a thrust through me which I knew signaled not my vanquishment but that of those I had known. On their march they had lost more and more of themselves, their identity, yet at this end that flared high and in the same moment they were taken—there was nothing of them left, just emptiness.

I fled that emptiness, running in sand which caught at my feet, until there was a band of pain about my body. Though I did not pause even then but continued to stagger forward away from those steps which reached upwards into nothingness.

The place of the ships was passed and now I faced cliffs which were like walls. There I leaned, one hand against the rock for support, gasping for breath, all of me darkened by fear which had grown even greater since I had felt that ending of our company.

Fear made of me a near-unthinking beast as I clawed my way along the cliff. Then I stumbled and fell into a rift in the stone. Not waiting until I could regain my feet, I went on hands and knees into that crack until I came to the end and lifted bleeding hands to search the stone for holds which would take me out of this. Always I waited also for some blow, some assault which would bring on me the mindless obedience to walk to my own death.

I went up and up and then sprawled out on a ledge which ran both right and left, the wall above that looking strangely smoothed when I ran my hands above to discover it held not a single fingertip hold. Thus I turned left, trusting that I was still fleeing away from the stair.

At length the cliff began to descend and the ledge sank also. Again I crept when I wanted to run for there was a mist below and I could see nothing but the roiling of those billows.

It was when I reached the mist and it closed about me that I knew I was no longer alone. Trapped in it was sound—sometimes a wailing or the gasping of breath one hears when a weeper is near exhaustion. Also there were louder voices which called upon names, of their fellows, or perhaps of gods. It was a clamor and yet it was strangely muted.

There came into my mind then another thought perhaps seeded by my fear. My comrades had been taken in a pack, but what if that which had taken them had thought for another day, or hour—or year—and would keep a certain part of its prey in captivity to serve it later? Had I not escaped but only prolonged the evil I had broken from? I raised my own voice in a hail, wishing to see someone of those I could hear, perhaps discover more of what we had blundered into.

I was not answered. Still the other voices cried, and moaned, and called for help. This clamor struck so into me that I wanted out of it and I turned to search again for the beginning of that ledge which had brought me here. Save that the curtain of the mist was so strong that I was utterly bewildered and could not say I had come this way or that.

I came up hard against some barrier and the surface of this was rough enough to afford me hand- and footholds so that I could climb. That I did and my head broke out of the mist. Then instantly all the voices I had heard were stilled and I was alone. The mist lay about me but beyond there were other places which might mark similar hillocks.

For the first time I saw others beside myself who had won free from the net of the mist. On a hillock not too far away there sat a woman and across her knees rested the head and shoulders of a man. There were blood-stained bandages about his head and his shoulder, and she held him tightly, rocking back and forth as might one who nursed a beloved child.

I called to her, for the relief of seeing those two was warm in me and I felt that I was shaking off for the first time something of that compulsion which had moved me. She raised her head to look and I saw features which were unlike those I had knowledge of. Only around her large eyes and about her lips was her very dark skin free from a featherlike down. That, too, covered her arms and hands and every portion of her body which was un-clothed. While her clothing was very thin, like the finest of veils, and had been rich, although it was now rent and bedraggled, with tears to split it.

She stared at me across the puffing mist which separated our mounds. Then she called in a voice which was a trill with no sound of words in it. Loosing one of her hands from the one she guarded, she raised that to wave to me.

Yes, I would go to her gladly, but if I descended now from my perch above the mist I would be lost again and could never be sure that I could find her. She must have sensed this as soon as my own thoughts formed. Carefully she moved the unconscious man she tended from her knees and got to her feet. There was a wrapping of cloth which sparkled here and there about her waist and this she loosened, proving it to be of greater length than I would have thought it measured. She shook this out and then stooped and made one end fast to her ankle. The rest she caught up in her hand and threw down into the mist. When she pointed to me and that and I was sure I had caught her meaning. If I could descend and reach that outcrop I would be guided by her girdle. It might be the most forlorn of chances but I was willing to take it, for to continue where I was until hunger or thirst, or that which commanded here, was moved to collect me, was indeed the most cowardly and useless of choices.

Yet it was not easy to descend until that noise-filled mist closed about me again. I had taken what precautions I could in the way I went so that I might be facing in the right direction when I was again below. I strove to keep going in that line in spite of the bewilderment with which the mist enfolded me. Twice I saw other shapes in the mist, blundering around, but I knew better than to allow myself to seek out a meeting with either. There was a shadow ahead and I kept on until I did indeed bump against the bulk of one of the hillocks. Eagerly I reached above my head seeking the touch of that rope of cloth. I indeed thanked the Wind Riser when I found it. After that it was a small matter to climb and rise up beside the woman and he whom she nursed. Her eyes, which to me were overlarge for her face, were on mine as I emerged and then she leaned across to jerk up the loop of cloth which had been my guide.

She motioned to the wounded man and gave more of her trills. I believed that she asked of me to see to him, but there was little I could do. Blood was drying on the bandages she had devised. He was clearly of her people as the same down on his skin was matted with blood along one arm where the shoulder wound must have dripped.

Now she made another gesture in the direction of the cliff which had brought me here and which arose as a dark blotch well away from where we were now. To think that we could get back there perhaps carrying the unconscious man with us was folly and she must have already seen that for the gesture which she had made toward that focal point was one of repudiation.

There was hardly room for three of us where we crouched. I looked in the other direction and saw that there were indeed other such perches as this but they could be as far away as the familiar sea on which I had voyaged for most of my life. She and I together might be able—with a great deal of luck—to reach one or two more of those perches. However, with the wounded and helpless man we dare not try any such moves. I think she had already guessed that for her head was bowed, the longer down which served her as hair flattened to her skull as she rocked once more the man she tended and crooned a series of notes such as might serve as a lullaby for a sick child.

Nor could I now go and leave her. She was not kin, nor had any claim on me. Still I could not leave her here in a place where death was certain to come. There must be some way out. I was a stubborn one; perhaps it was that very stubbornness which had given me the strength to resist the order which had set my comrades to climbing. I had won that much, perhaps there was a way I could win more. So I continued to eye the way ahead.

There was movement on another of the hillocks, one a good distance from us so that in this uncertain light I could not even be sure I had seen it. Then a figure did stand there and I realized that another of the mist entrapped had won temporary freedom. An arm was raised and that distant one waved certainly to us. He or she had a better position, for not far away was another, taller height rising and that appeared to mark the end of the mist-ridden lower land. It might well be that that stranger could win altogether to freedom. However, we could expect no aid—he or she was too far away.

After that first hail the other did not wave again. I could not see from our perch what he or she would do. Then the other held upward in both hands something which resembled an axe. With a show of strength the stranger brought that down to where wisps of fog licked up from the mist. And, as if those were tangible, they split apart, the head of the axe beginning to glow.

What I was watching might well be some form of hallucination but still my eyes assured me that this was happening and that the mist was swirling back from where the axe wielder stood. More and more of the hillock was revealed as the fog receded.

The other twirled the axe twice about his or her head. I heard sound, faint but unlike the voices entrapped in the mist. Nor was this the trilling notes uttered by my present companion but it carried rhythm in it—not unlike one of the chanties we of the sea sing to make some hard task a united one.

Out from the stranger's hold flew the axe, skimming above the mist so that the down-pointed blade of it cut a path across the billows. Back pressed that concealing fog on either side clearing a path which reached over hard-beaten clay covering the ground. Then the weapon thudded against the height on which we were perched and I snatched at it, my fingers closing about warmth, then folding into a hold which made it seem that I was well familiar with this weapon, that all its secrets had been always known to me. That it was more than any axe, of that I was sure. In this place it was easier to suspend disbelief, to accept that which hours earlier might well have seemed a story for the beguilement of children.

With the axe now firmly in my hand, I leaned down, kneeling on the top of the hillock to give me a firm base, and swung the weapon back and forth, watching the mist retreat as might a living thing sore threatened. The whole of the mound on which we had taken refuge was now free to its very roots.

So, we had a way of winning through the maze set by the mist, but even so could we try carrying the injured and unconscious man? How often need the axe be used? What if it failed once we were away from the doubtful safety of the hillock?

I was distracted from these dire thoughts by a sound beside me, and I turned my head to see the woman pressing her long, thin fingers to the injured man's temples, one hand on either side. There was a sense of fierce concentration about her. The man groaned a second time and one of his limp arms stiffened; he raised a hand uncertainly and his eyes opened. In the moment perhaps all he saw was her face and the complete resolution in it. He muttered a deep sound almost equalling a distant roll of thunder. Then, with her hands behind his shoulder, taking some of his weight, she got him to sit up. For the first time he sighted me and I met a measuring stare, that of a fighting man facing that of which he was not sure, but she trilled and his wariness slowly faded.

In the end, laboring together, we got him down from the hill, he aiding us when and where that he could. Then, with his arms about our shoulders, we went slowly, the three of us together, along the path the axe had cut. That I continued to swing in my right hand not knowing when I might have to use it.

Though the voices in the mist reached us, very faint and far-off, none who were imprisoned there blundered into sight in that corridor. We wavered on, though the wounded man was no light weight. I felt empty. It was a long time since food had passed my lips, perhaps it was even longer for my new companions. Still we crept ahead.

Then the power of the axe's first cutting began to fail and I saw the mist closing in ahead. I remembered how the owner of the weapon had used it. Dare I take a chance and throw it ahead to clear our way as had been done before? I could not leave the two of them; the man was now nearly a dead weight which I was sure she could not support. Otherwise I might have played advance guard and marched on to strike, axe in hand.

We had paused and I limbered my arm by swinging it back and forth. An axe was indeed a shipboard weapon but it had never been my choice and I was certainly not adept in its use. I swung at last and let the haft slip through my fingers. It did not fall to the ground as I more than half expected it might, instead it advanced through the air and once more cleared the mist it met with its cutting edge, we following at the best pace we could make.

The axe vanished entirely, which raised a sudden fear in me. If the blinding cover closed upon us again we would this time have no defense against it, we could only hope to reach that point ahead where it had gone to ground.

But the pace at which we stumbled along was so slow! It seemed to me that we must yet be far from the hillock where the axe wielder had stood. Were we never going to make that? If the stranger who had been so distant had been able to produce this marvel what else might he be able to do to free us all from this trap?

There was the rise of another hillock in sight now but the pathway to it appeared much narrower. The woman trilled and pointed to that, I guessed her concern equalled mine. In the end she and I were forced to advance partly in the mist and partly in the clear, only our charge hanging between us wholly free of its touch. It seemed to me that the stuff pulled at me, strove to break my linkage and draw me entirely into it, so that part of my now small share of energy must be wasted fighting that.

We came to the hillock's foot and a figure moved away from that towards us. Even as the woman and her charge were alien to any race I knew, so was this man, for I knew him at last for what he was.

He was naked to the waist save for some strings of colored beads inter mixed with curved things which might be claws, and the longer lengths of what must be fangs. His skin was a very dark brown but painted with brilliant color in elaborate patterns. The coarse black hair which covered his head had been coiled and knotted at the nape of his neck, kept in place there with a band of red cloth. Below a waist belt formed of discs of metal inset with blue gems he had on breeches which were also leggings, these fringed along the outer seams, plainly made of animal hide scraped bare of fur. While his feet were covered with boots very tightly fitting and also ornamented with beads and a few of the same talons appearing in his necklaces. He might well have been a barbarian such as traders tell about, but his dark eyes were shrewd and he was watching us with something of a propitiatory air. Swinging in his hand was an axe, surely the one I had tossed ahead not long before.

He eyed us up and down one after another, but he did not speak. Instead he gestured toward the right of the height from which he had descended, turned and threw the axe with a smoothness of long practice. Again that cut the fog and he started down the cleared path, not glancing back to see if we followed or offering us any aid with the wounded man. Perforce we did follow.

Luckily we were very near the end of that mist prison. We came out into the open and found our savior leaning against a rock, his axe again in his hand. Behind us lay the mist, night was gathering fast, and we had no knowledge of what waited before us. Food we needed badly and also water. Did he of the axe know more about this land than we?

He was striding on once more, finding passage between two outposts of stone, just as he had so confidently walked through the divided mist. Something crunched under my feet. I had trodden flat an arch of ivory—bones! They were lying thickly on the ground. We were making our way among and over relics of the dead! I caught one foot under another curve of ribs and took a fall, pulling the other two down with me. My body slammed hard against the bone-littered ground and—

Darkness, bewilderment such as is felt by someone being awakened too quickly from deep sleep. I was fleeing—

One me then another me, which was I? Memory untangled itself from the talent as I made myself breathe deeply and look about me. It was as dark as it had been when I—no, the owner of the knife—had come this way. I turned my wrist quickly and let that blade thud to the ground. That took with it the last tatters of otherwhere, other time. I was a Sulcar half-breed, not that youth who had by chance, and certainly magic on the part of another, won his way out of part of a trap.

Had he and those with him died here? I had found his knife, which I had used to unlock the door of knowledge.

Looking back now I could not remember where I had found it. Was it one of those still resting in a crumbling sheath or had it lain free? If so he might have dropped it in that fall and the four of them had defeated—at least for a while—that which kept the mist prison.

I looked around me. There were hillocks here, and an opening to the west ahead. Did that mist still hang there? Were there those who moaned and cried and called for help caught in it?

With the coming of the light tomorrow I must climb that cliff high enough to be able to see what lay beyond that rift. The scrying I had just incited was a warning. But for the moment I was too tired to even shift my body, though it ached. This use of the talent had been prolonged and I was already lacking in the strength which was born of regular food and rest.

I wriggled back, planting my shoulder firmly against earth and stone in such a way as to leave me facing the west. By my side, within easy distance for quick seizing, I laid my knives (save the one I had used as a scry guide and which I had no wish to touch again), the sword, and my rod. Though the night was still and I could see no curl of mist in the heart of the rift, yet I trusted nothing here.

As I leaned back I thought of that warlock—for at least he was master enough of Power to fit life of a sort into his axe. Many of the adepts of old were said to be men. It was only when those who fled the wars in Escore reached Estcarp did the gift become the possession only of women. He had resembled no one of any clan or kin that I had heard of—however, that was the south and we knew not what peoples might dwell here. I remembered that men who had been at the retaking of Gorm had commented on the fact that many of the alive-dead slaves had been strange-looking people of no known race.

How long ago had this happened, this escape from the mist? They had found skeletons here even as I had done. Was it so close to my own time that somewhere the four were still alive? That poor starving creature I had found—

she might well have escaped this same trap only to die in the barren land because she had no training to search out that which might serve as food.

Tomorrow—tomorrow I would know—I would climb and look and know!

16

I could deny sleep no longer. Thus I fell, thirsty and hungry, into a waiting pocket of darkness. What awoke me was as sharp as the call to deck and sail duty during a storm. But my famished body did not respond with the same vigor as might have been mine on one of the ships. I looked about—

Sleep had taken me by the hillock and with my weapons beside me, in that place of ancient death. Now I stood on my feet and around me was a dull, greyish fog which bewildered my eyes even as the tail end of rest left me swaying where I stood, unwary and unprepared.

That I dreamed was my first sluggish thought. So vividly had I relived that other life which had been shadowed by a like mist that I was once more caught by what I had past-seen or read from the knife. The knife! That was not with me, nor were any other of the weapons I had scavenged. I held only the rod I had earlier found.

Catching a bit of flesh on my forearm between thumb and finger I gave it a vicious pinch. That I had certainly felt! No dream then—but how could I have come into this place unless something had commanded my body during sleep to move me here?

I strained to hear—as had that earlier captive—the sounds of others caught within this blinding fog. But there was such a quiet as made me wonder for a moment if I were deaf.

Those three who had won out of here had had the help of Power. What was my own power—but the twittering of a bird compared to that the painted man knew—he with his axe. Also I was sure that whatever—or whoever—had pulled me here would soon exert more of strength to compel me to its will.

My power—no axe—I gave the rod a disparaging flick back and forth. Then I put hand to my shirt and drew forth the amulet. Instantly it blazed into almost eye-searing light. I pulled the cord on which it was strung over my head to flip the stone about. As it had done under the cutting edge of the axe, the fog retreated. It no longer enclosed me so tightly. I turned slowly, spinning the amulet by the cord in each direction, and the mist shrank.

Well enough, for now I had my own clearer of ways. There stood one of the hillocks not too far away, and I headed straight for that, keeping off the mist as I went. However, I needed a better guide—I wanted to gain the top of the cliff, even as I had planned the night before.

I was still listening for any sound to suggest that I was not alone here. Perhaps it was the thickness of the mist which made it so very quiet. I did not like the feeling which that silence aroused—was it a waiting, an anticipation of my coming within reach of that which saw me as prey? There were no bones on the hard-beaten clay of the ground here. I reached the hillock and once more settled Gunnora's gift in place, the cord safely about my neck. The light continued to blaze. The ground at the foot of the hillock was free. I climbed, a short pull and I was above the mist. It was midmorning by the height of the sun and the heat of its rays struck almost like a blow.

I was able now to see what I sought, the wall of the cliff lying to my right, and I made very sure, as I descended from my vantage point, that I was facing the cliff. Then, with the amulet in hand, I worked my way out of the blinding fog and saw once more tall rock. The surface was rough enough for me to be sure of handholds. I had gotten less than a third of the way up when I came to a part I remembered from my seeking. This was certainly the end of the ledge which the fleeing seaman had followed out of that bay of dead ships. I swung myself onto that, willing to return to the place I remembered so clearly from my glimpse into that other's life. Also, yes, it was certain—that was the same fatal bay I had farseen for our party much earlier.

Lack of water and food made me unsteady. At times I had to lean against the cliff wall which formed one edge of that road. But I forced myself on. Though it seemed that sometimes I could barely set one foot before the other, I came out at last to view the bay.

This I had seen from scrying and also through those other eyes. Now I could look at it in person and the sight was so overwhelming that I simply slipped down the cliff side against which I had leaned to huddle where I was, staring unbelievingly at what lay below.

I had thought Varn's harbor large. I knew that that which held Gorm itself and served Estcarp was probably the largest known in the north. But this—

Perhaps the fact that it was filled with ships—not ordinary ships swinging at anchor or waiting against a wharf for a promised cargo—made it seem endless. Though I could not see the far western end of it even from my place above.

Many of the ships had been beached, as if their crews had deliberately aimed them for the shore. Among those were some which were only bits of weathered wrecks for on top of them, grinding them down into the grey sand, were other vessels—later comers. Masts had fallen; their liens of rotting rope formed traps on decks.

Nor were these all sailing vessels—no, there were some—one very large—which resembled in part that ship Captain Harwic had brought into Gorm—ships which must have plied through the gate. Again this was a place of silence. As usual in this fateful south there were no birds. And certainly no one stirred on those decks below no matter how solid they still looked.

I turned my head to shut out the sight of that vast graveyard of ships and gazed inland. There was again my memory of this place from the first farseeing to tell me that this cemetery on the edge of the sea was not all-important.

Not too far from the cliff way there reached a wide stairway cut into rock set there as if armies of people came marching to whatever lay above. As the survivor of the knife had seen it, stone steps were worn in dips and hollows, by hundreds of feet during unnumbered years.

I looked upon that and there moved deep inside me a need for going up those stairs, for following all those who had marched that way before. Yet I also could sniff the evil from its crown. A mighty heap of refuse and filth might lay at the top, or back a little, for I could not sight such from here. However, the stench was sickening. The two-way struggle continued within me. I dropped from the ledge to the beach onto which ships had smashed. These must have been drawn by Power—a great Power which even nonliving products of men's hands could not resist.

The sand was below my bound feet when all the bemusement this place roused in me was pierced. I whirled with such vigor that I lost my balance and stumbled against boards spongy with rot, easily crushed by my weight.

"Destree!"

There was no mistaking that call from the Lady Jaelithe. I downed the mind barriers I had held while so near to this unknown danger.

"Hold!" came her order. "We are coming."

I tried to see between the wreckage of the ships if ours had entered that bay of disaster but I could perceive nothing of any movement on the outer fringe.

That my companions were using me for a guide I did not doubt and I quickly built up in my mind the picture of where I now was.

It was not from the ship-crowded bay they came, but as the Lady Jaelithe's touch grew the sharper and clearer, I pinpointed the source to the very beach on which I stood at a point farther westward. By the change in volume of linkage they were coming at a steady pace. I say "they" because I was aware that she was not alone. Others backed her, feeding Power that she might range the farther and discover more quickly what they sought. A shadow crossed my mind that what we now did might throw us open to whatever evil abode here. Instantly she reacted to that.

"Yes. No more!" The tenuous link between us vanished instantly. I remained where I was looking ever westward and waiting.

There was another who came first. Leaping down from the deck of one of the beached boats Chief padded through the sand to join me, pausing only to face the foot of those stairs and hiss, his tail fur straight out from the roots as he lashed that appendage from side to side. Then he was on me where I still sat in the sand, too weak to rise again. Purring loudly he rubbed his head back and forth on my breast where the amulet lay. I rubbed his ears, the very touch of his fur freeing me yet further from the pull of that stairway.

They were not far behind. The Lady Jaelithe, Lord Simon, Kemoc and Orsya, and, rather to my astonishment, also two Falconers and Captain Sigmun. The latter walked nearly sidewise so bemused was he by the sight of all those ships. Twice I saw him shake his head, and then rub his eyes with his fingers, as might a man who thought that he viewed something which was born only of clouds and sorcery.

So entranced was he that he kept backing even farther up the beach the better to see all which had been entrapped there, until he was nearly at the foot of that stairway, so that I cried out:

"No, Captain! Away from that stair!"

He swung about to meet my eyes, then glanced behind him. His forehead puckered by a frown, he straightway put a good distance between himself and the foot of that way to death—or so I believed very firmly that it was.

They had provisions with them and granted me a share of both dried fish and sweet water. Certainly no banquet, but to me now the finest viands I had ever tasted. When

I had finished I knew they awaited my story and I straightway launched into an account of all which had befallen me since I had gone into the sea.

I knew that at least the Lady Jaelithe could follow my words with mind touch and that she would so be able to attest that I spoke the truth. It was that portion of my story which dealt with the seeing brought by the knife which interested her the most. Though I had been aware that when I mentioned that first use of the amulet which had shown me the face of a woman of Power, she had seized upon that to store in memory.

My tale of the adventures of the single sailor who had escaped the fate of his fellows held them all absorbed. At the coming of the man of Power and his axe they were all caught and held by every word I spoke, even the usually unshakable Falconers. It was one of them who asked the first question when I had done.

"What chanced to them—those out of the mist?"

"Death?" suggested his fellow. "You found the knife among the bones."

"The fall which put an end to the sight—he may well have dropped it then," I returned. But would he not have rearmed himself, some part of me asked in chorus at that. Look at the weapons I myself had garnered from that place. There may not have been so many at his time of discovery but there should have been some. Had he just left the knife and went on, better armed with what he had found there? The old superstition that taking on another's arms also took on a part of the owner—I began to see that that might have been partly founded in truth. I had told my story in detail, but only when I had spoken of the scrying had it become different—I had been a part of him then, hardly aware of myself. What *had* happened after that tie had broken?

If they had survived, those strangely assorted four, what had been their final fate? Starvation in the barren country I had transversed before I headed southwest? I found myself hoping that the warlock with the axe had dealt better by them than that.

The Lady Jaelithe had seated herself, as she listened to my report, so that she faced the steps up which the captives had trod. Her mind touch withdrew. I saw tenseness in her figure, the fact that her eyes might not look but that she now called upon the inner sight. Lord Simon's hand went out to rest on her shoulder, and I knew that he was backing her with his own power. I could even sense the flow of force between the two of them.

My hand went to my worn and grimed shirt and I brought out the amulet. That rested easily, fitting itself perfectly into the hollow of my palm. It was alight—though that glow was blue and not the brilliant beam which had cut a way for me through the mist.

Kemoc sat cross-legged and Orsya half leaned against his shoulder. His maimed right hand was out, the first finger pointing to the stairs, his face also all concentration. Captain Sigmun and the Falconers had drawn a little apart.

I knew well the Sulcars were wary of this kind of Power and the Falconers owned to having no talents except such as bonded them for life with their birds. But with Chief it was different. He put one paw on my wrist and exerted strength to bring my hands down an inch or two. Then he leaned his head against my arm at the same place where his paw had rested. His eyes were wide open and glowing, fixed upon the stone.

Strength began to build. Slowly at first, like a single plank from one of the ships behind us floating on calm water. Then it picked up speed—the floating board could be motivated now by a rope attached and vigorously pulled.

Something had lain quiescent—it had . . . fed. Now it stirred a little, some faint warning might have reached into its half sleep to urge waking. I could not catch any clear picture. I did not think that any of us did or we would have shared it all at the moment it came into even one of the minds among us.

No, I "saw" no man, nor Witch, not even one of the monsters which had attacked before. There was a queer blankness about this thing of Power—it might be dead—lacking the spark of life which a user gives to the talent. Only it was not so—it was still able to function in a manner of its own.

I strove to reach above it with the farsight. Once again I hung above a solid block of sheer blackness. It might have been that all which provided life and color had been cut away here—leaving nothingness in its place.

Save that there was within that solid darkness something which sensed—sensed? How could that which was without life sense? Power, yes. It was a holder of Power, near filled with it. Until lately it had been emptied and it had to labor mightily to bring that to it which would once more make it ready to serve—to serve? What?

Then, as Chief might strike out with claws to defend himself before the enemy was fully aware that he knew of its presence, that which we were attempting to spy upon knew of us!

The amulet in my hand not only blazed light but heat sprung up from it. If that burning was some counter of that which we hunted to get me to drop what I had come to look upon as my personal defense it failed. I had had enough practice with the changes which might occur that I closed fingers about it and held on even when it became a live coal in the intensity of the heat it generated.

The Lady Jaelithe grimaced and then raised both hands. Her fingers moved as if she wove the empty air into living fabric. I saw Orsya's hands go out also and between them stretched two lengths of what could only be seaweed cords on which shells were strung. This burdened string she switched from side to side, lowering and elevating each hand one at a time. Kemoc had made no move of offense or defense but his face was closed, wiped clear of all expression.

There was movement though. The two Falconers, Captain Sigmun, were on their feet, starting towards the stairway. Their faces also were closed, their eyes staring straight ahead. I scrambled to my feet and lunged forward. The hand closed about the amulet thudded into

Captain Sigmun's back, bruising flesh against his mail shirt. From that touch a small wave of blue light ran, swept both up and down. He gave a cry, throwing out his arms, and then pitched forward, to lie unmoving in the sand.

With the Falconers it was otherwise. Their birds turned upon them, flying into their faces and screaming. I saw blood run from a scored cheek. As Sigmun had done, the men sank to the sand and their birds flew circles about them still screaming.

My amulet moved, striving to turn as if it would work itself between my fingers. I looked down upon it. Once more the well-remembered symbols incised there changed. I saw the face which was a skull, and this time the flesh it put on was scant cover. It remained closer to death's visage than that of the woman it had been before. There was baleful light in those skull Hole eyes, no smile curved those lips.

Lady Jaelithe jerked halfway around to face me. Her hands remained in the air but now they were still. I could guess what she wanted, but this was my battle. I knew only one way to fight it. I looked at the skull head and fought to summon Gunnora's grain sheaf and vine—that promise of fruitfulness which she was able to grant. This one was death—but Gunnora was life!

A small fear moved inside me. They said that I was of the Dark, the evil, Death's handmaid. However, if that were so I could not have stood even within the outer court of Gunnora's House. If this thing now in my hand was evil and thought to find me easy molding to its will— that was not so!

The grain, the vine! So stood the grain, tall, head heavy as it was in the field at harvest time. I had helped to cut such grain, to bind it into stocks, to feel its promising weight. There was the vine to fasten together—and the fruit that supposed was dark red, round plumpness from which, when one set tooth to break the skin, there burst that which refreshed after the heaviest labor, lightened the heart, gave hospitality to friends and weary travelers. This was life at its fullness—not death.

See it, I would, stock and vine, grain and fruit. That ugliness which hid it from me was not greater than Gunnora, to that I would in no way admit. Life—not death. I had no body, I was nowhere in the world—that inner essence which was me confronted the evil which was the skull.

It opened its fleshless jaws and it howled. I could hear that, the menace in it, just as I could feel it plucking at my will, striving to tear my determination from me. There was something beyond mere pain of body which slashed at me. Threat became deadly promise. Still I held. Grain and fruit, grain and fruit.

The skull became transparent in places so that I could see what I determined could be there. Once more it solidified and covered the emblem of life, lashed out at me so that I was near spent. But still I held.

Then both the skull and that which I had sought were gone!

My eyes were blinded; I was in the midst of a fire which roared and reared to enwrap the whole of me. There was no defense I had against this—nor was one needed. Instead all the pain which had gnawed at me was burned away. What was left was strong, able—held Power!

I blinked again. As when I had awakened that morning I found that I had moved unknowing from where I had been. For I stood at the foot of the stairway. That which I still held in my hands was no longer the stone which had come to me in Gunnora's shrine. Rather it was now a disc of gold through which moved motes of rich, dark red—the gold of the grain, the red of the fruit. And she who wore it was also changed, that I knew. But how and why—that I could not yet say. I was only sure that my feet had been set on another path, of which none knew much in those late days but which it was my duty—and my joy—to walk.

I did not move away from the foot of the stairway, but I half turned so that I could see the others. The Falconers and Sigmun had recovered to the point they were sitting up. However, the other four of our company had drawn up in a line in front of me.

I looked to the Lady Jaelithe and to Orsya and I held out my hands.

"Sisters, there is that which must be done."

Each came forward and accepted the hand I offered. I saw Lord Simon make a slight movement as if to stop his lady and Kemoc lay hand on his father's arm. Mighty were they both in different ways and well did the people of Estcarp and Escore give them all honor. Only this was an affair of women, at last I knew that.

She of the skull face might have been routed on her first attack but she had never been defeated and was not now in retreat.

The three of us began to climb those stairs. I could feel that which tried to wrap us around, to encompass us, first mind and then body. Those it had entrapped before, during all the eons of time it had been in existence, had not been as we. The man with the axe might have taught it caution if it had been able to learn. But the mind of this thing was limited, it did not live, was not able to change patterns of thought, except in the ways which were meant long ago to defend it against those who had no gifts.

Its attack upon us grew the greater the higher we climbed. If such as it could feel apprehension, I believed it must do so now. We were outside the pattern—the pattern of the Dark. Up we went, pitted step by pitted step.

We stood at the top of that stairway, high above the graveyard of ships from more than one time and world. Before us, dwarfing us, was that windowless, doorless block of a black so deep that it appeared to draw light to it and swallow it.

At that moment perhaps its uneasiness had grown to the point where it willed defense. Out of the sky came the winged monsters, shrieking aloud. They came and they sheered off, keeping a good distance as they cried out their hatred. The glow of the great jewel I wore grew ever brighter, surely a warning.

That which we had come to find was before us, but how we could enter into that dark cube was a puzzle. Shadows moved outward from it to begin a kind of in-and-out, weaving dance. Red eyes gleamed and they were gone. Talon paws appeared, to take substance, and then fade into nothingness once again.

"Aaaaiiieeee!" Out of the very air itself seemed to come that echo-arousing call.

17

He came from the east, to the land side of that cube, and he walked slowly, his shoulders a little slumped as a man draws in upon himself when facing the rigors of a winter storm. In his hands was the axe I had seen him use to such purpose, and he swung it slowly back and forth. Though there was no mist here, he could be cutting a path through a barrier which perhaps only he could see.

There was little change in him since I had seen him last through the eyes of the man he had rescued. He certainly was no older and his movements were the vigorous ones of a man of middle years. He was chanting as he came, the unknown words making a pattern which might be strange to my ears but which I recognized for what they were, sounds meant to set up a rhythm which energized his own defenses against this place of the Black.

It was Orsya who matched him—though her voice was not weighty, rather it began as the sound a river might make when it found its clear path half walled by rocks, and then it was the pelt of storm rain. However, it did not drown out his chant, rather became a part of it, filling out places, so that is was a smooth power, completely whole.

In my mind there grew a picture. This land was not barren after all, far within it there was that which would bear were it given promise of future harvest. I found myself humming the work song of planting in the fields. The Lady Jaelithe's hands were moving, translating into her form of Power all the force which lay in what our voices summoned.

It arose to a great crescendo of sound and then one of the Lady Jaelithe's hands pointed at the cube as if to guide what we had wrought.

Only that which confronted us here was awake now, and it was not angered, for I could not sense any emotion, rather it turned to its ever-abiding hunger for a weapon and it sent out a discordant wailing.

Instantly we were silent for what we had built here might well be taken over and used by that. I could feel the compulsion it would set upon us. This might be one of those from the Dark edging about a camp fire, seeking for one who sheltered by the flames to come forth to where it might take its prey.

We stood silent and quiet. Though I had never entered such a struggle as this before, I was ready to believe that the surest way to open a door to it would be to launch another attack.

What it wanted, I was sure of that, was not our bodies—rather our life energy. It was that upon which it feasted, which it had been set to draw to it. There had come fresh energy into it lately, but not enough, there was never enough. If it had so absorbed all the crews from all those ships, it had feasted well in the past, and it was slavering so to feast again. Yet it was not alive by any measurement that I knew.

A screeching broke the silence. The flying monsters coasted down about that great cube, though none alit on its crest. Nor did they fly against us. Had they come to view some deeds of their master? And who was that master?

My question might have been spoken aloud. On the side of the cube facing us there glowed a circle of light, grey as a bone which had laid in some murky place for untold years. And bone it was, for the light twisted and turned to form a sheath of bones standing upright. Those twirled and fell or whirled aloft and there was a full skeleton surmounted by a skull which I knew, no matter how much one skull might resemble another. This was she who had dared to use Gunnora's gift to print herself on my mind and memory.

Very slowly, as if it required infinite effort, she was building a form over those bones, but it was painfully thin—so that the visage and the body was like unto the woman I saw die of hunger in the rock land. I think that she struggled to reach a more tangible, better form.

She must, I though, be drawing on that which the cube had stored. It was only by fits and starts that she achieved more return for her purpose. Her head was fully woman now, and from it streamed hair which did not fall down across her wasted body but rather clung outward from her now hidden skull across the surface of the cube.

There was a suggestion of beauty in her face but that head above the skin-and-bone body was enough to arouse disgust and fear, not any awe or admiration.

Then, of a sudden, she left off her efforts. The bones and their thin grey envelope disappeared as though cut off at some source; only the head remained. That took on the likeness of youth and beauty such as perhaps few mortal women ever wear. Still this was of the Dark.

She smiled, and the tip of her tongue crossed the full redness of her lower lip. She had turned her gaze not toward us, but rather to the axe man. I think that was because he was a man and such she had found in the past to be ripe for harvesting. Only he showed a stone-silent face as one might see graven on some of the old statues in Arvon.

As we had earlier sang so now she trilled and the notes were sweet as the juice of a sun-riped berry, save more like that of a berry which had hung on the brier too long so there was a hint of decay beneath the surface.

Not only was her visage faintly foul, but that odor we

had sniffed from the beach arose about us here. The stench of a battlefield ten days old at the height of summer. I did not know whether I saw true or not but the cube seemed to shudder like a living thing so that foul stench could have been thrown off.

The axe man stood rocklike under her probing. Then the cube actually heaved. Out of it spun a long tentacle, whipping for his legs. I moved, the jewel of Gunnora's aglow in my fingers. But his axe fell clean and straight. The writhing appendage fell to the ground, to be gone an instant later.

The face on the cube lost something of its languorous smile. Now it mouthed words, and each of those appeared from those twisted lips like a fiery pellet of spit. From where they landed on the rock before the cube trails of smoke arose.

There was a rage there, so hot one could well feel it in the air. Those flying horrors screamed and arose in a body, flying back away from the cube, though I did not believe they had left the field entirely.

That rage was building and with it came something else—action I could not yet understand but which was fatal—if not against us, then others. The sun was darkening—or rather being veiled from us by clouds. I could *see* lines of energy rising from the four corners of the cube, slanting up, reaching for those clouds and the natural forces behind them. Darkness came as quickly as if night had shut down like the lid of a chest being closed upon its contents.

Yet the darkness was not complete, for around each of us as we stood there was a halo of sharp, eye-hurting light. That did not reach our bodies although that was what it was striving to do—to destroy those same bodies—and eat! The head on the cube stretched forward, the mouth open to show small, sharply pointed teeth. I thought of the were beasts and how some part of them showed their brand even while they walked in human guise and I thought that what I saw was not unlike a were. Was the woman a prisoner of the cube even as she believed herself to be in command of the power and mystery it represented?

We were not caught by that visible push of energy, but the sky opened above us. There came such a deluge of rain that we might have been standing under a fountain in full play. That in no way deadened or defeated the light; it passed directly through it to beat us. I put out my hands, allowing the amulet to hang in full sight, and I was grasped on one side by the Lady Jaelithe, on the other by Orsya. So linked we stood strong against that sky flood.

He of the axe had fallen back a few steps and set his shoulders against a rock. Unlike that brilliant, searing light which outlined the three of us, he had red flame encircling him, one in which tongues of the fire bent this way and that but were not drowned by the storm. I saw his lips move. Perhaps he was chanting again but the roar of the storm was such we could not hear him.

What I had heard of gates was that they were marked by age-eroded stones. This one, if it controlled a gate, was very different. But then perhaps a sea one would have to be.

I had not more thought of that when that glow was recalled from about us. It was no longer steady, rather it pulsated as if the energy which drove it was weakening. The rage was still there, perhaps the greater, since added to it was frustration. Long had what ruled this place been invincible, with no question or power raised against it. Even now it could not believe we were able to withstand its will.

My jewel's light spread out and out to encircle the three of us. Then it spun like a wheel, growing greater with every revolution, until it also enclosed the axe man and his fire. Having circled us at ground height it began, at a point directly before me, to rise, shaping itself into something not unlike a pointing finger. Only, before it reached the level of the face, that was gone.

The rain ceased, there were no clouds. The sun, now well to the west, lit the sky. Only pools remaining in rock hollows told us that what we had seen was the truth. On my breast the jewel called silently and the light it had loosed returned to it.

First of us to move was the axe man. He strode to a position before me just below where that face had formed. Raising his weapon he aimed a mighty blow, one which would have shattered even steel, I think. Yet his axe showed no harm, only it rebounded with such force as to near make him lose his balance. With his other hand he rubbed vigorously at the arm which hung limply at his side, though its fingers still grasped the weapon. I heard him give a grunt but we had no time to exchange any other sounds for the flying things were back, and this time they dashed themselves straight at us. Perhaps all our Power was weakened by our ordeal for nothing fended them off this time, and I flailed, vigorously with my rod, while the man before me used his axe, shearing off wings and feet so ably that I was sure he had fought just such creatures before and had learned well the trick of it. Lady Jaelithe also had a sword in her hand and Orsya whirled about her that bit of kelp rope which had strung on it the sharp-edged shells.

We killed and heard from the head of the stairway two battle cries. Then Lord Simon and Kemoc were with us and we drove off the flyers, nor had any of us taken hurt. It seemed to me that we had been very lucky, unless Power we had not consciously summoned was working for us now.

What we would do at the coming of night I did not know. I was loathe to leave this position by the cube, for I understood very well that one victory does not win a war. She whose face had appeared to us was not of the breed who surrendered. No, their commitment to what they would do is both full and final.

Lady Jaelithe was of one mind with me on that as she said:

"The dark can well be what leads powers of evil to wax, as the light for us. Therefore must we play sentry this night." Then she spoke directly to the axe man:

"Brother in Power, how is it with you?" For he was rubbing his left hand up and down his right arm, though he had used his axe valiantly moments earlier and the odorous dark blood of the flying things dripped from the blade of his weapon.

"Sister of Lightning." His voice was low and gutteral and he spoke the trade tongue with a thick accent, though we could still understand him. "What black magic holds in this place?"

She shook her head. "That I cannot tell you, knowledgeable one, for it is not of the path which I walk, coming instead from a different and darker way."

He nodded. "So does it seem, sister. This is not of man's magic, nor yet that of womankind's—though we have seen the face of her who calls up storms as a woman summons her sheep. She eats does this one and then grows strong enough to toss the land about and bring fires up out of the sea. Sometimes her catch is good and there are ships to come at her summons, and those aboard she takes for her own that she may fill herself once again—"

"She is Laqit." For that had come into my thoughts and I knew it for a true one. This was indeed the last of the guardians which Sulcar legend named, this strange horror at the end of the world.

They looked at me but it was the Lady Jaelithe who made first answer:

"So this be Laqit. Yet there was a greater who set her here." Now she looked back to the now bare wall. The sun was down, leaving only colored banners across the sky. Already shadows lengthened and it was Lord Simon who said my own thought aloud:

"Does darkness also feed this—this one?"

The axe man was ready with an answer: "Not so, except that it can watch and wait and plan. But it has not fed as it hoped and that will lead to the need of our being ever alert and on watch."

"It is not alive—you speak as if it is—" I said.

"Not with life as we know it!" the Lady Jaelithe said

quickly. "What do you do?" She ended with a swift demand as Kemoc moved forward, past us all. He had sheathed his sword, and his hands were raised shoulder high, palm out. Before any of us could move he had set those flat upon the surface of the cube, below where that head had appeared. His head fell forward a little, and I, who had moved to stop him, saw his eyes were closed and there was the strain of intense concentration mirrored on his face.

Not knowing what he would do I hesitated to draw him away. The others shared my uncertainty. We came close enough that we might catch him by the shoulders and draw him to freedom but we still hesitated.

I saw frowns, and the shadow of fear, determination such as a hunter might show though he kept to the chase in the face of great odds. Then Kemoc gasped and his hands dropped to his sides. He swayed and perhaps might have fallen had not Lord Simon and the axe man together steadied him and guided him back away from the cube.

He was drawing fast breaths, almost as if he gasped for air. Then his eyes opened.

"They are still there—those who have been recently taken. I have tried to call but they are so shaken with terror that they cannot hear. If we could break that, and get to them, that which uses them might well suffer. It is weaker—the feeding has been scant for a long time."

Perhaps it was that new strength within me which roused to that challenge. Knowledge I had always gained in snippets, under no tutelage, for there were none who would take me for teaching. Yet now I had such a store as I could not calculate. I had not been given time to count it all over, to sort this from that. Such an inner study might well take years when we had only a short and fleeting time here.

"Where is the ship—the derelict?"

They looked at me startled. It was Lord Simon who answered.

"We left it just without the south end sweep of the bay."

A long way, I thought, and then I though of birds' wings against the sky and the fact that the things which hindered a fast journey on land might not mean so much delay to one winged and aloft.

"There is that of the people gone which is still on board," I said. "Also, is it not true that that which has been worn much, treasured, kept by one person, is tuned to his or her spirit? Let us get what I left from the ship and see whether it can call to someone who is captive there." I nodded toward the cube.

"A falcon!" Orsya had caught my thought first. "Let the Falconers send one of their birds with a message to one of their own. That will not take the full night's time to reach there and back!"

Lady Jaelithe nodded vigorously. "Yes, that perhaps is the answer! It is one you and I have seen in part used." She spoke now to Lord Simon. "Remember when we called Power down upon the Kolders through that which was their symbol—how their allies fell away? Let us send for this!" She had taken two steps toward the stairway when she paused and spoke over her shoulder to the axe man:

"Does your talent do so, also, brother?"

He had put the axe down between his feet and was busy now at his belt where there were a number of small bags, all fastened by drawstrings pulled through loops there.

"This calling I have heard of but I have not seen. The gift the Above Ones have given me is different. Leave to me the guardianship of this place—it will not hold for long but there will be ones who shall stand sentinel for us."

Thus we left the stranger and went down the stairway. I thought as I went that many must have gone aloft by that way but perhaps we were the only ones ever to descend again. It was dark now. Gunnora's stone shone as well as any lamp but the spread of its diffuse light did not reach far. However, from some of the oldest ships, those which had been ground into the sand by the later comers, there was a glimmer. Almost it was the old tale of how the dread deathlights spring from the unknown graves where those dead by murder lay, to shine until they were granted justice.

By the light of that I saw the Falconers and Captain Sigmun. Each was seated and around him where he sat, well apart so that no line intersected another, there was a circle drawn in the sand. I would have thought that too soft to hold its shape for long, but these were still sharp and clear. The three men looked to Lord Simon and I thought that the stares of the Falconers were not far from cold fury. Their birds were on their wrists, heads under wings and they slept.

Captain Sigmun was the only one to speak. "How have you wrought above, warlocks? Your spells worked well here."

"Be thankful, Captain, that that was so," Kemoc snapped. "For there is that above which hungers and you would have been its meat!"

"So? Well, there comes a time for fighting and a time for standing aside. Have you gutted this eater so that we may now have our freedom?"

"Not yet. For that we must have your help—"

"Is it not true that we cannot stand against it?" One of the Falconers fairly spat that in Kemoc's direction. "Are we not bait?" He was sour of face even for one of his clan and I knew how jealous the Falconers were of what they deemed their honor. To be held a prisoner by his own side when a foray was made aloft must have diminished him and his fellow in their own sight.

"It is only your skill which can save perhaps all of us," Lord Simon cut in. I knew that he had ridden with the Falconers in the day of the Kolders and that since then he acted as a voice for them in the affairs of Estcarp, where they would not speak, since women judged there. To a Falconer a woman is a far lesser being than either bird or mount, to be kept from the consorting with man on an equal basis in all things. Perhaps it was because Lord Simon had long ago won their respect, in spite of the fact he was wedded and to a Witch, which worked on the pair of them now.

They had arisen and their falcons had awakened, one mantling as if ready for instant flight.

"What is your will, lord?" The younger of the two pointedly did not look in our direction, only to Simon. He beckoned to me. And as I skirted a broken timber half buried in the sand to come to him, the Falconers became stone faced again.

"There is this." I refused to be daunted by their attitude. "On the strange ship on which we have sailed into their waters there were many things which belonged to those vanished ones of her first crew. Most of those things we gave back to the sea lest they prove a draw of the Dark. Now we need what is left. With it we may be able to break the ensorcellment which holds this place and has squatted here to be the death of many.

"If you fly one of your falcons to the ship carrying a message, and that bird will return with what we need—it is small and easy to carry—then we shall be armed with an extra weapon which will serve us well."

Neither looked at me, but that they understood I knew. They were only following the long-held pattern of their kind. Then the elder nodded.

"Bold Wing is swift and the night is still young. He can be back by dawn if it is indeed true that what he carries is light enough."

"Good," Lord Simon said heartily. He took from a belt pouch one of those tablets made of a certain sleek stone, wafer-thin, on which orders can be written, erased, and written again. This he handed to me with one of the very narrow paint sticks.

I thought, trying to set my desire in as few words as possible. Then I wrote in the short word style of the Sulcar. It should be easy to find the boxes, take forth the jewels I had not been able to throw away. Perhaps that had been a foreseeing of a kind, and something within me had known that there would be a future use for such. I was very sure of one thing—that she who had worn those gems had treasured them, and they might well be the key to the lock of the cube.

Lord Simon handed the write-stone to the Falconer, who took great care to knot it into a cord he slipped over his bird's head. Kemoc went forward and with his sword, a very slender one which seemed to draw light into its blade, he broke through the circles set about the men so that the Falconer could step forward and loose his bird, which spiralled up into the dark and was gone.

18

It was a long night and twice during it I climbed those stairs to look upon the cube. The second time all fatigue had left me and I felt as strong in my own way as the rocks about. Though I kept a careful eye upon the place where that face had hung.

What the axe man had done amazed me the most. He was still busied about it when I had gone aloft. From those many small bags he had hanging at his belt he brought forth, a different color from each, what seemed to be colored sand near as powdery as dust. About the cube the rock of the cliff top was more level than it was elsewhere. Onto that space he dribbled sand from his clenched fist, first this color and then that. The colors I could be sure of, since the sand, even as the ship timbers below, gave forth a faint gleam. So he painted, one at each of the four sides of the cube, a weird figure which I guess was representative of some power he had learned to control. Then at the four corners, separating the territory of one of his designs from the next, he made other signs, not so detailed. Until, around the fortress of our enemy, he had set up this silent band of watchers born of colored dust.

I sat cross-legged and watched him. That this was no power of our world, I knew. Also I was as certain as if he had told me so this had in it something which was akin to Gunnora's kingdom—that it was born firstly of the earth and a deep respect for all which grew thereupon.

When he had finished the last of his sand-born symbols he came to where I sat and for the first time eyed me closely as if there was a need that he understand something which was unknown hitherto. Then he pointed to Gunnora's jewel with what he had held as an instrument for sweeping up any sand which dribbled awry because of some unevenness of the pavement.

"Corn Woman."

Whether he meant that name for me or for She for whom I now spoke I did not know. I answered with the name she was known to us:

"Gunnora."

He appeared to chew upon that as a man chews upon some viand he has never tasted before, trying so to judge whether it was to his liking or no. Then he nodded and seated himself some little distance away. Throwing back his head he began to chant again, but not raising his voice far above a whisper.

In me that thing I had felt since my stone had become a goddess's jewel stirred. I need not mind-probe to know that what he called upon was partly of Gunnora's own rule, the earth under us which could be fruitful or sere as Power employed it.

This was a place where I felt that no barrier might be eased. I had no time to go seeking inside myself for what I had been freshly gifted. I needed time, and solitude, and a way to work out my own road. None of those could I claim now. Still it seemed as I listened to a humming which was not of my own world, more barriers within me crumbled. I was not she who had started on this quest still fearful that the Dark might claim me—no, what I was—

I had listened to an old Sulcar sailor once who spoke of a queer land to the north, bordering on Alizon, of how there was a tribe of people whose leader could never be spoken to directly after he had taken on the circlet of rule, but had always with him a maiden to whom all words must be addressed, even though the ruler stood there beside her, and then he spoke to her and she to the petitioner. It had seemed to me a way of folly, but long-held custom often seems folly to those who look or hear of it unknowing of what actions it was born.

Would it—could it be that Power, also, had maidens or spokesmen who stood between the petitioner and what was wished? The Witches used Power as they would a tool—it was not personified for them. It had long been thought that it only was Dark power which drew serva-tors to it—remaining the shadow behind the High Chair in dealings.

What was I now? Surely a speaker for a Power whose strength I had no measure. I cupped my jewel and it was warm. Into me swept again that feeling of energy and purpose with which I had climbed the stair. The axe man chanted no longer, rather sat silent, his weapon resting against one knee. There was about him the air of a be-sieged who had made ready all possible defenses and now determinedly waited on attack.

"You are alone here, Brother-in-Power?" I asked. For it tugged at my mind that I wanted to know the fate of him whose knife had opened the seeing door.

His hands had been busy once again with another pouch at his belt. Now he brought forth a very small bowl to which was attached on one side a hollow, reed-like projection. He took from another pouch two pinches of what I thought might be dried herbs and those he packed tightly into the bowl. Then he had a very small splinter of wood which he rubbed across the rock so that there sprang from it a small flame and this he speedily applied to the contents of the bowl, sucking at the reed and then expelling from his mouth a puff of smoke. Even over the charnel smell of this place I caught that scent of that.

"There are others—" I do no know why he awaited so

long to answer my question. Was he still somewhat suspicious of us?

"Not all," he continued, "can be taken by that." He looked at the cube. "There must be something in them which it cannot touch. Inland"—he gestured eastward—"the living is hard but men can exist, and do."

I would have asked more, wanting to know of the three he had helped escape from the mist, but at the moment the Lady Jaelithe came up the stairs and walked slowly towards us, looking at the sand-and-dust drawings with wonder. With her forefinger she outlined in the air what was not unlike part of one of the figures and it flashed blue. I knew that she would not have duplicated the whole drawing for she might so drain away its power. The axe man was on his feet, the bowl of his smoking object in his hand, watching keenly. But after her action he made one of his own, raising his hand shoulder high, palm out, thumb moving back and forth across the fingers set together. I knew that for a salute between equals.

"You do not sleep?" she asked.

"Before Woman, that does not sleep." He nodded to the cube. "It is otherwise—planning darkness for us all—and perhaps more than us. It seeks food, for it wishes its freedom and that will come only when it is strong enough to break the bonds laid upon it."

"It is part of a gate," she said slowly. "But of a gate which was turned wholly to evil by the one who opened it."

"Laqit?" I asked.

She shook her head. "There were guardians set by some gates when the adepts who opened them went through. Then were orders given that such gates were to be held ready for retreat. Laqit was a guardian of this one, yes. But also time has passed, too many years. The adept is gone, that which was to follow a pattern which he set for his return is now acting erratically—perhaps because of the guardian who reaches for power and freedom of her own. She—it—can only be defeated when the pattern is completely broken."

"She reaches too far—and for too much." I stood up,
It was far too early to hope that the falcon had returned.
I was restless as one is before any great trial of strength.

"There are sentries," the axe man said, and inhaled
again from that which filled his pipe, puffing forth aro-
matic smoke.

"And potent ones, Brother-in-Power," agreed the Lady
Jaelithe. "Yet this is a long night and we shall all be glad
to see the end of it."

She stood for a moment at the head of the stairway as
if she expected me to join her. But I shook my head. The
axe man would commune with his messengers and guardians I knew. For me—I must somehow make peace within
myself, for a strangeness was astir until I thought sometimes that I must shout aloud or smite the bare rock with
my hands in order to contain energy building within. I
might not be a speaker for Gunnora, never had I heard
of any who were deemed such, but that I was now wholly
hers, blood and bone, mind and heart, that I would swear
to by any oath my people knew.

So I seated myself before that cube once more and I
deliberately thought of Laqit, of who or what she must
once have been—for that she was not of this world any
longer I was sure. As I thought I nursed my jewel between my hands and the colors within it swirled and spiralled. Though I had thought to put my full mind on Laqit
what I saw as a mind picture was something else. I was
aloft as one of the falcons above this rock-walled place
and the bay of dead ships, but there was one change—
that cube was but a square of broken walls and those
were crumbling into rubble, and the rubble to dust as if
time was here a weapon.

There were bodies which lay about those walls and I
knew if I wished I could see the face of each and every
one of them. I did not wish for I knew that I was foreseeing and always foreseeing meant ill to those about me.
However, I did not linger at the place where were the
controls of that fateful gate, rather I was swept, as if by
a needful fresh breeze, inland. I passed over that barren

ground where only the twisted deadly growth had been. There was springing from the earth healthy grass and shoots which would be trees. The dead was coming alive.

I saw a village of stone-walled houses and forms moved among those, but again I did not want to look upon faces. So my journey continued farther eastward from the sea. There was a river and across it the remains of a bridge and from that led still a road, one of the straight tracks which the Old Ones knew. While the land that led into was like unto an Estcarp where no war had come.

High on a rise above that road was a place which my heart leaped with joy to look upon. To it I would have gone, to give all that I had and take again that which I most needed. Only this I could not do and I knew that the time was not yet but, as always, farseeing had favored me.

Then I opened my eyes and what I saw was that skull face and it was laughing, its direful eyes upon me. I was sure Laqit had seen through my talent for that future voyaging, but she was dismissing all of it as a dream which would never bear fruit.

Whether I actually saw her or not I was never afterwards sure. But that she did know I had been questing and what I had seen I never doubted. Now her head was gone like a snap of the fingers. The axe man had vanished also. A moment later he came about from the other side of the cube. He was no longer smoking. Instead he had in his hand a length of carved wood, a little shorter than his forearm, and as he strode, along the far side of the figures he had drawn, he shook that. The wood bore two thongs on which were sprung bones or teeth and those rattled together in time to his pacing.

Back up the stairs were coming the four others of our command against the enemy. Lord Simon, hand on sword hilt, though it was not steel which would win this engagement now before us, Kemoc, Orsya, and the Lady Jaelithe. It was she who carried in one hand a small pouch which she offered me.

There was grey sky to the east; our messenger had

made better time than we had dared hope. It remained to be seen if the weapon he had brought was indeed that—arms to serve us—or whether I had guessed wrongly. But that I had not foreseen. Also I shut out of my mind what I *had* foreseen, the destruction of the cube, so that it might not bring any of us to grief as such seeings had done for me in the past.

I opened the bag and shook its contents free into my other hand. In the gathering light gems caught light from my jewel and brilliant sparks flew from them. The necklace I wrapped about my hand so that it would hold the other pieces against my flesh. I stood before the cube but first I looked to those five others who shared danger with me, for I was certain that, even if mine was the first move against the enemy, they would be a part of what would happen.

As Kemoc had done I advanced to the side of the cube, setting there my feet a little apart, bracing my full body as sturdily as I could. Then I leaned forward a little and put the hand which held the jewels against a surface which had not the feel of honest stone but rather a sleekness which made one think of slime and abominations. I loosed mind search.

I might have stepped on into the embrace of that dark evil. There seemed to be no solid barrier anymore. What lay within was a constant tumult, like the rushing of identities to and fro. I thought of Chief leaping into some narrow space containing a multitude of mice all of which strove to escape but found no way open.

To fasten on any one of those faint, stricken, dying identities (for dying they truly were) would avail me nothing. No, I might even be drawn also to the same fate. There was only one chance—

My thought had been a signal. Where my right hand might be, though I could not see it, there came a glow, first the merest trace of light, and then a small but steady flame. In my mind I fixed the picture thought of the gems—and bent all my Power (how much I might call

207

upon now I could not guess) upon the summoning of she who had hidden that treasure.

Those entrapped still spun and fled here and there, mindless in the last emotion left to them, abiding fear, on the very edge of madness, but not across terror, for this thing fed upon their thoughts and mad thoughts lost much of their nourishment.

The gems—I mind-pictured them again—not now in my hand held but rather on one whose face I had never seen and could not know. Around the throat the necklace, at the ears, on the finger the flash of jewels growing ever brighter.

She was there! I need not construct a thought shape to wear them; she who owned them claimed them. Straightway I plunged on into that one mind which the gem-brought memory had cleared.

There still abode fear, but another part of her thought caught mine.

Just as the blazing stone of Gunnora proved an anchor for me, so was what I offered fighting the wildness of her despair. Gifts—gifts of honor, or love—some of her thoughts were plain and open, others sealed to me. However, for now that which had her captive no longer played with her.

She was strong, was that stranger. The jewels were indeed a key for her, turning in a lock so that she could see a measure of freedom beyond this hell in which she ran captive and near mad.

Knowledge flashed between us. First she asked had freedom come? And I was forced to tell her in the openness of mind to mind that all freedoms save one were closed to her. I feared that I might lose her when I said that. She indeed retreated as one looking from side to side to find a way out.

Then she proved that she was indeed strong. For her thought caught mine and held tightly to it. If not freedom, save what lies beyond the last gate of all—then what was to be hers?

Again there could be no dissembling between us. I

thought of what must be done and I felt her mind grow hard and as keen as the blade of a sword as I stretched out before her the dangerous game which we must play—nor could I promise anything for its ending except hope.

There was anger in her and that was now fully awake. Women who have seen all they cherish fall in a raided village can rise to those heights of rage—it is cold, not hot, and it is deadly. I knew what the Witches had felt when they prepared to turn the mountains upon invaders. This was anger which could well be a potent weapon.

"Do what must be done!" That was an order and it was followed by a promise: "I shall do the same."

I sensed her reaching out to those silent, yet screaming, identities, searching, finding one, trapping it with fierce promise. Then I was without the cube, blinking in the rising sun.

They stood waiting even as they had been positioned when I left them. Though another had been added. Chief stalked forward, his ears flattened against his skull, his tail enlarged as was a ridge of fur along his back, and he yowled a fierce war cry. Before I could move he was past me, his nose pressed tightly to the cube. I heard him yowl again but the cry sounded muffled as if it came from far away.

When I stooped to pick him up he struck at me with unsheathed claws, leaving red rails on my forearm, and I loosed him quickly. He was back again in a moment. This time I used the mind send. Only, so different were our thought patterns, I could not match his level. There was a steady core at which he was aiming and I had hope that so he had found her and that she was doing what she could.

Thus we prepared for battle and under the sun's light we marched, mind with mind, to front that which had never been meant to be and must now vanish forever, if such as we were strong enough to stand against it—and if she within could indeed arouse one other, perhaps more to our cause.

Lord Simon drew his sword, putting it point down into

a crack in the rock, his hands clasped over its plain cross hilt. Kemoc had also bared steel, his head was well back and up, he was looking towards the sky as if there hung the weapon he favored. By his side Orsya twirled her ribbon, shuffling the shells along it, her lips also moving as if she told some tale of numbers. The Lady Jaelithe's hands were up; I saw what she held in one was that rod I had found in the wilderness but along it circles, tight rings of blue, speeding ever faster, to spring from its end into the air.

The axe man held that mighty weapon in one hand, in the other the rattle, and the sound of that broke through air which was suddenly heavy and stagnant, full of foulness.

I? I had Gunnora's jewel and what more within me I could not tell, only that it was growing. Chief drew himself away from the cube, retreating, still hissing, now and then growling. A strange band of warriors were we indeed; all we had in common was purpose.

On the side of the cube formed that circle of light, the skull, and then the fleshed head of Laqit. She was smiling and she favored each of us, even Chief, with a long, measuring stare.

"Little ones, flesh and blood, captive to the final gate—tied and held within one life—"

She mocked. We listened.

There was a fearsome crack of sound from above us and lightning struck—but not straight—deflected so it hit the cliff to the west. I saw Kemoc's face white under the mask of weatherbrowning and I knew that it was his Power which had broken that aim.

"The dead lie down with the dead and are at peace." Words came to me and I said them. My belief that I was now a Voice grew stronger. "Peace be with *you*, Laqit. He for whom you keep this gate is long since gone, nor will he return. Be at peace."

In that moment I knew that it was will in the greater part which held this danger together. The will of one long gone, the will of her who should be dead.

She spat much as Chief had done. The cube seemed to swell. Over us swept the edge of a thrust of energy which, had it hit us full on, might well have blasted us into nothingness—but Laqit could fight only in the design set for her.

There was a rumbling to the east. The ground under us quivered. A portion of the cliff was loosened and fell away.

"Now!" Lady Jaelithe's word reached me. My mind struck farther. I sought for her within the cube, touched—and then there was a barrier which crashed down between us.

We struck. Into the face I hurled all which was Gunnora's, growth, harvest, love and being, life and death, which is only another gate, peace and all the fair things of the world. Thrusts of light burst from Lady Jaelithe's fingers to strike the wall. Kemoc shouted and his voice filled the heavens as if all thunder known to our world answered him, while from the sky came lashing of lightning, not striking toward us but against the cube. The axe man twirled his weapon above his head; it might have been only fancy but I thought I saw giant figures resembling those he had drawn upon the rock come, each from a different direction, and their square-fingered hands reached for the cube.

Orsya whirled high her shell-tied strip of reed and again I felt a trembling under my feet. But what moved there were new courses of water hunting ways which led them under the cube.

So did we fight. But there were others. I knew when she who was prisoner within launched her own battle. Three of those others she had won to her, and united they stood. When the demand fell upon them for energy, they denied it. More and more and more anger beat—still they stood—though with each onslaught they weakened.

I saw Laqit's face twist, first with rage, and then in fear, and lastly in death, as such as she would know death, having surrendered her being to another way. Lightning struck full on the cube just as each of those giants from the sand paintings delivered also a blow.

There was a crack. I reached within, holding what Gunnora had to offer. She who fought did not claim it yet, but there were others and swiftly did that peace go to each whom the gate had not fully drained, last of all to her who watched me and smiled. She made a gesture and a bit of glitter came toward me. I threw back what I found now in my hands—flowers such as the Dales maidens wear at their bridals and are given them again at their last going forth. I saw her hands close about those and she was gone—there were no more half lives left

But there was still Laqit. From something she had built a body, though it was skeleton thin, and her head was pulled to one side. She came striding from the cube towards me.

"I always hated you." Her voice in my mind was a scream. "I swore that I would bring you down. There was no other reason for—" She gestured to the cube behind her where cracks ran now along the walls. "He promised me that I would in the end have you. And Yahnon was known to always keep promises. Therefore—"

She leaped for me, her bone arms out, her pointed fingers reaching for my throat. Out of nowhere there sprang a black-furred body. It struck full upon her shoulders and she did not reach me, rather fell at my feet.

"Go in peace." I knelt beside her and my jewel shed its light on her body so I saw how under its flash she appeared firm and smooth and how she became all woman and no longer a thing of horror.

She writhed over on her back and looked up at me.

"I—always—hated—you—" she said. "Leave me that—just leave me that!"

Then she was gone and there was only dust mingling with the colored sands.

There was no more thunder. Those giants who had come at the axe man's call were gone. The cube was falling in upon itself. From the center of it there upsprang a fountain and I smelled the flowers of springtime and not the stench of ancient death.

Thus was the gate closed and those it had slain were freed. Much came of our questing. The Sulcar ships sailed south and they found wonderful strange cargoes in the dead ships of the bay. Varn also ventured to that harvest and enough was recovered to rebuild much of their destroyed city.

The Lady Jaelithe and Kemoc set guards where the cube had been. They believed that it had indeed once opened the gate according to pattern but during the years had grown erratic—it needed always life force to feed it. That Yahnon Laqit had spoken of must have indeed followed a darksome path to have created such a thing.

There was one thing from the ruins which Chief brought to me. He had gone sniffing and hunting there, the first of us to dare such entrance—seeking I am sure one to whom he had been more than friend. When he returned he stopped before me and dropped what he held in his mouth—the ring from the set of jewels. That I slipped on my finger, which it fitted, and kept in memory of a very gallant one.

The axe man chose to stay in the place a handful of survivors had found after they escaped from the mist. We made a visit there but I did not see any among them like those with whom I had shared my own adventure though there was a man with down upon him who said that his mother, her brother, and his father had escaped together—so time defeated that wish of mine.

When plans were made for going north I made plain that I would stay. I had never had a place of my own—though now both the Lady Jaelithe and Orsya wished me with them. Instead I told them a little of that last foreseeing and of the search I must make for that place which is truly mine.

"Be it so," the Lady Jaelithe said then, "Voice, for we each have her own place and happy and lucky are we who find it." I saw her then look at her lord and there was that in her eyes which told me where her place lay.

This I have written at the bequest of Kemoc that it might be carried to Lormt and there set with the Chronicles which will tell the history of all happenings for those coming after. Tomorrow Chief and I take the eastern trail which lies so plain in my mind, and so shall we both come to our true inheritance.

That a place of such menace as that eater of life force from captured seafarers could exist was a strong warning that much might haunt our world of which we knew nothing. That it had been destroyed was indeed a blow against the ancient Dark and I set the account of she who now calls herself the Voice of Gunnora to the fore for the noting of those who will themselves begin new ventures. For with Kemoc and Ouen it was my thought that other such traps might well be hidden. Since after all we appear now to know very little beyond the world wherein we ourselves travel.

Still, after Kemoc and his lady had ridden on to Escore, I was not given much time to meditate upon such speculations for within a ten days after Kemoc's going there came another needing my aid. He was a Falconer and such had not ridden our way before (save for Pyra and she was no dour fighting man). Still I had met his comrades among the Borderers and had always felt well disposed towards them—though as all men they varied. Some being more approachable and others not welcoming any gesture of goodwill from those beyond their closed units.

This one wished of us histories concerning his own people. This also had been a mission of Pyra'a but I knew better than to call his attention to her. In fact she made some excuse to ride out the day after his arrival to go herb hunting. The strange situation between the Falconers and their women had long been a topic of gossip in our land and a matter of much speculation, some of it often lurid but never voiced near any of the breed.

The bird of this one bespoke Galerider and that awak-

ened the man's closer interest in me, I think. One night when he was wearied of much searching and little reward for that, he came to my quarters, which astounded me a little. The Falconers, even those best disposed to outsiders, seek no close speech beyond their own ranks. But sometimes the need to talk comes on a man and thus I recognized it was for him. I listened—still all his story I did not then hear from him because he saw it through his eyes only. The rest I gained in another way later on and it was indeed a tale which made even plainer how the travail of the mountain changes had altered our world.

Seakeep

by
P. M. Griffin

1

*T*here was no need of a fire this far into the spring, at least not by day. At night, it was another matter. Damp and sea cold still made themselves felt once the sun's warmth was gone, and so logs had been laid at ready in the hearth of the Holdlady's sleeping chamber to combat them.

Una's eyes shifted from the waiting wood to the smoke-blackened stone wall behind it. The absence of the familiar light and heat depressed rather than soothed her, and she quickly turned away again.

She sighed in her heart. She had reason in plenty for her low spirits, and she could not close out her bleak thoughts as she had the sight of the idle fireplace. The situation before her must be faced, and the decisions she made would mold not only her own fate and future but those of the people dependent upon her.

She did not think to rebel against the responsibility laid on her. She had grown accustomed to that weight, having carried it, with more than passing success, for year after year until she could scarcely recall save as a sort of distant dream the long-past days before war and the miseries that were its outriders had descended upon the Dales of High Hallack.

It had come upon them suddenly and unexpectedly, at least to outlying, virtually isolated Dales like those of this region, although the lords of the major holds to the south had indeed anticipated and tried to prepare against it. Even Harvard, that wily soldier who was her father, had not been concerned in that final year of peace about more than the happy fact that the lady who was his wife was at last with child. He had concealed his disappointment well when the infant proved to be female, rejoicing instead that his lady, whom he loved greatly, had survived the difficult birth. A scant two months after the child's formal owning and naming, Alizon had unleashed its hounds and strange weapons against the Dales.

Then had begun years of horror and loss. For the first time in their long history, the fiercely independent lords of High Hallack had united in common cause, for they had very quickly learned that if they did not, the individual Dales would be swept away one at a time until all had been devoured.

Even after their alliance, for a long time after it, the issue had remained at question, and hope was more a low, stubborn light that somehow refused to die than any sending of reason. Then the tide finally turned. The Dalesmen, in company with their mysterious, terrible allies, the Were Riders from out of the Waste, stopped and finally threw back the invaders, utterly defeating them and ruthlessly hunting down the last remnants of their once-invincible forces.

That work done, the army of High Hallack had disbanded, and its various units returned home. All too many had found little or nothing to greet them, for Alizon's forces had ravaged far and for a long time before they had been broken, and they had spared nothing, human or human structure, falling under their ruthless power. For many, the work of rebuilding, lives and Dales alike, proved as hard a war as that from which they had just been released, a war demanding an equal measure of courage and strength.

Seakeepdale and its neighbors had been spared all that. Remote and isolated, no armies had ranged and ravened in this region, and want had not battened upon the populace. The loss of luxury goods did not greatly affect holdings too poor to afford much in that line in the best of times. As for necessities, all the Dales in this locality were basically self-sufficient and traded for what they required or wanted chiefly among themselves, rarely venturing even as far as Linna either to acquire or dispose of goods. They had lost, aye, as had all High Hallack, but they had managed.

Una's chin lifted. Seakeep had managed better than any. With only a handful of old or incapacitated men to lend their limited strength and valuable experience to aid her women and young boys, her mother, frail and gentle as she was, had been able to keep her hold running and productive. Under her leadership, her people had maintained the various structures, had set and harvested their crops, seen to the more demanding working of the sea and the never-ending care of equipment and animals. They had succeeded so well that Seakeepdale had not only met its own needs but had been able to send some small relief to the Dales' hard-pressed army and set stores aside for emergency use besides.

Her head lowered, pride in her mother's accomplishment fading as other memories rose to replace those which had fired it. When the tragically few survivors had returned home, Lord Harvard had been with them, but he had ridden a litter rather than a horse. After all the fighting, all the plotting and maneuvering—the Dales' leaders had come to appreciate both his courage and his counsel, although he had not been a member of their inner circle—he had been felled, a spear through his back, in very nearly the final engagement of the long war.

For months, his lady and his people had tended him, despairing of his life. His will and heart were both strong, and he had lived, but never again would he use either his legs or his right arm.

Harvard had not broken in mind or spirit as many another would have done but had bent himself to the task of running and restoring his much reduced Dale. His own broken body would no longer serve his needs, and with the humility of a great heart, of one who could place responsibility above pride, he continued to rely upon his lady's proven abilities and ever increasingly upon the young, eager daughter who became the active agent of both.

The Holdlord trained Una well in duties not normally falling to a woman. No son would now be born to him, and it was both his wish and his lady's that the rule of the Dale not pass completely from the family which had held it since the first settling of High Hallack.

Una of Seakeep had proven an apt pupil, showing all the Holdlady's abilities but coupled with her sire's energy and a love of the land and its ways that was all her own.

Harvard, however, grew ever more heavy of heart as the years progressed. He could not blind himself to the potential for conflict and wasteful quarrelling should his only child and heir be left unwed when he at last went forth from this life and world. His lady's death after a brief illness at last painfully emphasized his own mortality, and he moved to secure Una's future and Seakeep's by giving her to the Lord Ferrick, an old and trusted comrade of his, a strong fighter whose mind was as sharp as his sword, a man well fitted to rule the holding that would one day come to him by reason of his union with its heir.

Arranged matches were the norm among the ruling families in the Dales, and Una of Seakeep had accepted her father's decision willingly, acknowledging its necessity and the wisdom of his choice. The marriage had been performed, and she, along with the rest of her people, had breathed a sigh of relief that one more threat had been brought to an end.

Only a few short weeks later, fate had struck High Hallack yet another vicious blow. Man's greed was not its instrument this time, but a foe even crueller, a sickness which had swept over all the continent with breathless speed and varying effect. To some Dales and some people, it brought but a few days of more or less mild illness. To others, it was devastating.

Nearly all this region's Dales had been badly hit, Seakeepdale among the hardest. The old, the very little ones, and those already weakened were all stricken hard, as was usually the case with any such epidemic, but this time the young and basically hale were cut down as well. They burned with fever, coughed, and in all too many cases developed a deadly lung fever from which very few recovered. With almost malignant precision, the disease had chosen the young men who had only then begun replacing the rents left in the population mix by the war and made them the targets for its most virulent attacks. Only a relative handful remained after the visitation had passed.

Una herself had gone to the brink of death. She had fought her way back, but when she awakened and some strength returned to her, she discovered she was bereft of both sire and lord.

Her grief for Harvard was naturally deep and sharp, but so, too, was the sense of loss which she felt for Ferrick. Una mourned him in heart, for herself and for Seakeep. He had been more of an age to have sired than to bed her and had been no more sensitive to a young girl's needs than any other man of his type, but he had used her gently according to his lights and even tenderly. As her father's close, though younger, friend, he had known her since her birth and had borne real feeling for her. That was more than many a Holddaughter could hope to find in the husband to whose chamber she was brought.

The woman's eyes flashed green fire. A good man had

died. That was a heavy enough evil. It was doubly wrong that his loss should result in further danger falling upon those he had striven to defend.

Una of Seakeep did not rail against the fact that she had been forced to officially assume the reins of control over the Dale in which she had been bred. She was capable of that and, in truth, enjoyed exercising the abilities she had more than proven she possessed. For several years, all went well. She ruled her Dale and worked with her people, and her efforts, their efforts, were rewarded so that Seakeep prospered and hope and the joy of life were once more fully alive in them all. Now, however, her widowhood was placing all she loved, all who looked to her and owned her authority, in jeopardy. To avert it, she would have to act decisively, knowing that she might well fail in her aim and that, should she succeed or only partly succeed, the potion she brought in for a cure might too readily prove a worse curse than the ailment it was meant to counter.

There was no help for it. She squared her shoulders and left her sleeping quarters for the slightly larger chamber adjoining it where she was wont to conduct the Dale's business and to meet with those who assisted her in running it.

A small boy was sitting at the broad writing table, frowning over the heavy book she had set him to studying to occupy his time and mind while waiting on her will. A fleeting smile touched her lips. Like her parents before her, Una believed that a holding was the stronger for having the bulk of its populace lettered, and this lad, despite his preference for more active pursuits, had proven quick and eager to learn.

"Bring Rufon to me now, Tomer."

"Aye, my Lady.—He will be right glad to hear it, too. He is full to the neck of those Ravenfield . . . people."

The woman nodded. It was easy to share her page's sympathy with the warrior and also his dislike for their arrogant neighbors. And his underlying fear. That lay as a pall over all Seakeep.

She gave no other indication of her feelings. "Run for him, then," she said mildly and composed herself for the meeting as soon as Tomer quit her, on the run as she had suggested.

It was not long in the coming. Rufon had been waiting impatiently for his liege's summons and was quick to respond to her call. He was a rather short, stocky man with rugged, not unpleasant features marred by a small, old scar on the chin. Only emptiness remained where the right arm should be.

The Dalesman drew himself up before her but waited for her to speak, as was seemly.

She gave him greeting, then turned at once to the business troubling them all.

"Our guests are still abed?" she asked him.

"Aye, but they will be up plaguing us for an answer soon enough. —You will have to give them one, my Lady," he added with a rough gentleness. He feared greatly that there was little real choice before the woman, that she would have to capitulate, to the ruin of them all.

She read that belief, and anger rippled behind the veil of her composure.

"I shall not deliver Seakeepdale to Ogin of Ravenfield. By the Amber Lady, do not even imagine that I could so betray my trust as to give that tyrant power over us."

"You will have to choose another lord, then, my lady, and quickly, or he will take that power unto himself despite your will."

"Choose whom?" she asked wearily. "Ravenfielddale is the strongest here. Ogin's father kept his forces well-nigh intact by the simple expedient of staying home when his neighbors marched to war. He could spare more men to the fever than the rest of us, and Ravenfield was granted a light visitation on top of that. He has a full garrison, while the other Dales have scarcely enough fighting men to maintain ourselves and prevent brigands from gaining a foothold in the region. Given that situation, which of our neighbors would risk, could risk, setting himself against Ravenfield by joining with me either himself or through marriage with a son? It is pretty well guessed that Ogin might be only too willing to find an excuse for adding a better Dale than ours to his territory.''

Her eyes flickered to the walls as if to peer through them to the world beyond.

''Seakeep is large in terms of space, but no man will grow rich on its produce. It would take a rank fool to put a Dale already in hand at hazard for it, at least until conditions become more nearly normal once more.''

There was always the holdlady herself, the man thought. Una of Seakeep was fairer than any other woman he had yet seen, maid or matron, surpassing even her own mother in beauty, and that last was no small accomplishment.

She was tall for a woman of her race, slender of build and so delicately formed as to give the appearance of fragility. Her hands were small as a child's; one of them laid at its full length would not have spanned the breadth of his palm.

Her features, in keeping with her slight bone structure, were very finely chiseled, exquisite rather than mirroring the slightly heavier ideal worshiped by the most of their kind.

Her hair was a rich dark chestnut. Even bound as it was in that single thick braid, it reached to the small of her back.

The eyes were the crown of her many beauties. They were very large and widely set and were fringed all around by long, dark lashes. Their color was a most astonishing jade green, doubly striking against a pale, subtly life-warm complexion.

His eyes wavered. Lady Una was right, of course. Lords wed for land and the power the ownership of land endowed, or else for a weighty dowry when no holding was to be had. Beauty in a wife sweetened the pot, but it counted for nothing when the marriage bargain was made, no more than did the worth of the woman herself. A pity, too, in this case, for there were few finer than

Una of Seakeep, or more able either, though it went somewhat against his sense of propriety to admit that last.

"There are still many lords in the Dales left without lands or place," he observed, "And many more men, proven fighters and leaders, who would not scorn a holding such as ours."

She shook her head emphatically.

"A stranger? I might only bring a second Ogin down on us. Besides, I need an army, not a single man, to secure my choice."

"What can you do, then, my Lady? You will have to give them some answer soon. . . ."

Una smiled.

"No, old friend. That is your part. Ogin sent emissaries to do his wooing for him. Seakeep's emissary, not its lady, shall make them reply."

Her eyes met and held his. She was grave now, but there was no hesitation on her, and it was apparent to him that she had some possible solution in mind, one she was prepared to act upon.

A quietness of bearing and manner had ever marked her, and now that her decision was made, that aura of stillness seemed to radiate from her, to rest on her like a mantle. Even her voice was soft when she spoke, gentle despite its firmness.

"You will inform Ogin's envoys that I am most displeased by their mission since I only last Yuletide specifically told him that my duties to my Dale and to my dead lord will require my full attention for a long time to come. Furthermore, one who seeks Seakeep's lady would do well to come to her himself."

That last statement gave Rufon a start, but a grin of appreciation spread across his broad face almost in the same moment. That peevishness was precisely what a man like Ogin of Ravenfield would expect of a woman. It would leave him satisfied despite Una's curt dismissal of his velvet-sheathed demand and would stand as partial explanation for a fairly lengthy delay in her willingness to entertain a renewed suit from him, a suit for whose final outcome he would feel absolutely no concern.

"You have bought us more time at any rate, my Lady."

"Time enough to secure ourselves if fortune smiles on my plans.—I must make haste now. I have already given orders to have the *Cormorant* put under sail, and I would be gone before our unwelcome guests awake."

The man frowned.

"Gone? Where . . ."

"Ostensibly to Linna to pay my respects to my lord's sister, although I would have our people keep the fact of my departure quiet for as long as possible. If I am overlong in returning, let it be made known that I chose to remain a little while with my kinswoman in the peace of the Abbey. That will be accepted if you also mention that I am trying to see if there might not be a market for some of our horses again."

He nodded. No one who knew her could imagine this one slinking away to cloistered halls in a foredoomed attempt to hide from a threat which must inevitably confront her, but Seakeepdale's superb horses had been prized throughout the region prior to Alizon's invasion. The herd, that nucleus of it which had not been sent off with the Dale's warriors, had been kept small during the years since out of necessity, but it was only reasonable that the Lady Una would now try to increase her stock and reopen trade for them.

Reasonable or nay, that was patently not her reason for going forth now.

"Where will you be in reality?" he asked.

"I shall see the Abbess Adicia in truth. There is love between us, and I do owe her the courtesy of a visit. After that"—she gave a shrug, as if submitting herself to fate—"Linna town itself and then home overland, with the help of the Horned Lord, or else south until I find what I seek." Una did not think it strange or amiss to call upon a being most commonly besought by soldiers and hunters since that was the work before her.

"What do you seek?" he asked, curiously and with a little concern.

"Mercenaries, a goodly company of them. Men enough to stand our cause until we can build up our own strength once more by one means or another."

"Lady! By all . . .—Do you recognize the risk you take? And how do you propose to pay such a host, even assuming you could find men willing to hire themselves to your banner?"

The woman sighed.

"There is peril, aye, but I know what I want. A company whose deportment shows that their pride and discipline are yet intact are likely to remain true to their oath. As for payment, that may not be as difficult to arrange as would have been the case a few years past. Life is still harsh and very uncertain, but open, large-scale warring is no longer the rule throughout High Hallack. With both lodgings and sea passage dear, escort or guard duty should not be too unwelcome an alternative for a party at loose ends while its leaders consider where next to locate.

"We must prepare to receive blank shields whether I do, in fact, succeed in binding any to me or nay. Let the lower chambers of the tower be made ready for their use, all save the great hall and the servants' places and their work rooms. That way, our people will not have to endure strangers being quartered upon them. We have too many manless families for that now, and there is room in plenty here."

She sighed to herself. The Amber Lady knew, they had room to spare. Seakeep's household had ever been small for the size of the tower, and it was smaller still since war and sickness had laid their lash on the Dales.

"As you will, my Lady," he responded, masking his surprise with some difficulty.

Una of Seakeep smiled. She was accommodating more than their own folk with those arrangements. She could have been far more specific with respect to the type of warriors she hoped to engage, but she did not choose to speak of that lest he believe her reason had been reft from her. She herself half believed that part of her plan to be sheer madness when she dwelled on it, but she was determined to make the effort. Her chances of securing Seakeep's safety would be fully trebled if she did manage to succeed.

Unlikely as that hope might be, there was still the possibility that it might come to pass—slight, perhaps, but real for all that. The Una who was as close to her heart as a sister of her blood might have been and who was her sole confidante in this matter agreed with her that the attempt must be made, as she agreed that the importation of mercenaries was Seakeep's only real chance of surviving as an independent entity during the period ahead, little though either of them liked the idea of bringing strangers onto the Dale's ancient soil.

Her head raised. The time for her to begin was come.

"Take you charge now, old friend. I shall return as soon as I can, hopefully with swords sharp enough to turn Ogin's greed."

2

All Falconers were trained from boyhood to handle themselves in and around water, and many of them loved the wild, alien element so well that they would not voluntarily seek a nonmarine commission. The mountains, the mystery and beauty of the highlands, held Tarlach too powerfully for even the awesome lure of the ocean to claim him that completely, but he had served aboard both war and merchant craft in the past and did not mislike the thought of doing so again should that work present itself.

He was undecided at this moment as to what course he and his comrades should follow, but he would have to choose, or allow fate to choose for him, fairly soon if they were not to see the merchants and innkeepers of this place devour the gains their swords had hard won for them.

Fortune had served them ill by freeing their swords this far from the centers of real trade and activity in High Hallack. Linna was not a bad town in itself, just too small and isolated to provide much opportunity for a company of this size.

Before the invasion by Alizon, Linna had been an insignificant village serving the few needs of the poorly endowed, rugged Dales of the surrounding region, but it had escaped the hostilities ravaging the greater part of High Hallack. It had possessed one of the few harbors remaining in the hands of the hard-pressed Dalesmen as well, a reasonably good one at that, and to it had come Sulcar ships, some blockading the coast to turn back Alizon's efforts to supply and reinforce its troops, some bearing much-needed supplies or equally welcome contingents of blank shields, often men of his race, eager to hire out their swords and battle skills.

Some of that bounty had survived the war's end. The harbor was deep and it was sheltered even when the Ice Dragon bit sharpest and roared the loudest, and sea captains found they could access a current not far off the coast which nearly doubled the power of the average wind to hurry them to the richer ports to the south. They continued to use the place, and so, too, had the merchants and traders drawn by the presence of their vessels. Indeed, many of them had established permanent dwellings and workplaces here, settling chiefly in the previously open area abutting the walls of the small Abbey where a handful of devout Dames had gathered to serve the Flame. Along with these additions to the community, a couple of new inns had joined the much enlarged original one close to the waterfront, all of which were still reasonably busy during the more temperate seasons of the year.

Apart from these changes, however, Linna had more or less resumed its old village identity and had all but reverted to the peaceful market town it had been probably since the Dales were first settled.

He sighed, and his fingers caressed Storm Challenger. The falcon did not move from his place on Tarlach's arm but raised his head to fix piercing, steady eyes on the human he had chosen as his comrade and mind-brother. He sensed the trouble on the man but opened no communication, knowing that was not wanted now.

Tarlach sighed again. It was right that peace should return to High Hallack, even as it was slowly returning to Estcarp across the sea. People everywhere had a surfeit of violence and wanted only to build and live their lives, each in his own way. Most would succeed in the end, and slowly the scars of pain, ruin, and death would be eased.

Not for the Falconers. When those thrice-accursed Witches had moved the mountains, destroying the Eyrie along with the invading army sweeping into Estcarp, they had sealed the fate of his race, or so he feared and believed.

His kind followed a lifeway most other peoples found harsh and cold in the extreme. In the far past, they had sailed north in Sulcar ships, fleeing the curse that still loomed over them. With them had come their women and young, but they had traveled together in the sense that others moved with their herds and in no manner as kin with kin. Estcarp, the realm of the Witches, was closed to them because of this treatment of their females, but they had found refuge and a home in the mountains on its border. There they had raised the Eyrie as the seat of their warriors, who earned their way as mercenaries, and had established the ever-perilous women in several villages where they remained apart, unvisited save at certain set periods by men who came on command to copulate with them to ensure the continuation of their race. In time, segregation born of need had been reinforced by hatred and contempt for all human and near-human females, and Falconers sought no alliances, permanent or temporary, with any woman apart from those brief encounters required for breeding the next generation of fighters.

That had worked well enough with villages and Eyrie set well apart from neighboring peoples, and even then some women had departed, slipping away from the mountains to seek richer lives elsewhere. How long could they be expected to remain in their present settlements within Estcarp? Another generation? Two? Hardly longer than that, he imagined. Falconer men would not stay bound to such a life with other examples and opportunities all around them, and, however little he might think of them, he did not believe their temporary mates would do so forever, either.

Once more, he touched the great war bird. Would the day finally come when no member of his species, not a single human being, would be able to share thought with these winged ones? If so, then their ancient foe had her vengeance on them for a fact even if she was never to regain the freedom to work it herself.

He gripped himself, trying to shake his spirit loose from the pall which had settled on him. The Horned Lord knew, he was tired! Perhaps all this only stemmed from that. . . .

Storm Challenger's soft greeting returned him to his surroundings. He looked up to see another man approaching, this one also wearing the high-winged helm and stark armor of his race. A black, white-breasted falcon rode his wrist with the ease of long custom. Brennan, his chiefmost lieutenant.

"What news, Comrade?" he asked, making himself speak lightly so as not to burden the other with his gloom.

"None. I came abroad early to enjoy the morning and saw you." He hesitated. "Something rides you, Tarlach?"

The mercenary captain shook his head.

"I was merely preoccupied."

"Deeply preoccupied for you not to have been aware

of our coming.—This has been so more than once of late."

Tarlach made him no immediate answer but rather fixed his attention on the activity already bringing the harbor alive. Three vessels were in port. Two Sulcar craft were unloading what looked to be kegs of wine or ale. The third, a vaguely disreputable-looking merchantman of no readily apparent origin, seemed to be making early preparations for departure.

"None of them is nearly large enough to serve our needs," he observed wearily.

"For the journey back to Estcarp or just southward?"

"I have not decided, but either way, we should do better than in our present situation. We have been here four weeks now without receiving an offer, nor are we likely to receive one the way I read it. Perhaps there are no suitable commissions left to be had anywhere in High Hallack."

Brennan eyed his commander.

"You sound less than desperate about that possibility. You want us to return to Estcarp?"

Tarlach shrugged.

"We could all use some time in one of the camps. We have been fighting now almost without break since we came to High Hallack." He straightened. "Whether we go or stay, it will be as a unit. We went forth as a company, and it behooves us to return so to the commandant."

The lieutenant started to agree, but before he could speak, both war birds hissed angrily and took to the air. Even as they did so, sudden shouts and clamor announced battle near to hand.

Instinctively, the two Falconers raced toward the source of the disturbance, a narrow alley separating two warehouses.

A band of seven men, a press gang to judge by their apparent unwillingness to damage their victim despite his resistance, had forced a lone traveler into the close space and were attempting to overpower him before anyone could become aware of their attack and thwart it.

Their target seemed to be a youth or a very young man. His hooded journey cloak was of a style which proclaimed that he had come from this general region. Much more they could not see, for he was standing at an angle to them, and the garment concealed his features and the greater part of his body. Only the sword glinting in his hand was clear to view.

One of the ruffians sprang in behind the lad in the hope of felling him with a blow from the stout rod he carried, but, to the surprise of all, the boy whirled even as he moved. The bright blade stuck home before the larger man could bring his weapon to bear.

The traveler's face was now partly visible to the newcomers. It was starkly white and stricken in a manner which suggested that he had not slain before, but horror of the killing had not fully crystallized in the enormous jade eyes before Tarlach drew sword and forced his way through the press gang, casting two of them roughly to the ground as he went.

He put himself between the attackers and their prey.

"Let him be."

"Try nothing foolish, carrion dogs," Brennan advised coldly. The second Falconer had kept his place at the alley's mouth but had unsheathed his own weapon in support of his commander's stand.

The gang hesitated only a moment before fleeing, taking advantage of the narrow path the lieutenant had purposely left free for their going. Their supposedly easily taken victim had proven something different in the testing, and the sudden appearance of the mercenaries altered matters still further. They were no match for those deadly, battled-tempered blades or for the falcons wheeling just over their heads. It was well known that those birds were trained to tear a man's face, his eyes, in battle.

Tarlach scarcely waited for them to disappear from sight before seizing the arm of the one he still took to be a boy.

"You are not injured?"

Una of Seakeep shook her head, too numbed by the shock of what had happened, what she had just done, to give him a verbal reply.

"Come quickly, then. If they return in force, we could be trapped here."

She could not repress a shudder as she was hurried past the body of the man she had slain but willed herself to give no other sign of discomfort or to speak at all even to voice her gratitude. Her companions were right. They had good reason to fear entrapment in here. Besides, they were likely to abandon her very quickly once they discovered that she was a woman. That, she must try to prevent, and she needed to be certain that her wits were fully about her again when she fronted them.

The Falconer captain slowed his pace once they had left the docks behind.

"We should be safe enough here."

Una drew away from him. He would not welcome physical contact with her once she revealed herself, as she must now do.

"Aye. Vagabonds of that ilk will not be anxious to face your like in any open place."

The men stiffened. This was not the voice of a boy, or of any male.

The woman dropped her cowl.

"Thanks given, Bird Warriors, and to your winged comrades."

"The service was slight," Tarlach responded harshly as he turned to go.

"It was of great importance to me."

He was hard-pressed to repress a smile.

"I suppose it was," he conceded.

"Hold, Captain!" she said quickly as the pair started to leave her again.

She did not know his rank, of course. She could not tell one man from the other behind those masking helmets, and there were few if any not of their race who could decipher the subtle markings on their clothing and armor by which they noted place and identity amongst themselves, but she had long ago learned that, when dealing with a strange warrior of unknown authority, it did not hurt to accord him a good rank. A certain amount of vanity was native to all her species.

There was no doubting, at least, that the man who had saved her was the senior of the two. Among Falconers, only the ranking officer of a party or the soldier of longest service actually dealt with those of other peoples among whom they moved, even in the tight quarters aboard a ship or with respect to those hiring their swords.

Although she trembled in her heart lest she lose this opportunity fate had given her, Una made herself speak quietly and steadily.

"You are blank shields?"

The man nodded. His grey eyes bore into her. Both her bearing and her manner of speech declared that the Daleswoman was wellborn, and her clothing was of good, though not extravagant, quality with little sign of wear. It was probable that she could afford to hire an escort for herself if she required one.

That she was such a fool as to imagine Falconers would swear allegiance to her was another matter.

"We are part of a larger force bound not to divide our number."

"I have need of such. That is what brought me to Linna." She drew a deep breath. "I had heard much of your kind's battle skill and courage and your quickness of thought from Lord Harvard, and I had hoped beyond hope to bind Falconers to Seakeepdale. What I have seen of you just now intensifies that wish."

Both mercenaries stirred.

"Lord Harvard?"

Relief swept Una. That had been her high die. They did know her late sire's name. Given that recognition, she felt they would at least grant her a hearing. After that, well, she could do no more than tell her story well and hope.

"I am Una of Seakeepdale, his daughter and widow of the Lord Ferrick, his comrade and chief captain during the war.—My need is real, Bird Warriors. I know you dislike having any dealing with a woman, but I ask you not to dismiss me before you listen to my tale. It will not take a great share of your time."

The Falconer commander's lips tightened. He turned abruptly on his heel.

"Come with us."

The captain did not break stride until he had reached the largest of Linna's three inns. Scarcely pausing even then, he threw open the heavy door and swept inside. Una followed after him and then Brennan, who quietly secured the way behind them.

The helmet-masked figures filling the big room within looked up at their coming. A deadly silence fell as they caught sight of the Daleswoman, and on every side she was conscious of their hostile, cold eyes burning into her, as if she were something vile which had just crept out of a Shadow-marred pit. Only the falcons seemed friendly, or comparatively friendly. At least, there was curiosity in the contacts she received from them and not the senseless resentment their masters evinced. She shivered in her soul and was glad that she had no Power to read that or to delve any part of these grim, hating minds.

Tarlach did not offer her a chair or bench on which to seat herself, but he did remain standing beside her.

"This is Lord Harvard's daughter, Una of Seakeep. She claims she has come to Linna seeking blank shields."

His disapproval was so strong that it was almost palpable. That was a bad beginning, she thought. What she faced was an interrogation, and she wondered if anything she could say would convince these men, or win their aid even if they did come to believe the truth of her words and the reality of her need.

The Falconer leader's eyes were hard as the steel of a prize sword.

"You are alone? That is why you are in boy's garb?"

"I am alone, aye. As for my dress, it offers me a freedom of movement which I should not otherwise enjoy. I was born in Seakeepdale, and I am well known in Linna town. If I had come in my own guise, I would have heralded my intention to all the country."

"Why do you feel it necessary to augment Seakeep's garrison now that Alizon's troops are no more? There is no warring in this region."

"Seakeep does not have a garrison," she told him flatly. "The fever hit us hard and took not only my sire and lord but most of our men besides. Of those who remain, the better part are youths scarcely of an age to be considered warriors, none of them with battle experience save against unorganized brigands. Only a relative handful of sound men are left to us, and it would be rank stupidity, madness, to imagine that the courage of women and children will stand against trained war skill and physical strength in any real test."

The Falconer was quiet for a moment.

"What is the nature of the danger threatening you?" he asked somewhat less harshly.

"It is only the possibility of danger as yet," she responded, "but it would take a fool to ignore it."

"There are more fools than you would imagine in this world," Rorick, next in command after Brennan, muttered. Too often, blank shields were hired weeks or even months after they would have been most effective. Sometimes, their services were not sought until hope was entirely dead.

Tarlach's glare silenced him. The captain's attention returned to Una.

"Who is putting the fear on you?"

"Ogin, Lord of Ravenfield, the Dale adjoining ours. He desires control of Seakeep. Thus far, he has contented himself with trying to win it through marriage with me, but when he finally realizes his suit is hopeless, we fear he may well try sterner means. His garrison, or his father's then, remained out of the fighting and was, thus, almost completely undiminished, and his Dale was

237

touched but lightly by the fever, the only one in our region so preserved."

"Why should he not move at once, then, without wasting time with wooing?"

The woman colored slightly, but her chin raised.

"I am not considered ill favored, Falconer. Ogin will wait, a bit longer at the least, if for no other reason than it would suit his vanity to have me capitulate willingly. He is an attractive man, certainly, and a strong one. By his light, he has good cause for hope, and it would pay him to gain his will thus. Even weakened as they are, he can do without alarming the neighboring Dales to the point that they might unite against him. Alizon taught us the worth of that tactic, and he is not one to forget such a lesson."

"Yet you say his efforts to gain you are in vain?" Tarlach questioned.

She nodded.

"That one is a tyrant and would be insuperable if he held any power in Seakeep. I could not deliver my people over to the like of him if there were nothing else against him."

"There is more, however?"

"Suspicion only, but it is sufficient to firm us in our resolve to fight long and hard before accepting defeat at his hands."

She pursed her lips.

"All this northern coast is rugged with few harbors and many deadly rocks, and storms rise with little or no warning. Vessels, great and small alike, have always run the risk of disaster when approaching it, and wrecks have never been uncommon for the volume of shipping involved, which, in truth, is not large even now. That holds stronger still with respect to our waters."

Her eyes suddenly hardened in a manner that gave him a start. There was both anger and the determination for battle without quarter in them such as he had only seen before in war leaders faced with a righteous cause and a difficult if not well nigh impossible fight in order to sustain it.

Una was not aware of the reaction she had provoked in the mercenary or of the change in her own bearing which had sparked it.

"Of late, there seem to be a great number of craft being lost in our region, literally lost, without a trace and without survivors to carry their tale. In nearly every case, the doomed vessels were merchantmen with full holds."

"Sea wolves?" he asked, his voice turning deadly cold.

"Worse."

"A black wrecker!"

The grey-eyed man all but spat out the words. One having served at sea, however briefly, could have no other feeling than the most unremitting hatred for renegades who lured ships to their destruction, usually slaying any the water would have spared, in order to strip them of their cargoes and other valuables. Such were less even than pirates, vermin fitted only for extermination. . . .

"We are in no way certain of it," Una cautioned. "There is little basis for our belief at all beyond the fact that the disappearances appear to have begun shortly after Ogin came into his inheritance, and there have been too few of them to give us a firm pattern.

"We add to that timing his strong interest in Seakeep. Mine is not a Dale which will ever bring great wealth, nor would it be of any greater help than Ravenfield itself in the fulfilling of an ambitious man's plans, but it is possessed of a long, rough coast, lonely and very well suited to dark work."

"It is best that this Lord Ogin be kept from your holding," the mercenary agreed. "Ravenfield does not border on the sea itself?"

"It does, but on a much narrower front. It is a wild coast even for the region, though, and it affords one good place where a small wrecker craft could be concealed. That cove would serve very well for his present low level of activity, but if Ogin hopes to make wrecking his road to power, he will need a better base."

"Which Seakeep can provide?"

She nodded.

"We have a harbor, small but very deep and with good shelter under all but the most extreme conditions."

"Such a one is an enemy to all. You could claim aid from your neighbors by right."

"They do not suspect him of this, though they are well-enough aware of the loss of ships in the area. As I said, it has always had a bad reputation. We of Seakeep are closest to Ravenfield and are the most involved with the sea, and so we have deduced more."

"You might have done well to share those deductions," he told her sarcastically.

"Suspicions, and coming from a woman?" she replied bitterly, but then quelled her annoyance. "Besides, could we in honor lay that shadow on a man without a shred of real or solid circumstantial evidence to support it, knowing he would be likely to carry the blight of it for years or for life?

"As for help, the other lords know him to be a tyrant with power to back his will and prefer to let him be, at least until they have recovered something of their former strength."

The man was silent for several minutes, a seeming eternity to the Daleswoman.

"What exactly do you want of your blank shields?" he asked slowly at the end of that time.

"Chiefly to act as a deterrent against aggression." She frowned, marshalling her thoughts to present them as logically and briefly as possible. "With each passing month, our own ability to resist increases as our youths work to gain skill and our older boys approach or attain manhood. You may well believe that they have been undergoing warrior training since childhood."

She eyed him.

"The same is true of our girls. I know you will not approve of that, but we had to use what was available to us during the war or leave ourselves completely naked for the future. This was but another uncommon duty they were forced to assume with our men gone, and they have done passing well, at least those young enough at the outset not to have been crippled by the belief that they are inherently not capable of such work.'' Her lips tightened momentarily. ''Fortunately, our women as a whole took better from the start to the heading and farming and to the fishing, or we should all have had a harder and hungrier time than we did.''

''Despite all, you do not want war?'' Tarlach questioned sharply. It was bad enough dealing with a woman like this. The idea of having to rub shoulders with a female garrison was less appealing still.

''We do not. Only to guard ourselves if needs be.''

Her face hardened.

''The Dales of our region have ever fought sea wolves from outside and brigands seeking to establish themselves on our coasts and in our mountains to the peril of all. If such evidence should come to light, then we would fight. Thus has it always been and must be, or we should soon be swallowed up by renegades unfit to bear the name of human.''

''Why Falconers?'' he asked bluntly. ''It is clear that you do not actually expect to discover such evidence, and even if you did, aye, we are fighters as you claim, but so, too, is every blank shield who came through the war and the times that have followed it. Few survived who were not.''

The Holdlady sighed. She had hoped this question would not be pressed. Her reply was not likely to please him, but she knew she had still more to fear from falsehood or half-truth.

She met his gaze steadily.

''I am not war trained, Bird Warrior, or accustomed to traveling with warlike men. Every blank shield is basically an unknown. If I chose wrongly and loosed a treacherous troop on my virtually helpless Dale . . .''

The green eyes fell, then raised again.

"There may be renegades among your kind, but as a whole, the word of a Falconer is known to be sound. Once given, it will not be violated in spirit or letter. So, too, is it with your discipline. I will do all in my power to see that you are not forced to have more to do than absolutely necessary with my people. You are professional fighters. We are not, and we will all be more happy to let go military duties, particularly during the summer months when our farms and animals and fleet will be demanding much of us. However, we do not want to have more trouble from the garrison brought in to defend us than they were hired to prevent. I need not fear that you, your men, will settle in as minor tyrants, treating my Dalesfolk as servants and slaves, wresting the fruits of their labor from them and viewing my wenches as stallionless mares handy to service their pleasure. They have proved themselves worthy of better than that."

A dark flush crimsoned Una's face, and her eyes did fall. It was not her custom to speak so bluntly on such matters, and it was beyond her power to conceal her shame.

Tarlach recognized her embarrassment, but saw something else as well, the quietness which remained with her despite her present discomfort and her desperate need to secure her will and secure it quickly. It was no absence of motion or feeling but rather a quality arising from within her to envelop her whole being. Were the others as aware of it? he wondered absently, and he wondered how anyone could be blind to this inner dignity and the strength it proclaimed.

He recalled himself sharply to the business at hand.

"There is the matter of payment." he said curtly.

She spread hands that seemed too small to have wielded a sword as he had seen her do.

"I cannot give what your company is worth in time of open hostility. Seakeep can offer the war price of a lesser unit along, of course, with your keep and that of your winged comrades and your mounts. They are not unjust terms since you are not being called to battle, merely to guard, with the probability of little or no actual fighting, but you could command more from a lord facing actual combat and needing a force as large as yours, and that I freely acknowledge.''

Several of his men stirred behind him, and the captain's own eyes slitted. There had been no change in her tone to indicate awareness of the shrewdness of her observation, but he believed that she knew full well what she had said. This Una of Seakeep had been managing her holding for a long time now, interacting with other Dales as well as ruling her own. Woman or nay, she knew what she was about.

"The duration of our oath?"

"Twelve months at the least. Longer if it proves mutually agreeable, but it would serve us ill rather than benefit us to take you on for less."

She waited now, making herself present an image of calm and assurance she was far from feeling. There should be no more questions, just the Falconers' response to her quest.

Their captain realized that the time of decision was at hand as well. His eyes swept his troops before returning to her.

"Your answer you shall have soon," he told her, "but not immediately. It is not my practice to bind our swords to any long-term service without first consulting with my officers."

"Of course, Captain. I shall return whenever you wish." She knew that they would wish to confer in private and would have been willing to accommodate that reasonable desire even had her own need not been so great.

"It will not take that long."

"Very well. I can wait outside."

Tarlach hesitated. If she did that, she might well draw the attention she was striving to avoid with her disguise. He owed her at least protection from betrayal whether they rode with her or nay, and there was also the possibility that the press gang might chance upon her again and attempt to exact vengeance for her earlier escape.

He pointed to a door to his left. It led to a smaller room intended for the use of highborn or otherwise privileged guests or those requiring a more private meeting place than the big common room. It was empty at the moment and was not likely to be wanted before time for the midday meal approached.

"You can wait in there, Lady, if you wish."

Una nodded and then took her leave of the mercenaries.

No one spoke for several seconds until the keen ears of their falcons reported that the Daleswoman had moved away from the door. Once they had that assurance, however, all eyes turned to Tarlach.

"Where did you meet up with that one?" Rorick demanded.

His commander tersely described the attack Brennan and he had thwarted.

The other snorted.

"A mare swinging a sword!"

"Her skill saved her a cracked head," Brennan pointed out indifferently, then dismissed the aberration from his mind and turned to Tarlach. "You are not seriously considering giving oath to her?"

"I am that, by the Horned Lord. Her tale is true as she sees it. All our winged comrades are in agreement on that, and they find nothing else amiss with her."

The war birds did not share their human companions' distrust of womankind, but they were sensitive as no man could be to falsehood or dark intent of any sort insofar as it affected their own company. They were, of course, instantly aware of any working of the Shadow or the true Dark, but that was not at question here.

"So?" snapped a voice to his right. "Let her take on blank shields of her own kind and her qualms be damned. Why should we concern ourselves with her difficulties, and for less than we could command, as she herself observed?''

''More than half our number served as young warriors in the war against Alizon. How many of us would be here to argue this had Harvard not proposed the change in plan which rendered the charge to which our company had been ordered needless? The end result would have been the same that day, but he alone had care enough of us, mere mercenaries though we were, to pull us from certain massacre. More, he then placed us where we could point the assault that broke the hounds' final strength.—To my thought, we Falconers are under no small debt to him, in honor if not by oath, and since we can do no better now than repay it to his Dale, so must be our service.''

His eyes swept the company.

''It is also to our benefit to accept this. As the Lady Una so subtly pointed out, there are not many lords in need of our swords at the moment, and perhaps that is to our good. We are tired. Our sick recover more slowly than they should, our wounded more slowly still. Our animals lack staying power, and our gear needs replacement and major repair. A spell at guarding would allow us to rectify all that, without paying out to innkeepers, and we would come away with a few extra coins to add weight to out belts as well, enough to pay our passage back to Estcarp without forcing us to draw on our major gains.''

The answering murmur which ran through those gathered around him was reluctant but not actually condemning, and he felt that he would have his will as he continued speaking.

''I will refuse if service to Seakeep is truly repugnant to you, but for my part, I think we would be fools to cast this offer aside.''

''We will go,'' Brennan replied gruffly. ''You know that full well. You will be getting the worst of it. It is you who will have to deal with the wench, not the rest of us.''

''What must be endured shall be, Comrade,'' he answered with a resignation which did not conceal his distaste for that aspect of their commission.

3

$\mathscr{S}$carcely two hours later, the Falconer company left Linna. They had settled their account with the innkeeper without having to ask their new employer to stand their debts but had used her silver, as was their right, to supply themselves for the journey ahead.

Una joined them outside the town, well away from prying eyes which might take note of their meeting and pass word of it to unfriendly ears. Ever in her mind was the knowledge that news traveled comparatively fast by sea, and they must perforce journey overland since there was no vessel available of a size capable of carrying her new army.

She herself was well horsed, better than any of the Falconers, on a gelding of Seakeep's own breeding. He had belonged to the Abbey, but her lord's sister had given him freely when Una had asked to purchase him or to have the loan of him for an extended period.

Warmth filled the woman's heart. There had been no questions, about this need or her strange garb or her hurried, sudden departure, merely a quick kiss, a fervent uttering of the Flame's blessing and Adicia's own, and an opening of the rarely used rear gate while the other Dames were at their private meditations.

Una raised her head. She was proud that she had been able to get away so readily and smoothly without forcing her escort to wait for her, and she was proud of her ability to handle her fine mount. It was a good beginning, that proof of competence, but one she knew she would have to maintain over the days ahead. The journey before them would be a long one, and she could not afford to weaken or lag during it. These cold men would be anticipating that, and if she fulfilled their expectations, they might well dismiss Seakeep along with its ruler.

The march was not a pleasant one for Una. It could not be completed in less than a good three weeks and could too readily stretch out far longer if they encountered any significant trouble. The Falconers pushed hard during the first stage of it. Ostensibly, they did so to make time while they could, before they reached the more demanding country that the Daleswoman warned lay ahead, but in reality, she knew they were trying her, or trying to break her down, to force her to plead for a halt or a slowing of pace. This she grimly set herself against doing, determined not to give them any part of their will. Pride and the necessity of remaining strong before them aside, needless delay was unthinkable. She would be away so long as it was. Maybe too long. . . .

Tarlach watched the Holdlady closely as the days went by, trying to gage what they actually had in her. She was showing some ability, right enough, he admitted grudgingly, but it was apparent that she was feeling the effects of the journey. Sometimes near the end of the day, it seemed more pride than strength that kept her in the saddle.

The fool! Would she really let herself be ridden into the ground?

A sense of shame touched him. That was unworthy. He would praise rather than condemn a warrior for similar stubbornness, and she had more than an unwillingness to give way before them to push her. It was not difficult to imagine that Una of Seakeep must be laboring under a sharp concern, fear, for her holding and what might be happening there. She was more eager than any of them to shave every possible moment off their journey.

Recognizing that, he reduced the pressure of their march. The Holdlady was carrying trouble enough without their adding to her difficulties out of mere spleen.

The Falconer company had not remained long in even nominally settled territory, and for the better part of their trek they found themselves forcing their way through a wilderness such as might never have known the tread of human feet before their coming.

Even for men of their experience and training, the way was rugged at its lightest, often so much so that they were compelled to dismount and lead their animals, and the progress they made, though constant enough, was slow and hard-won.

Scouts they sent out, as would any military column, but chiefly they relied on the sharp eyes of their falcons to bring them news. Always the report was the same— no sign of other parties, friendly or otherwise, and no change in the country ahead save that its difficulty inexorably increased with every passing mile.

Through it all, Una of Seakeep held her own with the mercenaries, neither delaying them nor asking their aid while on the trail, nor did she ever seek additional comfort or finer fare at night. At times, her face was drawn and pinched with weariness, her body ached with strain and the effects of the constant damp and mountain cold, but her eyes ever remained bright and her smile ready to greet any of her usually taciturn companions who chanced to approach her.

For the most part, that did not happen often. The Falconers did not fail in the courtesy required of blank shields toward the one hiring their swords, but in accordance with their established custom, it was their captain who handled all intercourse between his company and their employer. She soon came to know him well although he neither entrusted her with his name nor appeared unmasked before her. There were other ways to recognize and partially judge a man than the study of his face. His walk and stance, his speech, the set of his mouth, the sharp, ever-shadowed eyes all told a great deal. Above all, there was his falcon. Storm Challenger was a true lord among creatures, high even amid his own noble kind, and was a powerful testimonial to the worth of the man he had chosen for his particular comrade.

The mercenary commander often rode beside Una, for he wished to learn as much as he could about the territory his people would occupy for the next twelve months and over which they might be forced to fight.

He had expected little from such an informant when he began questioning her, but he quickly came to realize that he could not have wished or willed for better. Una's knowledge of her Dale and those around it was astonishingly detailed, almost minute in its precision, more in keeping with what he might look to find in the reports of a trained scout or ranger than anything he would anticipate hearing from the ruler of any holding.

Her love for Seakeep glimmered in her every description, a love so deep and of such strength as to be well-nigh palpable, but it was realistic for all its power. The Holdlady recognized and accepted her Dale's lackings and weaknesses even as she did its strengths and beauty. She knew and admitted its limitations and was content to live within the bounds set by its lack of major resources.

If more of her kind were of like mind, he thought rather grimly, there would be less of a call for his profession, less of the darkness and destruction which had torn this basically peaceful land for so long. The Dales and their lords had not been responsible even in small part for instigating any of that.

The Falconer supposed that such contentment had to come as an outrider to life in a backwater holding like Seakeepdale, but he had known something of Una's late lord and imagined it might be hard to achieve for a man with Ferrick's abilities, although his acceptance of both the relative solitude and the genuine hard work of running an economically marginal hold was readily understandable.

Even the most insignificant Dale was infinitely preferable to ruling none. A marriage such as Ferrick had made was the dream, the well-nigh unattainable dream, of every blank shield, of every wellborn but landless younger son venturing forth to win his way in a world where power lay with land and the ownership of land was concentrated in the hands of hereditary lords who carefully guarded their patrimonies, neither diminishing nor dividing them and delivering them over only into the hands of a single heir at the time of their own death. Only by bedding wisely and very well could any man not directly in line to inherit normally break into their carefully closed circle, and even in these days, with many Dales still in chaos and rightful lords dead, it was no simple matter to lay claim—and maintain it—on any holding.

Perhaps Ferrick had originated in the area. The quiet of the place would seem natural then and would not be as likely to chafe on him. Then, too, he had been no youth when he had come to power, not old, certainly, but well into his middle years.

Familiarity with him or at least his kin would have probably gone far in moving the old Holdlord to listen to and accept his suit for the hand of his only child and heir.

The heiress herself? Tarlach glanced at the woman riding beside him. Una of Seakeep would have been a maid scarcely out of girlhood when she had been wed. . . .

She had made no mention of her lord's people, but if the possibility of an alliance with them existed or if less formal help might be expected, he wanted to know about it. That could work greatly to their advantage in any confrontation with an overgreedy neighbor.

"Lord Ferrick, he was a native of your region or distant kin?" he asked abruptly.

Una looked at him in surprise. The Falconer had never questioned her about any personal matter before. She realized what he was about then and shook her head.

"He was a friend to my father, nigh unto a brother although Ferrick might have been the son of his youth as I was the daughter of his age. They had ridden together as blank shields for many years before my father came to Seakeep."

He looked at her sharply.

"Lord Harvard also bound his sword?"

The Daleswoman frowned, nettled by the completeness of his surprise.

"You Falconers may justly be counted the best of the mercenaries, but you are not alone in that calling," she responded testily, "nor do you alone excel in its arts. Father fought so well and had gained such wealth by his endeavors, and managed it so wisely, that he was able to woo and win my mother's hand, Holdheir though she was."

He stared at her, taking aback by her vehemence.

"I meant no insult to your sire, Lady."

Her temper cooled even as it had risen.

"I know. My weariness must stand as my admittedly poor excuse."

She reached out across the space separating them, then flushed and hurriedly withdrew her hand again as he stiffened under her touch.

"Your pardon, Captain!" She bit down on her lip. "I did not mean to break courtesy with you."

Her distress was so apparent that Tarlach cursed himself for having schooled himself so poorly.

"The breach of courtesy is mine, Lady. You have shown us by now that you wish to use us honorably."

"So do I intend, and so will it be with all my folk," she told him miserably, "but few of us are accustomed to associating with peoples other than our own kind or to accommodating ourselves to ways strange to us. There may be other violations of your custom, slight, perhaps, but offensive to your warriors."

He smiled, one of the few times she had seen him do so.

"Give us some credit for sense, Lady. Mercenaries cannot afford to be too thin-skinned.—We shall manage well enough unless I badly misjudge the worth of your word."

Time passed and more time. The company struggled along a difficult but obviously planned and maintained trail winding its way up one of the steepest slopes they had yet encountered. Had its grade been only a very little sharper, it would have been a cliff, a barrier impossible for their mounts to negotiate at all.

The crest topping it, in contrast, was surprisingly gentle, and there the Falconers drew rein.

Tarlach gazed out over the world which lay beneath, and his breath stopped a moment at the almost incomprehensible beauty of it.

He was looking down upon a long, rather broad valley which sloped gently into a miniature bay. Behind and to either side, mountains rose, tall, green-clad giants ever gazing seaward.

The ocean was a vast, brilliantly blue realm, her foam-speckled surface tossing and glinting in the golden sunlight. She seemed to quieten as she entered the bay. Here, her waves came dancing playfully over the pale sand, but beyond this single favored site, they rushed the land with awesome fury, roaring and breaking against the cliffs with eternal, implacable rage.

Their anger seemed most pronounced and, through that magic ever exerted by the great ocean, fairest at those points to north and south where mountain and water met in the long, low, narrow spurs which cradled and protected the tiny harbor. In these places, the sea was marbled with white even on this mild day, for a myriad of rocks and islets scarcely more than rocks themselves rose up to break its flow.

Above all stretched a sky high and blue, the perfection of its expanse enhanced rather than disturbed by a scattering of white clouds and by the flight of waterbirds.

To his weary eyes, this might almost be a vision out of the Halls of the Valiant were it not for the marks of human life and industry which were so much a part of the placid scene. The little bay was dotted with vessels, and cottages nestled on the green slopes above it where the fury of the waves did not reach. Cultivated fields and pastures stretched out around these to fill the whole of the valley, and overlooking all, slender and stately and formidable upon a high and yet sheltered pinnacle, soared a tall round tower.

Una had described this stronghold closely, but still the man stared at the actual sight of it. Never had he beheld anything of its like before, and he had seen much since the day he had first girded on a warrior's blade.

"What witchery is this?" he whispered.

The Holdlady heard that.

"None! It is old, aye, as I told you. It was old when my people first came to this place, but no working of Power keeps it sound, just the strength of the stone comprising it and the skill of the vanished folk who raised it."

Una's eyes caressed the tower lovingly.

"Save for that good rock, all the rest is of our working. Everything which had been there of wood or metal or materials more perishable still had crumbled to dust long before our arrival in High Hallack. We had to replace all that and have kept it in repair since."

"You mentioned another ancient place."

She nodded.

"The Square Keep. My forebears lived there before the decision was made to remove and settle closer to the greater bounty of the sea and land here. It had been put into repair then but is now a complete ruin again, all but the original shell. That is well inland and cannot be glimpsed from the valley, but you will doubtless visit it as you travel the Dale."

The woman fell quiet. She raised eyes that were somber and hopeful both.

"Well, Bird Warrior, now that you see it, how do you judge Seakeep?"

Tarlach said nothing for a moment. How could he tell her that his heart ached at the sight of it, that its beauty and the rightness and balance of the life revealed in even this first glimpse, the open peace and harmony of the place, drove through his inner being with the force of a spear after the violence and ruin he had witnessed all these last years?

"It appears to be a holding worthy of its ruler's care," he replied.

The Falconer's eyes narrowed as he scanned the mountains fringing the valley, gaging the peril they presented and their value as a defense. He knew that Seakeepdale consisted of all this now visible to him and twice again as much land, but only this one vale was arable to any large extent or permanently inhabited. His first task must be to secure this place, Seakeep's heart. After that, he would have to see what could be done to safeguard the rest.

That might not be an impossible goal despite the Dale's size and the relatively small force at his disposal. This was rough country, among the roughest he had encountered. The mountains presented an impressive barrier to anyone seeking to force entrance here, particularly to anyone attempting to lead a large company into it. Their own passage had of a certainty been anything but easy, and they had at least traversed a way which did some service as an informal road.

"Are there many other entrances like this to the valley?" he asked without taking his eyes off the distant peaks.

"No other except the sea. That is part of the reason my ancestors chose to settle here, as a guard against an invader's most probable route of attack. We had no idea what this land might hold then, you see, and there were signs in plenty to prove that it was inhabited, or had been at one time."

"What about this Square Keep? It has been my experience that men do not raise strongholds, most particularly strongholds fashioned out of great blocks of stone, unless there is either something to guard or guard against. You claim only this valley is fit for farming or pasture on a significant scale and that there are no major ore deposits in the region at all, so I doubt it was any quality of the land which drew the Old Ones to the place."

Una nodded slowly.

"Well said, Bird Warrior. I had temporarily forgotten it. There is a passage, but it gives entry only to the Dale, not to this valley, which truly can be approached only from here or by water, and it would be very easily defended."

"That would serve us little with no guard on hand to do it.—Any door to your domain must be viewed and treated with respect, Lady. Determined men can accomplish near sorcery with a supposedly insignificant breach."

Her fingers whitened on the reins.

"You are right. My carelessness might have cost Seakeep dearly."

She felt the grey eyes on her. For once, they were not cold but were filled with such sympathy that the control her responsibilities forced on her trembled, and she had to fight herself for a moment to maintain it.

"You must despise me utterly," she whispered.

"No!—Fate has laid a burden on you that you were never trained to carry. You had the wisdom to realize you needed the help of such as we and to seek it out." He smiled. "I presume you are as interested in our experience as in our physical abilities."

"More interested, Bird Warrior."

The gratitude she felt to him was enormous. This hard man had neither condemned nor patronized her with that response. He had acknowledged her position as it was and had acknowledged his own role with respect to it.

Tarlach's expression tightened as his attention returned to the valley and its strangely formed keep.

This was another matter. As he had already stated, Una herself was not to be blamed for the shortcomings of her Dale's defenses, but had she no advisors? There had to be some men down there who knew the ways of war.

"Whatever about the Square Keep, a guard must be set on this route at once. Had we been invaders, our swords would now be red with your people's blood."

The Holdlady smiled.

"Perhaps, but were I not with you and patently at my ease—and expected to be returning in such company— you would not be viewing any so charming a scene. If you failed to meet our challenges satisfactorily, it would be far fewer of you who would still be able to see anything at all, fair or ill."

The Falconer stiffened.

"Watchers?"

"Of course. Did you believe us to be complete fools? I thought you realized we were under observation for the last several miles." She saw him glance at Storm Challenger, who was perched on the mount fastened to Tarlach's saddle for his use. "The winged ones are not to blame. With strength in so short supply, we have had to fall back on care and stealth. Our youth know how to conceal themselves, and one does not sit on the top of a tree in mountain country where an enemy standing in a still-higher place might possibly spot his post. Even your comrades' sharp eyes are not likely to detect single, widely spaced sentries under such circumstances, particularly when they are not even radiating hatred or other strong feeling to alert their inner senses, which I believe to be more acute than ours."

The captain's jaw tightened. That failure had been a bad one. It could have been deadly, and he was mortified to have been caught in it almost at the instant of his arrival in the Dale he had been hired to defend.

He resisted the instinctive impulse to snarl at the woman. That would change nothing and would only serve to magnify his unit's blindness during their approach.

"Your people are to be complimented," he admitted rather sourly.

Una nodded to acknowledge the praise but did not press the subject. The incident could have opened a serious breach between them at the very outset of the mercenaries' service with her. That it had not was due solely to their leader's control, and she was not about to put that to any further test.

"Let us go down now. My folk should have readied barracks for you, but even so, it will take time to get you all settled, and the day is already old."

Una took the lead on the narrow, steep road which was the only approach to the round tower's single gate.

At first, only a squad of youthful sentries stood at attention to greet her, but then Rufon appeared at the entrance. She saw his jaw drop and then close with a snap, and she fought hard to repress a laugh. Apparently, those informing him of her approach had neglected to tell him the company in which she rode.

That gave her a moment of concern. She knew he had delayed to order food prepared, fire laid, and otherwise ready her chambers and the mercenaries' quarters for imminent occupancy. She had no doubt that he had prepared the barracks, whatever his private feelings about her chances for success, but would his arrangements be acceptable? Would anything provided by a Dale run primarily by women be satisfactory to house these men long-term?

There was no sign of that worry in the smile which she bent on her liegeman as she gave him greeting and accepted the hand he raised to steady her as she dismounted.

"Thanks given," she said as her feet touched the ground, speaking softly so that he alone might hear her. "I have brought us some help and doubtless some problems as well."

"Doubtless," the veteran agreed with feeling, then he shook his head in wonder. "By what sorcery did you manage this?"

"By fortune's stroke and very nearly my own disaster—but, I pray you, friend, do not use that word around them! They jump like kittens at the sound of it."

He chuckled.

"Never fear, Lady Una! We will take care to guard them well, feelings and person." His face softened. "It is good to have you home, my Lady."

"And good to be here."

She glanced at the keep.

"I want to settle our blank shields as soon as I bid them formal welcome. You have readied places for them

257

within the tower?" Of a certainty, they could not be housed in any of the cottages with Seakeep's families.

"I have, my Lady, as you instructed."

"Well done. Hasten now and prepare Lord Harvard's chamber as well. I would have their captain use that."

Rufon frowned but quickly recovered himself. He had loved the Lord Harvard, and he had no liking for allowing a hired stranger free use of what had been his personal place, but reason said this was a sensible move on the part of his liege. Their employer or nay, Lady Una would be little welcomed by those Falconers, and she herself would find no pleasure in venturing amongst them, but as ruler of Seakeepdale, she would have to meet, and possibly frequently, with their commander. This compromise would permit both parties to retain a greater degree of privacy than would otherwise have been possible, and, because of the man's race, there was small chance of any shadow's being cast upon her honor.

Una had anticipated some resistance, or at least disapproval, from Rufon and was both surprised and relieved to encounter none.

Perhaps because of the ease with which she had convinced him, she was completely taken aback when the mercenary spurned her plan.

Tarlach's eyes blazed before she had finished speaking.

"Officers and warriors of a Falconer unit remain together," he informed her with an icy finality that stung like the cut of a whip.

"Very well," she snapped, angry in her turn, "but I am going to have to have access to you, so warn your comrades that, woman though I am, they can expect to find me in their quarters fairly frequently. Rest assured, Bird Warrior, I shall not so far accommodate you as to bring you into my sleeping chamber when we needs must confer. My people have our customs as well!"

The Daleswoman gripped herself. Customs, aye, but her kind were not quite so ruled by irrationalities, practices and the hidden or open terrors which sparked them.

"A Holdlord's quarters are large. Two or even three of you could use the room in comfort, more if you accept crowding."

Tarlach was silenced a moment, first by amazement at the sudden outburst from the usually controlled Holdlady, then by mortification as he recognized its cause and what prompted her to make her second offer. Blank shields were not normally given a place among the blood household of those they served. Una had made exception for him out of consideration for his people's ways and had swallowed her annoyance at his rejection and opened her personal domain to still more strangers . . . because she believed he feared to be so separated from his own kind.

He held his temper. To allow it any rein would seem but overreaction, confirming her error in her mind.

Hoping that his masking helm would conceal the shame sweeping him, he raised his hand in a rough salute.

"There is no need for that. You have shown greater foresight than I, Lady Una. For that, I must offer thanks."

She nodded, but he could still sense the tension on her. He made himself smile.

"Blank shields are rarely used so well. You took me by surprise."

Now her expression brightened, resuming almost magically its customary ready openness.

"We of Seakeep have sound reason for welcoming them, do we not?"

Tarlach set his baggage down and looked around him. There was a feeling of solid comfort about the big chamber. It was amply furnished, the pieces substantial and massive in scale, well made but constructed of local materials and apparently by local craftsmen. He saw none of the exotic woods or costly inlay work favored by the richer lords to the south in the days when High Hallack was still free of war and they had resources to spare for such luxuries.

It was ready to receive him despite the lack of forewarning that it would be required, good testimony to the quality of the service Una of Seakeep commanded. The high bed had been made up and its hangings drawn back. A fire had been laid and now burned cheerfully in the hearth, its heat already reaching out to warm the air around it. Candles were in their sconces, waiting to give their flickering light when the sun finally set.

He walked over to the centermost of the three windows breaking the expanse of the outfacing wall and stood by it, gazing out over the valley and the bay beyond. The evening was now well on, and the sun was going down magnificently red.

A fine view, he thought, and this opening was large enough to permit him to enjoy it. Because the room was so high, greater access could be allowed to light and air than was permissible at lower levels, or anywhere in more conventionally formed strongholds. It had been so in the Eyrie as well. . . .

Heavy metal shutters had been fitted to each window to shield the interior in time of danger, but he had the feeling that they had never been tested by more than the violence of the savage storms which must occasionally roll in from the sea.

Sadness welled up in him. That could all change too soon.

It would not! It was his business to see that this peaceful holding did not suffer the same fate that had stricken so many other of High Hallack's Dales.

A knock sounded behind him, and at his word, the great oak door swung silently back.

He raised his hand in greeting to Brennan.

"Welcome. Come in and see how a lord of Seakeepdale lives."

"Passing well," Brennan commented, his eyes sweeping the heavy, dark furnishings and excellent tapestries; he, too, liked the amount of light entering here. "You will be living well, my comrade."

"Quite well.—Are the others settled?"

"Most comfortably. These Dalesfolk are not tightfisted

at any rate. We are not likely to starve while amongst them."

Brennan went over to the window.

"You would travel far to see finer than that," he remarked in admiration. "I wonder what else can be seen from this height."

"From the other side? A good bit of the bay, I imagine, and, of course, the mountain behind. The contrast between the two should be even more dramatic than this."

"Who else is quartered up here?"

"Only the Lady Una." His voice hardened instinctively, but then he shrugged. "She should not trouble me overmuch. She will be wanting her own share of peace."

His comrade laughed.

"You would find little of that below, right enough." His expression sobered. "What will be our course, Tarlach?"

"An easy one for the time being, for the rest of you anyway. I shall have to devote much of my attention to the Lady Una, and I will have to ride with her or her scouts to learn the Dale and something of those bordering it.—That learning is not my task alone. I want all of you to familiarize yourselves with Seakeep as thoroughly and as quickly as possible. Call on the younglings here to augment my reports. They should be more than willing to help."

The lieutenant nodded. This was a logical and common plan for a mercenary unit to follow upon entering into a territory where they might have to fight. Knowledge of their own and their enemies' lands always worked to reduce losses, sometimes significantly so, and frequently it was the edge that gave them the victory.

The commander returned to the window after Brennan had gone. He felt relaxed now that his duties to his command had been temporarily discharged, contented and enough at ease that he had no qualm about loosing Storm Challenger to the air in compliance with his winged brother's strongly declared wish.

All the falcons had responded with pleasure and their own excitement to this high, rugged country, so like their own lost home in many respects. It was good to be here and enough at peace that he could grant them the freedom of it.

It was good to have some share of that freedom himself.

4

*S*pring flowed into a gloriously perfect summer without a break in the quiet course of life in Seakeepdale.

Tarlach found himself thrown more heavily than he had originally anticipated into the Holdlady's company, heavily enough to give him pause whenever he thought to consider their enforced relationship.

That was not often. He had fallen under the spell of this beautiful, wild realm, and he had very quickly come to realize that there was no better guide to show him its ways.

The woman's familiarity with her domain was little short of phenomenal. She almost literally knew every foot, every aspect, of the huge Dale, and his wonder at the depth and intimacy of her awareness grew with every excursion he made with her.

So, too, did his own fascination with this world of mountain and sea, but despite his frank ensorcellment with it, he recognized as readily as did its ruler that Seakeep would not be a paradise in every man's eyes. It was not wealthy. Its territory was vast, aye, but it was poor in arable land, as Una had admitted from the outset, the most of that and all of the best being centered in the valley guarded by her round tower. Here, its people grew the staples and smaller luxury crops which sustained them and their animals, again, those common to most high, rough regions—small, dark cattle, the little black-faced sheep whose meat was so superior to that of the heavier lowland animals and whose wool was sparser but much the stronger, a few half-wild goats, hogs, mules and asses, and an assortment of fowl.

Only the horses were extraordinary, and these were of such quality and beauty that they seemed more creatures out of a bard's fancy than living beasts native to this ancient, many-sorrowed world. That notwithstanding, they were fine work animals and fine in the hunt or for exploring the roughest wilderness, and the least of them, properly trained, would be a war horse any Falconer would bind his sword for a full year to possess.

The mercenary sighed. He was not likely ever to own one of them, nor was any other of his race. The Dale's breeding program was small, producing enough animals to supply its own needs but no more. Markets where an acceptable price might even reasonably be anticipated were simply too far and the journey to them too difficult to make the effort of building the herd worthwhile. Even in the days before the invasion, horses had never been taken farther than the semiannual fairs at Linna.

That was just as well. Seakeep had never really been able to spare the men to send on long-term trading missions. There was no warring between the Dale and its neighbors, but this isolated, wild land was a lodestone to brigands, and its jagged coast called to pirate crews. These were the enemies of all and had to be fought by all, and they came frequently enough that each Dale maintained a well-trained, battle-tempered garrison to combat them.

The brunt of the ocean warfare had always fallen to Seakeep, since its harbor, though too small to support commercial fishing on more than its present scale or to entice merchantmen from the larger ports to the south, was the sole refuge for a fleet in this region.

None of that mattered, he thought, not economic hardship or danger from sea or land or human predators. A man could be happy here. This was a place in which to set down roots, to build and to grow, to meld with a world welcoming to those willing to work with rather than against her, a world where his kind could make themselves a home and grow strong and whole once more. . . .

His thoughts stopped, or, rather, they began to blur. The humming of the breeze and the muffled surging of the surf were working upon him in consort with the pleasant heat, and he was content for the moment to let his mind drift where their influence wafted it.

A high, distant call penetrated his mental doze, and he looked skyward, automatically homing in on the cry. Storm Challenger. An exultant joy filled him as he watched the falcon soar high in company with Brennan's Sunbeam. Unconsciously, his muscles tensed and strained as if he would join his comrade in body in the ultimate freedom of flight even as he joined with him in spirit.

This was just a playful flight, the birds' way of expressing their pleasure in a beautiful day, but they had soared for more serious and timeless purpose earlier in their stay, as had every pair in the company. These flacons were creatures of the heights, and Seakeep met their instinctive needs to the full. Their annual nesting had proven fruitful as no other had been since the last in the Eyrie, before destruction had come to set them wandering. Another such hatching, another year in the Dale, and the future of the black-and-white birds should be assured. That would be an accomplishment and a comfort even if the men who served with them must all too soon fade.

His breath caught suddenly. Una was on the beach as well. She had begun walking toward him but had heard the falcons' calling and had stopped to watch them. To his horror, she raised her arm in the distance greeting used by his people, and they—they responded, with a true welcome and not merely an acknowledgment of her presence.

She understood! That accursed female understood what they said and did!

He reached her in a matter of moments. Seizing her

roughly by the arm, he spun her about, forcing her to face him.

"Witch! Dare you try your spells against them?"

Una struggled an instant to free herself, but when she could not, she stood still, quiet save for eyes blazing like cauldrons of green fire in her fury.

"You have strange standards of judgment, Falconer! For you to do this is but natural communication with members of another species. For me, it is an aberration, something vile to be feared and condemned."

Her contempt was a lash into his face, but he did not give way.

"For your kind, it is unnatural."

"Then it is most difficult to understand why no animal has ever refused me greeting and good wishing after the manner of its kind."

His hold loosened enough for her to jerk her arm out of his grasp.

"It is true that this is not a usual gift of my people, and I have had to take care during all my life lest I be branded an oddity or worse among them, to the detriment of my house. I had not intended revealing myself to you, either, but I thought it no harm since the falcons themselves answered me as they did." She turned away from him. "I suppose I was wrong to expect better than this from you."

Her voice both thickened and trembled at that last, and she hurriedly strode back along the way she had come.

Tarlach cringed in his heart, realizing there was pain as well as anger on her.

Justified anger. He did not need the reproach he was receiving from the two falcons to tell him that.

"Lady! Lady Una, wait!"

The Daleswoman halted and faced him again but gave him no verbal reply.

He came to a stop before her and stood in the manner of a shieldman before his liege.

"I overstepped my right . . ."

"Aye. That you did." Una eyed him coldly. Her shoulders squared. "Prepare your mount, Captain, and order mine prepared. The question of sorcery appears to be ever in your mind and accusation of it ever on your tongue. All this area is well-nigh free of that, but I do have a friend whom you would find distinctly suspect. She is no follower of the Shadow, but you shall judge that for yourself. If you read it otherwise, or if your fear of her proves too great, then go, and do not waste more of my time and resources."

The mercenary's hand went to his sword, and he had to will himself to leave it sheathed.

"Take care, woman. We are oath-bound to serve—"

"Your oath be damned! Of what use would you be to me if you come to hate me more than my enemy? Ogin is a man, after all," she added bitterly. "What matter if he may be luring ships to their deaths in order to increase his store?"

"That is vile judging!"

"You do not think it amiss to use me so. Ready yourself to ride, Falconer. I must have your decision now as to whether you and yours remain in my service or not."

5

*T*he pair rode from the round tower in black silence. Tarlach wondered briefly if he was acting the fool in telling no one what he was about, in coming with this woman at all, but he dismissed that thought in the next instant. Pride and anger were driving him, aye, but it was his duty to investigate any local conditions which might affect his company, and that, unfortunately, included sites and sources of Power activity. As for Una, Storm Challenger rode with them, and the Falconer commander knew that, whatever else she might be capable of doing, this one would not purposely lead him into harm. Or himself. Treason of that kind was not part of her. That he was forced to admit despite all his hard feeling of the moment against her.

The heavy quiet continued between them, and as time went on, the mercenary grew more and more uncomfortable under it. He had never been conscious of the Holdlady's pressing her conversation on him, but he realized now how much he had come to enjoy her response to her holding, her observations of the land and the amazingly rich variety of life it supported, her often surprising reaction to his own comments, and with that exchange abruptly terminated, he felt as if he had suffered an irreparable loss, all the more painful and poignant because the break between them had been of his making.

At last, he sent his horse forward until the stallion drew abreast of her mount.

"Is my crime so very black?" he demanded sullenly.

"No. You cannot be blamed for being what you are. I chiefly resent that your attitude has forced me to do this."

Her eyes rested somberly on him.

"Women have their friendships, too. We cherish them as much as any of your kind do yours, cherish their closeness and confidence.

"I value that more than most, perhaps, since I have been privileged to have but one such companion, one single sister of my soul. I had no siblings, and even were there girls of my age in the neighboring Dales, distance would have prevented much interaction between us while we were very young. As for our own people's offspring, my father did not believe it well for me to mix too freely with them, the more so once he had reconciled himself to the fact that there would be no son to rule after him.

"I filled my days well, but still I longed for some true comrade as I grew older, someone to share the experiences of life and growth with me. It was as if the Amber Lady had wielded her Power for me when I came across the place to which we are going and discovered there a girl of my own age who loved Seakeep even as I did and who held interest in many of the things which gripped my heart and mind. She even shared my name."

She smiled at the memory of their meeting but almost immediately grew grave again.

"She is not human, or entirely human, as we define ourselves, and even then, as a child, she knew enough to want to keep apart from our kind, a shyness she still retains."

Una heard the quick indraw of his breath and nodded.

"There might have been very great peril for me in that meeting, but I was fortunate. I was also not an utter fool. As dearly as I yearned for this friendship, I went to both my mother and my nurse, who was a wisewoman of very great ability. They met my other Una and gave their approval to my continuing to visit with her, but they are the only ones I have ever brought to see her."

Tarlach's eyes were dark with trouble.

"If this . . . Una is innocent of evil, why have you thought it necessary to conceal your association with her?"

"Partly because it was her wish, as I have mentioned, partly because of my own position. A Holdlord's daughter must always act and think with respect to her Dale, and I was heir as well. I could not afford to let myself be thought too strange or have it rumored that I had truck with things better left alone. That I have a strong gift for healing which extends well beyond the training every wellborn girl receives in that art as part of her education was welcomed since that is both a distinct benefit to all and is an accepted duty of my sex and rank, but no other ability or connection that so much as hinted of Power would be so regarded."

"No speech with animalkind and no friendships among the Old Ones?"

"Either might be sufficient to have caused objection to my coming into my own."

"Power in one form or another shows in many Dale families," he reminded her. "It rarely appears to arouse much resentment."

"Aye, but that comes as a gift—or curse—from of old. There are no such traditions in our house, no ancient melding with those not of our race or kind."

"What is hallowed by time elsewhere would meet a very different reception here as a present-day innovation?"

"Given the nature of most people, aye, particularly now. The fact of a woman's holding rule to herself so long is in itself an oddity resented to some extent by many."

His eyes measured her.

"Yet you are willing to bring me to your friend?"

"I must. I cannot have you unsure of me if it comes to pass that you are forced to fight for me. You have to be certain, in your heart at least, that I stand with the Light and not the Dark."

His head bowed.

"I would I could tell you I entertained no such suspicions against you."

"You must have them, being what you are."

"We do have reason, Lady," he said softly.

"I do not even imagine otherwise, not after having come to know you a little," she said with sadness.

"You do not ask those reasons?"

"I have no right to ask," Una answered. "That is Falconer history and Falconer business alone."

Tarlach was silent for several minutes.

"Before we came to the land where we established our Eyrie, we, the men of my race, were enslaved." His eyes closed at the recalling of that ancient horror. "You cannot conceive of the depth of that bondage forced on us by an adept of the Dark path. It was an Old One, not human though human enough in appearance, who held us in such thrall, but for all her store of Power, she was unable to work her will on us directly. To accomplish that, she needed to use our females. Every woman was a vessel to serve as her tool, and those she utilized became even as she, dark and cruel, living only to exalt themselves and to grind and degrade . . .

"Eventually, at great cost, we broke free, and the surviving remnant fled north, borne in Sulcar ships, taking with them those of their women that were still alive but treating with them even as we do today.

"We had escaped, you see, but our victory was only partial. The Dark One was foiled. She was captive, but she was not dead. Her will lived and ever sought the woman who would shed for her the blood that would release her. Then she would be after us again.— Apparently, no other race could serve her particular needs.—We durst not let ourselves grow attached to or involved with any woman again, for it would be through such close association that her Power would close on us again should she indeed gain her release. Over the years, the centuries," he shrugged, "need became virtue, I suppose. Contempt and hate took the place of any longing our forebears must have felt for a warmer, gentler life among our own. That ill feeling soon expanded to include all of your sex, as was probably inevitable considering the number of women who are wielders of Power in Estcarp, the great number of women who are potentially most perilous to us."

He stopped speaking suddenly as a thought came to him with all the force of a diving falcon.

"Our females must be afraid of her return, too, more intensely than we. Maybe that is why they never made an effort to seek other lives in number, although Estcarp lay near enough for them to have gained refuge there." He stared fixedly into the distance. "They have worse to dread than us. We were enslaved, but we remained still men, still ourselves. Those who served her purpose were not what they had been. Identifiable traits remained, aye, but in person, in soul, they were altered even as those who accepted the Kolder's jewels were changed and bound."

"All your women were so chained?" she asked softly.

"No. Our history is clear on that. She attempted to seize only the ones she specifically required, and most of those she did call refused her, dying of that refusal, but always a few responded or were compelled to respond. That was her Power and our undoing, that no Falconer woman could deny her, or survive making good that denial, and each one so claimed could then chain the men associated with her."

"So, once out of the trap, you determined to allow yourselves no associations at all?"

"Could you risk drawing that doom down on yourself a second time?" he countered.

"No. I could not, even at so great a price." Una was still for a moment. "Perhaps your answer, for male and female alike, lies in taking partners from among other peoples. You indicate that your foe seemed to want or require those of your blood to work her will." She eyed him pensively. "A species unable to change to some extent is doomed, for the time when some change is required will inevitably come. That holds true for people as well as beasts, I think."

"Perhaps, and perhaps some of my kind might eventually be convinced to risk that course rather than face complete extinction, but, Lady, do you see the women of any other race coming to us? Our ways are viewed with a hearty dislike by your sex, and who would be foolish enough to imagine a yielding to need also guarantees an altering of heart? It would be too much to think that attitudes generations in the building could be banished in an instant because some of us accepted the necessity of such a move and broke with the rest of our fellows to make it." Were banished by the rest . . . "It will not come to that."

"No? Then I do fear for you. Your villages are in Estcarp now. Old history will not hold forever against the examples of another, richer life open for the viewing but a short ride away. Add to that the losses your men must have suffered since the Kolder came, and your kind is in major, maybe mortal, trouble, whether you admit and face it or nay."

She studied Storm Challenger for a moment as he sat regally upon the perch before the man.

"I should not be sorry to see some of your ways gone, but, Falconer, what you have achieved with these valiant birds must not be lost. That would be to the impoverishment of this whole world."

Tarlach did not know whether to stare at the woman in awe or curse her for naming this fear of his as accurately as if she had drawn it directly from his mind. A chill ran through him at the sudden thought that she might have done precisely that.

He chose silence and a quick move from the sensitive subject before she should also divine his pain and his hopelessness of ever rising from the blow dealt to his race by the destruction of their base.

"What must be endured shall be," he told her with a finality that allowed for no further discussion. "But what of yourself, Lady? I am . . . curious about your gift. You can apparently treat with the falcons much as we do. Can you do as much with all other animals?"

"Aye and no both. Each kind is different, and the thoughts of some touch more readily than others with mine. Your falcons are wonderful. I had never imagined to find mindways so complex and deep in any other being save a cat, and I usually do not draw very closely with birds."

She hesitated.

"I meant no harm or insult to you in addressing them. Since they returned my initial courtesy greeting without reserve, I assumed I did no wrong."

"You concealed from us your ability to talk to them," he pointed out.

"From habit, as I do from everyone. It was no evil intent or deed that I was trying to hide."

"I yield to that," he said after a moment. "You can speak with all or most warm-bloods to some extent. What about things whose blood runs cold?"

"With some of the scaled ones and those creatures dwelling in both water and on land, but I have no contact or almost none with insects or fish or other beings like to them." She guessed the question he did not voice. "I have no such ability whatsoever with our own kind."

The man had the control and the grace to mask his relief.

"You have formed no individual friendship such as we share with our winged brothers and sisters?" he asked.

She shook her head.

"I have not been so blessed. Though all will speak with me, none have permitted me to come that close.—Your falcons actually do choose the warrior with whom they will ride, do they not?"

"Aye, but they are also taught from the egg to seek such a comrade among us. Other creatures do not expect that sort of relationship from humans. Try making the initial move yourself. Choose a being you respect and can love and reach out to it." He paused. "A cat would be a sound choice. You indicate a preference for them, and they are regarded not only as acceptable companions for humans but ones for whom a great deal of fondness can be shown. With one of them, you need not reveal the true nature of your association." Tarlach smiled. "They are small as well. That is a distinct advantage if you want to keep your comrade beside you in hall and bower."

She laughed.

"A point well taken, Bird Warrior! I shall bear it in mind." She sobered. "And the rest of what you have said. If such a friendship can truly be mine, rest assured that I shall do all in my power to win and be worthy of it."

The silence between them was different now, companionable and ever ready to lift, as it frequently did under the wonder of the country through which they were riding.

This was the high-mountained interior of her rugged hold, and Una, knowing the Falconer's delight in such terrain, set a course up a steep slope to a crest from which they could see for miles before them. Higher peaks behind hid the ocean from them, but the rocks and forests, the barer, sweeping expanses of heather, furze, and fern, the small, wild streams racing into impossibly clear lakes, the low places green with sweet grass or dark with bog growth were as grand in themselves and tore at heart and mind with all the sea's more familiar force.

Tarlach felt a twinge of guilt at the strength of the emotion rising within him, as if he were betraying the Eyrie and all his dead stronghold had meant.

"There are other mountains far higher," he said sharply to counter it.

"Probably, and grander, too," she agreed, "yet I think I should not love them as well if I were set in their midst now. These have been my friends since my infancy, and their beauty has become my standard for all that is fair."

He forced himself to relax. Una had done him no wrong. She was not responsible for his weaknesses and should not have to bear with his temper if some difficulty of his own momentarily discomforted him.

"It is so with me as well," he told her. "I was born amidst highlands, and I am drawn by them to this day." The Falconer smiled softly and naturally. "Since coming here, though, the ocean has managed to put her spell on me as well, which she had never been able to do before."

He glanced at her.

"Your Seakeep has magic, Lady Una. I grant you that."

The woman looked out over her world.

"Aye," she murmured, "magic that can set one's heart at peace."

Una's attention was fixed upon her Dale, but it was at the Holdlady herself that the mercenary captain was looking, and she glanced at him with some surprise when she sensed the direction of his gaze.

"Is anything amiss?"

He flushed a little, for he had not realized he had been studying her so intently.

"No, Lady. I was thinking about your relationship with your land," he added hastily. "It is most uncommon."

"Surely my feeling for that is not so strange? I should imagine most Holdlords share it."

Tarlach shook his head.

"No," he replied slowly, "that is not true, at least not among those with whom I have had contact. They see their domains with the eyes of rulers or farmers or herdsmen and, naturally, as soldiers, and all, of course, see in them their homes and their roots and cherish them for that reason, but your look just now was that of a lover."

A sudden chill gust of wind caused him to glance skyward. Dark clouds seemed to be materializing out of the erstwhile vividly blue dome.

Tarlach sighed inwardly. Storms came on very quickly in these mountains, and by the look of it, there was no hope of returning to the tower before this one opened up. They would have to go to earth somewhere and wait it out, that or ride on and take a soaking.

He turned to his companion.

"Do we run or dive for cover?"

"Both. Our goal is near and will provide us with good shelter."

Hardly had she finished speaking than she sent her mare over the crest and began racing downslope at a pace which would have frightened many a fairly daring man.

The warrior watched her a moment before following after her. Whatever her other talents or lack of them, Una of Seakeep was as skilled with a horse as anyone he had ever met.

They had not been traveling long at this furious pace before the woman's mare leaped, almost flew, over a high hedge and disappeared from his sight. In another moment, Tarlach had joined her.

His eyes widened a little. They were within a very small field enclosed on all sides by a tall fence of mixed growth, its lowest point being that at which they had made their entry.

The grass was high and had obviously never been seriously grazed, but it was the wall of vegetation surrounding them which held his attention. Holly, fuchsia, mountain ash, and rhododendron rose up together in one seemingly continuous mass, while heather, broom, and an almost bewildering variety of smaller hedge plants, many brilliantly flowered, filled every space the larger growth left free.

Roses were here, too, wild roses, and, along the wall facing them, tiny, deep pink climbers that had clambered to the very top of the trees supporting them and were cascading in vivid sprays through their branches. In other places fragrant patches of honeysuckle provided a similarly dramatic display.

"This is incredible," he said softly after a moment's silence. "But how came it to be? You could never have done all this. Not even the roses could have been brought to this state in the full of your lifetime, and these trees . . ."

Una laughed.

"Of course I did not set them! I have done some pruning, right enough, but that is the extent of my interference with nature's handwork here."

"She had some other help, then. Many of these plants may be feral now, but they are not so in themselves. Human hands, some hands, put them or their ancestors in this place."

Several great drops of rain struck them, and Una caught his hand.

"Come, or we shall be drowned despite all our horses' efforts!"

"What about them?" he asked as he allowed himself to be drawn after her.

"They shall be fine. See, they are standing under cover already."

She led her companion into the shelter of a great holly. The leaves and branches were thick around and above them and seemed to form a natural tunnel leading into the very heart of the hedge.

They followed this to its end at the base of the ancient tree. Here, the branches lifted so that there was room in plenty for the mercenary to stand erect. A low, rather long grey rock stretched before the trunk, its top slightly rounded and comfortably smooth.

The Daleswoman seated herself on this and smiled up at him.

"Welcome to the Bower."

He sat beside her. It was an effort to conceal his nervousness, although objectively, he found nothing amiss with the place. What Una had already told him about her namesake was enough to set him on edge.

"When did you discover it?"

"As a child, shortly after I found the field. I was a dreadful little thing for burrowing in those long-gone days. Listen! You can hear the rain falling all around us, but scarcely a drop is coming through. It takes a proper deluge to penetrate this far."

Tarlach shivered and drew his cloak more tightly around himself.

"Enough of the wind seems to make it in."

She smiled.

"Not in proportion to the whole. Look at how the branches are dancing in the top layers above us. Besides, you would gladly take a lot more cold than this and a soaking outside with it to what we would be enduring in here from the biting clouds if the air were still."

"Biting clouds?"

"You must know them. Tiny, flying insects. They swarm by the thousands and ten thousands in dim places when there is little or no wind to keep them off."

"I do indeed! We call them the bitter motes."

The man shook his head ruefully.

"I remember one night—it was during my first service as a blank shield, too—my company was stationed in ambush awaiting an anticipated invasion of the holding to which we were bound. It was a hot, muggy evening in late summer without the barest breath of a breeze to stir the air. . . ."

"And the clouds were out?"

"Red raving, and we were under a command of total silence. We did not dare move so much as a hand to try to keep them off us, not that it would have done us much good."

Una laughed sympathetically.

"You poor things! Did the invaders come?"

"Not at all. They arrived a month later by an entirely different route."

She tried unsuccessfully to mask her smile.

"That must have been enough to make you consider seeking another lifeway."

"Just about," he admitted.

Another gust of wind reached them. Tarlach saw his companion shiver and burrow farther into her cloak. She straightened abruptly, with purpose, and his stomach muscles tightened. They had come here seeking more than shelter.

"Where is your friend?"

"In her own place, of course. You did not think that she lives here? This is merely the spot where we normally meet since we both love it so."

"How do you summon her?"

"It is not a summons really. Una is my friend, after all, not a servant. I just call to her with my mind, as she calls to me if she is the one to initiate the visit. Usually, I am the one to do it, for there is almost no delay in her response, whereas I must ride far to reach the Bower."

She stood up.

"I had best begin."

"Aye."

Una looked at him closely.

"Are you sure you will be all right?"

"Aye!"

She cringed mentally. That question had been a mistake, but she knew enough about him to realize that he was definitely not happy about any of this.

That could not be helped. They would have settled nothing if they rode home again without having fulfilled their mission.

Closing her eyes, she set herself to issuing the call that would bring her friend to her.

* * *

Tarlach watched uneasily for several minutes. He was beginning to feel relieved as time continued to flow by with no perceptible change occurring in their surroundings, but then Storm Challenger's warning hiss told him that it was only the weakness of his human senses which made it appear that all was still normal in the Bower.

For nearly a full minute longer, he could detect no difference, then the air before him began to shimmer, to stretch as it were, until he seemed to be looking into an inconceivably eerie passage.

A figure materialized at its farther end, indistinct at first but growing ever clearer as she approached, appearing rather to float than to physically walk. At last, all too soon for him, she stood before them, as real or seemingly real in the flesh as they were themselves.

The Falconer came to his feet in shock. His mind groped for and found Storm Challenger's, but the bird evinced only a surprise similar to his and the natural uncertainty engendered by this eldritch situation in which they found themselves. There was no fear on him and nothing at all of the anger all his kind instinctively displayed when confronted by any taint or work of the Shadow.

The newcomer was very alien, all the more distant despite and because of her beauty and the fact that she might almost have been human. Most frightening in his mind was her resemblance to Una of Seakeep. In face and form, they might almost seem one woman divided by some accursed enchantment, but closer observation revealed that the depth and breadth of a great ocean lay between them.

This being showed an uncommon stillness as well, but the calm in her expression was not that of one who accepted and had come to terms with a life that held its share of weight as well as joy and the ever-present potential to crush utterly. Hers was the empty peace of someone who had not been tested at all and who neither feared nor faced any threat of trial in a future maybe infinitely long.

The fair features were lovelier if anything than the human's but were somehow oddly chiseled, as if another race had a part in their fashioning.

The green eyes were at least alive, and if he could not fathom all that they held, he thought he could read something of the emotion flickering within them, a sadness and a hunger whose cause he wondered if any human might delve or comprehend.

That vanished in the moment of his identifying it, for her eyes, her whole face, lighted with pleasure when they rested on his Una. Whatever about his other doubts, that response told him that the bond between the two was quite real.

That, too, changed rapidly. The strange Una spotted him, and a veil dropped over her inner being.

She glanced inquisitively at the human woman.

"Sister?" Her voice was soft, like the Holdlady's but somewhat oddly though not unpleasantly pitched.

"This is the captain of the force who have come to help us. I thought it best that he meet with you to assure himself that we of Seakeepdale have no traffic with the Shadow."

The magnificent eyes fixed on him.

"I hope your mind is now easy on that score, Captain, or that it soon will be. This Dale and its people have ever been free of taint, from its earliest history right through the present moment." She smiled. "For my part, I love Seakeep as well and am grateful for this chance to give you my own thanks for your service." She made no mention of the fact that he was patently a blank shield, well paid for that service, no more than Una had drawn his profession down during her introduction of him.

Tarlach gave her salute, but he was glad to take refuge in his people's custom and make her no verbal reply. He was unsure of her, not of her allegiance to the Light, which both Storm Challenger and his own instinct affirmed, but of her purpose, and he did not know how much she might be able to read into the feelings behind any response he might make or what her reaction to his uncertainty would be.

He stepped back several paces into the living tunnel, leaving the pair to speak together in privacy as would be expected of him. He was, after all, no more than Una's escort. . . .

He watched them from that vantage, fighting the urge to force his way back in there and thrust himself as a sword and shield between the Holdlady and her almost-image.

More than an image! His heart gave a vicious leap. By the Horned Lord! That one was something far more!

It was a battle after that to restrain himself during the eternal minutes which followed, but he knew if he intervened now, whatever hope he had of reasoning with the Daleswoman would probably be ended. He must hold his peace for the moment, unless the stranger made some open threat against which he might rightly act, though to what effect, he could not even begin to hazard.

At last, after what in actuality was only a very few minutes, it was over. The alien woman withdrew down her passage as she had come.

No sooner did Una stand alone once more and his comrade had confirmed that the gate was truly closed than the Falconer was at her side. He seized her hands.

"What does that one want of you?" he demanded harshly.

The Holdlady started to answer sharply, but then she saw the tightness of his lips and read that which burned in his eyes.

"Nothing. She is my friend."

"She is you!—Una, she is your own self, different, aye, but you in spite of that!"

She stared at him as if he had gone mad.

"We are not the same, not in thought or totally in likings, and though we do look alike, I do not have quite her store of beauty. I know that is of no importance to your kind, but surely you must see it. The rest, you cannot know unless you accept my word, but that is before your own eyes."

"I have admitted that you are not the same and praise the Horned Lord for that, but yet, you two are one. I cannot explain how or why, but it is so. As for your appearance, Una of Seakeep, you judge yourself ill. You are fairer in any man's eyes than that strange . . . thing could ever be. You have shared human life. You are strong and weak, warm, because of that sharing . . ."

He stopped speaking. It was impossible to express concepts, to describe comprehensibly a situation so completely outside anything he had ever encountered or heard described before. He fully believed that even the Witches of Estcarp, with all their vaunted Power and learning, would have been utterly baffled by this, though for the first time in his life he heartily wished they had one of them here with them to help them front this mystery.

"Una, she is not of the Dark. I give you that, but still, I—I fear that she is trouble, and dire trouble, for you. Do nothing, grant her nothing, without careful and long thought lest you thereby take a step you might be powerless to retrace."

6

*T*arlach was in his usual place on the beach the following morning, standing in the shelter of a great rock. The sign of the previous day's storm was still on the sea, and he did not envy those manning the small boat far out in the bay whose antics he had been observing for some time with that part of his awareness not locked into his memory of that other Una.

He had been thoroughly surprised and much relieved by the Holdruler's response to his declaration. He had anticipated fury and well nigh a battle of wills with her—reason almost demanded it after so incredible a statement—but that had not occurred. Una had staunchly defended her friend, right enough, as he supposed was only to be expected, but once her initial astonishment had subsided, she had not set her back against him. She had neither condemned him nor dismissed his fears outright. Rather, with real humility, she had admitted that she herself had none of the answers necessary to refute him and no knowledge in the ways of the Old Ones. Given those limitations, she had acknowledged the wisdom of conducting herself with the circumspection he advised.

She had thanked him for his quickness of mind in detecting a potential for peril which neither she nor the two people she had most trusted in her life had even envisioned.

His head lowered. He had been so sensitive to that danger only because the strange Una was female and because she either possessed herself or could otherwise control enough Power to permit her to open a gate at will. How much credit did he deserve for that? He wondered what sort of response he would have made had their positions been reversed and the Daleswoman had found it needful to caution him in some relationship of his. To his shame, he knew full well that he would not have heard her with the same fairness and respect, that he probably would not have used her with courtesy at all, not even that which was her due as the one to whom his sword was bound.

His preoccupation was not so deep that he failed to hear the welcoming call Storm Challenger reserved for his mate. He looked up as the falcon left his shoulder to join Sunbeam in the air above, and he raised his hand in greeting to Brennan.

The lieutenant acknowledged it.

"I knew I would find you in this place."

His commander smiled.

"I am here often enough. I love to watch the way the bay changes with each new shading of light and hour."

The other looked at him.

"You are very drawn to this Dale."

Tarlach nodded.

"Seakeep has much to offer a man." He sighed, his mood sobering. "I hope war does not come here. It deserves better than that."

"I doubt it shall. There has been naught but peace since our arrival."

"Aye, but it is during the autumn and winter storms that a black wrecker will be active, not now."

"Assuming one is operating in this area at all. We have seen nothing to suggest that there is, no more than there has been any trouble with this Lord Ogin. We have not had so much as a sight of him."

"You knew it would probably be thus through the summer months," the captain replied in surprise. "As for the Lord of Ravenfield, he would logically remain quiet for a while and then begin pressing his suit with the Holdlady anew using other tactics."

"Aye, there is the Holdruler.—You were long in the returning yesterday."

Tarlach stiffened.

"What do you say?"

"Nothing."

"The storm caught us, and we took refuge against it, then had a long wait before it blew over." There was a sharpness in his tone which was rarely loosed on any of his own. "Do you imagine I would violate one to whom I am oath-bound, by violence or through seduction?"

"Seduction can be a mare's weapon."

The captain's hand struck the hilt of his blade.

"I would kill any other for that," he snarled.

Brennan stepped back a pace. He did not need the suddenly alerted falcons now swooping very close to the two men to tell him the depth of his friend's anger. Most righteous anger. He had done him ill in speaking as he had for no better reason than his annoyance over his commander's disappearance the previous day.

"Pardon craved, Comrade. It is just that more than one of us had begun to grow uneasy by the time you returned. You had given no one word of your plans, and we did not even know where to begin seeking you."

Tarlach's outrage cooled.

"That was foolishly done," he admitted. "In truth, I had allowed our employer to provoke my temper and acted under its lash." He shrugged. "That is done. Our purpose was sound. She gave me report of a place of Power, and I went to examine it, using her as my guide."

"What! I thought Seakeepdale held no such canker."

"The activity is intermittent."

"Tainted?"

"Neither Storm Challenger nor I detected any sign of that."

The Falconer leader found himself reluctant to reveal what had happened in the Bower. It was too strange for him to offer either explanation or assurance, and yet he felt to the depth of his being that the woman from beyond the gate represented no threat to anyone but the Holdlady of Seakeepdale. On the other hand, Una's position would of a certainty be compromised in his comrades' eyes if the story became known.

That must be avoided. She was already somewhat suspect, apparently, or Brennan's impatience would not have been expressed in the terms he had used just now, and the company was growing restless under the lack of real work and the seeming absence of the threat Una had described as her reason for hiring blank shields. Technically, that should not matter. They were sworn to give a twelve-months' service here, but the fact that they were bound to a woman might put stress on the strength of that oath in the minds of some, and he did not want to face the task of imposing obedience and discipline on any of his warriors. This was too good a unit to be so weakened.

Fortunately, his lieutenant seemed to accept his appraisal as he had spoken it, and to help forestall any further questioning, Tarlach turned his head to the sea, once more fixing his attention on the small vessel tossing on the still-angry water.

She was much nearer now, and he frowned as he continued to study her.

"Brennan, you had more time at sea than I. What do you make of that boat? I have been watching her on and off for about half an hour. Sometimes she travels fast, sometimes slow, as if with the wind, and occasionally she turns broadside to the waves as she is doing now, although she always eventually heads into them again."

The second man watched her closely for some minutes.

"She is probably sound enough, but I do not like the look of her. She is not moving right, as if she were only partially under control at times."

Brennan's head snapped up.

"She is in trouble! See, she is flashing something white, a sark perhaps."

"Rouse the Dalesfolk! They have probably seen her as well, but we cannot chance that they have not. I shall keep watch on her here."

Brennan nodded and raced for the nearest of the cottages, but he had not gone ten yards before he saw several girls and a couple of youths running like young coursing hounds down the beach toward the moored boats. Knowing matters to be in good hands, he returned to his commander after raising his hand to the Dalespeople to acknowledge their control of the emergency.

The strange vessel was soon taken in tow and brought ashore.

The three men aboard her, all well known to the Seakeep people, were tired but sound. They reported that they had been fishing off their own shore when their rudder had struck a submerged rock they admitted they should have avoided easily had overconfidence in the face of a too familiar danger not made them careless. They had rigged another rudder with their spare oar but had drifted out of their Dale's waters by then and had made for here with the intention of putting into Seakeep's harbor to properly complete their repairs.

When the sea had proven a little too rough for their makeshift rudder, however, they had grown afraid and had begun signaling for help. There were few other landing places beyond this point besides Ravenfield's single small beach, and all three readily confessed their unwillingness to venture into that territory, which had always been known as a dangerous coast and had gained an even worse name for wrecks and lost ships in recent years.

Tarlach's eyes met his lieutenant's as the eldest of the fishermen, he who was telling the tale of his vessel's adventures, made that last statement.

Brennan nodded. That was the sign the Falconers needed. There was no doubting the sincerity of the seamen's fear, their acceptance and avoidance of a locally acknowledged peril, and there would be no further thought of leaving Seakeep before the term of their service ended.

7

With the willing help of Seakeep's fisherfolk to speed their work, the strange fishermen had soon completed the repair of their boat and were gone again before the afternoon had moved very far toward evening.

The new feeling of purpose they left behind them in the mercenary warriors would hold firm, and already the Falconers looked upon their routine guarding as a matter of need and of some importance. Perhaps the still-quiescent Lord of Ravenfield might not prove to be the source of the peril the three had so casually confirmed, but someone was, and there was no question about the need to keep this harbor secure against that renegade.

Despite fortune's solving that trouble for him, Tarlach's mood remained dark all that day and continued dark into the next so that he was glad enough to keep to his quarters, out of sight of his comrades and the Dalesfolk alike, while he attended to the record keeping that was the bane of every commander responsible for more than a mere handful of warriors.

He was not pleased to hear a soft, almost secretive knock around midmorning but gave the call for admittance.

He scowled when the Holdlady entered, but a high-pitched meow drew his attention to the minute kitten she was holding against her, and he glanced into eyes glowing so brilliantly that they were well-nigh aflame.

The Falconer came to his feet and hastened to meet her.

"You have bonded with your comrade already!"

"I have indeed!" She hesitated. "I am sorry to intrude on your work, but there was no one else to whom I could introduce her." Once more, excitement overcame her. "I never imagined it could be like this!"

He laughed.

"It was the same with me when I was first so chosen, my Lady."

Tarlach stroked the tiny animal with his forefinger. She was a tortoiseshell, seemingly all fur and with huge, very round, and quite fearless eyes.

"She is a delight and should be a beauty when she grows." He glanced at the woman. "She is very young, though. What made you seek out an animal so immature?"

"I did not, not intentionally. I chanced on her this morning. She was defending herself claws and teeth against one of the dogs, who had cornered her. He meant business and would have ended the matter in another few seconds had I not intervened, but there was no cringing or thought of surrender to him or to death on her."

"You did not haul the brute off her?" he asked quickly.

"Hardly! My skin is still whole.—I should have done that had I been forced to it, but I merely told him in mind to be about his proper work and not to trouble again those who should be his charges. He went off suitably chastened."

"And your little friend was grateful?" he inquired, masking his relief.

"Much more! I asked where I might find her mother to reunite them, but she refused to tell me or to leave me." The woman smiled indulgently. "She is very strong-willed."

"You are well met there," he said dryly. "What have you named her, or was she kin-named already?"

"I called her Bravery. After that stand of hers, she merits it."

"In truth."

Tarlach took the little creature and examined her carefully.

"A fine animal. She should prosper well. Remember, though," he added, recalling his own excitement with his first chick, "it will be a while yet before you can take her adventuring with you."

"I think my maternal instincts are quite intact, Captain," she told him tartly as she retrieved Bravery from his hold.

Their hands brushed together during the transfer of the kitten, and the Falconer stiffened.

He glared at the Daleswoman.

"You have brought me the queerest commission I have ever had the misfortune to hold," he told her savagely.

Tarlach stopped himself.

"I am a fool," he said, "and an arrant boor besides. All this must be twice as difficult for you."

"I do not find your company unwelcome," she answered, turning her face from him. "I have come to see you as a true friend rather than merely as an ally."

The color rose a little in the cheek visible to him.

"If I wrong you by saying this, I pray you pardon me. You know that I—I would not insult or lessen you."

"Insult? Your regard is not that."

He took a step nearer her.

"Una of Seakeep, you would be the delight and strength of any lord fortunate enough to win you for all that remained to him of eternity. Too often I have heard you indicate otherwise in your speech. That is an injustice to yourself and to Seakeep; such thought can move you to choose for your lord a man less worthy than you and your Dale merit and should gain."

He turned away.

"It is not my right to speak thus to you."

The woman smiled.

"You have every right. Have I not called you my friend?"

The jade eyes studied him speculatively.

"Your comrades have been giving you trouble?"

His quickly masked start gave her the Falconer's answer although he himself was unwilling to admit the accuracy of her guess.

"Why do you ask that?" he inquired evasively.

"Because it almost needs must be so. Your people do not appear to enjoy idleness. You have had more to do than the rest of your command since coming here. Now that the others are rested and have gotten some feel for the Dale, they cannot find the guarding of the one overland entrance very challenging. They do not even have responsibility for watching the gorge at the Square Keep since you have set your falcons that task. They would have to be wanting something to properly occupy them, even without the irritant that I must represent." Her eyes fell momentarily. "Idleness must be aggravating that, too."

"You are sharp, Lady. Your reading of us is not far off, but have no fear that we shall break faith with Seakeep." His eyes glinted coldly. "Your fisherman neighbors have thoroughly convinced my warriors of the need for our presence. We are all one in our hatred for sea wolves and black wreckers, and we regard both as our rightful prey."

"Thanks given, Bird Warrior," she said in a voice husky enough to tell him that she had been more than passing concerned on that subject.

"Our oath would have kept us here," he told her stiffly.

"I know, but it is better, infinitely better, that you hold to it willingly."

For several moments, neither spoke. The man found the silence oppressive, but a constraint had fallen on them both, and he did not know how to break it.

Bravery cried then in a voice astonishingly loud for her size, as if to express her disapproval of this change in the atmosphere around her.

He smiled again and once more stroked her.

"If you can bear to part for a while from this little one, I should like for you to ride with me. Although I have studied the gorge several times, I have not actually entered the Square Keep. In that, I have been remiss. It doubtless still has potential as a defensive position usable either for or against our cause."

"I shall have put on riding garments by the time you have ordered our horses to be made ready."

The Falconer scowled as he headed for the stables. It was indeed his business to check out the old keep both for its military potential as he had stated and to see if it might show any sign of use by forces of either the Light or the Shadow, but he knew the way right well without having to call for a guide.

He shook his head angrily. Did he jest with himself? Like it or not, after that meeting in the Bower, he was going to have to keep very close to the Holdruler of Seakeep. He did not know precisely how far his oath to defend her actually extended, but to his mind, it included shielding her to the best of his ability from the effects of possible ensorcellment as well as from plain cold steel. To do that, he would have to make sure that she could not be summoned to another such rendezvous while he was at some distant place and unable to reach her.

It was important to him that he succeed. The strength of that importance surprised and troubled him a little, but there was no point in denying that he cared about Seakeep. He did not want to see disaster strike here, and he did not want to see it strike the Holdlady herself, so much so that he had been moved to speak as he had earlier though it went against both his own training and his position here. If Una set up the wrong man as lord in Seakeepdale, the result could be as bad as an invasion. It could be worse.

In a sense, it was a pity he was what he was. Seakeep's last two male rulers had ridden as blank shields . . .

Tarlach stopped in mid step, then he began to laugh softly. The men of his race had often been accused of taking themselves too seriously by a mile's march, and if he was not the proving of that now, no one ever would be. Was he another Ogin, then, with an opinion of himself so inflated that he imagined his suit would be welcome beyond any question of its success? The idea of his seeking a Holdlord's place was so ludicrous that it was funny only. He could not bring himself to so far dignify it as to chide himself for having entertained it in the first place.

The course they followed was a rugged one, and they had to cross a good part of it on foot leading their animals, but the Daleswoman moved along it with nigh unto the same ease as she would have shown negotiating an overgrown walk.

The pair made reasonably good time, and since there was no need for haste on them, they stopped to rest after traversing a particularly difficult stretch although they had not scheduled a break at that point.

Una sat on the thick heath and breathed deeply of the sweet air, drinking of it as if it were wine.

The man settled himself beside her, as glad for the chance to stop as she was.

"No wonder you were able to endure so well on our march here after training over such ground."

"Am I going too quickly?" she asked contritely. "I know this area so well that I am not very troubled by it, but you are new . . ."

Tarlach only laughed.

"You forget that every land is new to me. This pace will not try me overmuch."

He looked at her curiously.

"How is it that you have learned to move through a wilderness like this? I have never before seen such ability in a Daleswoman and rarely anything approaching it in one of your men, apart from trained scouts or hunters."

She smiled, pleased but a little embarrassed.

"I was always one for exploring, and my father instilled in me the belief that one who would rule a Dale must be knowledgeable about it and all its workings."

"It was Lord Harvard who had you taught the use of a sword?" he asked curiously.

"Aye. It amused him at first, but I think he was less than pleased later when I proved good with the weapon." She sighed. "To his credit, he let me continue to train with it. He was a firm believer in maintaining a sound body, and he did not consider wielding a needle or strumming a lute an effective substitute for physical exercise."

"That is why you also ride so well?"

"In part, though all Seakeep people have that ability to some extent. Our horses are such that they demand perfection from us. Anything less than skill with them would be a desecration." Her eyes sparkled. "He even insisted that I learn how to swim and sail because those were skills useful to a seabound folk."

Una's brows furrowed.

"He never thought I might have need of battle skills, though, that I might have to rule and lead an imperiled Seakeep."

"Those can be learned," the Falconer told her. "You have the basics already to judge by the way you handled yourself that day we met."

She looked quickly away, biting hard on her lip to keep it from trembling. That was a memory she did not cherish.

The captain's hand just brushed hers.

"Forgive me, Lady," he said gently. "The first slaying is ever harsh even for those of us trained to such work."

She smiled, grateful for what he offered.

"Does it ever truly become easier?"

"Aye, but for most of us never a pleasure. We all know to beware the man who takes joy in bringing death."

Tarlach saw that she was ready to go and, coming to his feet, gave his hand to help raise her. They set out at once and soon fell silent again, devoting their attention to the mountainside rising before them.

They had traveled thus for some two hours longer when the woman came to a halt and silently pointed with her small hand.

The thick forest through which they had been riding ended abruptly at the place in which they were standing. A tall cliff rose up above them, and on its summit stood a most strange ruin, its sturdy walls still strong despite the weight of the years, of the centuries, resting upon them.

It was a keep, square in shape, its stern face broken by a very few narrow slits scarcely large enough to allow a bowman space to aim and discharge his weapon.

Her eyes ran proudly up the forbidding, powerful walls.

"The Square Keep was discovered much as you now see it by the first of my people to reach Seakeep after coming to this land and beginning what we now call our history.

"According to the tale he told later, the spirit of this land came to our lord in a dream in the form of a noble maiden, or came in her own self as some would have, and told him that this place was his and his line's for the taking if he willed to have it, but that if he did so, it would be with the understanding that his blood would be carried through his daughters.

"He did so will, and his heirs—all daughters as foretold since no male child has ever been born to our house— and the heirs of the people who followed him have dwelled here even unto the present day."

"Ravenfield and the other Dales?"

"They were settled at the same time, quietly as ours was, but they were spared even so much contact with those who had ruled High Hallack in the far past. We were all fortunate in that respect. In many other places, men have been seared and their lines cursed by brushes with the Old Ones and their works.''

"You read that truly," Tarlach agreed readily after a short silence while he studied the ancient building.

"The keep, can we enter it freely, or is that dangerous? You have said it has been a ruin for a long time.''

"Very long, but, aye, we may explore if we use reasonable caution.''

The old fortress proved most interesting although they were not actually very long in the exploring of it.

The ground level consisted of one great chamber. The floors above, three of them, were linked to one another and with the first by a narrow, ever-twisting staircase running upwards through the incredibly thick walls. The chambers inside, those they could see, since the woman's fear of venturing too far out onto what little remained of the ancient floors kept them to the outer parts of the keep, were all dank with the barren cold born of centuries of disuse, and dim, for the few narrow windows admitted little light to the interior.

The stairs ended in a slender doorway that brought them out onto the ramparted roof.

The view from this high place was spectacular, but more than that, it showed clearly along its entire length the only passage piercing the high wall of mountains forming Seakeepdale's inland boundary in this area. At the opposite end of this gorge lay Ravenfield.

"I want to scout it out again since we are so near," the warrior told her. "Our falcons' reports are good and complete, but it does a commander no harm to observe a position firsthand now and then.''

"Very well, Captain. Let us go. The way down to it is easier than the one we followed coming to the keep.''

8

*R*avenfield's lands differed very little in appearance from Seakeep's, mountains stretching out on every side wild, forbidding, and beautiful. There was more and richer arable soil in Ogin's domain and much less seacoast, but neither fact could have been ascertained from this place where the two Dales met.

"An invasion could be mounted through here," the mercenary told his companion, "but I would not like to be serving under the commander desperate enough to lead it. A dozen men set where we are standing could annihilate an army trying to reach Seakeep from this gate, and it would require precious little warning for us to place the ambush."

"And if they did pass through here, they would still have to cross all the country between, much of which can be readily defended, and would then be faced with the prospect of taking the road into the valley itself."

He nodded.

"Not an easy task, but any man capable of black wrecking is not one to be underestimated."

The Holdlady gasped suddenly.

"Speak of dark dreams, and one's sleep is shattered!—Do you see that vale to the right on our side of the gorge? A stream runs through its center."

"I see it. There is a rider on the farther bank. One of Ogin's people?"

"Ogin himself unless I am badly mistaken. He has an odd seat although he is a fine horseman."

She watched the Lord of Ravenfield for several seconds.

"He cannot see us. Shall we slip away or confront him?"

"Is there wrong in his being here? He is on your land."

The enforcement of boundary integrity varied greatly from section to section and even from Dale to Dale within a given area.

"None at all," she replied. "Border jealousy is rare here. There is too little to spy out or damage save around the keeps themselves. He could legitimately be seeking animals strayed over here, hunting, or merely enjoying a ride."

"Or he could be reconnoitering the territory even as we," Tarlach said grimly. "He has heard of my company's presence in Seakeep by this time and cannot but have divined the cause of your hiring us. He could be preparing to strike the first blow in the hope of crippling us through surprise."

"Aye, or that."

The Falconer's eyes narrowed for a moment.

"I would meet this neighbor of yours. Let him come upon us, though. We shall see if he chooses to hail us or withdraw unseen."

They slipped away from their vantage point and, mounting their horses, carefully worked their way down so that they would not be observed before they were ready to show themselves.

Both tensed as they at last moved into the open, wondering how the interloper would respond to their presence.

Ogin was not long in spotting them. Either his mission and heart were indeed light, or his nerve and speed of decision were those of a master general, for he called out to them almost at the moment of sighting, or, rather, he called to Una, whom he obviously recognized as readily as she had him.

He was a striking man, Tarlach saw as they drew near him. Of average height, Ravenfield's lord was of a stocky build, all muscle with nothing of fat upon him. His face was square in keeping with his body. Its complexion was ruddy beneath a deep tan. Ogin's eyes were dark under heavy, black brows. His hair was very dark as well with a pronounced wave. It showed the barest hint of thinning at the crown. His features were well formed except for the lips, which were uncommonly narrow, making his mouth seem no more than a hard slit across his face.

He inclined his head toward the woman in a courtly fashion.

"You are far from home, Lady Una," he remarked pleasantly after exchanging greetings with her.

"As are you, my Lord."

"Indeed, and I am a trespasser besides. I was rough-training this colt when I caught sight of a fine hart and gave chase."

"I am sorry to have broken your hunt, then."

He laughed.

"You but spared my pride, Lady. My horse was too inexperienced for such work in this country, and I lost the beast."

The shrewd eyes flickered to the mercenary, who had remained silent and a little behind his companion during the exchange.

"What fear has come upon you, Lady Una, that you ride your own lands with warrior escort? That had never been your wont."

"Only the times, my Lord. Too many have been sent wandering and running whom it would not be well for a woman, or a man either, for that matter, to meet while traveling alone."

He eyed the Falconer's winged helm coldly. It was a chance and perhaps a reckless one, but this meeting just might be made to work for his good.

"A single warrior, my Lady?—That one will be of no use to you. All this solitude is wasted on his sort—"

Ogin said no more. He wanted to swallow but dared not lest the needle point of the sword pressing against his throat penetrate the flesh and the windpipe beneath.

"My charge includes defense of my liege's name as well as her person, Lord Cur," Tarlach said with an icy fury in which the other man read the will to his death. "You have made assault on that, and hers is the right of judging your fate.''

''Let him go free,'' Una commanded.

Her own voice, her face, were fixed with disdain.

''This now closes the question that was between us, Ogin of Ravenfield. Your insult to me I shall not forgive, and more unpardonable still is the slur you cast at this warrior who has bound his sword in honorable service to me. You may leave unharmed now, but if he or any of his comrades should take you again on my lands, he may exact whatever penalty his honor demands from you.—Now go, before I alter my command and allow him to loose his blade on you!''

The Holdlord eyed the lowered but still-ready weapon in the mercenary's hand and the falcon already circling his head and made no issue of the matter. His gamble had miscarried and more violently than he might have imagined. He could only count his losses and lay other plans to gain the end he was determined to secure.

Without a word to either of them, he jerked his mount's head around and turned back toward his own domain.

The Falconer glared after him.

''The bastard,'' he muttered savagely. ''I should have cut him down where he sat!''

''He was angry at my having outmaneuvered him by blunting the threat he represented, and perhaps he hoped to drive a wedge between your people and your oath.''

''He is a fool as well, then. Because he is void of honor, does he imagine we are all of his ilk? My race must be harshly judged indeed if that is the way we are viewed.''

''It would have been an ill deed all the same to fell him for a word.''

Tarlach looked closely upon her and saw the tightness of her manner; she had not enjoyed the insult. Like himself, she had reined her anger, aye, and her slashed pride as well. This one was worthy to have command over others, as worthy as was any lord under whom and with whom he had served throughout the years of the war and since.

"The break between you is open now," he observed.

She sighed.

"That was inevitable once he spoke as he did. I suppose he knew my answer anyway, and my determination to resist force, once he learned I had brought blank shields to Seakeep. Our folk made sure that news spread where it should go as soon as you arrived."

She sighed again.

"It is probably for the best that it happened. Now he will either have to take direct action against us, which he is not likely to do with your company to stand our defense, or else content himself with his present base and level of activity."

The captain straightened.

"Activity which I hope we can soon put to an end," he said quietly; if he had ever doubted it before, he firmly believed now that the dark-eyed Dalesman was fully capable of doing all the people of Seakeep suspected of him. "Let us go, Lady. It is growing late, and I would not make our camp too near this place."

Una nodded. With his hope of obtaining Seakeepdale through marriage shattered, Ogin of Ravenfield might well consider some work of treachery against them.

They rode as fast as the terrain would permit for the rest of that day and well into the evening, concealing their trail with all the cunning bred and trained into the Falconer over the long years when his life had at times depended as much or more upon his ability to move silently and quickly as upon his skill with a sword.

There was only so much that even he could do, however, with their destination and general direction known, and the captain frowned darkly when they finally ceased their run for the night. No camp could be so carefully hidden that it could not be discovered.

"Come," he said suddenly after they had finished eating the portion of their supplies allotted to that evening's meal, "we shall make our bed in the branches above."

Una started but followed him without protest.

He led her some distance from the area they had disturbed before stopping beneath one of the forest giants towering high above them. Using their belts to help them grip and hold the smooth-grained bark, they climbed to the lowest branch and from there to the one above, a limb so broad that they could have walked erect upon it for a full third of its length had they been so daring as to make the attempt.

The woman was glad that her companion was not so inclined, and she was relieved when he indicated that they would not have to go any higher. She gingerly maneuvered herself until her back rested against the solid roundness of the trunk and from this position of relative security rather unhappily surveyed the place where she was to pass the night. She had no fear of heights, but neither did she like to dwell upon the fall she could take with the slightest loss of balance.

If Tarlach was aware of her unease, he gave no sign of it. Moving as cautiously as she had before him, he settled himself beside her.

Una steeled herself and slid a little to her right to give him more room.

His arm closed around her.

"Stay still. There is space for both of us up here. If we take it in turn to watch so that one of us is always alert, we should have a secure if an uncomfortable night."

She smiled despite herself.

"Ogin willing."

"Ogin willing," he agreed, "and I believe he will leave us in peace to enjoy it."

"That is why we are perched up here like a pair of nestless birds?"

He laughed.

"I live today because I learned early to guard against even unlikely peril, but if I felt we were actually in danger, I would not have permitted us to stop at all."

Una sighed to herself, knowing he was right.

"In any event," she said after a moment's silence, "the first watch is mine."

"Do you think I would allow you to sleep through?" he asked a little sharply.

"Maybe you would, maybe not, but I do know that your senses are better trained than mine and will be needed in the darkness of the late hours and in the strange light of predawn. We should have little to fear during the first part of the night. Ogin had no warriors with him, and he would not attempt to ride after us alone. Even if he had a company waiting fairly close by, he would still have to return for them, then come back again, discover our trail, and follow it. Despite our stopping, he can hardly overtake us very quickly. In fact, I am more concerned about the possibility of some sort of ambush near the tower than I am of any direct pursuit."

The mercenary looked at her with new respect.

"You read it as I do.—Have no fear. We shall be watching for any such trap, although I truly do not think we shall meet with one. The Lord of Ravenfield could not have known we would be riding here, and I do believe that he was traveling alone. You have told me that is the practice here save when it is known that brigands are active in the area, and lack of an escort precludes an impromptu ambush." As if to emphasize his words, he yawned. "For now, my Lady, it is best that we try for whatever rest we can find."

The Falconer did not sleep immediately although the weariness of an active day was full upon him.

He was resting partly against the tree, partly against his companion. He had no fear of falling. The slender arm around him was strong in its support and would hold him should he begin to slip, at least long enough for him to become aware of and avert his danger.

He looked up. Even his night-trained eyes could discern no more than a shadow profile of the Daleswoman, so thick had the darkness become.

That was enough, more than enough.

Tarlach closed his eyes again and allowed his consciousness of her to sweep through him.

The nearness of her was as a flame, lighting every nerve, every instinct, within him. He longed to close that lovely body in his arms, to lie beside and with her . . .

A fury of self-loathing filled him, and he crushed the unwelcome passion. Was this the best that could be expected of one of his race, then, this rapid capitulation to the forces working on all men, and in a manner utterly degrading to his honor? It was vile beyond any violation of discipline to even think of so using one dependent upon his protection. Una of Seakeep needed him now. She trusted him, and she must never come to suspect the extent to which his supposed strength had failed him.

9

Their precautions were either totally successful or quite unnecessary, and the pair reached the round tower unmolested late the following morning. There, they separated, Una to apprise Rufon of all that had befallen them, and Tarlach to make report of this first meeting with their potential enemy to his own comrades.

His tale ended, the captain flung himself into the heavily carved chair Brennan drew up for him, his expression threatening and dark.

"That one merits the hating," he muttered.

His fury against Ogin of Ravenfield had returned in all its force during his recounting of their exchange, and he felt little need to mask it among these men.

"Is the man feeble-brained?" Rorick asked. "What could he have hoped to accomplish by provoking you two like that?"

"Probably precisely what the Holdlady suggested, to force a wedge between us with that slur on her name. It would have been to his benefit to strip her of defense again by driving us off.''

Brennan laughed without humor.

''He erred, then. I have rarely seen you with your back up like this.''

''I dislike someone trying to manipulate me as if I were a witless child,'' his commander replied hastily. ''How do you accept it?''

''None of us care for insult. I think Ogin of Ravenfield may discover us rather more interested in the fight than he might otherwise have found us if it comes to that now.''

''Aye, and he recognizes his mistake. Be assured of that. He does not strike me as one who habitually so fouls his tactics, either.'' He shook his head. ''I pity anyone giving him cause to vent his spleen at the moment.''

''What is your judgment of him?'' Brennan questioned. ''Apart from your dislike of him, how would you class him as an opponent?''

Tarlach paused, choosing his words carefully.

''Intelligent, capable, willful and quick of temper but, I think, usually in better command of himself than he showed us—a dangerous man and, I believe, one with the ability to induce others of his ilk to fight well for his sake. He is not an enemy we dare ignore.''

''You believe that Seakeep does have cause to fear him, then?''

He nodded.

''I do, and after our meeting yesterday, that fear may not be very far from being confirmed in action.''

His lieutenant was frowning.

''One thing I do not understand. We have heard the explanation of how he comes to have a strong and able garrison when those of his neighbors are all much reduced, but a crew capable of black wrecking is another matter. The Dalesfolk here and the admittedly few outsiders making use of the bay whom we have observed all seem to be honest, human people, right poor material for such work even if they were compelled by force to undertake it.''

"Such can be hired. Ogin has left his Dale on occasion since he gained possession of it with no explanation of his destination given to his neighbors. He could well have been gathering the renegades he required to him and settling them in his chosen lair. The Ravenfield folk would by and large have been kept ignorant of their presence and purpose, and any happening to learn about them would have been slain outright or silenced by terror.''

Tarlach went to the long table which served the mercenaries as a desk and spread a map on its ample surface. Ogin's wrecker activities were the most hateful of his presumed offenses, but they must be relegated to a secondary position in their regard for the moment; it was his possible role as an invader to which they must now address their attention.

The Falconer company was still together, clustered around their officers and deep in discussion, when Rufon entered the barracks.

Tarlach gave him a nod of greeting and looked inquisitively at him. The veteran had assumed the role of liaison between the clannish mercenaries and those people of Seakeep needing to deal with them, and he thought that the Dalesman might be acting as Una's messenger now. Although her position gave her the right to do so, she had never yet intruded upon them in their quarters.

That assumption proved accurate, and he soon found himself in the great hall. Una was standing near its center, alone for the moment, a pillar of quiet set amidst a scene of uncommon activity.

The man's eyes narrowed. There was no panic, but this bustle went well beyond the normal press of activity usually to be found here. That seemed to bespeak some sort of trouble.

He was even more convinced that something was seriously amiss when he reached her side a few moments later and saw the grave cast of her features.

"What is wrong, my Lady?"

The green of her eyes seemed to deepen as they fixed on him.

"Are Falconers permitted to do work not related to battle?"

"What work?" Tarlach asked in surprise.

"A storm comes, one of the sea's mighty gales, though it is very early in the season for those, and the most of our harvest is still in stacks upon the fields. If we cannot bring it in before that tempest strikes, our animals will feel hunger's lash this winter."

"You wish us to help you draw it in?"

"Aye, if you would not find the task demeaning. Without your help, a good part of the crop is certain to be lost."

"We are not like those lords who think the labors supporting their domains are somehow beneath them, Lady, and we, too, love our animals, though they be less fine than yours; we have no wish to see them hungry. The help you want is yours, but it shall come from only half our number, the others I shall have to hold in reserve for our defense."

"Ogin can read the signs as well as we. He will not mount an attack now."

"Not if he is still within his keep, perhaps, or very near to it, but if I were he and already well en route, I would press my assault, hoping to come upon my enemies while they were laboring in their fields and unprepared for treachery and then shelter my army in the captured tower or in the cottages and outbuildings if that still held out when the gale struck."

"You are right as always in these matters," the woman conceded with admiration, but then she shuddered. "How terrible your life must be for your mind to ever have to flow to war and the work of death."

"My life is a blank shield's, and my thoughtways are a major reason for your having hired my sword."

"Aye, and yet I am sorry you have not known more of peace."

The man smiled.

"We, too, have our times of quietness. If that were not so, I should hardly be able to appreciate, much less enjoy as I do, all I have found here. It is just that other peoples rarely see us in such moments. They are not likely to come often during our periods of service with you."

The grey eyes shadowed.

"This commission has been an exception to that, and soon even Seakeep may become prey to violence and hate. . . ."

"Perhaps the Amber Lady will spare us that," Una said quickly, "or the Horned Lord, war being his province."

He threw the mood from him.

"Maybe they shall, but they mean to test us all the same in another way if your reading of the weather is sound.— Let us be away, my Lady, and see to this work of harvesting."

The mercenaries labored all that afternoon and evening beside the Dalespeople, racing the ominously darkening sky and rising wind to bring what was an unusually rich harvest under cover before it could all be swept away.

Every cart was pressed into service and every available beast, horse, mule, ox, and ass. Many drew the wagons with their loads of saved hay and oats. Others slung the great stacks in, hauling them out of the fields by rope without the aid of any vehicle.

Workers stationed in the barns and sheds piked each load inside, straining to have one in its place before the next was delivered.

Although ever threatening in its aspect, the weather continued to hold throughout the afternoon and evening, and when Tarlach at last stood at the window of his chamber which gave him the best view of the cultivated area, it was to look upon gratifyingly empty meadows, half of which would still be full had it not been for the aid furnished by his command.

Night was nearly upon the world, for the black clouds choking all the sky gave little room for an extended twilight, but the waning sun still provided enough illumination to reveal the tight patchwork of Seakeep's fields.

The greater number and also the smallest were the gardens bearing the Dale's fruits and vegetables. These had not been emptied of their crops, which had not been ready for harvesting even had there been time to take them in.

Such tiny fields, he thought, and now more than ever, he appreciated the wisdom of those who had made them thus, minute plots surrounded by high, firm stone ditches which would protect the crops growing within from the gale's anger and hold the carefully tended soil in its place despite heavy rains and steep slope. So it had proved since the settling of Seakeepdale, and so, he believed and hoped, it would prove tonight.

He shivered. The big room was cold despite the roaring fire. After setting the siege shutters firmly in place over each of the windows and securing them, he returned to the inner portion of his quarters and prepared himself for bed. There would be no point and less pleasure in remaining up very much longer this night.

10

*T*he rain began soon after he had retired but remained no more than a particularly heavy downpour for a long time. Then, two hours after midnight, such a blast of wind struck the tower that the warrior snapped awake, grasping the sword which was never beyond the reach of his hand.

Even as he took hold of it, he released it once more, recognizing the source of the disturbance.

The man rose quickly and went to the screened window nearest him. He opened the observer's port set into the shutter but could see nothing beyond save a seemingly infinite blackness.

His eyes shut as a searingly brilliant flash of white light filled all the world around him, and he hastily closed the tiny port once more lest he be soaked by the cascade of rain forcing its way through the small opening.

Tarlach went back to his bed. He did not return to sleep, for the hammering of the gale-driven torrent, the almost continuous lashing of the lightning, and the exploding thunder were overwhelming in their violence and would not be dismissed from his awareness. Lying there, listening to the tempest's fury, the mercenary commander did not believe he was alone tonight in welcoming the thick stone walls around him.

He must have dozed at some point, for when awareness again returned to him, it was to find Storm Challenger tugging at his hand impatiently and none too gently with his cruelly sharp bill.

Tarlach heard it then, a knock scarcely audible against the chaos raging outside.

He sprang from his bed. The light from the still-flickering fire was sufficient for his needs, and he did not bother to reach for a candle. Since the war bird told of no danger but rather pushed him to action, though without explanation, he hastened to the door and drew it open.

Una. She was fully clad in the garments she had worn before retiring and was holding a candle, whose flame danced wildly despite the shelter she tried to give it with her cupped hand. Her eyes were huge and her face too white for its pallor to be explained by the hour and dim light. He saw that Bravery was clinging to her sleeve.

The Falconer ushered her inside, carefully closing the door behind her.

"My Lady, what has happened?" He did not even think to insult her by asking if it was the storm that was troubling her.

"She came to me. My sister. The other Una."

He knew that he whitened himself. Although the room

was cold and he was bare before her to the waist, he forgot his intention of drawing his cloak around himself.

"Here?" he whispered.

She nodded.

"Aye. She said she actually has the freedom of any of the Old Places."

He led her to one of the two chairs in the chamber.

"What did she want?"

Una drew a deep breath to steady herself.

"I had remained up to make record of our harvest and to attend to some other business I had let lapse a while and was about to prepare for bed—"

"You were alone?"

She nodded.

"Except for Bravery. I often work late and always dismiss my waitingwoman when I do."

"She came then?"

"Aye, and in haste. She had all but stepped from her passage before I was aware of its opening. Once here, she quickly told me the purpose of her visit, first describing her nature and then confirming what many have come to believe about this world, that the forces of Light and true Dark battled fiercely here at one time and that at long last, after awesome destruction, the forces of Light partially conquered, not totally but securing supremacy enough to impose the balance of life once more and to put checks upon those many servants and works of Shadow and Dark which could not be utterly overcome."

"This other Una, what was her role in that war?"

"None save that of a distant victim." She shivered, and not from the chill. "You were right about her in a sense. She is me, or, rather, she is what I would have been had the Shadow never found entrance into this world, but she is not whole. She has no actual substance and no real place in this time or any other time."

Una bit down on her lip, fighting to retain hold on her composure before this man whom she feared would have small patience with any display of weakness or hysteria, although it was pity, grief, and not fear that was chiefly driving her.

"She was content to remain as she was and to make herself accept that role and—and just hope that better might eventually come, but conditions around us have changed to the point that she felt she could no longer do so. The old balance has been troubled. Not only in High Hallack but throughout all this world, Power has been wielded and forces awakened which have long slept, to such an extent that she says the time left to all of us might well be short, so short that she feared if she was ever to have life, real human life, she was going to have to claim it at once."

She saw Tarlach stiffen, as if he knew what she was about to say and rejected it utterly.

"Una wished to meld her spirit with mine so that she would become part of me and I of her—"

"No!"

The woman shook her head impatiently, silencing him.

"It would mean the life she so craved, and I should have knowledge and the key to the Power she says lies within me."

"No!—Una, you did not . . ."

His fingers bore into her shoulders so that she winced although she would not permit herself to cry out. He seemed scarcely to notice but did ease the pressure of his grasp.

"Una, what answer did you make her?"

The Holdruler's head lowered.

"I wanted to grant her wish. She pleaded and reasoned so passionately, but I was afraid. Something deep within myself rebelled against the very thought of what she required of me. I battled myself and my selfishness, but I could not bring myself to agree.

"Bravery struck then. With her mind and all the strength of her body, she tried to force me out of that room and here to you. That was when I recalled my promise to you, and I told Una that I could make no such decision in a moment, based only on emotion and excitement, that I must weigh it in all its aspects when my mind was cooler and more open to reason.

"She grew angry, naming me a coward and the falsest of friends, then told me to stay as I am and face life and what it might throw at me with the weapons I might have had forever tight sheathed. After that, she—she flung herself into her passage and vanished."

"The Horned Lord be praised," he whispered.

Tarlach realized his hands were shaking and hastily withdrew them. He had been blind, he thought dully, intentionally blind, but this infinite peril had stripped away that comfortable denial. He knew now what Una of Seakeep was to him. He did not merely long to satisfy himself with that beautiful body. He wanted the woman for his companion, to cherish and guard and grow ever closer to her for the whole that remained to him of life and to center that life around her.

"Una, that offer was of the Dark. Had you yielded, you would have been lost, and so, too, would your . . . sister."

"No! She is not—"

"Herself, no, but the Shadow's ways can be seductive. Think what she suggested. Was this not the fate that befell our women in those ancient days? They, too, became, not individuals any longer, but extensions of another." He paused lest his voice begin to tremble and betray him. "Her purpose for asking this does not matter. Each creature comes into being unique. Anything which destroys that individuality, anything which eliminates or adulterates mind or will or spirit, strikes at the very basis of life, at its greatest glory, its greatest strength, its very core. Your loyalty and generosity nigh unto delivered both of you into a trap which neither of you deserved or devised."

"Neither of us? Do you really believe that after what you have just said?"

"If you are somehow one, then I cannot accept that she would intentionally have wrought that black evil."

"Thanks given for that," Una said softly. She looked

up at him. "I owe more by far than my life to your good sense and to Bravery's."

"Do not forget your own. That core within you which protested your granting her plea was no cowardice, Lady."

"Perhaps not, though it was not reason, either.—Do you think she was right? About the old balances being disrupted and our having maybe only a little time left? You have had more experience with Power than I, having lost so much because of its use and even fighting beside the Were Riders if what Rufon tells me is true."

"It is true," he replied stiffly. "As for the rest, I do not know, Lady. That vast amounts of Power have been unleashed and old forces awakened, aye, to that I can testify, but to say more . . ." He shrugged. "No man has the reading of the future."

"Perhaps that is to our good."

The Daleswoman came to her feet.

"I have troubled you long enough, Bird Warrior, but I felt it was your right to know all this."

"My name is Tarlach," he said wearily, as if in defeat. He scowled at the door.

"If you were Holdlord, I would not permit you to go from this chamber tonight after what you have already endured in your own."

"I cannot remain," Una told him softly.

Nor could she. Even here, tongues wagged fast and some minds ever ran in a kennel. A lord might do much not permitted a woman without loss of his people's respect, and if he did alienate himself from their ways to the point that he was bereft of that, he could usually still retain his power to command them. With Una, it was different. She needs must keep her name unsullied, or her authority would be seriously compromised, a risk she durst not take at a time when Seakeepdale most needed to stand solidly behind its leader.

His own position would not admit of scandal either. His Falconers would not smile at such a rumor as a company of another sort would do, and explanation at this point would do him more ill than good. The fact that he had concealed their first encounter with that other Una would have to be revealed, and that deception would of a certainty be most harshly judged.

"Leave your door ajar. Between them, Storm Challenger and Bravery should be able to alert me if she makes another attempt to reach you."

"You believe Una might try to use force to compel me?"

"Hopefully not, but the despair of deep disappointment has driven many a one to deeds not normally within their nature, for good and for ill.—Have you an amulet of Gunnora?"

"I do, a gifting from my mother."

"Wear it, then, if you do not have it about you now. I do not know what the Lady could or would be willing to do for you since your spirit sister is not herself of the Dark, but we cannot afford to forgo any defense."

"I have it on."

"Good."

He looked at her. She seemed so slight and vulnerable in the flickering light that he wanted only to take her into his arms to shield and comfort her.

His fingers reached out and gently brushed her cheek before dropping away again.

"For your trust, thanks given, Una of Seakeep. I shall prove worthy of it, if I must spend the life of my very soul to see you safe."

11

All through the following day—if the dull twilight permitted by the massive clouds could be so termed—the great storm raged and then through the night after it.

The Falconer captain spent much of his time watching it while the dim light held. The uncontrolled and uncontrollable violence of it fascinated, awed, him and also frightened him a little, whatever the security of his refuge. There was something in this tempest which reached the very core of him, touched in him some primal spark, the ember of a time when there had been no shelter save a covering of hides or brush or, at best, a cave discovered more by chance than by foreknowledge.

It was the enraged ocean which kept drawing him and holding him to his window. He had seen storm-flung waves, great waves, before, but never had he imagined to find in Seakeep's harbor the like of those boiling there now.

The usually peaceful little bay was utterly transformed. It looked larger, for the two arms of land partially enfolding it were submerged at their tips, although both places were of an elevation which normally kept them visible during the year's highest tides even when reinforced by a gale of considerable strength.

The ravening waters had rushed far inland as well, covering most of the lower pastures. So high did they come at one point that he began to fear for the cottages set nearest the beach. The people were still within them if the lights told true, and there could be no thought of flight to higher ground now. The wind would almost certainly sweep anyone attempting that.

The dwellings and the planted fields around them remained inviolate, however, further testimony to the knowledge and foresight of those who had originally chosen the sites for them. The ocean threatened, she took the rough lands below, but Seakeepdale's homes and gardens were spared.

Tarlach slept soundly that night and would probably have slept well into the next day had something not caused him to come full awake shortly after the eight hour.

He lay still, trying to discover in his waking state what had roused him. There was no sensation of danger, and no warning of anything amiss from Storm Challenger . . .

There was a change, a lessening, in the sound of the tempest, he realized suddenly. The wind no longer pummeled the round tower so wildly. He had grown accustomed to its scream over the past hours, and this alteration in its force was more than sufficient to have thus activated his warrior's senses.

The Falconer dressed rather slowly and then cautiously opened the observer's port at which he was wont to stand.

The storm was indeed much reduced, although it was still a power against which no sane man would care to pit himself. Wind and rain were both at the level of a more average gale, and the waters had receded almost to the beach once more. The spurs on either side of the bay were nearly completely exposed now, with only their very edges and outlying rocks still submerged.

The ocean retained her anger, however, and if the breakers crashing onto the shore were no longer so awesomely high, they remained fully as deadly to any mortal forced into joining battle with them.

The man stiffened then and, throwing back the shields, leaned forward as far as possible into the narrow window, oblivious of the rain clawing at him through the uncovered slit.

There was a vessel out there, a merchantman by the look of her, and it required no sailor's eye to see that she was in serious trouble. One mast was broken, shattered approximately at its center. The ship listed sharply, and she rode ominously low in the water so that her deck was almost constantly awash. Even at this distance, he could see that her movements were sluggish, as if she were heavy with water and unable to respond well to the commands of those trying to control her.

All this flashed upon his mind in an instant, as did the knowledge that, conditions being what they were, it was very unlikely that any other had seen her.

Tarlach raced from his chamber and, calling to the ever-present sentries, raised the alarm within the tower.

The demands and terrors of the ocean were bred into

the people of this seagirt Dale, as much a part of them as the limbs which bore them up or with which they performed their lives' work, and word of the imperiled craft had been carried throughout the valley within minutes of the captain's having sighted her, the storm notwithstanding.

There was little anyone could do. The boats were ready and their crews beside them, but they could not be launched. They might have braved the seas farther out in the troubled bay, but nothing could pass the churning, crushing madness of the breakers. It was not even possible to light a signal fire or beacon; the drenching rain smothered every effort before the fuel could begin to take light.

The Falconer officers joined Una and Rufon in her office chamber, watching the agony of the broken vessel, each in agony himself because of his helplessness.

"She is trying to make the harbor," the Dalesman said at last with a kind of deadly calm, "but her master does not know this coast. She is dangerously near the cliffs as it is, and if she continues on her present course, she will surely ground on the north spur or on one of its outriders. Once that happens, she is lost and her crew with her; there is no way of getting a boat out to her to take off any survivors."

That grim prediction proved to be all too accurate. The merchantman limped toward the bay, toward the unguessed peril of the submerged spit.

Her captain was wise in the ways of coastlines, or else he sensed something amiss, for he strove to bring his vessel farther out and did, indeed, clear the spit itself. The threatened ship passed into the very heart of the miniature islets and rocks surrounding the landmass, however, and within minutes of doing so, the inevitable occurred. She grounded with a crash rendered inaudible by the roar of wind and waves and a jolt which rent the very souls of the watchers.

She was ripped completely open. Scarcely had the

shock of striking left her than her bow rose into the air, and she settled stern first into the furious ocean.

The very rock which had doomed their ship gave added moments of life to those of the crew fortunate enough to have been on deck and somewhat forward at the moment of impact. It remained within the tear it had made and so wedged itself that it held the prow a little above the level of the water. To this clung some fifteen hapless sailors.

Theirs was not a comfortable refuge or a secure one. The prow was no great distance above the ocean at its highest point, and every few minutes a huge sea would wash over it, completely covering it for the instant of its passing. Only the fact that, compelling though they were, these were still rollers and not yet full breakers, preserved the castaways at least temporarily, but at best their respite would be short. Hands bruised and numbed by cold and strain would gradually weaken, and their hold on the slippery, steeply inclined wreck must eventually break.

It took time, longer than might have been expected but that the mariners realized they were very near to tower and cottages and hoped against the stark witness of the tempest that help would somehow reach them. An hour passed without visible change, then a massive wave covered the prow, and when it was once more clear to view, three of them had vanished. An hour's quarter later, another five were taken.

Tarlach turned away from the window.

"They are not physically so very far from land. If a rope were carried to them, they should be able to climb along it to safety."

"Aye," responded Rorick, "but how is it to reach them? The distance is too great for us to throw it out even if the wind were not against us."

"A properly directed dive from the cliff would take a man beyond the white water. He would have to be a strong swimmer, but granting that, he should be able to make the wreck."

Una paled at the suggestion.

"That part of the sea is filled with obstacles. No one would dive into it from there even in the calmest weather when the ocean herself presented little danger. A would-be rescuer stands nearly as much chance of being broken against some submerged rock . . ."

"It is the risk of one life against the certain loss of many, Lady," Tarlach replied quietly.

Una nodded, although she knew who the swimmer would have to be.

"Tell us your plan, Captain."

"It is simple enough. You are right in stating that only by purest chance could anyone survive a leap from the crest of the cliff, and even more difficult, more impossible, would be a successful climb back up to it along a rope by already exhausted men, yet only thus can escape from the wreck be accomplished.

"See that ledge there, the broad one about a third of the distance from the water? There is a fairly easy ascent to it from the fields above the beach, and men could be stationed there to assist the survivors."

His companions nodded.

"I shall make my jump from the smaller one immediately above it. The rope can be fastened to some point there so that the castaways need but drop into your peoples' arms once they are over land and not be forced to attempt any scaling of a final rocky lip."

"It is as good a scheme as can be devised," Brennan agreed reluctantly, "yet I would not have you be the one to make the attempt."

"The plan is mine, and I am the strongest of our company in the water." He glanced at the Holdruler. "It is nearly certain that none of your folk could be considered, Lady. The most are yet too young, their adult powers undeveloped."

To that, she was forced to yield, though it tore her to the depth of her soul to do so. She lacked the strength of muscle to take this on herself, and she knew that Tarlach's reading of her people was accurate. Indeed, there

were few of them who might have made the attempt even
had that not been the case. In accordance with the superstition shared almost universally by fisherfolk, most
of Seakeep's inhabitants were unable to swim. As for his
taking the task upon himself, since his own comrades accepted this as Tarlach's role, she could not gainsay him.

12

*E*ach moment might bring disaster to some or all of the
desperate mariners still clinging to the prow, and the captain made no delay. Leaving his mount at the base of the
cliff, he ascended the rough but easily negotiable natural
path to the ledge below that from which he would soon
leap and from there clambered the ten remaining feet to
the one above.

This last was not an easy climb, and he was breathing
heavily by the time he reached his goal.

He did not pause, that notwithstanding, but cast off his
cloak as soon as he had gained the level place. He retained the single, tightly fitting garment he wore beneath
it. Fashioned in one piece of supple leather and covering
all his body, it would keep the cold from him and should
provide some protection as well from the tearing of the
obstacles with which he would inevitably meet.

The Falconer made fast the light, strong rope he had
carried with him to a tall pinnacle of stone so perfect in
shape and width that he might have imagined it had been
formed specifically for this purpose had its surface been
less rough. As it was, he was forced to tie his line carefully so that it would not rub and fray against a sharp
ridge running nearly its full length.

The free end he bound about his waist, fastening it with
a knot that would resist pressure but would rip easily
when he willed that it do so.

There was a movement below, and he bent to help Una over the edge and onto the ledge.

She rose to her feet with his assistance and drew the hood of her short cape over her hair although she was well soaked. He recalled absently how she disliked the feel of rain running down the back of her neck.

He saw with some concern that she had Storm Challenger with her, huddled beneath the cape and grasping her left arm tightly lest the wind sweep him despite the protection she was affording him. Although most of the mercenary company had gathered to watch their commander's attempt, their falcons had remained within the tower, away from the frigid rain and the violence of the gale, which still had more than enough power in its higher gusts to fling one of the birds against the cliff or outward and down into the ocean.

He realized in the same moment that the Daleswoman fully appreciated the danger and had his comrade well secured, and his worry eased. Una of Seakeep could be trusted to see that no harm befell the winged warrior.

"You should not have come here," he chided. "You would both have better shelter below."

"We wanted to wish you fortune's blessing," she said simply.

She also wanted to be with him as he went into what might well be his death, but that one could not say to a man such as this.

Perhaps she might not be able to speak what lay in her heart, but Tarlach was glad of her presence. The Lady of Seakeep realized this and knew she had done rightly in coming to him.

He closed her marvelously tiny hand in his and held it a moment while he studied the foaming madness below.

It was so far, he thought, so desperately far to the quieter water beyond. His daring plan did not seem very feasible now, when he looked over his proposed route from this high vantage that was to be its beginning.

Feasible or nay, he must start, or none of those poor

devils out there would see the sun rise on the morrow. Rise? They would not be alive to watch it go down.

He was frightened, aye, but his fear was neither unnatural nor excessive, and he made no attempt to disown it within himself. No reasoning man could put his life in peril unmoved, and it was not any sword that he faced but all the might of an enraged ocean.

Tarlach straightened. She was a worthy foe, and it was a worthy death he would meet if that was to be his fate.

He looked swiftly upon the woman beside him, and a pang of loss tore him as even his fear could not.

He released her hand, and, turning from her, he made his leap into the maelstrom below.

For all its suddenness, the dive was excellently executed, and the man cut the water cleanly in the place where he had intended to put himself.

He went deep before braking his descent and leveling off. The seas were rough and very strong even out here beyond the white line of the breakers, and he thought it best to remain as much as possible beneath them. He had another reason, too, for keeping well below the surface. Tarlach had guessed that the water beating against the cliffs with such awesome fury must retain some of its power in its return to the outer body of the ocean. By catching that undertow, availing himself of its strength, he should be able to counter in a great part the forces seeking to drive him back against the shore.

So it proved, and he rode the submerged current as long as possible, leaving it to face the madness on the surface only when his lungs' demand for air became too incessant.

The Falconer took care not to penetrate the backwash too deeply, however. There were places where such hidden streams were so strong that a man becoming trapped within one could neither rise nor descend out of its grasp; he was unwilling to chance that it might be thus here.

He was a good swimmer both on the surface and under

water, but this was no light task he had taken upon himself, and his progress was slow and painfully won.

Although the rain had lessened considerably, the storm clouds from which it fell allowed precious little light through to pierce the troubled waters, and visibility was poor, almost nonexistent. Only the sightings he was able to take when surfacing to breathe gave him any real warning of close obstacles, and it was the brief glimpses he managed to catch of his goal during those moments coupled with a highly developed sense of direction which kept him on course.

The rope he carried weighed upon him and increased the drag of the water, and it was in constant danger of snarling. He had foreseen this peril and bore the slowly unwinding coil strapped to his chest rather than on his back to keep better control over its release, but there was little he could do to protect the ever-lengthening line trailing behind him. He tried to regulate the speed at which he loosed it, but beyond that he could only pray that it did not become entangled before it lifted out of the sea.

His exertions were such that the chill of the water did not affect him very greatly, but he was tiring rapidly, and the injuries he had already taken made him wary in his swimming, slowing him still further.

Whatever his care, Tarlach could not avoid all of the jagged rocks littering this section of water. His slow pace helped, for he was able to alter his course fairly readily in the few seconds given him after sighting each fist of stone, enabling him to avoid sustaining serious damage, but, despite that mobility and the considerable protection afforded him by his leather clothing, his near blindness while submerged and the strong and sometimes strange action of the sea caused him to hit hard several times, and soon his body, particularly his shoulders and arms, was heavily bruised and bloodied.

The mercenary ignored his injuries. They were not significant individually or in total. It was exhaustion that he had to fear.

The wreck was still a goodly distance away, and he was well-nigh spent. There was a very real danger that he would grow so weary with battling storm and water that his battered limbs would cease to obey his will.

Time passed. The wreck was near now, perceptibly nearer than it had been when he had last surfaced. That fact gave him new courage, but the increased confidence it provided, or, perhaps, a weariness past full control— he himself would never know which—rendered him careless. His course altered unknown to him during his next dive, and he rose to find himself in the white water fringing the outmost face of a minute island.

A gauntlet of wind lashed him, and with it came a wave as angry and crushing as was possible in a sea not yet a true breaker.

Before Tarlach could move to avert his peril, he was lifted high and slammed against the stone wall with a force that drove the breath from him.

He must have lost consciousness momentarily, for when he was next aware of himself, he was under water and choking on the bitter liquid he had begun to swallow and draw into his lungs.

Struggling against the blackness still threatening to engulf his mind, the mercenary fought his way to the surface, in the end literally pulling himself up the face of the rock.

Dazed as he was and despite the burning agony in his chest, he forced himself to move diagonally instead of directly upward so that, when he broke through at last, it was on the lee of the islet that he found himself. The shelter there was poor enough, but it was something, and the jagged stone gave him a place to which he could cling for a short while until he was again able to swim, or else until he could ready himself to die.

He pressed tightly against the wet surface, not caring that the viciously sharp barnacles further ripped his already rent garment and cut into his tormented flesh with each rise and fall of the sea around him.

It was his left arm that held him in place. The right dangled uselessly by his side. He did not know whether it was shattered or merely numbed by the shock of the impact. As of yet, he felt no pain, although he could see that he was bleeding heavily from a deep tear in the shoulder.

If that or the arm beneath it was broken, he thought, he was slain. He would not be able to reach the wreck as he now was, much less make the crossing back to the cliff. Even with the lesser injuries he could now perceive, he doubted he would be able to do so.

That made no difference for the immediate moment. He was too dazed to do more than cling to his place and hope that his senses would soon right themselves.

He shook his head violently in an effort to clear away some of the blood pouring from a scalp wound just above the temple, then closed his eyes. He had succeeded only in increasing its flow and had made himself desperately ill besides.

Gradually, the sharpness returned to his mind, and the crippling sickness passed from him. He gingerly tried the damaged arm and found that he could use it again.

Tarlach impatiently wiped some of the blood from his face and away from his eyes. It was still coming, but only in a trickle now, and he did not think the injury would give him further trouble. Such cuts always bled freely, even the most superficial of them.

The Falconer looked for and located the wreck. It was very near. He knew that he should not have to dive more than a couple or three more times before reaching it.

The rope was his most immediate concern. It had saved him by catching on this rock in such a manner as to prevent his sinking while stunned or being carried back in the direction from which he had come, but if it were too badly entangled or if it were frayed, he might yet be lost and those he sought to save with him.

Thought of them drove the last clouds from Tarlach's mind. He released his hold and, diving, began working his way back along the line.

Fortune had been kind. The rope had embraced the rock in one clean loop, which he easily freed.

That done, the man made for his goal. The brief pause—only a few minutes had actually passed since the accident—had served him well. It was not sufficient to restore him completely, of course, but the distance he still had to cross was short, and the rest he had taken was enough to carry him over it. He dove twice and on rising the second time found himself within an arm's length of the dead vessel.

He reached the prow, tried to clamber upon it, but the wet, slippery wood and steep incline defeated him, and he could not have scaled it without the aid of those already clinging there.

Tarlach had barely reached their side when a shout warned him to take hold. Almost in that moment, a huge swell rolled over the wreck. He felt the wrenching force of it and shuddered, realizing what the battered sailors around him had endured this day.

Incredibly, no more of them had been taken since the eight had been swept, but, then, he had not actually been long in coming to them, and hope had renewed the strength and holding power of the survivors, two of whom, he saw with a numbed sense of shock, were females. They had seen him and knew no man would make such an effort unless he bore with him the means of their salvation.

They had no time to cast away, however, and he described his plan even as he made fast the rope, shouting to make himself heard by all.

The mariners were grim-faced when he finished speaking, for the road he proposed would have daunted men rested and full in strength, but these were Sulcar, bred to the demands of the sea. This was their only hope of safety, and so they steeled themselves to take it. When the mercenary refused their offer to let him go before them, the first woman grasped the suddenly fragile-looking line and began moving hand-over-hand along it.

13

*U*na watched Tarlach's progress in an agony of suspense, never taking her eyes from him when he was visible above the waves, following his progress when he was not by watching the strand of rope ever rising out of the water behind him.

Because he was submerged when they occurred, she was spared the sight and the knowledge of most of the accidents which befell him, but the last she witnessed in all its terror.

The Falconer himself was stunned by the impact and was unaware of much that was happening to him in that instant, but she who saw the manner in which he was cast against the stone fang thought that his body must be utterly shattered. When he slipped beneath the water, she believed to the depths of her heart that it was never to rise again.

The woman could scarcely credit the evidence of her eyes when he clawed his way to the surface, but even her joy could not blind her to the fact that he was hurt, perhaps seriously hurt. He was holding to that rock in a way which told that he was incapable of doing more to help himself.

The man's strength or, she amended, his courage, was astonishingly resilient, however, and he dove again an incredibly few minutes later.

There were no further mishaps, and he quickly reached and clambered up the side of the dead ship—only to find another danger confronting him.

Fear mounted in her as each succeeding wave swept over the prow. Distance prevented her from observing the extent of the captain's injuries, but Una had witnessed his failure to scale the wreck unaided, and she could see that one of the survivors was helping to hold him in his place, as if the fastening of the rope had taken the last of his strength.

She shuddered. Would he be able to cross when the time came, or would he have to remain where he was, himself a sacrifice to the storm from which he had saved the others?

The first of the mariners was crossing now, moving slowly, painfully, up the rope.

It was a hard, agonizing task, but the work of a seafarer is of a kind that builds solid muscle, and at last she came to the ledge below Una and dropped off into the arms of those waiting there to receive her.

A cheer went up from the Dalesfolk which Una imagined was echoed by the survivors waiting their turn on the wreck out in the bay, although, of course, no such sound could reach her.

The second sailor had begun his crossing, but she felt sure of his safety, and her attention stayed more with Tarlach than with him. Was it but her hope, or did the mercenary appear to be taking more of his own weight?

By the time the third man had reached the ledge, she saw that this was indeed so and relaxed a little for the first time since he had parted from her.

Seakeep's lady stiffened suddenly. The fourth man was about a quarter of the way across. He appeared to be having no more difficulty than any of the others, and yet something seemed amiss to her. More than amiss. Something was dreadfully wrong.

She frowned and forced herself to concentrate on the scene before her, trying to discover what was giving rise to this sense of alarm.

The rope! There was a strangeness in its motion, an added violence in each jerk that it gave.

Desperately, her eyes ran its length from the wrecked merchantman to the place where it was bound to the ledge.

Una grew pale as death. The line had slipped, not far, but enough that it was now in contact with the axe-sharp ridge of stone. With every motion made by that unsuspecting seaman out there, another few strands parted. Only moments remained before his support was entirely severed.

She called out to those below her but knew she had not made herself heard.

What could she do? She doubted she could so much as reach the lower ledge before the rope went.

It was snapping!

With the speed of desperation, she leaped and caught hold of it. The break was in the coil, and enough length remained that a man might have refastened it or at least have drawn it about the pillar so that the stone would have taken the most of the mariner's weight.

Una's strength was not sufficient for that. She twisted the line about each of her hands, then cast her arms around the rock, thus completing the loop with her own body, in the very moment that the rope finally parted.

She screamed as it jerked tight on her hands. The pain was incredible, unbearable, yet she must endure it or see the rest of those people die, see Tarlach die and make his death a nearly useless gesture.

The Daleswoman gave fervent thanks that she had been given both the foresight to seek the support of the rock and the time in which to claim it. She could not have held this weight unaided and would only have been drawn off the cliff herself had she attempted to do so.

She pressed her forehead against the pillar, sobbing in her agony, but she only wound the punishing rope the more tightly around her crushed hands.

She was to have no respite. Una had hoped to secure the line properly when the man crossing it reached safety, but the next had begun to move before he dropped from it. She must remain as she was until the last was over.

She had to stay conscious as well, and so she battled furiously against the blackness which would have brought her the ease of oblivion.

It went on and on, a seeming eternity of crushing, wrenching torment, then, abruptly, the pressure left her. She looking up, half dazed, to see the tall figure of a Falconer keeping tight hold upon the rope. Another worked feverishly to secure it to the stone once more.

The very release from pain was a torture in itself, as was the sudden rush of returning circulation, and the woman wept bitterly although it shamed her to do so. Because she keenly felt that shame, she fought herself until she once more had herself in full command.

The mercenaries finished their work and came to her. The nearest she recognized as their lieutenant and the other as the one second to him.

Brennan knelt beside her and cradled her bruised hands in his own with a gentleness which seemed foreign to a man of this stern race.

"Rest, Lady," he told her. "Rest easy. You have given them their lives, the Horned Lord and their own strength willing."

"How did you know?" she managed to gasp through the haze of her pain.

"The captain's falcon. He had to wait until there was enough of a lull in the wind to permit him to come to us, but fortunately, he was not delayed too long.—He waits our commander's return below," he added, forestalling her next question. "He took no hurt in his flight, although he had scarcely reached us before the wind rose again."

As if to emphasize his words, a gust harsher than most lashed at them, momentarily taking their breaths and setting all three shivering.

The second warrior placed a cloak around her. She recognized it as Tarlach's and protested, but the man only laughed.

"We will not leave him wanting, Lady. Never fear for that."

He lifted her then and, because her injured hands prevented her from making the descent herself, bore her to the ledge below.

There, she suffered the rope cuts to be bound but refused to leave. Her mind was clear again, free of the cloud left by pain and effort and alive to all that was happening around her. She would not seek shelter and comfort herself until the Falconer captain was once more safe upon this shore.

14

With the securing of the rope, the mercenary fulfilled his purpose in coming to the wreck, and in that moment, the strength which had been sustaining him vanished. He slumped wearily against the prow, knowing the next wave or the one following it would sweep him.

An arm closed over him with the grip of braided steel. He looked up to find that the mariner nearest him, a tall, powerfully built man, had seen his trouble and had moved to aid him.

Tarlach flushed because this one who had already borne so much must thus spend what remained of his strength. He offered no protest, however, and only nodded his thanks. The alternative was death, and he was not prepared to go down to that while hope of life remained.

The other had little difficulty in reading his thoughts and grinned broadly.

"Think of it as some small return for the use of your rope, Landsman," he said, then braced himself to receive the onslaught of the next wave.

The first of the castaways was inching her way along the swaying rope. The Falconer watched her progress as breathlessly as any of the others, and if he was still too spent to cheer with them when she reached the ledge, the joy and the triumph in his heart more than equalled theirs.

The crossings went smoothly, with the survivors moving rather more quickly than the mercenary had anticipated.

He studied each one carefully, noting his movements and trying to discover the major difficulties of the ascent and how best to counter them. His own turn would come all too soon, and he would have to know then exactly what to do and how to accomplish it as rapidly as possible. His strength was too uncertain to brook much delay—if it would be sufficient to take him across at all.

At least it was returning to him. The big mariner had given him the respite his body had needed to restore itself after the multiple shocks and strain he had suffered in reaching the wreck, and he had taken the most of his weight upon himself again before the fourth survivor had gained the shore.

He was all too well aware, though, that his recovery might be a false one, or, if genuine, short-lived, as the last had been. He had taken injuries, some of them of unknown severity, and any one of them could affect his ability to cross that slender rope. The torn shoulder concerned him particularly; it could very easily prove bad enough to cripple him.

Tarlach closed his eyes. All the open lacerations were troubling him now. He did not have pain in the sense that he had known it in the past, but the salt water was acting on them, and they burned wretchedly. He was cold, too, and shivered violently, as did the others still on the wreck. Exposure weakened a man, he thought as he cringed beneath the lash of a fresh squall, and, if prolonged enough or severe enough, it could kill him.

He felt the seaman beside him stiffen and look up.

The last of the castaways save for this one was now almost across.

The Sulcar glanced speculatively from the rope to the Falconer.

"Let us go together," he suggested.

Tarlach shook his head.

"No. That cord is thin. I would not trust it to take our combined weight.—Go. I shall use these last minutes to rest and then follow you."

The other nodded once and took hold of the rope.

The warrior watched him closely. He made good progress and seemed to have less difficulty than any of his comrades although he had remained longest on the wreck and had borne the newcomer's weight as well as his own for part of that time. The man's strength and powers of endurance must be prodigious.

Tarlach sighed. He would wish heartily for a share of both before very many more minutes had passed.

There was no help for it. His turn was come.

He worked his way along the slippery wood until he was in position to take up the rope. He paused while a sea, the largest in some time, passed over him, then he grasped the line.

For a short while, the lower portion of his body was submerged, but gradually, he rose beyond even the most eager of the waves.

His imagination had not played him false in anticipating the difficulty of this ascent, and Tarlach could only wonder that all of the others had been successful in reaching the shore.

They could not have done it had they not been relatively sound, but, then, neither could anyone significantly injured have held his place on that wave-washed prow for so long. Those who had suffered physical damage of any importance in the sinking of their vessel had either gone down with her or had been among those taken earlier.

Even unhurt, he wondered how every one of those mariners had borne this. He had thought himself hard, his body trained to endure and to conquer pain and difficulty, yet he did not know if his arms could hold. The shore was far, so infinitely far, and there was no relief, no moment's ease, along the whole of the way to it, just endless, wrenching agony which intensified each time the rope rebounded under the pressure of his movements.

Had he been able to establish a smoother rhythm, he would have spared himself much of the jolting now ripping his muscles every few seconds, but his injured shoulder made that impossible. It would not accept his full weight for more than the barest fraction of a second, and so he had to depend on the left to support him save

333

in that instant when he must release his hold to grasp another place a little farther along the line.

Soon all thought left his mind, everything except his concentration upon this awful, creeping climb and the will which lashed nerve and muscle to accomplish what sane consideration would have declared to be impossible.

Thus it was that he started somewhat when he found himself suddenly very near to the cliff, as if he had just wakened to reality out of the mists of ensorcellment.

The sight of the corrugated, all-but-perpendicular wall cheered him, fired his courage. With hope to spur his waning strength, he crossed the remaining distance more rapidly and even more smoothly than he had the great length now behind him, although this final stretch was far steeper and more difficult to negotiate.

The moment at last came when he was over the ledge where the Seakeep people and his Falconers waited. So powerful had been his will's control that it was another instant before he was able to force his fingers to relax their hold; then he was down, standing once more on the firm heartstone of the mountain.

For several seconds, he was aware only of the reality of his escape, that and Brennan's supporting arm.

Tarlach leaned heavily on the lieutenant. With the press of danger at last gone, the forces which he had marshalled to meet it were also ebbing, and both mind and body were demanding payment for all he had inflicted upon them.

The mist cleared suddenly from his mind. One he expected, wanted, was missing.

"Una?"

She was with him then, forcing her way through the blur of faces around him.

"I am here, Captain."

Her voice was brisk, that of a healer with her patient before her, and he did not think it an accident that she had addressed him by his rank rather than the name he had confided to her. That one's mind retained its grasp. . . .

He dimly heard her telling those with her to bring him down to one of the cottages rather than wasting time making for the more distant tower, but he was content now and glad to give over the command of his affairs to these others. A veil of darkness had enveloped him in its soft, impenetrable embrace even before she had finished speaking.

15

𝒯he mercenary commander woke slowly. He was in a strange room with whitewashed stone walls and heavy, simple furniture. The angle of the light streaming in through the small window opposite him showed it to be very late morning.

That surprised him, and, without thinking, he sat up. The sudden movement brought with it such a surge of pain through the whole of his body that he fell back again with a gasp he was not quick enough to smother.

Storm Challenger swooped down from his perch in the rafters and alighted on the bed, alternately crooning softly in concern and scolding his comrade for his carelessness.

Una was beside him in the same instant.

"Easy," she told him. "Even a Falconer must expect to pay for the abuse you meted out to yourself."

Tarlach made no answer. His eyes were fixed upon the heavy bandages binding both her hands from the wrists to the knuckles.

"What happened to you?" he demanded.

She shrugged, wincing a little as she did so, as if her own muscles were sore.

"A few cuts. I shall have a more appropriate covering put on them as soon as I leave you. There was no time yesterday."

335

"You lie! Your eyes show red. Has pain set you weeping?"

"No. I am merely weary." Her head lowered. "I have wronged you. For that, I crave pardon."

He sat up again, oblivious this time of his protesting muscles.

"What ill have you ever done to me?"

"I have tempted you with Seakeep."

The Holdlady made herself face him.

"I knew your people loved highlands and played upon that liking to cement your agreement to aid us."

"The Dale is fair, my Lady, and my commission demanded that I observe it closely, as your duty demanded that you display it to me."

"Display it, aye, but I opened to you the Seakeep of my heart, endeavored to share that love with you. I succeeded overmuch."

"There is no disgrace to me if you did. Seakeepdale is a holding fit to win the respect and heart of any man worthy of the name."

His breath caught in a sudden rush of horror. What else had he told her? Or the others?"

"Was I so ill last night?" he asked carefully, almost afraid to trust his voice to speak.

"Ill? No, but you were restless, and I thought it best that I be the one to remain with you." As a healer, she had that right, and not even Tarlach's comrades could gainsay her.

"Lest I reveal the existence of your spirit sister?"

"In part."

There was also her own need. She had come to feel for this man what no other, certainly not the lord to whom her father had given her, had ever before roused in her, mind and heart and body. His proposing that deadly plan and taking the execution of it upon himself had wakened to her awareness what must have long been living within her, the knowledge that Tarlach of the Falconers, this strange, stern warrior whose face she had never fully seen before they had stood together on that ledge, was her chosen lord, so named by her heart and her will alike.

Of that she dared not speak and would probably never dare to speak.

The woman made herself smile.

"I need not have worried on that account. You said very little, save of your feeling for Seakeep, and you claim that is not damaging to you among your own."

"It is not," he averred again.

He shifted uneasily. Her concern warmed him, but he felt uncomfortable because of it as well. Una had troubles enough of her own without his adding to them.

Tarlach frowned slightly as another question rose in his mind.

"My injuries are light, or I would not feel as well as I do," he said slowly. "Why was it necessary for someone to stay with me?" Even now, he realized suddenly, she was watching him very closely, as if seeking for something amiss.

Una touched the bandage crossing his temple.

"We had reason to fear a hair-thin break and dared not leave you."

Her manner changed.

"Do you have any dizziness now, any blurring of vision?"

"None."

"Pain?"

"No more than is to be expected."

The cool fingers brushed his forehead.

"There is no fever, either."

She smiled.

"I think it is quite safe for you to return to the tower now and let its owners reclaim this cottage."

The man saw that a fresh uniform had already been brought for his use.

"As soon as I am dressed."

"I shall have your mount prepared."

He glanced at his shoulder, recalling the trouble it had given him. It, too, was bandaged.

"This?" he asked.

"A nasty but harmless cut. No more than that. There is no sign of poisoning, which would have been your greatest danger from it."

The jade eyes darkened.

"Slight though it is, it might have slain you. . . ."

"That is over now," he said softly.

He flexed his shoulders, being careful of the injured one, and was relieved to find some of the stiffness beginning to go from them.

"How are the survivors?" he questioned her.

"Well, all of them. They are waiting to thank you."

She shook her head ruefully.

"Beyond exposure and the shock of their experience, none of them suffered nearly as much damage as you did."

Tarlach merely nodded. Her answer but confirmed what he had already figured.

Una moved toward the door.

"Your lieutenant has been most anxious for you. Shall I send him in?"

"Aye, of course, or he will believe me hurt for a fact.— Hurry back with my horse," he told her. "I would not have the people of this house grow too tired of Falconers and those who hire them."

The captain was already nearly dressed when Brennan entered the room.

He pulled on his tunic, wincing as his bandaged shoulder protested this new range of movement.

"I shall have to put up with this for a day or so, I suppose."

The other laughed unsympathetically.

"Be glad that you are here to endure it, friend.—How do you feel?"

"Sore," he admitted, "but I am quite sound."

"The Horned Lord was with you," Brennan said gravely.

Tarlach faced him.

"How did the Lady Una come to be hurt?"

"She did not tell you? But, no, she would not."

The lieutenant described all that had happened on the high ledge.

"That rope had cut her hands to the bone before we reached her," he concluded. "It is only by a miracle that it did not sever some nerve or tendon and leave her a cripple. As it is, all she faces is some insignificant scarring."

He shook his head, grudging his admiration but compelled to give it.

"Few of our number would have had the will to hold on as she did."

The commander sat on the bed. His face had gone starkly white.

"What manner of man am I," he whispered, "to keep her here all night, and she wounded herself?"

Brennan shrugged.

"Your need was the greater, and she willed it thus."

"I never even noticed she was hurt."

"You were in poor condition to notice anything."

There was a knock, and, upon receiving the captain's permission, Rorick joined the pair.

"The Lady Una ordered your stallion readied and brought to you."

He studied his commander critically.

"You are looking better than you did yesterday evening, I am pleased to say."

"I imagine that still leaves ample room for improvement," Tarlach replied dryly.

He drew his cloak around his shoulders.

"Come. I have inconvenienced the people of this place long enough."

He stood a moment in the door, observing the scene before him.

The sea was still high and angry-looking, but all other sign of the storm had vanished from the world. The sun was bright and yellow, the air almost amazingly clear and pleasantly warm despite a fresh breeze.

All color seemed to be intensified, whether in the varied hues of the surviving flowers, the vivid blue of the sky, or the startling emerald of the fields.

The latter appeared to be in good condition, gardens and pastures alike, with the exception of those which had actually been flooded. The high walls had successfully defended the tiny areas in their keeping; Seakeep's people would not be wanting for their produce this winter.

Tarlach was readily identifiable for once because of his bandaged arm, and as soon as the Falconer officers stepped outside, every eye fixed on him.

His own warriors grinned as they stiffened into formal salute, but, ever remembering that they were among those not of their race, they did not call out or approach him.

The Dalesfolk stayed back as well, but it seemed that they could not lift their eyes from him, and the look they bent upon him was little short of adoration.

If he were truly an outside lord, he thought, and coming into Seakeep through marriage with the Holdheir, he need not fear for his acceptance now.

Angrily, he drove that thought from his mind and silently cursed himself for his weakness in supporting a desire which could never be fulfilled.

More to distract himself than out of any feeling of impatience, he mounted and put his horse into a trot which quickly brought him to the gate of the round tower.

16

Tarlach was soon introduced to the mariners whose lives he had saved, all but their captain, and he guessed that this one was probably with the Holdlady herself in one of the chambers which she favored for her own use, probably that in which she ate, given the hour. Una rarely took her meals in the great hall unless some ceremony or gathering called for her presence there.

That assumption was soon borne out by Rufon, who came to him with the invitation to join the Holdruler and her guest at her board.

The Falconer went at once. He owed much to the man whose strength had held him on the prow of the dead ship, and he wanted to offer him his thanks, that and his sympathy for the losses he and his people had sustained.

Even as he entered the room, the Sulcar rose from the place he had been occupying at Una's left and hastened toward him.

He was an imposing man, handsome in feature and possessed of a well-proportioned body which had all the grace of a soaring falcon despite its extraordinary size. His fair hair was bleached almost platinum by the constant working of sun and water and looked nearly white against his bronzed skin. The eyes were a pale blue.

The grasp of his fingers was firm when they closed on Tarlach's hand.

"I am glad to find you well, Captain. I am Elfthorn, master of the *Mermaid Fair*."

The mercenary returned the pressure of his hand.

"And I am pleased to see you thus and your crew as well."

"Because of you, we are sound. I give you thanks now in my own name and for my comrades."

The warrior grimaced.

"I am sorry I could not arrange a more pleasant journey for you."

"Anything that took us off that cursed prow was paradise itself."

The blue eyes darkened with a pain that would not soon leave them.

"I should not speak of the *Mermaid* thus," he said softly. "Even in death, she strove to serve us."

"She was a gallant ship. I grieve with you for the loss of her."

The other forced a smile.

"My life was spared to me and part of my crew as well. That is far more than we had reason to expect."

That speech took courage, Tarlach thought. The Sulcar rode the waves as a clan, the women working their vessels beside the men, the children learning their ways almost from the time they could walk. So would it have been aboard the *Mermaid Fair*.

None of those children had survived the wreck. This people lived by the sea and did not bewail what she took from them in her cruelty, but mourn they must, in solitude, in their own hearts and souls, even as Falconers bore and suffered their own losses. This was a strength and a pain he readily understood, and he grieved with Elfthorn as truly as if those the storm had riven from him had been of his own company. He held his place, however. He would not worry those deep wounds by forcing further response from the man.

While the meal, which had been delayed until Tarlach's arrival, was being eaten, the Sulcar told how his vessel had been caught in the mighty tempest and how she had ridden it successfully until a freak, twisting wind had snapped her mainmast even as a gigantic sea had swept over her in such a manner as to rip her hatches open, all but swamping her and carrying off so many of her crew that the hopelessly overmatched pumps could no longer be properly manned.

The outcome had been inevitable from that moment, and he had been seeking for a place to beach the doomed vessel so that those still remaining might preserve their lives and perhaps part of their cargo as well.

He gave a great sigh.

"Gunwold's fortune is made now."

"Gunwold?" Una asked blankly.

"A man of the Old Race but one of the best sea captains I know. He is master of the *Dion Star* and my chiefmost rival. We were each racing to deliver a cargo of silks to the markets in the south, for conditions here are still such that there are not likely to be buyers for two such shipments, and we both knew that only the first vessel in port would dispose of her goods with profit. The pilot must have brought him through this region and sent him on his way long since, unless fate struck him some blow like that which brought us down.''

He misunderstood the silence which greeted his statement.

''The *Star* reached Linna a few hours before the *Mermaid*. There was only one guide ship in port of any interest to us, and Gunwold was quick to engage her.

''To give him right credit, he offered to divide the cost with me, knowing the reputation of these waters and that I would follow him blindly, for there is no hatred in our competition, but the pilot refused to take two ships, claiming he would be unable to serve either properly if the weather should turn at all.''

He looked from one to the other of them, frowning deeply now.

''What is amiss?'' the man asked sharply.

''There is no pilot servicing this coast,'' the Daleswoman told him quietly.

Elfthorn's mouth hardened at the implication of her statement.

''A pirate?''

''We suspect a black wrecker,'' she replied, ''though in this case, the two are well nigh the same.—Did you see her captain at all, speak with him?''

He nodded and described the man as closely as his memory permitted.

She shook her head.

''It is not Ogin.''

''He would not show himself there,'' Tarlach interjected. ''He is too well known for that. Another, some stranger, would have to contact potential victims for him.''

''We must forget him for a moment,'' Seakeep's lady told them, determination firming in her voice. ''The *Dion*

Star needs our attention now, though I very much fear there is little we shall be able to do for her. All too many ships, large and small, have vanished in this area since Ogin became master of Ravenfield, and even without the possibility of treachery, a storm such as we have just weathered could have shattered a fleet. We have no way of guessing where or how far it might have swept her or where he might have led her."

"We can only wait for some word of her fate, then?"

"Not so," Tarlach answered. "The sea is still wild today, but by tomorrow she should be calm enough for the boats to go out, as they naturally would in the aftermath of a major tempest. Una and I shall be aboard one of them and shall explore the Ravenfield coast. That would have to be part of any search we would undertake considering the deadly name and general isolation of the region. It is my understanding that Ravenfielddale has few boats for such work."

The Holdruler nodded.

"Very few, and none of them are large enough to effect an even moderately difficult rescue in deeper waters. Seakeep has traditionally taken this duty for them."

"Our course is plain before us, then. We will leave as soon as the sea permits."

The mercenary leader joined Una after they had quit the feasting hall.

"If the ocean continues to quiet herself as she has until now, she should be calm enough for us to sail by dawn."

She nodded.

"I shall order the boats to be ready to leave with the first light."

"In the meantime, I suppose we must inspect the valley."

The woman looked at him sharply. There was a dead note in his voice she did not like.

"I must inspect it. You are to rest after your ordeal yesterday."

Tarlach started to protest but then shrugged, seeing she

had read the weariness which had suddenly come over him.

"How can I be so tired?" he asked. "I have done no more than ride from that cottage to the tower and eat a good meal, and I was late abed . . ."

"Your body has been repairing itself. That is wearing work. To judge by some of those scars you bear, you have been wounded severely enough in the past. It must have been the same with you on several of those occasions."

"It was." He sighed. "Hopefully, this will not be quite so long a process as it was with a few of them."

She smiled.

"Give yourself a couple of hours' ease, and all should be right with you again."

The Holdlady took her leave of him, promising to see him again later in the day.

The captain raised his hand in farewell, then went to the level where his quarters were located.

He entered his own chamber, closing the door carefully behind him so that he should not be disturbed.

It was with no little relief that he stretched out upon the bed and closed his eyes, but his thoughts remained active and were full of concern. He was as utterly drained as if he had taken no rest at all since he had returned from the *Mermaid*'s prow. If he could not regain some measure of vitality before morning, he would be of little use either to himself or to his comrades.

Despite his worry, he dozed and then slept deeply, not waking again until three full hours were gone.

The Falconer felt refreshed and himself once more and hastened from the room in search of the Lady Una.

He found her, as he had anticipated, in one of the recently flooded pastures.

"How bad?" he asked after exchanging greetings with her.

"They will do for sheep," she replied. "That is fortunate since we shall have to close some of the higher fields. We seem to have been lucky otherwise. No one was hurt and none of the animals, and the buildings took only minor damage. The boats and their equipment are all sound as well."

"The crops?"

"I have not examined the gardens yet, but according to my people, most seem to have come through well. We lost some fruit, but not as much as we expected. The other things, staples and luxuries, appear to have survived more or less intact."

Thus it proved when they toured the gardens a little later, and both were justifiably pleased by the time they again prepared to part.

Their separation would be short. Tarlach wished to meet with his warriors regarding his upcoming mission and then rejoin the Daleswoman as quickly as possible so that she could brief him in greater detail than she had heretofore done on the coastline they would follow.

Tarlach did not spend much time with his Falconers. They were to have no role tomorrow, and he merely wished to tell them what he had learned from Elfthorn and the course of action they had determined upon as a result. It was the stark confirmation of the reality of the danger threatening not only Seakeep but all this region, all the coastline, and it gave them a purpose beyond the earning of pay for being here.

He was a little surprised when Rorick followed him outside but fell into step with him.

"Why are you permitting the Holdruler to accompany you tomorrow?" the warrior asked without preamble.

The captain looked sharply at him, but his anger died as it was born.

His stupidity astonished him. He had not even thought to begin this search without having Una of Seakeep beside him, yet with the question thus brought before him, he could not wonder at the lieutenant's surprise. It would have been a strange move even for a warrior of some other race. More, he could be sailing into a measure of danger, although it was information and not trouble that the Seakeep vessel would be hunting. Dare he, had he the right to, expose Una to that?

He shook his head, ending his argument with himself.

"She has to come. Lord Harvard or Lord Ferrick would if they were still living, and she cannot afford to do less."

"I suppose you are right," the other conceded. "I had not considered that. Rule must be harder to maintain for the like of her.—You will not ship any of us with you?"

"No. Boats from Seakeepdale will be expected to appear in Ravenfield waters on their search for storm victims. The presence of Falconers would tell Ogin that we had some very different purpose in mind."

"He will never allow you to come upon his victim if she is still on the surface," the other pointed out.

"Why not, with such a storm to serve as a reason for her presence? Besides, he will not expect us to arrive so quickly. We are altering the search pattern enough to bring us to Ravenfielddale's only harbor a full day before we could normally anticipate reaching it. He will believe he has time in plenty to erase all evidence of violence before the wreck is found. The cargo he can strip at his leisure, as would be his right, claiming his own people had come to check the beach and had also discovered what was left of the *Star*."

"The wrecker ship will be kept well out to sea, I suppose."

He nodded.

"Of course. Ogin would want no part of our sighting her."

"You might come upon his renegades as they raped their prey."

"That would mean a fight," he agreed grimly. "It is not likely given the care Ogin will be exercising, but, aye, the chance does exist, and it is one against which we must guard until we are full sure we can take them. Our vanishing along with all his other victims would be of no benefit to our cause."

17

A bright morning dawned to reveal a world utterly at peace. The temperature was mild, the breeze brisk without anger, the bay more like a sheltered lake than an inlet of the ocean. Even the open sea beyond was quiet and gentle, as if she had never been ruffled by more than the present soft undulating of her surface.

The Seakeep fleet weighed anchor with the first true light, each boat setting out upon her assigned course. Every vessel's route was so planned as to cross that of at least one other in several places, thus forming a reasonably tight mesh over the whole of the area to be searched.

The round tower's own craft joined with the others. There were two, slender, fast little ships very different from the heavy fishing boats used by the Dalesfolk. For all their seeming daintiness, however, they were strongly built and larger than most of the latter, and it was to these that the longest and most difficult and dangerous runs were given, those through the Ravenfield waters.

Tarlach would have preferred to use the *Tern*, for he judged her to be possessed of the greater speed and maneuverability, but she was much the bigger craft, and her place was farther out, beyond the sight of land.

Her superiority was but a matter of taste on their present mission, and he felt no qualm or real disappointment when he stepped aboard the *Cormorant*, giving his hand to steady Una, who crossed the narrow plank immediately after him.

He surreptitiously studied the Holdlady, seeking any sign that her own ordeal might have left upon her, but she seemed quite as well recovered as he. Only the bandages circling her hands remained as tangible evidence of what she had endured, and even these had been reduced to narrow strips hardly worth the noting.

They waited in the stern until the mountain spurs which had been so deadly to the *Mermaid Fair* had closed the harbor in behind them and then made their way to the prow, from there to keep their watch for the missing merchantman.

They would do so in comfort. The *Cormorant* was the round tower's pleasure craft, and seats had been fastened to the deck with an awning raised above them so that the Holdruler could enjoy the freshness and beauties of the ocean and coastline without enduring discomfort from the strong sun.

The pair would not have to concern themselves at all with the handling of their vessel; her full complement of captain and four crewmen were aboard and would see to her needs and management. All were mature and well experienced, and all were male, a fact which Tarlach regarded with relief although he had the grace not to say as much to his companion.

At first thought, five hands seemed a large company for a ship this size, but she often made voyages of such duration as to require two watches, and occasionally part of her crew was needed to defend her, although it was the more aggressive *Tern* which actively sought out and battled pirates when packs attempted to establish themselves in the isolated region.

The mercenary's grey eyes fixed on the lands they were passing, great, towering cliffs crowned with green, and, above them, the greys and purples of the mountains.

Pain sharper than a sword thrust twisted his soul. Eventually, he must lose all this, go from it . . .

He did not realize how open was his grief until he felt the light touch of Una's fingers on the back of the hand he had unconsciously clenched on the rail and turned to find her looking upon him, not with pity, but with a sympathy as deep as all eternity.

"Surely, it need not be forever," she said softly. "Seakeep will always be open to you."

The man only shook his head.

"I shall not return once I leave here, Lady. To do so

would but add to my torment." He glanced back at the shore. "I want this land," he whispered fiercely, "and never can that be for one such as I."

The Daleswoman pressed him no further, and for a time, speech ended between them.

Both kept watching the waters around them for sign of the *Dion Star* although neither expected to find anything, not until they had crossed into the sea touching Ogin's domain.

Perhaps Rorick was right and they might find too much there, he mused. If the merchantman had come to grief either through the storm or through treachery, her cargo was still likely to be inviolate, assuming she had not gone under altogether. The wrecker, which would have to be a small ship, certainly no larger than Seakeep's *Tern*, would not have been able to unload her in the heavy seas of the last hours. They might well meet with her as she came for what her victim had carried.

His eyes slitted. What should be their response in that event? Under normal circumstances, they should be able to overpower her, for the *Cormorant*'s crew were capable fighters as well as able seamen, but might it not be wiser to avoid conflict a while longer, to pretend ignorance as to the killer craft's nature? Ogin and his people certainly had every right to sail the ocean bordering their hold and every right to inspect a derelict discovered there, claiming what she contained should all those aboard her have perished.

They could not pretend to imagine the vessel was come out of Rosehilldale, Ravenfield's farther neighbor. That big domain was possessed of no harbors at all and had no fertile, sea-touched valleys. Thus, it had no ships.

"What is the Lord of Rosehill like?" he asked suddenly, feeling a little uncomfortable because he should have questioned her about the man long before, when he had interrogated her regarding the domain itself, but had failed to do so.

"A good man, both able and kindly in his ways. Markheim is quite young, but his youth has not damaged his

Dale; it has prospered as well as any in the area under his rule, which began with his father's death two years ago.''

''Wed?''

''This last year and a half. His lady is now awaiting her woman's time, being greatly enwombed by him.'' She smiled. ''That seems strange in a way, for she looks scarcely more than a pretty child herself.''

''Markheim has some solid reasons for not wanting any of this region's Dales to become a black wrecker's lair. It is a pity his seat is so far. We could use such an ally if Seakeep were badly pressed.''

''Aye,'' she agreed grimly. ''He would require three days' forced march just to reach the Ravenfield stronghold—if it could be done in that time at all—and longer still to come to our tower, and that only after a messenger had been received at Rosehill with word of our need.''

''He would come, though?''

''Of a certainty. His house and ours have always been more than passing close.''

The Falconer was silent only a moment.

''I think it is time that we speak with him,'' he said slowly, ''and with the other lords as well. Even if we discover nothing now, even if Ogin is completely innocent of all we suspect, Elfthorn's tale is proof enough when coupled with the recent increase in the disappearance of vessels that something is very wrong in this region. Seakeep does not have to work alone in eradicating that evil.''

Una nodded, her lovely face grave.

''Your suggestion is a sound one. We are so isolated here and so accustomed to depending upon none save our own selves that we sometimes fail to see the obvious solution to a problem when it requires active cooperation with our neighbors. A coalition such as you describe would bring the added benefit of powerfully discouraging aggression against any of us. Ogin would hardly invade one Dale when he knew he would merely be calling the united power of the others down upon himself."

"Unless he struck quickly only to slaughter and then withdrew again, taking with him all clues to his identity."

The woman looked at him sharply.

"You think he would act so?" she asked.

"A man capable of black wrecking?—If he is guilty of that, which I believe likely, and from what I saw of him in our admittedly brief meeting, aye, I think he could take that vengeance for your work against him, particularly if he managed or believed he managed to keep his name clear of taint and hoped to gain at least part of Seakeep's lands in the event you were all slain."

They continued their discussion a long time, for the creating of a workable, efficient alliance among the far-lying, individualistic Dales was a complex task even in the preliminary discussion. Only when the sun reached its zenith and they observed that preparations for the midday meal were almost completed did they allow the matter to drop from their attention since they did not yet wish to reveal the full direction of their thoughts to their companions, who would be eating with them in accordance with long-established custom aboard both of the round tower's vessels.

When the meal was finished, all returned to their duties.

Those were not heavy despite the seriousness of the *Cormorant*'s mission, not yet at any rate. The gentle breeze and quiet sea made the mariners' work light, and none of them anticipated either sighting the *Dion Star* or meeting with peril themselves while they remained so far within Seakeep's waters, which they must do for the remainder of this day. If for no other reason, they could not afford to forget the possible need of neighboring vessels because they sought for one particular ship, and the *Cormorant* would have to follow at least an approximation of the search pattern normally assigned to her in the aftermath of any major tempest. They maintained careful watch for their prime target, certainly, for storms show no respect for man's boundaries and might have broken the merchantman anywhere, but the pressure they would feel on the morrow did not grip them now.

Because a hunt such as that on which they were engaged could not be pursued with the world cloaked in darkness, the small ship dropped anchor once night fell, and those who were not on the late watch retired to their resting places, cabins or crew's quarters.

The former were almost incredibly small, containing only a bunk and a sea chest, which also served as a bench.

Tarlach went below along with the others, although he would have been better pleased to remain longer outside; there might well be little opportunity for rest the following night, too little to waste this. He left the door widely ajar, though, despite the damp chill of the night air. The tiny chamber otherwise far too closely resembled a tomb for either his liking or his peace of mind.

18

The day was not very old before the Seakeep vessel set out once more.

All the crew and the two passengers were on deck when her anchor was weighed and remained there although this was not nearly so warm or calm a morning as the last had been. There was a feeling of tension, of expectation, on them. They would cross the Ravenfield border about midmorning, and then . . .

All that morning, they watched the water and the coast for sign of the missing ship. The nature of the shoreline was changing rapidly, with the cliffs becoming ever steeper and more forbidding and places where an illegally acquired cargo might be landed ever scarcer. Such spots would soon vanish into almost nonexistent rarity, and Ogin could reasonably and easily have chosen to avail himself of the resources of this little-visited segment of his neighbor's Dale.

They found no indication of any such use, no hint whatsoever that their mission need be anything more than a gesture sparked by the humanity of Seakeep's people. That notwithstanding, the mercenary's heart leaped up in his breast when they rounded a narrow, breathlessly steep finger of mountain very distinctive in its configuration. They had passed the Point of the Lords, the boundary between the domains of Una and Ogin. The shore now parallel to their course was Ravenfield's.

The Holdlady, who had been standing beside him at the rail, released the breath she had unconsciously held and deliberately turned her back on the land.

"Let us eat now," she advised, "although it is still early. There is but one place of which I know on all the Ravenfield coast which would be a suitable lair for a wrecker vessel, and we are not very far from it."

She had already described for him the cove to which she referred, a very narrow inlet leading to a cup of white sand, well sheltered and with easy access to the cliff tops far above. It would have been an admirable base for legitimate shipping, although its size precluded any large operation, but the entry channel was blocked in its center by a huge submerged rock called the Cradle from its form, which was revealed during the year's lowest tides. At all other times it lay concealed, an invisible, deadly menace to any vessel attempting to pass into the harbor.

No craft could sail over it. The two high points, the Headboard and the Foot, were only a few feet from the surface, the former being almost visible during ebb tide, and, since the rock lay lengthwise across the channel, only a very slender vessel—even the *Tern* would have been dangerously large for the attempt—could hope to bypass it.

Granting proper size and maneuverability and a daring crew familiar with the passage, however, a ship would be hard-pressed to find a more sheltered or secure port.

She would be almost entirely invisible save to one looking directly into the inlet's constricted mouth, and the
high, closely encircling cliffs would break the killing force
of nearly any wind, nearly any wave, even those generated by the terrible storm just ended.

Both Una's description and the map he had studied told
him the cove was well concealed, but even so forewarned, the man had to quell an exclamation of surprise
when the *Cormorant* rounded yet another of the seemingly endless mountain spurs to find himself staring into
the natural refuge, or, rather, at something blocking the
entrance to it, a badly listing derelict grounded upon the
deadly Headboard of the Cradle.

She was big, considerably larger than the *Mermaid Fair*
had been, and no sign of life was apparent either on her
deck, the small part of it visible to them, or on the beach
beyond.

It was the Daleswoman who broke the silence which
gripped them all for several long seconds.

"Were they all swept?" she whispered.

"Perhaps," he replied. "The impact would have been
bad, and she would not be getting full shelter out here.
Any survivors would likely have gone ashore by this time
anyway. The bay is dead calm, and the cliff is obviously
easily scaled."

The *Cormorant*'s captain joined them.

"Not so, Bird Warrior. Aye, the beach is easily reached
and the mountain climbed, but how would men strange
to this region know where to go from there? Even if they
could locate it, a vast wilderness separates this place from
the nearest human habitation. They would not be supplied or equipped for such a journey, particularly if any
of their company were injured. Were I in their place, I
would hold my ground a while and hope for a search
such as we do, in fact, conduct in the aftermath of so
major a storm."

"Well reasoned," Tarlach agreed. "They either perished to a man, then, or the survivors are still on the
Dion Star.—The Lady Una and I shall board her at once.

You shall remain on the *Cormorant*, Captain, with two of your men. The others are to come with us."

The Seakeep vessel went in close to the wreck and stayed beside her until the four had gained her deck, then moved back, a safe distance away from the killer rock.

The deck of the *Dion Star* sloped so sharply that the members of the boarding party at first found it difficult merely to hold themselves in place, much less cross it. They soon gained their balance, but even then, all four preferred to keep handholds well within reach.

Tarlach more than any of them. It was only by the lash of his will that he was able to release his grasp on his support and force himself to stand erect. His mouth had gone as dry as if his tissues were shriveling for want of water, and his legs trembled so badly that he wondered if they would continue to bear him up.

He laughed at himself then, and all righted with him once more. This derelict might not be an entirely secure refuge, but she was hardly that bit of a prow to which he had clung a few days previously.

A glance at Una told him she had not become aware of his momentary terror, and he turned to the work before him with good spirits.

The dead ship sloped directly toward the beach, away from the cove's mouth and the open sea, and the four had not left the rail very far behind before they were cut off completely from the sight of the *Cormorant*.

This did not entirely please the warrior, although it meant that his party would be screened from observation during most of their search. They would also be blind to approaching danger, and he was all too conscious of the fact that the wrecker could return at any time, at any moment.

Despite that danger, he hesitated to send Storm Challenger aloft. The bird's sharp eyes would give them good warning of any approaching vessel long before she came near enough to threaten them, but sailors, too, were keen of sight, and the most of them were well familiar with the flight patterns of sea and shore birds. There would be no doubting the falcon's nature if he should be spotted in his turn. Even if he were too high and distant for the wreckers to distinguish his distinctive black-and-white plumage, it was likely they would be suspicious enough to investigate any raptor's presence near their lair with all possible speed. The hiring of the Falconer company by Seakeep's lady was well known, and men of the wreckers' ilk would not like at all the thought that the mercenaries might be taking part in what was supposed to be a simple voyage of search and rescue. They would feel compelled to find out what, if anything, had been discovered about their own secret work.

His party would be forewarned of their coming and would easily avoid a confrontation, but harm would still have been done. Ogin would then be alerted that Seakeep's ruler was suspicious of him and that her suspicion was both accurate as to detail and ran very deep, and he would be a stark fool if he did not simply cease his activities until Una's blank shields had taken their leave of her. At that point, he would probably attack and reduce her Dale as Tarlach had suggested he might. Even if he did not go so far, he could still resume his attacks on shipping, secure in the knowledge that there was little his neighbor could do against him provided he acted with enough caution to give her no real or no good circumstantial evidence against him, at least until he grew so powerful that he no longer need fear her or any of the others.

That must not be allowed to happen. They had to keep the Lord of Ravenfield's sense of security intact, work and watch until his guilt could be confirmed and he and his killers be taken. If they could accomplish that now, or part of it, all the better.

Despite his acceptance of that necessity, the Falconer remained uneasy about keeping the war bird with him. They could be trapped all too easily. . . .

He feared for the *Cormorant* as much as for themselves. In open water, the Seakeep vessel had good hope of outfighting or outrunning any adversary they might expect to find here, but the narrow mouth of the channel gave her precious little room in which to maneuver. They would just have to work quickly and get away as fast as possible to report the *Star*'s death and to make their plans in accordance with the nature of the evidence they uncovered here.

He shook his head as a feeling of frustration swept him.

There might be no black wrecker, no danger at all. The *Dion Star* could have been separated from her escort during the tempest and, seeing the cove, have made for its shelter, oblivious to the peril lurking just beneath the waves.

If that had been the case, fortune had been hard on her, for the huge seas would probably have carried her over the obstruction at its center or at the Foot. Only the Headboard remained too high, and it was across this that she had attempted to come.

His expression hardened. She could have been sent across it. A wrecker would not have dared to attack during the storm, but Ogin or his agent could easily have lured his victim to this place and let the Cradle do his murder-work for him.

He grimly pulled his mind back from speculation. That availed nothing. The merchantman herself would have to tell them what had happened.

There was little to be learned from the deck. The great waves raised by the tempest had swept it clean of all small or loose items. Of everything, only one lifeboat, in reality no more than a tiny dory, had somehow managed to stay in her moorings, probably because the angle at which the *Dion Star* had settled had given her good shelter, but nothing else remained. If men had died here, the ocean which had slain them had carried their bodies away with her.

"Try the cabins," the mercenary suggested without much feeling of hope; he had pitched his voice low, although there was ostensibly no reason to maintain silence or secrecy.

After signaling Una and the two sailors to hold back,

he made for the nearest of the two deck cabins, that which would most logically have been utilized by any survivors because of its location and size.

As he approached it, Storm Challenger suddenly stiffened on his shoulder, spreading his wings and extending his head with an angry hiss.

Tarlach stopped. So. There was no fear on his comrade, but something was decidedly amiss within.

He stepped out of line with the opening. Cautiously reaching over, he tried the door. It gave no resistance and swung wide with the first gentle pressure of his hand.

He stood still a moment as he gazed inside, his eyes hardening in a way no enemy would have been comforted to see.

The storm had spared some of the crew, then, for there were men in the cabin, dead men who had met their end through the violence of their own kind and not through nature's mindless fury.

One lay near the door, his skull so crushed by the blow of some heavy object that his brains were mixed with the blood fouling the floor beneath him. Swords had felled four others who had been seated around a table and had been cut down as they tried to rise and defend themselves. A final man was lying on a makeshift bunk to the right of the entrance, his left leg immobilized by rough splints. His throat had been cut, as if in an afterthought by one rushing past him to down his more active comrades.

It was the sight of the last which caused Una to sway and turn her face away when she and her companions joined him a few seconds later, but she was strong and quickly steadied herself once more.

"They never expected what they received from those who entered here," she whispered savagely through set lips.

"It was help, friendship, that they were anticipating. That much is evident from their attitudes," the warrior agreed.

His arm came around her, as if he were unconsciously seeking to shield her from any similar danger.

Tarlach himself was quick to recognize the unnecessarily protective nature of the gesture and hastened to release her again.

He glanced toward the door.

"Let us be gone," he said briskly. "I little like this place."

"Should we not examine it, Captain?" the man nearest them, Santor, questioned. "We might learn much from it. The log . . ."

The Falconer shook his head.

"That will have been taken, whatever else they left for future attention.

"I want to have a look at the hold and then cast off before the wrecker returns. We cannot face her with our force split and with no room in which to conduct a sea battle."

"Perhaps they have stripped the cargo already," the second mariner suggested. "They had all of yesterday in which to do it."

"I doubt it, not completely. Ogin's ship needs must be small, and I do not imagine she would make more than a couple of runs in any one day unless really pressed. Her crew would not be able to bring much more than that up the cliff, however easy the climb might be for unencumbered men, and the risk of damage is too great to leave silks out on an open beach for very long."

He looked to the woman.

"There are no dry caves at sea level?"

"None, or I should have mentioned them."

He did not question her certainty. Seakeep's people knew all this coast intimately, Ravenfield's and Rosehill's as well as their own, a knowledge which had been the salvation of many a storm-caught or otherwise imperiled fisherman over the years. That knowledge included land features as well as those of ocean bed and currents.

The four left the bloodstained cabin, Tarlach carefully shutting the door behind them.

The Holdlady hastened toward the seaward rail to acquaint those aboard the *Cormorant* with the news of their discovery and to inform them of their plans. The others followed after her, for all of them still preferred availing themselves of the side's support to crossing the length of the steeply slanting deck without aid.

Without warning, the falcon let out a purposely low-pitched scream. Tarlach flung himself forward, catching Una as he went down, throwing her to the deck as well.

"Drop!" he hissed to the two men coming up behind them.

They obeyed, too surprised for either protest or question.

After a moment, the mercenary began to snake his way up the sloping deck until he had reached the rail. The rest followed him.

The side of the derelict was high and solidly built, but the storm and impact had broken it in several places, and stress had warped the boards comprising it so that cracks had opened between them. Through one of these last, they saw what had alarmed the war bird, a slender, black vessel even now bearing down on them.

Not on them. On the *Cormorant*.

The newcomer's prow looked strangely heavy for a craft of her size. Reinforced. She rammed her victims, then.

Those aboard the Seakeep ship recognized their danger as well and strove to avoid it, but the attacker was between them and the open water, and the wreck prevented them from slipping into the harbor itself quickly enough. They had only this one small area in which to move.

It was not enough. Undermanned as she was and taken by surprise by a speedy vessel obviously well used to this method of attack, the *Cormorant* was all but foredoomed. The killer struck her squarely, driving and pinning her against the solid structure of the big derelict.

She held a moment, then splintered under the double impact.

One man, the captain, died instantly, crushed in the crumbling of his vessel.

The others reached the water but had scarcely surfaced again before arrows raced down to meet them, arrows flying with an accuracy and assurance that proclaimed familiar custom on the part of those sending them forth.

Tarlach's glare silenced the bitter curse begun by the sailor nearest him. If they gave themselves away now, they, too, were slain.

His face was grim. The wreck was certain to be searched. They would not be able to conceal themselves effectively, not all four of them, and to attempt to do battle with so many was but suicide.

"Slide back down," he commanded suddenly. "Into the water."

Una started to move at once, but the men held in place, staring at him.

"What keeps you?" he demanded impatiently.

"I can swim a very little," Santor replied, "but Nordis, here, cannot."

"Can you tread water?" he questioned this second seaman.

"No."

"I will bear you up if needs be, but the Headboard should give us support.—Make haste now, or we shall be sighted going over the side!"

The pair still looked decidedly unhappy, but they were without choice and slithered down the deck until they had joined the Daleswoman at the opposite rail. The Falconer was with them in another moment.

Tarlach and Una moved first, flipping themselves across the railing quickly and quietly and then lowering themselves the full length of their arms.

This part of the wreck was much nearer the water than was the other side, and they had but a short drop after releasing their hold.

The woman immediately swam into the darkness created by the overhanging vessel, not stopping until she had reached her very side. There, her feet found purchase on the stone fang impaling the *Dion Star*, and she raised an arm to signal the warrior that he had reasoned accurately concerning it.

A few moments later, the mariners were in the water as well, and all three men were huddled beside her in the shadow of the dead ship.

Theirs was not a comfortable position, standing upon that submerged rock and supporting themselves by leaning against the great hulk which would become their death if she shifted only a little farther in their direction.

Death walked the deck above them as well. Even as the captain had reasoned they would, the wrecker crew boarded the derelict seeking survivors from the *Cormorant*.

There was no mistaking the man who led and ruled that band. His voice reached them clearly above the gentle lapping of the waves. They knew it, all of them, and their hearts burned with hate and an impotent longing for vengeance.

Tarlach's lips moved in silent thanksgiving to the Horned Lord that he had been given the foresight to close the cabin door when his party had returned to the outer deck and that they had disturbed nothing during their brief exploration. The killers were searching thoroughly, and they apparently knew what signs to seek, but nothing had been left behind for them to discover.

So it proved, and the wrecker crew at last reassembled on the deck.

Once more, Ogin's voice reached the fugitives.

"No boarding parties, then. That is well for us. Una's people would not have been such easy targets had we found them armed and prepared, as these would have been."

"What were they doing so far into your territory?" another with the accent of a southlander asked. "Do they suspect you?"

The Holdlord gave a contemptuous laugh.

"Hardly. The storm drew them. Seakeepdale's residents are a humane race," he explained in a mocking tone. "They always send their boats out as soon as possible after a tempest on the chance that some vessel or other might have come into trouble. That is why I have insisted that we keep at sea and away from here. We might have had considerable difficulty in taking them had they become suspicious, especially that ship. She was fast and easily handled."

Ravenfield's lord turned his attention to the cargo.

"We shall have to finish here before anyone comes seeking the *Cormorant*—"

"Another ship can be sunk as easily," a rough voice cut in.

"Do not be a fool! How many can disappear here in a week's time without our coming under suspicion? Why did you imagine I have let rich ships go by me in the past if not for fear of alerting our neighbors to our operation? Ravenfield cannot fight every Holdlord and ship's master in High Hallack, and remember well that if I go down, you cannot survive for long without my protection and support."

The southlander, who appeared to be next in command to Ogin, broke in at this point, as eager to avoid one of the lord's tempers as he was to press on with their work.

"We shall have to make haste in any event. I know nothing of clouds if those are not storm dogs above us."

Several others agreed and cursed angrily at the delay more foul weather would force upon them, that and the danger of the *Dion Star*'s breaking apart with the better part of her valuable and delicate cargo still aboard. That had happened to them once already with another merchantman they had lured onto this rock.

Before they began, however, the Lord of Ravenfield had his killers take the corpses from the cabin and, after weighting them to assure their remaining on the bottom, cast them over the side, thus destroying the most obvious evidence of what had taken place. Soon the *Cormorant* would be sunk as well. After that, even if another Sea-keep vessel did come upon the derelict before she was scuttled, her crew would have no reason to suspect any evil save the violence of nature and would not search for the bloodstains marring the cabin's floor.

19

*U*na shuddered as each of the dead men struck the water. One dark whim of fortune, and four more would join them. One small sound could be enough to betray them. The clarity of the voices, the distinctness with which they heard the movements of the wrecker crew, was evidence enough of that.

Tarlach had taken her into his arms almost from the time they had reached the wreck's side, for the place on which they had to stand gave but poor purchase for their feet, and she labored under the additional disadvantage of being several inches shorter than her companions, but now he pressed her closer to him. He knew what she endured, the sick fear that helplessness brings, the shame of being forced to witness grave wrong without being able to take action against it, the sheer misery of constant, piercing cold.

That last was bad now and would grow ever worse as the water in which they were immersed leached more and more heat from their bodies. Even Storm Challenger, who was spared an actual wetting as he clung to the *Star*'s side, trembled constantly under the ever-more-vicious clawing of the penetrating damp and wind-powered chill.

This they could endure and must endure. Neither the temperature of the ocean nor of the air was low enough to slay them in the length of time they could expect to be here, although the violent muscle contractions which cold could induce might well bring death by rendering them incapable of swimming when the time came to leave their refuge.

They feared that possibility as they feared discovery by

those above, but these mishaps must be counted the curse of chance. A more immediate danger threatened them. Their enemies would work long this day, and even after they had quit the *Dion Star*, the Seakeep fugitives durst not leave their hiding place, not while any daylight remained. All that while, the tide would be rising. Already, it had begun to turn. The change was not yet noticeable, but soon, desperately soon, the level of the water would climb until it left them without a place on which to stand and perhaps to the point where it would fill their shelter entirely.

It was a fear that proved its accuracy all too quickly. The rising sea reached his neck, his chin. The Falconer bowed his head to give his helmet clearance in the space that remained and finally removed it altogether, letting it sink into the depths of the ocean.

Una looked up at him and then clung the more tightly to him. He seemed vulnerable without the masking helm, as if he stood naked before the world, and unconsciously, she offered herself as a shield against whatever darts it might fling.

They stayed thus only a short while before Tarlach was forced to release her in order to take charge of Nordis, he who could not swim. The woman found herself similarly occupied, for Santor, though he could support himself for a brief time, was possessed of small skill in the water and little endurance, and it was upon her that he must depend for his life during the long hours of waiting before them.

Fortune blessed them in that the day had not been young when they had boarded the derelict. The wrecker crew made one hurried trip from the *Dion Star* to the beach, but then the westering sun forced them to devote themselves to the cargo they had salvaged lest the tide, swelled as it was by the unsettled weather, take it from them.

Their going all but freed the fugitives from the danger of detection provided they did not leave their hiding place. This they could not do, not yet, with the dead vessel still in clear view of those black-souled men working on the beach and on the cliff above it.

Only after night had spread her friendly mantle over the world did Tarlach cautiously move out from under the shadow of the derelict, towing the Seakeep mariner after him.

Darkness had fallen none too soon, for the water would shortly have filled their sheltering place entirely, but the mercenary was quick to realize that the tide was serving their cause despite all the discomfort and concern it had given them. The rail of the *Dion Star* was now near to them, within relatively close reach. Had the sea still been low, they would have been hard-pressed to board her from the water, particularly weakened by cold and tension as they were.

Even with the help fortune had thus given them, the task was a hard one. He tried and failed to climb the outward sloping side, and he failed to leap up to it from the water.

Nordis, now resting in the Daleswoman's charge, watched him fall helplessly back. He had almost succeeded, but the distance was a little too far. Some support, some solid place against which to brace one's efforts, was needed if one was to gain the deck by that means.

"You are strong in the sea, Bird Warrior," he said. "If you were to hold me, aid my spring, perhaps I could reach it and then draw the rest of us up."

"Aye, it could work," the mercenary replied quickly.

Scarcely had he spoken before Una and the second man came on either side of him. Trusting himself to their support, he took hold of Nordis and gathered himself.

The mariner nodded.

"Now!"

As he leaped, the captain cast him upward with all the strength left to him.

For one bitter instant, Tarlach thought this attempt had failed like his own, but then the man's hands closed over the edge of the rail. He hung there a moment but soon began to struggle upward. The deck was not yet won.

His arms were powerful, though, and he knew the ways of ships, and it was not long before he disappeared over the side. Several interminable seconds passed, then a rope snaked down to the remaining fugitives.

The second sailor went up next. Una and Tarlach had literally to be drawn aboard. Their strength had been spent in fighting the cold and the water below both for themselves and for their less able comrades, and, once they were no longer buoyed by the sea, they found themselves nearly helpless.

The wind was now high and very sharp. It cut through their soaked garments like a thousand daggers.

Aye, it gave the pain of knives, the Falconer thought, and it would soon prove as deadly, but there was nothing he could do to defend against it save to sink down beside the *Star*'s high side and hope the sturdy wood might break some of its force.

The mariners would not permit that. They had known all the horror of helplessness below, but their own strength had not been squandered, and they now kept their companions on their feet.

"It will be better once we are out of this wind, Captain," Nordis said in a low voice, ever mindful of the ease with which sound could carry. "You can rest in the cabin."

Within minutes, they were inside, and the door was closed against the night.

The Falconer was walking more steadily by then but still dropped gratefully onto the chair the sailor drew over to him.

The temperature of the air was not so very low in itself, and he began to feel more comfortable almost immediately and almost to feel somewhat ashamed that he should be sitting at his ease while their party remained in peril.

He started to rise, but Santor grinned and placed a restraining hand on his shoulder.

"Let you and the Lady Una stay where you are a while, Bird Warrior. The turn to work is ours. Besides, I think we know more of a ship's cabin than either of you, even on a vessel of this size. Another chamber lies beyond this one. A man lived in it, and there will be things of his that we can use. Those bastards do not appear to have done much in the way of general looting."

"They have had no time for that yet.—Go to it, but guard your lights well."

"There is no port inside, and the moon is candle enough out here."

The two men were gone some time, but their arms were gratifyingly full when they did return.

"Fortune smiles," Santor declared triumphantly. "We found plenty for all of us, good-quality stuff, too, but that should be true, this being the master's quarters."

"I do not imagine he would have grudged us the use of them," Tarlach replied, stripping off his own soaked garments even as he spoke.

He dressed rapidly, then sat back, closing his eyes. It was an ecstasy merely to be dry and truly warm once more.

Una had changed as quickly, turning her back to her companions while she slipped out of her own and into the dead seaman's clothes.

Facing the others once more, she smiled broadly.

"That is a vast improvement, my comrades. Now, if we can just discover some food and drink, we shall be well fortified for our escape."

That proved to be a vain hope. They did find some wine, a little, but nothing at all of food in the cabin, and a hurried search showed that the galley and the hold containing the vessel's stores had been completely flooded.

The mercenary shrugged. That was a disappointment but not a danger to them. They would have won home or be dead from other cause long before hunger became a threat to either their lives or their health.

Thirst could be a very different matter, but he thrust

his fear of it from him. They must act now whether drink was available to them or not.

The dory was their only possible means of escape. None of them looked forward to a voyage in her, Tarlach least of all, but there was no choice before them if they were to give any battle at all for their lives. Had his companions been Falconers, combat trained and superbly capable in the water, they just possibly might have boarded and successfully made away with the wreckers' vessel even outnumbered as they were, but those with him certainly could not accomplish such a feat.

No, it was to this small craft that they needs must look to bear them on their coming journey.

She seemed incredibly fragile even to the sailors' more experienced eyes, yet they knew her to be a lucky vessel, having survived both the tempest and the rigors of shipwreck. Perhaps some of that fortune would flow to them when they took to her.

It was well that they could think of her thus, for the threatening storm was fast approaching now. The seas were becoming short and high, and heavy clouds filled in most of the sky, closing off what had been a brilliant moon. To set out in so tiny a craft into such weather seemed little short of suicide.

To remain was an even surer death, and all four preferred perishing in an attempt to gain their lives to being butchered as had the crew of the *Dion Star*.

The memory of those slaughtered men served to strengthen their resolve. If they made the try, they might win through, one of them at least, and carry testimony of all they had seen and heard. Dead, they could not confirm Seakeep's suspicions of Ogin's guilt.

Silently, the seamen examined the dory and found her sound. Even her oars remained. Any other equipment she might have held had been swept off, but she was such a tiny thing that it was doubtful very much had ever been stored in her. Santor and Nordis sought out several buckets to be used as bailers, for these they deemed to be essential, then declared her to be ready.

Tarlach ordered that they use the wine at once. It was not worth the saving—there was scarcely half a cup for each of them—and they had need of its strength.

Once more, the Seakeep mariners took charge, launching the dory smoothly and silently despite the choppy waves in whose midst they set her. They gave one glance at the menacing shore and crouched down as far as possible as they began rowing toward the open sea.

20

*A*lthough all of the fugitives kept low in their boat until they had left the wreck considerably behind them, none of the four had much fear of detection now. The night was dark with a trace of fog to further cloak them from unfriendly eyes which might turn on the *Dion Star*, and the wind was high enough to mask any modest noise they might make in rowing.

All the same, it was with relief that they drew out of the narrow channel and rounded the spur of the mountain, out of sight at last of the dead merchantman and of those who had murdered her.

To his comrades' surprise, Tarlach ordered that they continue moving seaward rather than immediately assuming a course parallel to the land.

"This is no deep-water vessel, Captain," Nordis ventured, "and with heavy weather coming on . . ."

"We shall be driven against the cliffs or onto the rocks if we remain here."

Una straightened suddenly, guessing the hope he had not dared voice.

"We might even be picked up by the *Tern* farther out."

"The *Tern*! Aye, she will stay at sea since there is no port to which she can fly quickly enough!" exclaimed Nordis.

"This blow will not be anything to drive her in search

of one," Santor said eagerly. "It should prove no more than any of those the fleet has weathered many a time. Even at its worst, it will in no way rival the last."

There was a grimness in his tone despite the hope of early rescue Una had given him. Neither he nor any of the others needed to be told that the gale, comparatively mild though it might be, would be impressive enough for people attempting to ride it out in this pitifully tiny vessel.

"Forget the *Tern*," the Falconer warned sharply. "If we meet her, we can indeed rejoice, but it would require more a miracle than kindness of fate to accomplish that. It is on this dory and on our own strength that we are going to have to depend, and on nothing else."

His words cut down his companions' newborn elation. There could be no gainsaying the rightness of them, and if the Daleswoman still nurtured some little hope in her heart of connecting with the second round tower vessel, she did not attempt to argue its cause. They did better to forgo the brightness belief in such discovery could give their spirits now rather than risk its almost inevitable shattering later, at a time when physical exhaustion and the lash of the elements might make its breaking the breaking of their will to fight on.

The Falconer commander and the Lady Una claimed the oars. The sailors made no protest, knowing that these two could handle them, at least well enough to bring the dory beyond sight of the land and start her toward home. After that, their greater experience would be needed, and they must be fresh and ready then to assume responsibility for their party's lives.

The storm did not break suddenly but rather crept upon them as if it were half afraid to show itself. The rain began soon after the dory had left the wreckers' cove but remained no more than an unpleasant drizzle for a long time. The wind, though bitterly cold, only gradually assumed the properties of a true gale. The ocean was more responsive to what was to come, but even she delayed some time before displaying her full anger.

What she did unleash was bad enough. Tarlach's muscles ached with the strain of battling swells so short and sharp that the boat seemed to make no progress at all, but he stubbornly refused to surrender his place at the oars.

Pride would have kept him there even if duty did not. The Holdlady, slender and fragile as she was, did not cry out against this same labor. While she held firm, so, too, would he until his skill was no longer the equal of the work before him.

It was only after the rain had become an almost continuous downpour and the wind had roiled the water around them into a fury that the pair gave way to their more able comrades.

The mercenary huddled in the rear of the boat, cradling the falcon on his lap to give him what little he could of heat and shelter. His comrade was dying. He knew that, although the crisis was still some time away, and he despaired because of his powerlessness to do more to preserve him. He could not even keep the rain off him. There was nothing he could do to help any of them, Tarlach thought listlessly. He was scarcely able at this point to rouse himself enough to intelligently watch the progress of the oarsmen.

Una was beside him. He could not see her face, for she was sitting with her head lowered, but from the limp way she held herself, the droop of her usually straight shoulders, he knew that she was even more exhausted than he.

Little wonder, that. The Daleswoman was fighting what must be fairly severe pain as well as weariness and the effects of hunger, thirst, and the never-ending cold. The salt and constant wet had gotten to the numerous cuts striping his body, and, although none of them save that on the shoulder, which was now giving him considerable trouble, were of any significance, each one of them felt sore and angry. He could imagine the torment to her seriously damaged hands, could well-nigh feel himself what each stroke of the oars had done to her—

The shock of frigid water brought a gasp from him.

The swell which had broken on them was passed, but a second followed fast upon it, sweeping over the foundering dory.

"Bail!" Nordis roared. "Bail, or we are downed!"

He leaped to obey, the Holdruler beside him. They worked with the desperate speed of their need, and soon they had the boat enough lightened that she could respond once more to the commands of the rowers.

There was no returning to rest, however, not then, not in the hours which followed. The rain increased until it fell in an almost solid sheet, a deluge sufficient in itself to fill the open vessel, and it seemed that every third wave poured over the dory's sides.

Nordis and Santor proved their skill and their courage that terrible night. It was they who fought the bucking vessel, guided her, tried to keep her facing into the waves so she should not ship water with every swell. Many were the times the two in the stern saw them raised almost vertically above them as their craft climbed some mighty wave, their bodies clearly visible in the eerie, frightening brilliance of a lightning-illumined sky, or below them as they raced into some stygian trough.

Tarlach rested the bailer on his knee after clearing the boat for what seemed the thousandth time. The respite would be all too short, he knew, before he could be compelled to take it up again.

It was then that he became aware of the emptiness. No other mind touched his.

"No!" It was a moan. There was no body. He had failed even to preserve that.

"Not so!" Una's icy, bloodied fingers closed on his hands. "Do not believe that, not yet.—One of us would surely have felt his dying, Tarlach. Neither of us did. He—he was not really that low when you last tended to him?"

"No."

He looked at her, wanting to hope and fearing to

chance this pain again if he did so and it was proved useless.

"Where, then . . ."

"Gone for help, perhaps."

"In this gale?" he demanded contemptuously.

"Grant him that much, that he would strive with his last strength, even as we. He could not aid us here, but if he could still fly despite those wet wings, can you believe he would not make the trial?"

"Flight should still have been possible," he conceded after a moment, "and this storm is not like the other, perilous force though it is." His eyes closed. "The Horned Lord guide and help him."

"And Gunnora . . ."

A bitter jolt of water silenced her, and they threw themselves back into their endless fight to keep the sea from closing over them all.

Dawn broke and grew old before the storm showed signs of abating, and the morning was well on before the rain entirely ceased.

All four slumped in their seats, too spent for the moment even to feel cheered by the lessening of their sufferings.

Tarlach's mouth tightened. No, that was scarcely accurate. The nature of their discomfort might have altered, but it was in no way reduced. They still had to combat high seas and sharp wind, and if there was no rain to torment them, thirst would soon make them long for its return.

Una saw him lick the salt from his lips and touched his arm.

"I managed to catch a little of the rain."

She held out one of the bailers to him.

"I am sorry there is only enough for a few swallows, but it was impossible to collect any until we stopped taking so much water, and the rain had almost ended by then."

"Sorry? Lady, you have revived our souls! That could be the saving of us in the distance we must go."

He took the pail from her. There was indeed only a small amount of liquid in it, and he took but a single sip. This he rolled around his mouth before allowing it to trickle down his parched throat. The taste was decidedly brackish, but he would not have relished the finest wine as much in a time of plenty.

The Falconer did not delay in returning the bailer to her. She, too, drank, taking no more than he had, then she held it out to her companions.

Both realized how little it contained and shook their heads.

"We shall be home soon enough, my Lady," Nordis told her. "Do you drink for us."

"Take it, both of you," the mercenary commanded sharply.

The Seakeep men stiffened.

"It is not our custom to deprive one weaker than ourselves . . ."

He raised his hands in a gesture of peace.

"It is our strength that your Holdlady needs now. We should be serving her ill to further reduce that even for her temporary comfort."

The mariners' eyes fell, and they accepted the water, the last any of them was likely to have until they won through to safety, the last they might ever have if they failed to do that very quickly.

The hours passed slowly. The fugitives had been nervous at first, fearing pursuit from the cove, for the storm, though violent, had not been such as to intimidate a vessel of the wrecker's size if her master's purpose were strong, but they soon relaxed. They had been careful to leave no sign of their presence aboard the *Dion Star*, and the loss of the dory, if noted at all, would be laid to the rough weather. The missing garments would not be marked since there had very obviously been no close examination of the cabin from which they had been taken, and their own discarded things they had brought away with them. No, they had nothing to fear from Ravenfield now unless some freak twist of chance brought about their discovery.

The warrior and the Daleswoman claimed the oars to give the others a chance to take some rest but were so weakened themselves that they could keep their places no longer than a couple of hours before having to surrender them again.

The work of rowing was brutally hard, and yet they dared not leave the oars idle for more than the few seconds lost in changing the team manning them. The storm of the previous night still kept its grasp on the sea—indeed, it was probably not truly ended at all but merely in a short-lived lull—and the waves continued to hurl themselves at the dory, as if enraged that she had outfought them for so long. It took the full of the fugitives' waning strength, the full of their skill, just to keep their tiny craft afloat; to make any real headway toward their goal was impossible.

Their spirits fell as time went on, precious time, time they could ill afford to squander. The overcast sky spared them much of what they might have endured from the blistering rays of the sun, but they were granted little else in the way of ease. Salt-fired thirst was a torture now, a draining torture that took power from muscles and mind alike, and ever in their thoughts was the knowledge that the return of the tempest, which by all the signs would not be long delayed, would mean at the least another day like to this if they could survive its pummeling a second time.

Because of the constant strain of their labor and their rapidly deteriorating physical condition, it became necessary to change rowers every half hour lest they grow too exhausted to function at all.

Tarlach took Una's hands in his after their third such turn. The bandages covering the palms were soaked with blood.

He made no comment as he pressed the cold, white

fingers between his, trying to give them warmth from his own meager store of heat.

How much more of this could the Daleswoman take? Her will was strong, and so, too, was her body, remarkably strong for one of such delicate appearance, but all they were enduring would soon bring down the most powerful man, much less this slight lady. The fact that she was possessed of no great reserves of fat or muscle was in itself enough to doom her . . .

"A sail!"

He looked up at Nordis' cry. The very tip of a mast had just risen up over the horizon.

His tongue ran over cracked lips. Should they attempt to hail her? They needed help, desperately needed it, yet even a strange vessel, one having no connection with Ogin of Ravenfield, might not be safe transport for the fair woman beside him.

The two sailors and the Holdlady herself were no less aware of their possible danger.

Santor gave voice to the fears of all.

"Pirates do occasionally sail these waters, as do those who might not treat kindly with folk in dire trouble, but such are rare, and we cannot afford to forgo the probability of assistance because we dread meeting with them."

"Let the Lady Una and you, Bird Warrior, since she will have need of your aid, conceal yourselves in the water as we approach the ship. If she proves false, you two, at least, shall still be alive and free."

They agreed because there seemed no other choice before them, although all realized they would not survive their companions by very long in the event of such misfortune.

The fugitives waited tensely as more of the sail and then the vessel herself hove into view. At the same moment, Tarlach sat erect, relief and joy sweeping through him as Storm Challenger soared high and proud against the westering sun.

"We can spare ourselves a dunking. She is the *Tern*!"

21

The mercenary tried to crush the excitement swelling in his heart. The Seakeep ship was still very far away, and their dory was but a minute speck on a rough ocean. They might not be seen at all except by his winged comrade, and with no Falconers aboard to whom he could rightly deliver his intelligence, the war bird might not be able to communicate his discovery to those manning her even though he had somehow managed to draw them in this direction. Santor did say that she was well off her assigned track . . .

The others were aware of that black possibility as well. The tunic Nordis had taken from the *Dion Star*'s cabin was white, and this he stripped off and began waving violently in the direction of the *Tern* while the other men rowed as rapidly as they might toward her.

Whatever their efforts and the falcon's and the prayers burning in their hearts, it seemed for a long while that they would not be noticed, that they would be left to face storm and water alone as they had all these interminable hours.

Just as their hope was plunging to its lowest ebb, however, the larger vessel weared. Not very many minutes passed after that before they were standing on her deck with a crowd of curious, concerned mariners around them.

The Falconer almost savagely silenced the questions being fired at him. Una was beside him, in part leaning on him despite herself, and he could feel the tension in her, the strain of her effort to hold herself erect.

"See to the Holdlady first," he snapped, "and to these others. There will be time then to talk."

Dry clothing, food, and warm drink wrought a near miracle in the four, and soon Tarlach, as military leader

of the *Cormorant*'s survivors, was recounting the tale of
their adventures in close detail.

His audience was quiet when he finished speaking. His
description of their discovery of the murdered crew
aboard the derelict had sparked angry growls from the
Seakeep sailors and even more so the tale of the *Cormorant*'s death and the slaughter of the men left with
her, but the story of the fugitives' escape and ordeal silenced them, and it was several seconds before any of
those who heard it found voice.

"We of Seakeep have blood-work before us and a heavy
blood-price to claim," the *Tern*'s master said at last, "but
that must wait for now. We have not yet seen the end or
the worst of last night's storm. I suggest that we run before it and lay our war plans in Seakeep when the Lady
Una and the captain have rested.—Is this agreeable to
you, my Lady, Bird Warrior?"

The Holdruler nodded.

"Aye, unless the captain feels it wiser to attack Ravenfield or the wrecker crew at once."

"No, nor have we the strength to do so now even if I
so willed."

He sighed.

"It is better thus. When we do move, I want to be sure
of taking that black company quickly."

His voice became cold, frozen by a hatred so bitter
that all those present shuddered in their hearts to hear
it.

"Ogin of Ravenfield is going to die. It may be by my
sword or under my eye or by another's hand while I am
held in some other part of the battle, but from this moment forth, he is no more than a corpse. I vow that upon
my very soul."

Tired as he was, sleep would not come to the Falconer
captain. Dark thoughts filled his mind, grim accusations
from which even the violence of his hatred for the Holdlord of Ravenfield could not screen him. He had accomplished so little since his coming to Seakeep . . . No, that

softened his guilt. He had failed in so much, had failed so many, he who had sworn to guard . . .

Storm Challenger flew from the place he had chosen at the footboard of the bunk to come within reach of his companion's hand.

Tarlach stroked the bird. The mariners had treated him well and correctly when he had come to them battered and soaked from his flight through the gale. They had wrapped him in a towel, drying and warming him, and had fed him well. More, they had shown him the respect of recognizing that he had news of import to deliver and of trying to comprehend him until he had been able to lead them to the survivors.

His fingers stopped in mid-caress. This one could well and rightly quit him for the blunder he had made, yet in his friendship, he made no accusation. A man could search far and long before finding the like in a fellow human.

The falcon's head turned back toward the door, and he gave a soft call.

The man sat up. Una was lying awake as well and had used her ability to communicate with Storm Challenger to ascertain that Tarlach did not sleep and to request that he come to her.

The mercenary threw a cloak over the tunic the *Tern*'s captain had given him and hastened down the narrow passage to the cabin which he knew to be the Holdlady's, staying close to the wall lest he be thrown down as the vessel rolled and shuddered under the battering of the storm once more raging outside.

A sick dread filled his heart. He knew the reception he merited from Una of Seakeep, the justice of her outrage, even to her dismissal of him, though her need for blank shields would probably preclude that last. Intellectually, he accepted the consequences of his misjudgment, but he knew, too, that if she met him with contempt—or, worse, with disappointment—it would break what little remained to him at the moment of spirit. He did not even have the will left to resent that her regard had come to be of such immense importance to him.

He was before her door. He hesitated only a moment before knocking. There was no point to cowardice. This meeting must take place, now or within a few hours. It was better to have it over, to have his fears confirmed or laid to rest, as quickly as possible. Even despair was preferable to this accursed uncertainty . . .

Una was resting upon her bunk but was still fully clad. She was relaxed now and comfortable, and even in her male attire she looked remarkably winsome. He realized quite irrelevantly that he had never before been inside an intimate chamber of hers.

She motioned to the chest which was apparently part of every such cabin's furnishings and then moved to the foot of the bunk so that she might sit near to him.

His eyes went to her freshly bandaged hands.

"How are they?"

"Perfectly at ease. They suffered no real damage, though I suppose the scarring may be a little worse now.—What of your own hurts?"

He shrugged.

"They are insignificant."

His voice was muffled despite all his effort to conceal the weight riding him, and her fingers moved quickly to grasp his as they had on the dory when he had believed Storm Challenger lost.

"Tarlach, what agony is on you? I saw it before we parted earlier, and it has doubled in that little time."

His eyes fell, but he did not attempt to conceal his misery. It seemed that he could not, not before her.

"Even now, I lay trouble upon your troubles," he whispered bitterly. "It was mine to shield you, Lady, to see that no peril or discomfort ever came nigh to you, yet I have brought you only danger, hardship, and suffering."

He touched the bandages covering her palms.

"You gave me my life there on the ledge, and it was

very nearly bought with your disability and disfigurement. Since that night . . ."

"I am the rightful ruler of Seakeepdale. I will not abdicate the responsibilities laid on me, not any of them, and I most assuredly cannot refuse the duties binding all human beings."

"I had my duties as well and have failed to perform them adequately."

"In what sense?" she demanded sharply.

"Had I sent Storm Challenger aloft when we boarded the *Dion Star*, we should not have been trapped there. I had feared he might be sighted and identified, thereby revealing the extent of our suspicions, and I judged that a greater danger than the possibility of actual surprise and attack. My misreading of the true situation caused three men to die and inflicted upon us all that we have endured since then."

The woman stared at him, then anger flashed in the green eyes.

"You are either playing the fool, or you are proud to the point that it interferes with your reason," she told him, giving full vent to her irritation. "You erred, perhaps, but we, at least, live, and with the definite knowledge of Ogin's guilt."

"By chance, we live."

"By chance and your good management. Life is a chance.—Can you allow yourself no mistake, Tarlach of the Falconers?"

He averted his face.

"Not with such a charge laid on me."

Una's lips parted. She should have known—he had all but declared it on more than one occasion—but that it should be so deep . . .

She bowed her head lest he read the recognition in her. Any response to this on her part, whether that of her heart or of cold wisdom, could only serve to increase his pain, to render his position the more difficult. She must and would continue with this interview as if he had not betrayed himself to her, as if they were no more to one another than comrades linked by strong friendship and common cause. Even that was much and too much for one such as he to admit.

The Falconer had come to a very similar decision, and when he faced her again a few seconds later, she found him apparently completely composed and easy of spirit.

"For your understanding, thanks given, my Lady," he said and then seemed to close the matter between them. Of a certainty, she saw with relief, he did not realize how much else he had told her.

The Daleswoman thought he would leave her immediately, but he remained beside her, watching her closely.

"You said but little when I mentioned the action we must take against Ogin," Tarlach said at last. "I would know your thoughts concerning it."

"Even if they are contrary to yours?"

"Even so, Lady. It is active war which we are discussing, not merely defensive guarding, and you speak for your Dale."

She sighed, knowing and hating the confirmation she must give.

"I do not wish to see this ancient land bleeding anew, and I most particularly do not want Seakeep to be the Dale responsible for once more bringing the curse of war upon it."

Her slender body straightened.

"My desire is irrelevant. A terrible evil has taken root here. It must be eradicated, whatever the cost."

The man nodded and then smiled faintly. He felt easier in his mind now. Seeing Una looking so well after her ordeal and hearing her acceptance of his part in it had raised much of the depression which had been crushing his heart, and her support of the course he needs must recommend reassured him, for he, too, had little love for the thought of loosing more bloodshed and violence over High Hallack and had even begun to doubt against the dictates of reason his right to do so.

He rose to his feet. With the double weight lifted from his spirit, his weariness was taking hold of him at last, to the point that he was becoming perceptibly light-headed. He must leave her now, or he would be unable to do so at all.

"I had best go," he told her. "We shall both need our minds fresh when we reach your tower."

"Rest well, my comrade," she replied softly. "You have battled long and hard already for Seakeep's sake."

22

All that night, Tarlach lay locked in a sleep so deep that it might almost have been a shade of death itself, utterly oblivious of the lashing of the tempest outside, oblivious of the valiant and at times bitter struggle of the crew against it.

When he woke at last, it was to sunny skies and an ocean once more gentle and loving.

He lay still for several long seconds, allowing himself the nigh unto hedonistic pleasure of orienting himself slowly, as a lord might have done in his own bed in a time of peace, since he, in truth, did know where he was and his every instinct proclaimed the world to be quiet and secure around him.

He rose in the end and dressed himself in the garments laid out on the sea chest, again moving with deliberate slowness.

His muscles gave surprisingly little protest when he tested himself, and he wondered absently if it were possible to condition oneself against abuse even as one did against the rigors of a blank shield's life.

It was the *Tern*'s master who greeted the captain when he came out on deck and described for him the storm of the previous night. He then gave him their position relative to their destination.

"You were out so long that we were beginning to fear

we would have to carry you into the tower," he finished, grinning broadly.

Tarlach smiled.

"You would have managed to wake me somehow, I think. I would be rather heavy cargo."

He glanced about him.

"Are any of the others up yet?"

"No. You are the first. They should all be stirring shortly."

The captain realized he was famished and requested food, which was brought to him with a speed that declared this need had been anticipated. He and Storm Challenger had scarcely begun eating before his companions from the *Cormorant* joined them.

The afternoon was old when the thrice-welcome sight of the round tower and then the cottages and fields nestled in its protection at last lay open in their eyes. A short while after that sighting, they were ashore.

Tarlach went immediately to the tower, delaying only long enough to place the passengers and crew of the *Tern* under bonds of silence with the exception of Una, who needs must face the nearest kin of those she had seen slain. Seakeep's code would not permit these ones to be unnecessarily kept in concern and suspense or that they learn the truth through rumor, and so the Holdruler went privately to each household to inform its members of their loss and to bid them to hold their grief in silence for a brief time yet.

The Falconer captain summoned Brennan and Rorick to accompany him to what both guessed from his manner was to be a council of no small import. Rufon he called as well, but once he had them assembled, he remained quiet, saying only that Una must be present before they could begin. None pressed him, although the grim cast of his expression, his very silence, bespoke news that was both harsh and significant.

His grey eyes darkened when the Holdlady finally appeared. Her set, too-white face told the difficulty of the task just behind her.

He hastened to her. His fingers closed briefly over her hand. This was a pain he knew too well himself, and his own heart sickened to think how often she might be compelled to repeat it before the horror that was to come could be brought to an end once more.

Every eye was on him, and the mercenary made no further delay in giving his report of all his party had seen and endured.

He spoke tersely, without any display of emotion, for he did not want to drive his listeners into ill-considered action. The crimes which he described were grave, and grave were the measures necessary to prevent their repetition. It must be reason's decision whether to accept or reject his proposals, reason only, and not an outraged heart.

As had been the case aboard the *Tern*, all were silent a long time after he had finished speaking.

The first to address him was Rufon.

"You believe attack is our only answer?"

"I do, as I have said. To spare this Ogin now would be the equal of nurturing the seeds of plague in your house. A man such as he could never be trusted even if fear of reprisal kept him human for years, for decades. One day, he would strike out again."

The Dalesman looked to his liege.

"This is my thought as well, my Lady, but war is no light matter, as we all know to our sorrow. Do you agree with this?"

"I know the grief which can, which almost certainly must, come of our choosing this day, but the Lord of Ravenfield has made our decision for us. Such work as he has wrought cannot be permitted to continue. I stand by the captain, as I have already declared to him."

The Holdlady turned formally to Tarlach.

"So let it be, Captain. Seakeepdale is at war, and yours is the waging of it. I only would I were able to do more for my people and for yours than send them into peril with my blessing."

"Your part, you will do. As for the rest, the waging of war is my company's work. Our swords would not otherwise have been bound to Seakeep's cause when you perceived the shadow looming over you."

"Seakeep's warriors shall be with you all the same," she told him firmly, "in whatever capacity you choose to use them. We are not a race to permit others to carry horror in our stead."

"This, I know," he replied, smiling for the first time.

"How do you plan to conduct this war, Captain?" the veteran asked him. With their course determined, only the laying of their plans—and bringing them to fruition—remained.

"As quickly as possible," the mercenary answered with a speed which proclaimed the thought he had been giving to the effort ahead of them. "A long campaign would be all but disastrous for Seakeep, but if we can move rapidly enough, we should be able to spare our people and Ravenfield's much slaughter and destruction."

The grey eyes were bright now, piercing like to his falcon's:

"You have said, Lady, that Ogin has no close kin to take Ravenfield after him?"

"None," replied Una.

"Tell me, Rufon, would his Dalesfolk fight stoutly or yield if he were proven slain and a strong force was before their gates?"

The older man thought a while.

"Yield, if they could feel at all sure they would be spared. They have had to accustom themselves to submitting under Ogin and his father before him to a degree that has ever been unacceptable to any other Dale in this area."

"Is he allied with any of the neighboring lords?"

The Holdlady shook her head.

"No. He is not liked and his house is not, it being a fairly new line here whose rulers have not fit in well with our ways. His grandsire married into Ravenfield, you see, and brought in a lowland lady a few years after when the Holdlady died in unsuccessful childbirth.'' She smiled rather ruefully. ''We highlanders are slow to accept change.''

''There must have been ties with the original house. Who would have taken Ravenfield had the outside woman not come?''

''Seakeep. We have no claim against that of true marriage, though.''

''No, Lady, nor do I suggest pressing such an argument, but it may well help us in winning the Dale and establishing a quick and stable peace there once we take out Ogin if memory is held long here, as you state.''

Rufon nodded.

''You intend to go after the wrecker crew before marching on the stronghold?'' he asked.

''Aye,'' Tarlach replied. ''Theirs is the crime, and theirs must be the payment. I want them brought down before they can either hide themselves or flee the region entirely. Ogin in particular must be felled quickly. If once he can hole himself in his keep, we shall have a long and bitter struggle in front of us which might well be the death of both Dales.''

''Are you not assuming much in building our plans around the possibility of the Holdlord's being with his killers when we strike?'' Brennan asked, interrupting for the first time. ''To my mind, it would be more likely that he should pass the greater part of his time in comfort in his keep.''

''That would normally be true, but he knows that Seakeep boats will be out seeking the *Cormorant*, and I very much doubt he will trust his murderers not to attack if any of them come uncomfortably close, particularly if the *Dion Star* is still intact.''

''If he is not with them?'' the lieutenant persisted.

''Then we brace ourselves for a siege and hope it will be short-lived.''

''His people are too cowed for us to hope they will rise

against him even after learning the cause of our attack," the Holdruler warned.

"Aye, but they should also be incapable of courageous resistance against us, nor do I imagine they would wish to offer such battle."

The Falconer captain strode to the window slit and peered out at the bay for a moment before facing them once more.

"I want the *Tern* repainted grey, mottled over with black and touches of white. Cover both sails and hull in this manner."

"It shall be done," the Dalesman assured him. "The other vessels?"

"Send them out at once as they are. Let Ogin grow accustomed to seeing Seakeep craft. I plan to hold the *Tern* offshore until twilight. The growing dusk coupled with her camouflage should keep her invisible until we are all but upon the wreckers, but if we are seen, I would prefer that their suspicions be lulled concerning our purpose."

"If the *Dion Star* remains?"

"The boat or boats first finding her must explore her, of course. There will be nothing left to arouse suspicion by then, and our people will be able to carry on with their play. I would say she will be gone by now, though, either through the storm or deliberately scuttled after having been stripped."

"The wrecker might come upon our search parties."

He shook his head.

"Ogin will not make that mistake a second time. She will be staying well out during the daylight hours. That is another reason why I wish to penetrate her harbor late, to give her time to get inside herself." He frowned. "There is a slight chance that she will remain at sea altogether, but I believe her crew will prefer the comforts of a snug harbor enough to have their will in that matter. She is designed for quick raiding, not long-term dwelling, and the ocean is still unsettled enough to make staying aboard her unpleasant unless she be secured in a place of good shelter.''

"Perhaps she will wait until full dark before seeking her base," Rorick suggested.

"I think not. She is rather too big to risk running the Cradle at night."

"So is the *Tern*."

Tarlach nodded.

"We must be inside before then ourselves."

He fell quiet a short while as he envisioned the attack in his own mind.

"We shall have to strike quickly and conquer quickly. Ogin's men know that harbor intimately. If we give them time to maneuver, they could draw us into disaster. The *Tern* is large for work in that bay.

"If it be possible at all, we must prevent anyone from escaping up the cliff to warn the stronghold, or our task there will be the harder. Sending in a landing party simultaneously with our attack should accomplish that.''

"Once the wreckers are overcome?" questioned Una.

"We march on the stronghold, bringing any of the killers still living with us and also Ogin's body." His mouth hardened. "That one will never permit himself to be taken living."

"The capture of a keep with the number of warriors the *Tern* can carry is a large assignment even for Falconers," Brennan commented dryly, but his eyes were smiling, for he knew his commander well enough to realize he would have a ready answer to that objection.

Tarlach grinned.

"So it would, Comrade, but the remainder of the fleet shall return home once the mock search is over and sail again for Ravenfield. They should reach the cove some six hours after our arrival, bringing with them supplies and the rest of our company. Seakeep's warriors shall march overland, bringing our horses with them, and meet with us en route.—Perhaps you might suggest the best place for our rendezvous, Lady, Rufon?" he added.

"There are a number of good possibilities," the Dalesman replied. "If I might have a map, my Lady, lest my memory fail me on some point, and the captain can choose from amongst them?"

She herself brought the chart to him, and it did not take long to select the most suitable site.

Tarlach remained looking at the map for several seconds, as if troubled by some thought. At last, he sighed and, raising his eyes, fixed them on the Holdruler.

"The overland column will be comprised of your own soldiers, my Lady. I know it is much to ask, but I would have you march with them."

That brought violent protest from the other three men, but he silenced them impatiently.

"Think, will you? What people would give themselves over to a band of blank shields, even when accompanied by neighboring Dalesfolk? Lady Una rules Seakeepdale, and her house has had the respect of the region for generations. Her presence could go far in convincing the Ravenfield garrison and those they defend to yield quickly to us."

"I will go," Una interjected before further discussion could take place, "but not overland. I sail on the *Tern*."

"Lady . . ." the commander began.

"Now you think, Captain! Where will a healer serve your wounded best, with them or with another band miles distant?"

For a moment, she feared that he would still deny her, but then his head bowed, albeit all could see that he gave way most unwillingly. Her skill was simply too great for him to deny his warriors access to it.

All were silent some time after that, then Una glanced at the mercenary leader.

"What if one of our supposed search craft should happen to chance upon the wrecker?" she asked. "She could not pretend not to see her."

He smiled.

"Well asked. It is unlikely but could happen.—She shall hail her and ask if she has seen any sign of the *Cormorant*, as well as making the other inquiries to be expected at such a meeting. Our enemies will most assuredly have a convincing set of answers prepared for such an eventuality.''

The Seakeep leaders remained together a long time until the plans for the conducting of their attacks were settled, then they separated, Tarlach going to his Falconers and Una to address her people and prepare the fleet as the captain had instructed.

23

It was the middle of the following day before all was at last in readiness and the assault force was preparing itself for departure.

Una came to Tarlach's chamber to go over any final details which might have occurred to him since their last meeting.

He had assumed once more the dark cloak and high helm of his race, and her heart twisted in her breast at the sight of him, although she had known it would be thus. The uniform rendered him stern of appearance and distant.

When she looked into what she could see of his face, however, the feeling of loss left her. The man had not changed with his costume.

They spoke together only a short while—the council of the previous evening had covered just about everything that needed to be discussed—but the mercenary did not seem eager to quit the apartment to join their comrades below, and so she stood beside him, watching the activity boiling around the loading area of the harbor.

Tarlach's eyes went to the vessel they would soon board, and he shook his head in something of wonder.

"Your people have done well," he said to his companion. "I know where the *Tern* is moored, and yet I must half convince myself that I am seeing her. She will be nigh unto invisible to those not expecting her coming."

"I pray it may be so."

He turned away from the window abruptly, as if he could no longer bear the view.

"I would you were not coming with us."

"I must."

"I know, but you are not fit for war despite your ability with a sword."

The woman nodded.

"That, I realize. I shall stay out of the fighting, unless, of course, the issue goes so far against us that I have no option but to defend myself."

The Falconer's hand whitened where it rested against the stone wall.

"It wonders me that you can entrust yourself to my care again."

"I would trust you with my immortal soul," she whispered fiercely.

At that moment, the kitten Bravery squalled and hissed. She had been curled up on the foot of Tarlach's bed where she had climbed after Una had put her down upon entering the room, but now she was on her feet, her little back arched, her ears laid back. Even as she moved, Storm Challenger gave his more formidable battle cry.

The humans whirled about. The air before them was shimmering.

Tarlach put himself between Una of Seakeep and the disturbance. He knew it for what it was, a gate such as he had seen open in the Bower.

There was no escape. He dared not try to force their way through it to the door, and so he drew his sword and, heart pounding, waited to front whatever was to come.

As before, the figure of a woman materialized, approaching them as if from a great distance.

The spirit Una stepped into the room and stood surveying them. The Falconer could not fully read what lay in her expression, but he did not believe anger to be there or even very great surprise. Comprehension, perhaps, and maybe something of impatience.

"Have no fear, Bird Warrior," she said in her oddly pitched voice. "I have come with a warning, not to make further requests of my sister."

He inclined his head in acknowledgment but blocked with his left hand the Holdlady's instinctive move toward the other.

"We bid you welcome in that event, but all the same, it is best that you remain some distance from us. Sit if you will, Lady. There is a chair behind you."

She frowned.

"Is the round tower now yours to command that you give greeting and issue orders to those who come with business to conduct here?"

"The tower, no, but these are my quarters."

The newcomer smiled at that and in smiling seemed well-nigh one with Una of Seakeep.

"I stand corrected, Captain."

Tarlach waited until she was seated. Her expression had grown grave again almost immediately, and he did not doubt that her purpose for coming to them was indeed a serious one.

"You mentioned a warning, Lady," he prompted at last.

She nodded slowly.

"I did.—You have both noted that, unlike the most of High Hallack, there are no active relics of the Old Ones, in this area, that the ruins here are but that and no centers of half-sleeping Power?"

"Aye, this we know."

"It is by no accident but through the individual and collective courage and the determination of those who once lived here that this is true.

"The populace of all this world was larger and richer, far more varied, in those distant days, with many non-human races sharing place with those like to our own kind. Humans held this area, people strong in Power, men and women alike, though the last possessed and wielded it in by far the greater measure.

"An adept dwelled near to them, in a tower he had raised by his arts atop a rock straddling the mouth of a small inlet—"

"The Cradle!" gasped Una.

"Even so.—Like all too many others, he, in his arrogance and his hunger for ever more Power, ever more knowledge, drew upon forces better left untapped, tried gates never meant to open into any living realm such as ours. Because he himself was so dark of spirit, the results of his meddling proved direr than those which cursed so many other places, for himself and for all around him. He called and was answered, not by a thing of the Shadow but by a lord of the true Dark. His stronghold and all within it vanished in a blast of fire and bitter wind in that answering.

"The inhabitants of the region had been forewarned of his experiments and had deduced that trouble only would arise from them, though none had guessed the magnitude of the disaster he would summon. They had united to stop him but had moved a little too late. Before they could act, he had met his doom, and the Dark had been loosed upon the land."

She paused, as if to collect her thoughts, then went on.

"The full horror of what had occurred was soon brought terribly home to them, and they realized this massive evil must be stopped at once or all the world and perhaps other worlds with it were lost. They separated then, the women and the men, each party knowing they would not see the other again.

"The sorceresses fronted that lord of the Dark in their united Power and fought it in such a battle as had not been waged before or ever since in all this realm. In the end, their aim was achieved. They opened a gate into its own place and succeeded in driving it back into it, but in order to seal the passage permanently, they were forced to follow after their foe into that nightmare land. They completed their work and saved our realm, but for them there was no return. They remain, preserved in that dread prison by their ensorcellments and maintaining their sanity, which was otherwise lost, by lying in a sleep like to a living death.''

"Their men?" Tarlach asked.

"There was the original gate remaining, that which had engulfed the accursed adept and his keep. It had to be closed as well, but it was guarded. The Dark thing had left its Dog to hold the passage. This they had to defeat before they could begin their labor, in the full knowledge that if it could delay them long enough, its master would come, and all they had striven to preserve at such awesome cost would be lost.

"They were already few in number, having been badly decimated by earlier encounters with the adept's hirelings and the lesser things he had drawn to him, and their enemy was forewarned by the vibrations of its master's battle, even then raging in all its fury. It was prepared for trouble and prepared to return it in full measure.

"Most of the attackers perished in the assault, but the handful remaining drove it back into its gate and, with their last strength, sealed the entrance, dying to a man of that effort and the wounds they had sustained in the battle preceding it.''

"Their children?" the human woman asked. "There must have been many too young to fight.''

"None were left. All of them had been slaughtered, along with those tending them, in the first wild rampage of that dark force. It was this massacre, the manner of the killing, which had alerted the adults to the nature of that which they and their realm faced.''

Both her listeners said nothing for some while after she finished speaking.

"A dread tale and a proud one," the Falconer responded at last, "but how does it affect us save as an example of courage?''

"Because those men, for all their bravery and sacrifice, had not been strong enough to succeed fully in their aim. The Dog was not sent back through that passage but was,

397

rather, trapped within it. It was weakened by the wounds it had taken and further reduced by the lack of sustenance over the interminable ages since its imprisoning, but now blood has been shed at and around the Cradle, and pain and fear and anger have been released and the blood-lust and greed of the murderers. The Dog has fed well and tries its bonds. Only a little more of such offerings, a very little, and it will break free once more. When it does, be assured that its master will not be long in following.''

Her eyes met and held each of theirs in turn.

"There is no company now extant possessing and practiced enough in the wielding of such united Power as to be able to chain those things again. Even Estcarp's Witches at the height of their strength would have been hard-pressed to do it, and they have not yet nearly recovered after their moving of the mountains. No individual human being can hope to withstand either of them. If that gate opens and they gain entrance here, this realm will see a riving such as it did not endure during the worst days of that ancient war.''

"Do you warn and in the same breath tell us that we are foredoomed?" the Falconer asked. "Was this the meaning of your statement to Una that our time was short when you tried to draw her to your will?''

"It was not, to answer your second question first. the peril I foresaw then came of reason only and was of a more general nature, stemming from the disturbance of old guards and old balances taking place all around us. This other situation has just come to my attention, for only the most recent slaughter at the Cradle made of it a threat sufficient to activate my danger senses. Before that, I was as ignorant of it as you.''

Her eyes measured him, as if wondering if he was in any sense fit to carry the charge fate had laid on him.

"No, I do not say you are foredoomed, but take care to end this man's evil quickly, then seek aid from both the Amber Lady and the Horned Lord—who is her consort, Falconer—to help cleanse the place and set secure seals upon it.

"Above all, Una, my sister, see to it that this rock is not again used as an altar to receive the blood and the lives of butchered men."

Once more, she became still. Her look was sorrowful when she gave her attention back to the mercenary.

"I have no certain information for you or yours, Bird Warrior, but I am possessed of knowledge not open to you of shorter memory, and I can tell you this much. The curse which you have so long feared may someday relatively soon be brought to an end, either that or come to life once more. For my part, I believe it shall be the former since many races populate this realm and no other is as susceptible to that doom as your own."

She saw him start and nodded.

"Your history is known to me. It was the Shadow and the destruction its coming caused which was responsible for the loss of so much of our world's lore, and I am what would be had we been spared that plague. Your people are old in this realm, one of the earliest to reach it, and you should be one of the best fitted to live with it. You have been blighted, and now the shade of extinction looms over you all. I say this to you, though, as a gate once brought you to this place, yet another may be your saving, or the saving of those and that which is best amongst you."

She turned to Una.

"From you, sister, I crave pardon for my earlier, harsh words. You were right to fear what was of the Dark. Only believe that I had not seen the supposed solution to my hunger which I proposed as such until I pondered our break. I wronged you, and yours is the right to shun me, yet our association is old, the friendship of two lonely little girls and, later, of two lonely women. I would not see that shattered even for so strong a cause."

"It is not," the Holdlady replied firmly. "The place you have ever held in my heart is yours still."

"Thanks given, dear sister, for that and for all your

regard. We may not meet again, and I would wish you now fortune in the struggle ahead and fortune in your life, be it long or very short.''

With that, almost without warning, the alien Una rose to her feet and stepped into her passage gate. In another moment, she was gone from their sight.

Tarlach held the Holdruler against him, as if fearing she might even now be swept into the closing gate. Only when all sign of it had vanished from the chamber did he release her.

''Una, I would have you march with your people. . . .''

Her eyes locked with his, and there would have been more yielding in the heartstone of Seakeep's mountains.

''Under no circumstances will I allow you to take that weight of responsibility upon yourself. We share it between us, you as my war leader, I because it is my Dale and my will that presses this war, and we shall witness and share the consequences of our warring since continue with it we must.'' Her voice softened. ''Would I survive long if the Dark were loosed, Tarlach?''

''No. If the gate opens, we are all slain,'' he conceded. ''Soon or late, it would swallow us.''

''Then say no more. I, for one, prefer to know and meet my fate at once.''

His shoulders squared.

''It is time to go.—Would you have me tell the others this news?''

Una thought for a while.

''No,'' she said in the end. ''Not my folk, at least. They must fight in any event. Why throw this added terror on them when naught they can do will alter what we risk?'' She paused. ''It may be otherwise with your comrades. They will press the attack at the Cradle itself.''

He shook his head.

''Like you, I would not blight their spirit with the dread of a possibility over which they have no control. Let them remain free to concentrate on fighting men without having to bear the fear of waking ultimate evil.''

The pair found all in readiness when they entered the great hall. They quickly made their farewells to those who were not to accompany them and then started for the door and the vessel which would carry them to battle and, perhaps, to the deciding of their world's fate.

Elfthorn was standing with his crew at the entrance of the tower, but instead of merely wishing them fair fortune as did the rest, he matched his pace with theirs.

"A boon if you will, Captain."

"What would you have of us, friend?" Tarlach asked, already guessing what he would say.

"A crewman's place aboard the *Tern*. I told you Gunwold and I were rivals and that there was no hatred between us, but I did not say that we had lived as fosterlings on one bark. I would avenge his death and avenge also the suffering this Lord of Ravenfield has caused you both, who gave me and mine our lives and then received us so kindly."

"The place is yours and a place with the boarding party as well. Your strength and courage will be welcome to us in the fight ahead."

24

Tarlach stood on the deck of the *Tern* watching Ravenfield's harsh, beautiful coast. He had lain aside his helmet once more, and the cloak in which he was wrapped was one such as any of Seakeep's mariners might have worn. With their mission so near its crisis, he would do nothing which might announce his true intentions to his enemies. Most particularly, he did not want to reveal the presence of Falconers aboard this vessel before the time of attack was upon them.

He had felt somewhat nervous at first, remembering his short-lived but paralyzing panic aboard the *Dion Star*, but the unpleasant reaction had not recurred, and he felt sure now that he was free of it.

All the same, his spirits were low. If his plan failed, there could be months of slaughter before the Dale he had come to love. That was a dark prospect and one on which none of his company liked to dwell. Of that, he was certain.

He could be sure of little else regarding his comrades' feelings about Seakeep. That they liked the holding he knew, but he would not be greatly surprised to find that all or the most of them fully shared his own attachment to it. The power of these highlands was very great. . . .

He shook his head. Perhaps he was but covering, excusing, his other, greater weakness by trying to lay something of this outrider of it upon the rest as well.

His eyes closed. The terror he had been battling surged through his defenses, gripping him so powerfully that he had to grasp the rail to keep himself from doubling over under its lash.

What did any of this matter if the slaughter soon to take place near the Cradle should prove the final feeding that demon Dog needed? He believed the spirit Una. He believed the sincerity of her warning and the accuracy of her reading of the threat looming over them all, and he trembled that this assault he commanded might open the gate to doom for High Hallack and perhaps for the whole of this world. It was too much. Too much responsibility for any man to have to bear. . . .

"Tarlach?"

His head turned at the soft call. So engrossed had he been in his thoughts that he had not heard the Holdlady's light step.

"It was bad enough before," he told her, paying her the compliment of not concealing the fear that he felt. She endured it as well, after all. How should they not quail? No sane being could face this challenge without dread.

"We did rightly to keep this from our peoples," she said. "I have no experience in the waging of war, but I think the knowing would only reduce their ability to fight even against men." She drew a deep breath. "Should we go on with it, Tarlach? Una told us to stop Ogin, but the cost could be the ending of us all."

"We must," he replied firmly. "His continued existence and that of his butchers must in itself feed the Dog since they have gone so far in rousing it. If I did not feel certain of that in my very bones, I should not risk a contest in the cove, even if it meant letting both him and the wreckers escape our vengeance."

His head lowered, and he stared unseeing into the ocean.

"That is one of the great torments of our situation. So much rides upon us, and yet we have little or no choice as to the action we must take."

The captain shivered and huddled deeper into his cloak as a sharp blast of wind bit through the heavy material as if it were no more than a layer of summer lawn.

He glanced skyward in some alarm but found no threat there. This cold breeze was but part of the rapidly advancing fall and not any signal of a coming storm.

Una shared his thought.

"It looks as if winter will be early this year and harsh when it does come."

"Aye."

"If the fighting drags on any length of time . . ."

"It is not my intention that it should drag on," Tarlach responded rather too sharply.

He gripped himself.

"Your pardon, Lady.—Try to rest easy on that point at least. Assuming fortune favors us at all, we should be able to bring Ravenfield to terms before the Ice Dragon bites at us in earnest."

He raised his eyes to the shore and studied the great cliffs somberly.

"Prepare yourself now, my Lady. There is only a little time left before our assault must begin."

* * *

Both Seakeep leaders were on deck once more as the small vessel glided noiselessly toward the deadly cove.

Tarlach's heart hammered in the wild, sharp manner he always associated with imminent battle, and he silently sent forth the short, intense prayers of a man who might soon be seeking admission into the Halls of the Valiant.

A few minutes more. Only a few . . .

The all-too-familiar curve of the headland screening the wreckers' harbor came suddenly into view, only the tip of it, but he knew it at once. Its form was not likely to fade from his memory for a long time to come.

Others came up from below, Falconers and crew. Working in a silence as deep as death, they loosed from her bindings the launch which had been riding the *Tern*'s deck like some great barnacle and, when she was fully manned, lowered her into the sea. She would follow after the larger vessel, landing her cargo of warriors to secure beach and cliff while the mother ship engaged the black wrecker.

The evening was well on, and the darkening sky stained the ocean beneath a deep grey. Tarlach comforted himself with the thought that it would take eyes as keen as his falcon's to spot the two tiny craft against such a background. Their worst danger lay in skylining themselves, and even that risk was minimized by the artful mottling which broke the outline of the sails.

The daylight, although fading, was still more than sufficient to give them a clear view of the tiny bay.

Nothing blocked its entrance now; the *Dion Star* had vanished as if she had never been.

No visible barrier lay between them and the harbor, the captain amended in his mind. The Cradle remained, a dire menace waiting under its concealing cover of water for its next victim.

He shuddered despite himself. With the tide high as it was now, scarcely an abnormal ripple troubled the surface to reveal its lair to even the most practiced eye.

His thoughts did not stay long with the obstacle nature

herself had set there. That was the concern of the mariners. His work was before him.

The wrecker vessel was in and apparently moored for the night. She was resting in the center of the harbor, held in place by her anchor, and her sails were furled. A few men moved about her deck with the casual air of those who anticipate no trouble from weather or their own kind. The others were most likely below. None were on the beach, which was almost covered by the tide, and he did not believe there would be any in whatever shelter they had constructed for themselves on the windswept cliff above. Of sentries, he saw no sign, nor had he expected to find them. Life here had been too secure and unruffled for anyone to feel much inclined to court discomfort in apparently needless guarding.

The Falconer's hand was on his sword. They were very near now. How much closer would they be able to come to their quarry without being sighted?

No farther! One of the seamen aboard the wrecker looked suddenly in their direction and stared as if he believed madness had seized his mind, then he shouted the alarm to his comrades.

The *Tern* was in the channel, almost parallel to the Headboard, by that time.

Tarlach's mouth was dry. Would she pass? This was the route the wrecker followed, but the Seakeep ship was somewhat larger and deeper of draught.

The *Tern* was through, sailing freely in the bay. Without pause or delay, she bore down upon her prey.

The defenders strove desperately to ready their craft for combat, but the attack came too swiftly. The invaders were upon them before they could do much more than weigh anchor.

The captain recalled all too well the efficiency of their archers. These were felled at once by his own bowmen, then eager hands made fast the two ships, and his warriors leaped to the killers' deck.

The fighting was furious, vicious, for the wreckers knew the fate awaiting them if they were taken, and Tarlach had not misread Ogin's power to induce men of his own ilk to do battle for him. With his presence to rally them, they fought as they might not otherwise have been capable of doing.

The Falconers warred as was their wont, hard, cleanly, and with consummate ability, though they did conduct their assault with more fire than was usual with them. The crimes of which their opponents were guilty were particularly repugnant to them, as they were to all who frequently rode the waves, and each of them felt a personal need to avenge the *Cormorant*'s death and the sufferings their commander had endured in its aftermath.

For Elfthorn, hatred and the will to vengeance were paramount, although never did he permit himself to grow careless or wild in his desire to exterminate the renegades who had betrayed and slaughtered the crew of the *Dion Star*.

He used skill and raw strength in equal measure. Tarlach saw him drive his blade through the breadth of a man's body, lift him on the sword, and then cast him over the side as if he had been no more than a small ham gone putrid.

That was one of the few coherent glimpses the captain managed to get of any of his companions during the course of the engagement. He had been the first to leap aboard the killer vessel, springing into the very midst of those clustered on her deck to resist the assault. He succeeded in drawing their attention for that moment from his comrades, allowing the first of them to gain their target relatively unscathed, but he himself was surrounded, and so he remained.

His position was a bad one. The men before him, around him, were capable fighters, and his own comrades could not break through their massed ranks with any speed. The wreckers appreciated that whatever little hope they had lay in their ability to support one another, and they battled mightily against the newcomers' efforts to separate them into smaller, more readily dispatched groups. Their determination gave Tarlach neither hope of release nor respite in his struggle to remain alive in their midst.

As seconds wore into minutes without help reaching him, his situation grew ever more desperate. No man could shield himself simultaneously on every side, and he knew his death would soon claim him.

He parried a thrust coming at him from the right. It turned from his trunk but sliced through his upper arm. A moment later, he was struck in the back. It was a glancing blow, readily deflected by his mail, but it unbalanced him, leaving him helpless for a moment before the one facing him.

The wrecker lunged, but his wolfish grin of triumph turned to a scream of terror and agony as Storm Challenger dove, a fury incarnate so rending face and eyes that his ravaged victim died gladly in the next moment on the Falconer's blade.

The press against him eased abruptly. Brennan and Elfthorn each forced their way through to him, the latter using both the power of his arm and his sharp sword to throw his foes down.

Now Tarlach was able to look about him, seeking the one man his hate demanded that he kill.

He soon located him and began cutting his way through the struggling throng in order to confront him.

The Lord of Ravenfield was a doughty swordsman in his own right, and several warriors had gone down by his hand before the mercenary leader was able to reach and challenge him.

Ogin did not know who it was that he faced. He did not even suspect that anyone had escaped from the *Cormorant*, and, like most of those not of their race, he could not tell one Falconer from the next and so did not recognize Tarlach as the warrior who had ridden escort to Una the day they had met near the Square Keep.

He did read all too clearly the cold, implacable purpose in the mercenary. His death was determined in those half-shadowed eyes, and his own heart chilled. He knew he was not likely to walk away from this encounter.

Even without the purpose that seemed to be driving his opponent, Ogin recognized that the disadvantage was his. He was no longer fresh. He had been wounded in the earlier fighting, and now pain and lost blood combined to give a still-sharper edge to the Falconer's basically greater skill.

For all the bitterness of his hate, Tarlach did not play with his foe once he realized the victory would be his, for that was not the way of his kind, and they strove together only a few minutes in all before the wrecker lord fell to his sword, dying before his body struck the deck.

The few remaining killers were quickly brought down after that, none seeking quarter and no quarter being offered them.

On shore, too, the battle had raged, although on a much smaller scale. The captain had erred in believing no guards would be stationed on the cliffs, but fortune had been rarely lenient, and the watchmen were there only to defend against possible damage to the perishable cargo by vermin or other wild intruders should the storehouse be left unattended. All had been asleep at the time of the assault, and the invaders were up the cliff and upon them before they realized anything was seriously amiss. They died rapidly, without inflicting much of the damage which had potentially been theirs to wreak.

All experienced something of a surprise, almost a disappointment, that the long-anticipated engagement should be ended so soon, but that feeling passed off even as it was born, and the mercenaries raised their swords high in the victory salute of their race.

It was a salute twice given, each man first lifting his own weapon, then lowering it again while the blades of those unable to wield them were held aloft. There were several of these last, for the victory had not come without its price, some belonging to the slain, the rest to the gravely wounded.

25

*T*hat gesture released Una. She had watched the battle from the *Tern* as Tarlach had bidden, in an agony of fear for the Falconer captain that overrode even her disgust at the slaughter she was witnessing. Now that it was ended, she wanted only to fly to him, to feel his arms around her and to assure herself that he was truly all right.

No such display was possible. She held herself to the degree of haste and purpose appropriate to her rank and her healer's art.

She crossed over to the bloodstained wrecker, accepting Santor's steadying hand, and started for the group of men comprised of Elfthorn and the Falconer officers.

The woman's pace quickened when she saw the blood on the commander's shoulder. When she reached him, she pulled aside the rent leather.

"Clean and bind this," she told Brennan crisply, although she breathed an inner sigh of relief; the wound was no more than a gash, long but not deep.

She turned back to the captain.

"Where have you laid your sore wounded?"

"On the deck over there until we can see to them, all but one man on the cliff. They can be moved to the *Tern* and brought home once their injuries have been dressed."

Una's eyes flickered to Storm Challenger, but her question regarding him was spoken merely to conceal her gift. She knew already that the war bird was unhurt despite his bloodied appearance.

Two of his kind did need her aid, as did a number of the human blank shields, and she delayed no longer in going to them. She had no fear as to her reception. Falconers knew how to take care of battle damage, but a healer of her competence was not often to be found, and she knew they would welcome her help for their more serious cases rather than merely submit to her right to give it.

As for the dead, the mercenaries' own would be brought back to Seakeep. Their enemies would be buried here in a single grave, all but Ogin, whose body they would take with them to Ravenfield to stand as proof of his death.

Because the sole casualty resulting from the assault on the cliff was too gravely wounded to be moved to the *Tern* as he was, the Holdlady accompanied the Falconers and Elfthorn when they went ashore to inspect the beach and warehouse and examine the materials stored therein.

She was with her patient a long while, and when she at last rose to her feet, it was with drooping shoulders and a lowered head. She had succeeded in making him comfortable, in inducing the sleep which had, astonishingly, eluded him, but healing was beyond her ability or, she believed, beyond the ability of any other. A spear had pierced him, slicing the bottom of the stomach and then traveling obliquely through his body so that it cut his intestines not once but through several folds.

His falcon sat on the shelf above the bunk where he had been laid. She, too, knew the nature of the wound, had known even before the woman examined him, and she was whimpering so piteously that her grief wrung Una's heart. Would she do this to Bravery if she should somehow be slain? she wondered. Would she suffer so if she should lose the kitten?

She took the bird up on her arm, stroking her feathers, giving what comfort she could, which was only that of sympathy and understanding, but she did not attempt to persuade her to leave the place with her. These two would remain together until the man died. After that, she understood from Tarlach, the falcon would be united with another warrior following a period of mourning if she would choose to accept one.

Since there was nothing more she could do for him,

the Daleswoman committed the dying mercenary to the care of his comrades and prepared to return to the beach and then to the *Tern*. If there was no further help she could give to this man, there were several aboard her vessel who would profit well from her skills.

Elfthorn helped settle the wounded and arrange for their care during the voyage back to Seakeep harbor, then reported to the Falconer commander that all was in readiness, although he knew it would be some time yet before they would be able to depart. Tarlach had forbidden the *Tern* to try running the Cradle before she had at least the light of a perceptible dawn to guide her.

The merchant captain did not envy him that decision. Several of the wounded were heavily hurt, two to the extent that the delay in reaching permanent quarters and full care could possibly ensure their deaths. He, himself the commander of a closely bound unit, readily understood how such an order could—must—tear a man, as he knew that no other could ease or lift the burden of it from the Falconer.

Tarlach's eyes strayed to the place where the *Tern* was moored. He wondered how those aboard her were doing and if the gravely hurt men would survive the night and the voyage home. The next several hours were critical for them, he knew.

It had been a costly engagement for one of its magnitude, he thought. Seven warriors were dead, and twice that number were significantly wounded, two of them grievously. The company would not remain an effective unit for long if it continued to sustain losses like that.

He sighed. At least they had the good fortune to be pledged to Seakeepdale. Many other holds did not treat so well blank shields felled in their cause, but they had no fear of neglect from Una's people.

His pulse leaped suddenly, but then he frowned. It was hours yet before even the first precursor of dawn should be visible. Why should the two ships out there be so readily visible?

Why should the sky be brightening in the west?

He knew the answer in his sick heart, and the next moment confirmed it. A lurid red glow materialized out of the blackness above the Cradle. It quickly strengthened, first into light and then into fire, an evil, lifeless fire that seemed to defy nature, aye, and possibility itself.

The others were aware of it as well. None of them suspected as yet that they were watching the coming of doom, but no one could doubt that this was a happening of great Power and that its origin was not likely to be any wellspring of the Light. They were afraid, but for now, they drew sword and waited. Even the falcons did not yet know the true scope of this disaster as they screamed their challenge to the Dark.

He saw her then, the Lady of Seakeep, walking purposefully down the beach. She did not pause until she had reached the edge of that place where the land stretched farthest out into the sea. There, she stopped and stood facing the burning gate opening above the Cradle.

"Una, no!"

The Falconer scarcely realized he had begun to run until he came to a halt beside her.

"What do you think to do?" he demanded harshly.

"Whatever I can. My sister told me I had a store of Power—"

"Sleeping and untrained!"

"The attempt must be made, Tarlach. At the least, it will be better to die trying to stop that thing than merely cowering in terror before it.—By the Maid and Matron!"

Within that unnatural fire they could see something, or the suggestion of something, a great, misshapen head that appeared to be all jaws, jaws filled with row upon row of fangs. Even from here, they were clearly visible.

Tarlach's eyes closed but opened again in the next instant. His terror would not permit him to shut out sight of the monstrosity.

The Dog was not yet free. He could see it struggling,

fighting to rip apart the last thin shields holding it away from the realm of life it had longed for so great an expanse of time to ravage. Soon now, probably within minutes, it would have achieved its freedom.

Una of Seakeep looked up at him.

"You should be with your comrades," she told him gently. "Go back to them now."

"My oath is to you."

"I release you, Tarlach. This goes beyond anything you plighted yourself to face." There was no hope of life in that, but she might perhaps win him a few more seconds.

"There is more binding us than an oath."

"There is more," she agreed quietly.

"Then grant me this, that if I am to meet my death on this beach, it shall at least be at your side."

He turned once more to the sea and the doom growing ever stronger there. He would die, but it would be in Una's cause, striving to defend her in the short time remaining to him. Above all, he vowed to himself that he would give her an easier death than she would meet from that horror beyond the gate, that he would give her fine spirit a true and clean release.

Storm Challenger and the other falcons he tried to dismiss, for their wings might win life or extend life for them, but all held fast to the bonds uniting them with their comrades. They, too, would attempt to stand their world's cause against this thing of the Dark.

The gate was giving way!

He was startled to see Una spring forward and only barely restrained himself from throwing himself after her when he realized the Holdlady was still in her place beside him.

The spirit Una!

The one his lady had named sister moved through the waves, on the waves. She advanced steadily until she had crossed half the distance between the shore and the opening gate. There, she stopped.

For one instant, she stood, still as a pillar of stone, then she sprang even as the gate tore open. It was not a seeming woman that leaped forth but light itself, fire, a blistering arrow of green flame which ripped into that dread passage and struck squarely that which sought to emerge from it.

The night exploded in light and sound as green flame and red fought together on the sea and above it, each struggling to devour the other. Thunder rent the sky, and the air around them turned, not hot, but bitterly cold.

At last it was over, and whether the battle had lasted minutes or many hours, none of the watchers would ever be able to say of his own self. The superphysical lights vanished, the red abruptly, the green first weaving itself again and again through the air above the Cradle before fading gently into oblivion, leaving behind it only the rich velvet blackness of their world's night.

Una sagged against Tarlach. She was weeping softly.

"We would not grant her the life she craved, and yet she spent her life thus for us."

The man gave her no reply save to hold her closer to him, but it was not the excess of brilliance they had endured which set his eyes streaming.

26

It was some minutes before he trusted himself enough to turn quietly away from the ocean. With his arm still about the woman in support and comfort, he started walking back toward his comrades.

Elfthorn hastened forward to take charge of the Holdlady, but the glare Tarlach fixed on him made him quickly step away again, nor did the Falconer leader remove his arm from her until Una herself straightened and took her own weight back upon herself.

Explanation had to be made, and the Daleswoman described the warning they had received from their spirit informer and detailed their reasoning for keeping this intelligence from their warriors even while she apologized for having done so. Of her relationship with the other Una prior to that last, fateful visit, she did not speak.

Only a few questions were directed at her despite the similarity between the spirit and herself, and she was soon able to take her leave of the fighters and seek the rest her body and mind and soul so greatly needed.

There was no such mercy shown to Tarlach. His comrades were angry over his silence, and he knew that if he did not satisfy them, the company would cease to exist as a unit with the conclusion of this commission.

Patiently, he reiterated what Una had already told them of their reasons for keeping the news of the true danger they faced to themselves.

"What would your knowing have accomplished?" he asked in the end. "We could not have fought that thing, and the fear of waking it would only have rendered you less able against those who did lie within the scope of our ability to defeat.—By the Eyrie, what do you imagine drove me to throw myself into the middle of those wreckers as I did if not my dread that any delay in concluding the battle might rouse the Dog? Fortune was rarely kind to let me come out of that one alive."

"All right, Tarlach," Rorick said hastily. "I suppose you are right, but that thing put the Ice Dragon's chill on all of us."

"You should have been feeling the way I did," he muttered.

That brought a sympathetic laugh from more than one of his companions. The lieutenant smiled as well, but his eyes remained somber.

"What connection did that spirit thing have with the Lady Una? Their resemblance proclaims that there needs must be some association."

A silence was on the assembled warriors. Their captain's possible answer to that, the depth of his knowledge concerning it, was a matter troubling to most of them.

"Am I supposed to be the Holdlady's confidant as well

as her hired sword that she should discuss such a subject with me?" he responded irritably.

"Perhaps you are."

That came from one of the outermost of those gathered around him. Tarlach's head snapped toward the man.

His already ragged temper broke.

"The Lady Una shared the knowledge of our peril. I know too well what she endured since we learned that, and it is logical to assume that there was some sort of feeling between her and the being who saved us. If we are not capable of acting with compassion, then I do not know what titles we may lay on ourselves, but humanity cannot be numbered among them!"

His eyes swept his companions. There had been enough truth in that to set their minds at rest, and he took hold of himself. It would do no good and perhaps might cause much harm to press the question further.

Pleading his very real and apparent weariness, he separated from them. Tarlach found a sheltered spot near the cliff wall and drew his cloak around himself. Within minutes, he had sunk into the deep, dreamless sleep of exhaustion.

Brennan woke him shortly after dawn.

"Sorry, Tarlach, but you had best be moving."

"The fleet is in?" he asked as he sat up, rubbing his eyes.

"Aye."

"How does the landing progress?"

"Well. All should be ashore by the time you have eaten."

"The *Tern* is gone?"

The lieutenant nodded.

"With the first light as you commanded."

"Excellent.—The wounded?"

"They are all living. We can credit Una of Seakeep for that."

His commander came to his feet.

"Good news. I had not really expected it."

He studied the busy scene around him with satisfaction.

"It goes well indeed. We will move out as soon as everything is fully ordered."

Falconers fought and traveled mounted whenever possible, but, as they functioned effectively at sea, so, too, could they perform well as infantry. Their march over Ravenfield's wild highlands was swift and smooth, untroubled by either natural difficulty or human opposition.

They kept careful watch against the last but had little actual fear of it. The remoteness and rugged nature of their route would have made discovery unlikely in any Dale, and Ogin's people had been trained to keep within their village and the circle of cultivated land around it. They had no reason to wander out so far, and few of them would have had the desire to do so even if they possessed the courage or the folly to thus defy their lord. The company could be nigh unto certain that they would be able to pass through unsighted and unhindered.

Such excellent progress did they make that they reached the rendezvous site somewhat before schedule and were forced to conceal themselves nearby until the Dale unit arrived to join with them.

Their wait was not long. The column out of Seakeep, Rufon at its head, had been able to hold a fast pace as well, and the two forces were united hours in advance of their proposed meeting time.

With their army at full strength at last, the invaders no longer buried themselves in the wild lands on Ravenfield's outskirts but moved on a straight course toward their goal, bearing themselves in battle readiness.

So swiftly did they march that the villagers and garrison had no warning of their coming until they broke suddenly upon the Dale's pasture lands in the early morning as the herdsmen were leading out their animals to feed.

The Ravenfield warriors and the people nearest their keep were able to take refuge within, but then had to flee, leaving their livestock and goods behind. Whatever stronghold contained in the way of foodstuffs would have to suffice for the duration of the siege.

Then began day upon weary day of talk as Una and Tarlach strove to negotiate Ravenfield's surrender.

Ogin's body was displayed to prove that there was no longer any need for either fear or loyalty to him, and the story of the *Cormorant*'s death and her survivors' escape was told in explanation of this assault.

Oaths were sworn that the lives of the Dalesfolk and garrison would be spared and that there would be no pillage of lands or goods, a fact borne out by their treatment of those who had been unable to gain the shelter of the keep.

It was a difficult task, and for a time it seemed they would fail in it, but the captain had judged rightly the effect of Una's presence, the weight and power of her word and the respect in which her house was held, and in the end, the banner of Ogin's line was lowered in admission of defeat.

Moments later, the great gate opened, and the steward came forward. He stood before the stronghold, waiting.

Seakeep's lady looked to the mercenary commander.

"Let us go to him, Captain."

"That is not my place," he replied curtly, mindful of his comrades' earlier suspicions.

Una's eyes fell.

"You are right. It would not be well to thus risk both Seakeep's leaders."

Tarlach and those of his Falconers near enough to them to hear the woman's low-voiced reply stiffened as if struck, but the captain saw from her expression that Una had not reproached him. She considered his statement a rebuke, and she accepted it as just.

"Forgive me that," he said. "As your military commander, I needs must accompany you even if it were not my duty to guard you."

"Will you have an escort?" Brennan asked him.

"No. That might frighten them back behind their walls. We would never budge them then without a long fight.

Have the archers stay within range and at ready, though," he added grimly, "just in case thought and word are not the same with them."

He raised his hand in a gesture of farewell, and he and the Holdruler mounted their waiting horses.

The Falconer kept pace with her and rode at her right in violation of custom for so solemn an occasion, but he wanted to be able to use his shield to best effect to cover her should those in the keep send a shower of darts at them.

That ride seemed to take an eternity, short though it was in actual distance. Both were acutely conscious of their vulnerability to any attack despite the falcons soaring high above and the bowmen set to fire at the first signal of danger to their leaders.

There was no treachery and no mishap. They met with the steward, and after yet again assuring him that his charges would come to no harm from either her people or her blank shields, Una of Seakeep received Ravenfield's surrender and formally took power over the defeated Dale into her hands.

27

*S*ome time was spent in ordering the captured Dale under the stewardship of the man Una named to assume that role, but these were people accustomed to accepting the commands of others, and the transition of rule was accomplished more rapidly and completely than might otherwise have been the case.

Once the Seakeep leaders felt certain all would remain quiet in Ravenfield, they departed for home, leaving a small, temporary garrison behind.

The enthusiasm of their reception was little short of astonishing, and the Falconers were amazed in no small degree to find that the welcome given them fully equalled that accorded the warriors native to the Dale, for such was not usually the case. Those who hired their swords out for gold could expect little more than gold as their reward, however hard or well they fought.

For the Lady Una, there would be small respite from strain in the weeks and months ahead. She sent couriers mounted upon swift steeds to inform each of the neighboring Dales of what had taken place in Ravenfield and of the events which had brought it all to pass. These same riders also carried her assurances that she had no designs for waging any war beyond that which Ogin's crimes had forced upon her.

The Holdruler sighed wearily as she watched the last of her emissaries depart. Assurances were easily given but far less readily accepted, and she realized full well that it would be long months before any of the domains around her relaxed again. She had already extended her agreement with the Falconers to cover the dangerous period ahead when fear of attack might grow into panic and move some of the other Dales into active hostility against Seakeep if there was no strong force on hand to deter them.

Her jade eyes darkened. They needed the mercenaries more than ever, and she hoped to the depths of her soul that she would not mishandle her proposal to Tarlach, for that could only result in his immediate departure and his warriors with him, whatever his promise of service, yet neither she nor her house could lay claim to honor or to humanity if she did not make him this offer.

A great sadness filled her at the thought of him. It could have been so good between them if he were a man of any other race, but she accepted that all the richness which might have been must be allowed to wither and die stillborn.

Had she been a girl, buoyed by the confidence and intolerance of youth, she might have expected him to follow his own wish and join his life with hers, damning an old and narrow custom, and she would of a certainty have reacted with anger when the failure of his courage prevented him from acting in accordance with the dictates of his heart.

As a woman, she could do neither. For a Falconer, the brotherhood he shared with his comrades was everything. Apart from the strange friendship they shared with their war birds, they quite literally had nothing else. Even the Eyrie, which had been their pride, was now gone. He loved Seakeepdale, aye, but he would really value actual possession of it only insofar as it might offer a secure and fitting seat for his kind.

Could she expect that a relationship with her would be sufficient in itself, that it could take the place of all he would lose to gain it? Until she was able to answer that and answer it affirmatively, she must hold her peace. She loved Tarlach far too much and respected him too much to do that to him. Her eyes closed. She could not risk that he might in the end come to hate her or she to pity him. No wanting or need of hers was worth that.

One vow she did make. Tarlach of the Falconers was her true lord, and however hopeless was her longing to join her life with his, he would remain her only lord. She would set no other man over Seakeep in his stead, and if she thereby doomed her direct line, so let it be. She would never voluntarily carry another's seed or accept another's caress.

The Falconer captain received with no little surprise the Holdlady's request that he attend her in her own chamber at his earliest convenience, but he went to her at once.

It was not without some nervousness. Neither of them had mentioned again the declaration they had made on that Ravenfield beach with a terrible and seemingly inevitable death only moments from claiming them. He had not wanted to set out upon his final road without having told her that, and he still felt the thrill of joy which had sprung to life in him despite the doom shadowing them when she had acknowledged a like feeling for him, but what was possible to admit in dying could not find fulfillment in life. He had believed, in truth still believed, they both accepted that.

His eyes fell and raised again. Of course, they accepted it.

They were not without some solace. They had been working more closely together than ever since their return to the tower and would do so for many months to come. They could take pleasure in that association, and if the ending of it would be painful, well, that they would have to face when the moment of separation was drawing upon them. They need not dwell on it now.

Una answered his knock with a quickness which told that she had been waiting for it.

Tarlach looked curiously around her apartment, not knowing what he had expected and feeling slightly disappointed because it fitted so well his concept of the private quarters of any highly born woman.

The furniture was more delicately fashioned than he had seen elsewhere in the tower, and some of the pieces differed to a greater or lesser extent from their counterparts in his own chamber to meet her different needs.

The various hangings and bed dressings were feminine in character, gracefully blending intricate floral displays with scenes depicting breathtakingly real-looking animals and birds. A frame containing a partly worked piece of needlecraft stood in the strong light by the window.

Only in one corner was there evidence of her responsibilities and heavier interests. Here stood a desk similar to his and behind it a closed cabinet of a type designed to hold maps and books and the records a Holdruler must maintain.

A number of closely inscribed papers lay on its surface. Una must have been working on them before he had come in, but he smiled to see the speed with which Bravery had claimed right of place once her companion had moved. She was now seated regally upon them and was calmly but intently watching the two humans, as if she were vitally interested in the outcome of their meeting.

Given her relationship with the woman, that was very possibly the case.

His mouth hardened, and his attention riveted upon Una herself.

The lady was standing at the centermost window.—The view beyond was all he had imagined it would be and more.—She was gowned in wool, as the season now demanded, a dress the very shade of her eyes. Its sleeves were slashed, revealing a lining of the palest green. As with most of her costumes, this gown clung tightly to the narrow waist and flowed freely from there into a soft, wide skirt. Her hair was bound by a broad ribbon of the same jade color, which was drawn through its dark mass in a complex lacing. When she turned at last to face him, he saw that there was what looked to be a fine emerald on her center finger.

His heart twisted painfully at the sight of her. She was so beautiful, all that could be desired in person or in body.—Had she attired herself like this on purpose, to wring his resolve and force him to repeat the declaration he had made and carry that declaration to fulfillment?

Shame filled him. Una of Seakeep would not use him, any man, thus.

Recognizing and admitting that only sharpened his grief, his awareness of all he must surrender. Whatever her intent, the Holdlady had driven a barbed sword through him by bringing him to this place, where he longed to come by another, richer light.

The man let no sign of his misery escape him. He gave her salute.

"You summoned me, Lady?" he asked, since Una herself seemed uncertain how to begin.

"I asked to see you," she corrected. "Elfthorn has been given what remains of the *Dion Star*'s cargo?"

He nodded.

"As you commanded and is fitting. He and Gunwold were fosterlings, and his grief is real and sharp."

Both fell silent again, uncomfortably so.

Una struggled to find the best approach but still could

think of no way that was completely without danger. Perhaps she did not, in truth, want to find a way to make the offer that would seal her loss.

It was so much harder to deal with him here, she thought. Throughout the rest of the tower and the Dale, they were Holdruler and comrade, but this place was private and her own, and the Falconer captain was her own true lord. . . .

That did not matter now. It could not be allowed to matter. She loved this man, and it lay with her to prove that love.

Her head raised, and her eyes gripped his.

"I have a proposal for you, Falconer, one which can benefit both our peoples, but yours far more than mine."

"Name it," he said, cloaking his surprise and also his relief, for he had not been entirely certain of his ability to resist her pleading if she turned that against him; he knew in his heart that he would sooner face a slow death by fire than see her under the lash of pain, of body or of heart. Such testing would not have been likely anyway, given what he knew of her character, and her words just now confirmed that. It was not an impossible union between them which she wanted to discuss. No good to his comrades could come of that.

"I am now possessed of two Dales."

The mercenary smiled despite himself at the grim note which entered her voice as she spoke.

"Many a lord would find pleasure in that fact."

"Many a lord has no objection to the shedding of blood!" She steeled herself, then plunged ahead. "Between them, Seakeep and Ravenfield contain a vast amount of land, easily the equal and probably the better of what you Falconers controlled before the mountains moved. It is terrain similar to that which you once had save that it also has the advantage of providing ready access to the ocean.

"If I were to cede Ravenfield to you and enter into binding treaty regarding our joint use of Seakeep's wild lands, it would give your people a place in which to establish themselves, to build and grow strong once more.''

"Do you know what you say?" he gasped, scarcely crediting that his ears had brought him her words aright.

"Falconers face eventual extinction as matters now stand," she answered evenly. "I have seen enough of you to know that this must not be permitted to happen. The means to prevent it has been given me. I may not control a gate such as my sister mentioned, but land I have, land that can mean both life for you and a real home again in this world.''

Her eyes slitted when he gave her no response, either in word or gesture.

"Can you think I am laying some sort of snare for you? I speak the truth. Ravenfield I do not want. The very thought of retaining possession of it after having gained it in such a manner is repugnant to me, however righteous my reasons for doing so. As for the rest, to stand back unacting and watch a people, any people, flicker into oblivion whose star I have the power to keep in this world's sky would be a stark evil, a work of the Dark itself. By my lights, I am without choice in making this offer!''

"I believe that, Una of Seakeep," the captain said very quietly. "But what of your own people and those of Ravenfield? Are you not risking doing them a mighty hurt?''

"Once before I said to you that life itself is a risk, but, no, in this case I do not believe that you or the generations to follow you will foul the oaths you take. I would not make this offer to any other blank shields, Tarlach, or to the lord or leader of any other people. Only Falconers have the proven honor to make the suggestion feasible.

"One stipulation I do make at the outset is that my Dalespeople must be used with complete respect, male and female, warrior and craftsman alike, both my own folk and Ravenfield's. I will not have any of them subjected to abuse or insult because of some of your less desirable ways.''

She hesitated again, then once more pressed on.

"For this reason, because it is proven that we two can work well and reasonably together, I shall give over Ravenfield to you yourself rather than to your people as a whole or to any other of your leaders, and you shall represent and decide for them in the treaty we shall develop and in all matters concerning it thereafter."

"Una!"

She stopped speaking to give him a chance to recover himself. If the first part of her proposal had taken him unawares, this last had stunned him outright, perhaps for cause greater than mere amazement.

"It is permitted for individuals of your kind to hold land in their own name?"

"It is not forbidden," he responded slowly. "The question has never arisen amongst us.—We cannot trace descent," he added as an afterthought.

"I doubt the arrangement will continue in perpetuity." Her eyes fell. "It is just that I trust you above any other, Tarlach, and—and I do not want to have to treat so closely for all of my life with a man I know despises me."

She hesitated again.

"Would you have trouble dealing with Falconer officers of higher rank?"

"Some. All men are subject to pride, but we are not unreasonable, whatever you others believe of us. If once I can convince them to accept my role as Holdlord, they should be willing to permit me to act in that capacity with respect to Ravenfield. Seakeep, too, since few of them would want to associate on such a basis with you."

He eyed her.

"The benefit to us is obvious. What gain will Seakeep have?"

"Not as much," she answered frankly. "We will have the permanent protection of the finest mercenaries to range our world at least since the departure of the Old Ones and perhaps before that, as shall be detailed in our treaty.

"Apart from that, your gold and your trade will be most welcome."

She smiled at his look of surprise.

"You have called our horses the finest you have ever encountered. With your companies, your columns, as a ready and constant market, we could at last build our herd to fit the capacity of the land, as both animals and Seakeepdale merit, and you would be mounted as no Falconers have been since your race first crossed into this realm."

"It is not the final answer," he said slowly, as if to himself, "not even if I win enough support to bring at least one of the villages here."

"No," she replied, "if you mean that your women will not remain forever quiescent in the old way. You could hardly expect me to aid in maintaining them in such a state, could you?"

He smiled faintly.

"No, Lady, of a certainty, I could not."

She sighed.

"This will buy you time. You cannot continue long as a viable, separate people living at the sufferance of others. With land of your own, you can again maintain yourselves as you did in the past, and you would have the chance to face and try to resolve the difficulties besetting you.—That you must do yourselves, Tarlach. No one else can find the answers for you."

"Much less implement them," he agreed bleakly. "I very much fear we shall not find some of those solutions easy swallowing."

The captain was silent for a long time after that.

"There is merit in what you say," he told her at last, "merit in every word."

His voice sounded strange, as if the words were being wrenched from him under the compulsion of the rack, and what she could see of his face was drawn and white.

"There is heavy risk for you in this, is there not?" she questioned gently.

His eyes closed.

"If I place such a proposal before my commanders and they reject it as being a woman's accursed wile, I shall be no more than a rabid dog in their sight."

"Do you believe this will prove the case?"

He shook his head.

"Not entirely. My company will support me, I think, if I present my case well, as should many of the columns, but there are some who will not, those who have ever been strictest in their isolation from other peoples. They form a good part of our number, and they will never condone this." His voice seemed on the verge of breaking, and he looked hurriedly at the window. "I have friends amongst them, comrades of my youth . . ."

Una placed her hand on his arm.

"It is not necessary for you to become involved. I can make the offer directly and deal with whomever your leaders appoint."

The man turned to her once more.

"No, Lady. What must be endured shall be. Falconers are trained to accept our responsibilities. That they at times carry with them danger greater than that of death or physical injury is of no significance."

"We of Seakeepdale are as powerfully trained not to inflict such peril on others when the power to alleviate it is ours."

He smiled sadly.

"It would be useless, Lady. No other Falconer would consider such a proposition from a woman, and I should still face the same wrath, the same penalty, for supporting it."

He straightened as she had often seen him do before embarking upon some difficult course.

"The task is mine to carry, my Lady of Seakeep. Its importance to my people both now and in future times is such that I cannot even consider refusing it."

The Daleswoman's eyes dropped, then lifted again.

"It is settled, then," Una said, speaking slowly, wearily, as if she had spent herself in a bitter struggle, "though I suppose it will be long before we beat out the final treaty."

"Perhaps not so very long. You are mindful of our needs, and I shall endeavor to be as considerate of your people's."

They both fell quiet. There was nothing more to be said on this subject, which now required deep, private thought on the part of both.

Tarlach did not move to take his leave of her but rather turned to the window. Una had given so much, not merely the awesome gift of a Dale but that of life itself to his harsh race, and he had returned nothing. That he so valued her action and so appreciated its import that he was willing to place himself at risk of banishment and ultimate disgrace was no offering to her. It was but a warrior's duty in the face of his people's need.

Slowly, his hand went to a small leather pouch on his belt. Perhaps he had unconsciously intended to do this, he thought, for why else would he have chosen to carry the Talisman today instead of wearing it as he had always before done in all the years since its making?

"Una, I have no lands or gold to bestow in my turn, but I ask that you accept this from me."

The woman took the pouch and carefully opened it. She drew forth a slender, silver chain. Depending from it was an object which drew a gasp of delight and wondering appreciation from her, a small but exquisitely wrought silver falcon portrayed diving with a blood-red jewel grasped firmly in his talons.

"Oh, Tarlach, this is indeed beautiful!"

"It is more than that," he said in a way which caused her to look swiftly upon him.

"Power?" she asked incredulously.

He nodded.

"Of a sort. Every Falconer fashions one of these when he attains manhood, and he may possess only one at any given moment in his life. They can be gifted, as I am doing now, or suffer natural mischance, but they cannot be beguiled from their owner or otherwise taken without the full consent of his will, a virtue which passes to a true recipient, though not to a chance discoverer in the event of loss.''

His eyes rested somberly on the Talisman.

''The possessor may also claim the aid of any Falconer or Falconer unit, provided only that his cause be just and in no violation of our honor.''

''Thanks given, Tarlach,'' Una said softly. ''I shall never of my will abuse this gift.''

So saying, she clasped the chain around her neck, then quietly slipped the falcon beneath the material of her gown. His giving of this had been open, as had been his earlier gifting of his name, with no stipulation or request that she hold her possession of it close. Her doing so was an offering of her own, her acknowledgment of his confidence and her assurance that it would not be betrayed.

It broke the control he had forced on himself. Tarlach turned from her to conceal the anguish twisting his face.

''Una,'' he whispered in a muffled voice, ''I swear to you, by the Horned Lord, were it not for my people's real and desperate need, I would offer you more than this, or seek to offer more. I would ask more of you . . .''

The Daleswoman came into his arms. His mouth covered hers and found there a mirror of all his own passion and longing.

His hold tightened. They might make the dare this once, take and give what was their desire and need. Una was no maid, but a widow who had known a man's embrace. . . .

That thought died even as it was born. It took the lash of his will, for his body was aflame, but his arms loosened, and he stepped away from her. Gratification was not what he, what either of them, wanted, and he did not believe in his heart that the woman would willingly have yielded herself, for all her love, had he demanded that of her.

Una's eyes raised to his. She, too, had battled the desire burning within her, and she had to fight now to keep the tears brightening her eyes from welling forth.

"I would give you hand and hold, my own lord," she told him almost fiercely, "and while will remains mine, no other man will ever gain either from me."

Her shoulders squared.

"Nor will I entirely abandon hope, Tarlach of the Falconers. We of High Hallack learned the value of holding to that despite reason's grimmest sentence during our war with Alizon, and I would not see you surrender it, either. No one knows what web fate has woven for him—or what may be done with the threads as yet laid out for that weaving. We may still win through to what seems an impossible goal now."

The Holdlady drew one long breath, then she smiled at him.

"Let us be gone, Captain. I know little of him if we do not receive a visit from Lord Markheim very shortly. We had best prepare ourselves to greet and reassure him, and the others who will be following fast upon his heels."

They left the chamber together, each realizing the days ahead would be full of challenge and each prepared to meet that challenge and the whole of the life to which their decisions and their deeds would bring them.

This tale of Seakeep was more than one night in the telling. Having once begun it I could sense that he who lived it must press on to voice the rest. Perhaps so he made clear to himself certain feelings and questions he had not faced before.

When he finished it at last I was moved to throw the crystals. The pattern did not form falcon eyes as it had for Pyra, rather there was a jagged red line and above it grey so that I knew ill was close upon him. I would have spoken so to this bird warrior save that a message came to him that the Lady Una had come at last across the sea to join in his quest. And straightway he went forth from Lormt to meet her.

Only I was oddly shaken and once more I paced out-side the walls of Lormt, with Galerider and Rawit as my only companions. Twice it seemed to me that shadow

431

clouds gathered strangely—not in the east where Escore knew those Dark skirmishes and danger which might burst swiftly out of nowhere, but westward—over that land where we thought war was safely over.

My sword hand itched and I reached for that weapon I no longer wore. I found myself listening for a Border horn to sound downwind. Then I knew within me that, for all my thought of being one who no longer had any active part to play in action, strange destiny still lay ahead.

No—the end of the fight was not yet, nor would that pass me by.

FANTASY BESTSELLERS
EDITED BY ANDRE NORTON

☐ ☐	54715-2	MAGIC IN ITHKAR 1 *edited with Robert Adams*	$3.95 Canada $4.95
☐ ☐	54745-4	MAGIC IN ITHKAR 2 (Trade Edition) *edited with Robert Adams*	$6.95 Canada $7.95
☐ ☐	54749-7	MAGIC IN ITHKAR 2 *edited with Robert Adams*	$3.95 Canada $4.95
☐ ☐	54709-8	MAGIC IN ITHKAR 3 *edited with Robert Adams*	$3.95 Canada $4.95
☐ ☐	54719-5	MAGIC IN ITHKAR 4 *edited with Robert Adams*	$3.50 Canada $4.50
☐ ☐	54757-8	TALES OF THE WITCH WORLD 1	$3.95 Canada $4.95
☐ ☐	50080-6	TALES OF THE WITCH WORLD 2	$3.95 Canada $4.95
☐ ☐	51336-3	TALES OF THE WITCH WORLD 3	$3.95 Canada $4.95

FANTASY BESTSELLERS
FROM TOR

☐	55852-9	ARIOSTO	$3.95
☐	55853-7	*Chelsea Quinn Yarbro*	Canada $4.95
☐	53671-1	THE DOOR INTO FIRE	$2.95
☐	53672-X	*Diane Duane*	Canada $3.50
☐	53673-8	THE DOOR INTO SHADOW	$2.95
☐	53674-6	*Diane Duane*	Canada $3.50
☐	55750-6	ECHOES OF VALOR	$2.95
☐	55751-4	*edited by Karl Edward Wagner*	Canada $3.95
☐	51181-6	THE EYE OF THE WORLD	$5.95
☐		*Robert Jordan*	Canada $6.95
☐	53388-7	THE HIDDEN TEMPLE	$3.95
☐	53389-5	*Catherine Cooke*	Canada $4.95
☐	55446-9	MOONSINGER'S FRIENDS	$3.50
☐	55447-7	*edited by Susan Shwartz*	Canada $4.50
☐	55515-5	THE SHATTERED HORSE	$3.95
☐	55516-3	*S.P. Somtow*	Canada $4.95
☐	50249-3	SISTER LIGHT, SISTER DARK	$3.95
☐	50250-7	*Jane Yolen*	Canada $4.95
☐	54348-3	SWORDSPOINT	$3.95
☐	54349-1	*Ellen Kushner*	Canada $4.95
☐	53293-7	THE VAMPIRE TAPESTRY	$2.95
☐	53294-5	*Suzie McKee Charnas*	Canada $3.95

Buy them at your local bookstore or use this handy coupon:
Clip and mail this page with your order.

Publishers Book and Audio Mailing Service
P.O. Box 120159, Staten Island, NY 10312-0004

Please send me the book(s) I have checked above. I am enclosing $ _____
(Please add $1.25 for the first book, and $.25 for each additional book to cover postage and handling.
Send check or money order only—no CODs.)

Name _____

Address _____

City _____ State/Zip _____

Please allow six weeks for delivery. Prices subject to change without notice.

MORE BESTSELLING
FANTASY FROM TOR

☐ ☐	50556-5	THE BEWITCHMENTS OF LOVE AND HATE *Storm Constantine*	$4.95 Canada $5.95
☐ ☐	50554-9	THE ENCHANTMENTS OF FLESH AND SPIRIT *Storm Constantine*	$3.95 Canada $4.95
☐ ☐	54600-8	THE FLAME KEY *Robert E. Vardeman*	$2.95 Canada $3.95
☐ ☐	54606-7	KEY OF ICE AND STEEL *Robert E. Vardeman*	$3.50 Canada $4.50
☐ ☐	53239-2	SCHIMMELHORN'S GOLD *Reginald Bretnor*	$ 2.95 Canada $ 3.75
☐ ☐	54602-4	THE SKELETON LORD'S KEY *Robert E. Vardeman*	$2.95 Canada $3.95
☐ ☐	55825-1	SNOW WHITE AND ROSE RED *Patricia C. Wrede*	$3.95 Canada $4.95
☐ ☐	55350-0	THE SWORDSWOMAN *Jessica Amanda Salmonson*	$3.50 Canada $4.50
☐ ☐	54402-1	THE UNICORN DILEMMA *John Lee*	$3.95 Canada $4.95
☐ ☐	54400-5	THE UNICORN QUEST *John Lee*	$2.95 Canada $3.50
☐ ☐	50907-2	WHITE JENNA *Jane Yolen*	$3.95 Canada $4.95

Buy them at your local bookstore or use this handy coupon:
Clip and mail this page with your order.

Publishers Book and Audio Mailing Service
P.O. Box 120159, Staten Island, NY 10312-0004

Please send me the book(s) I have checked above. I am enclosing $ _____
(please add $1.25 for the first book, and $.25 for each additional book to cover postage and handling.
Send check or money order only—no CODs).

Name _____
Address _____
City _____ State/Zip _____
Please allow six weeks for delivery. Prices subject to change without notice.